To choose

She wanted the Traulander. He was the best fighter because he was arena trained. That alone made him more ruthless, more dangerous than the others. He was loyal, perhaps to extremes. He was fierce, as fierce as Hovet any day. He was strong, with incredible stamina, and he healed quickly. He had been a champion, which meant he was a survivor, yet he possessed integrity and honesty. He was intelligent and perhaps sensitive. There was nothing of the brute in him, although his manners needed work.

He was ideal for her purposes, but she dared not select him. . . .

Besides, she was extremely disconcerted by her personal reaction to Caelan E'non today. Disconcerted and angry. Passion was not a quality she expected to find in herself. She would not permit it to exist if she could not feel it for her husband.

No, Caelan was too dangerous, in too many ways . . .

Ace Books by Deborah Chester

REIGN OF SHADOWS
SHADOW WAR
REALM OF LIGHT

SHADOW WAR

DEBORAH CHESTER

ACE BOOKS, NEW YORK

SHADOW WAR

An Ace Book / published by arrangement with
the author

PRINTING HISTORY
Ace mass market edition / January 1997

Copyright © 1997 by Deborah Chester.
Cover art by Dan Craig.
Cover design by Rita Frangie.

ISBN: 0-441-01169-1

ACE®
Ace Books are published by The Berkley Publishing Group,
a division of Penguin Group (USA) Inc.,
375 Hudson Street, New York, New York 10014.
ACE and the "A" design
are trademarks belonging to Penguin Group (USA) Inc.

PRINTED IN THE UNITED STATES OF AMERICA

10 9 8 7 6 5 4 3 2

SHADOW WAR

Part One

Chapter One

THE FANFARE OF trumpets came at last, a bugling summons that filled the arena and reached all the way down into the subcaverns below. The milling activity in the preparation rooms, barracks, and passageways briefly ceased as attendants, scrub-boys, healers, trainers, and gladiators lifted their heads to listen. Even a momentary hush fell over the guards at their posts.

Inside his private ready room, Caelan E'non was pacing restlessly back and forth, aware of time passing, his blood raging in anticipation of what lay ahead.

He heard the trumpets, faint at first, then growing louder. They sounded for him.

Caelan stopped pacing in mid-stride. His heart soared toward the sound. For a moment he could not breathe. Swallowing, he tipped back his head and gazed at the ceiling. Even all the way down here he could hear the dull roar of cheering. The stone structure around him absorbed the shouts of acclaim until the walls themselves seemed to vibrate from the force of so much sound.

They were screaming for the champion.

They were screaming for him.

An endless day of waiting came down to this moment, glory and anticipation all tangled together.

Caelan's mouth went dry. He longed for a drink of water, yet did not touch the dipper in the pail. He could swallow nothing.

As three-time champion of the private gladiatorial seasons, Caelan was the star attraction in the final event of today's spectacular display of combat and slaughter. He had come here to the old public arena at dawn, brought in all the pomp of a closed chariot bearing him, his personal trainer, and his slaves, the whole flanked by guards on horseback. He had been fed, massaged, and oiled. An hour past, he had been dressed for the arena in a leather loincloth and fighting harness. The slaves had braided back his long, blond hair. He wore a leather headband across his brow to keep the sweat from his eyes. Now he stood, tall and muscular, his broad shoulders square, his loins narrow.

Orlo, his trainer, had long since dismissed the slaves and cleared the room to allow Caelan his privacy. It was Caelan's habit to wait alone, pulling deep within himself, wrapping himself in concentric rings of mental readiness. He performed drills in his mind, making the moves over and over. He also limbered his secret gifts, first *severing* himself from all emotion and thought until he stood at the center of a cold, still void, then shifting back to the warmth of *sevaisin,* the joining of completion and harmony.

Today, however, concentration proved difficult to maintain. It had been well over a year since he'd been in the old public arena. It seemed antiquated and foreign to him now. He was used to private quarters, efficient sluice bath facilities, and his own entry into the ring hung with his ivy crowns and trophies. But here, the subcaverns were cramped, ill lit, and dank. The place reminded him of dark times, of when he'd first been brought to Imperia and sold at the gladiator auction. Ill trained and harshly treated, he had been expected to die in his first combat.

Drawing in deep breaths, Caelan forced the memories away. His thoughts scattered like dry leaves in the winter wind. Despite his efforts to remain calm, his blood was pumping. Even his constant pacing had failed to keep his muscles as loose as he wished. Now he felt the edge, the excitement rising in him with cold chills. His body thrummed with impatience, and he circled the small room to face the door. Time for the guards to open it. The trumpets sounded again, and he wanted to cry out something savage and wordless in response.

Instead nothing happened. No guards came to fetch him. Orlo did not return. It was time, past time. The crowd was calling for him. He walked the edge of readiness, and this delay irked him.

Frowning, he tried to curb his annoyance at the slipshod manner in which this old arena was run. What was behind the delay? Had one of the gates broken? Had one of the fighters gone berserk and broken into the crowd?

Stupid to be here in the first place. This wasn't part of the regular season, which had already ended. The public arena was for the dregs of the fighters, men broken and desperate, prisoners of war, criminals who were condemned to spill their life's blood for the enjoyment of the masses.

Like all privately owned gladiators, Caelan held little but scorn for a ramshackle place like this. It was beneath him to be brought here.

But he had no choice in the matter.

In honor of the coming coronation of his empress, Emperor Kostimon was holding a day's worth of games offered free to the public. All businesses had closed. All workers were dismissed for the day in order to attend the games. This was the biggest arena in the city, and the emperor's personal favorite. As champion, Caelan had to appear in today's contest, unless his owner wanted to cause a riot. Caelan was the citywide betting favorite, known to everyone. There would be thousands of people present today who ordinarily could not afford the entrance fee to see Caelan fight. Through the generosity of the emperor and the graciousness of Prince Tirhin, Caelan's owner, the people would have this single opportunity to come and watch the fighter whose fame was growing across the empire.

According to the guards, the arena was packed to maximum capacity and beyond.

Why did no one come for him? Caelan's frown deepened, and he resumed pacing. It took but five minutes to clear corpses from the arena and rake the sand. Why sound the trumpets if he wasn't going to be let out?

His hands worked at his sides, and he longed to have a weapon in his grip. As champion, he'd earned the privilege of carrying his weapons into the ring. It helped calm him to have his sword in hand ahead of time. But here, the strict rules forbidding such liberties remained, with no exceptions.

Even Orlo hadn't returned, and he should have been back long ago. Caelan reached out and struck the door with his fist as he paced past it. Even as he did so, he knew he should have curbed the urge. He was expected to stay loose, to keep his mind clear and empty.

Instead here he was, making another circle, feeling increasingly grim and impatient. Bad enough to wait all day for the last event. But this delay was an insult.

As champion, his responsibility was to keep nerves of steel. If he let himself look worried or nervous, the odds changed immediately. There were bookmakers' spies everywhere; impossible to keep them out when even the guards were willing to take bribes to turn informer. Banging on the door should give them something to talk about.

It was the mark of an amateur, not a veteran such as himself. Orlo would be furious when he heard about it, but then his trainer should have been here instead of wandering off to spy on Caelan's opponent.

The door burst open. Even as Caelan turned, Orlo—

bald, stocky, and swinging his club—came striding inside with a scowl on his face.

"Murdeth and Fury!" he said and kicked shut the door in the faces of onlookers crowding behind him to catch a glimpse of Caelan. "Damned tricksters! No wonder the emperor's entry was kept such a close secret."

Caelan hated to talk just before he went into the arena. It spoiled his mental preparation. However, now he stared at his trainer with a frown of his own. "Who is the challenger?"

"An unknown." Orlo spat in the corner and shook his club as though he wanted to bring it down across someone's shoulders.

Once he used to regularly beat Caelan with it. No longer.

Caelan shrugged. "What does it matter? If he's green—"

"I saw the brute. He's a Madrun."

Caelan's careful edifice of detachment crumbled. "Great Gault!" he said in astonishment. "How did he get one of those?"

"Prisoner of war," Orlo said bitterly. "Brought in chains, with half of his handlers clearly afraid of him. He's not even gentled, by the looks of him. Certainly not trained for the arena. Bah! I hate these political gestures. Why couldn't you be pitted against a decent fighter instead of a barbarian?"

In spite of his alarm, Caelan had to smile. There was a time when Orlo had considered *him* a barbarian. Still, to go in against a Madrun . . . Caelan looked at Orlo and frowned.

Orlo's expression changed at once. "Never mind," he said gruffly. "It makes no difference. I'm just angry at the unfairness of it. Just when you have finally developed some finesse to show off before the lords and ladies, along comes this savage. Bah! What good is all my work?"

Wryly, Caelan nodded. Orlo was a master of under-statement when it came to the days and hours of grueling practice drills he'd put Caelan through, simply to learn the extra flourishes that played to the crowd. Even to days when Caelan faced weak, ineffectual opponents, he had to make the contest look good. Moreover, he had learned how to in-flict wounds that looked fatal, when in fact often the healers could save the defeated men.

"You can't prance around today," Orlo said. "This isn't an exhibition game. The Madrun will maul you if he can. He's big and solid, a good match. It will be a tremendous spectacle, but you must stand prepared for his speed and strength, which may be close to yours. Business only. Keep well focused. Match his savagery with every dirty trick you know. Understand?"

"No rules in the arena," Caelan quoted softly.

"You've become a cynic."

Old bitterness soured Caelan's mouth. Considering the kind of life he led, how could he be anything less than cyn-ical?

Caelan changed the subject. "What is the delay? I heard the trumpets sound. I should be going up."

"Not yet."

Caelan snorted and clenched his fists. He wouldn't complain; it did no good. Usually Orlo would be complain-ing for him, but the trainer was still scowling into the dis-tance.

"When do I get my sword?" Caelan asked. "I thought you would bring it in with you."

Orlo roused himself from his thoughts. "No chance of that today. With the emperor here and the whole city in the stands, the guards are terrified there will be trouble. Old women, the lot of them. No sword until you enter."

"Fine," Caelan snapped, losing his temper. "And am I

to be blindfolded and manacled like the old days? Prince
Tirhin could have saved himself the entry fee, because I
won't—"

"Silence!" Orlo roared. "You've been insulted little
enough, and no one's going to put you in shackles."

Caelan heard the trumpets again, and with them came
a roar that seemed to shake the stone walls. The sound fed
into Caelan, pulsing through his nerves.

Edgy and tense, he swung away from Orlo. "How
long?"

"It's not quite time," Orlo said. "There's some sort of
entertainment being staged in the emperor's honor. Find
your patience and keep to it."

A knock sounded on the door with unexpected courtesy.

Surprised, Caelan opened his mouth, but Orlo spoke
first:

"Enter."

The door opened, and two men stepped inside. One had
brown leathery skin and cold eyes that stared intently at
Caelan. Robed in a saffron tunic that reached to the floor, a
leopard hide across his shoulder, and his sleeves banded
with brown stripes of rank, the priest was clearly someone
of importance, although Caelan did not know him. He wore
a wide collar necklace fitted with the gold emblem of the
Vindicants in its center. His long-fingered hands carried a
staff tipped with the same emblem at its top.

Gazing at the man, Caelan felt a strange chill tingle at
the back of his neck. It took all his innate stubbornness not
to step back.

The other man was black-haired and handsome, with a
mustache and chin-strap beard. He wore a blue velvet tunic,
a snowy linen shirt, and a gold-embroidered cap perched
rakishly on his head. It was to this man that Caelan bowed.

Inside, he felt a rush of pride. Prince Tirhin rarely visited him before combat. This was a tremendous honor, a mark of the highest favor. Even so, that cynical inner voice whispered to Caelan that the prince came only to reassure himself that his champion would give his best today. The visit meant nothing more than that.

Squelching such thoughts, Caelan raised himself with a small smile for his master alone. He felt ready now to take on as many entrants as dared to meet him.

Pulling off his gloves in the doorway, the prince glanced back over his shoulder, and Caelan caught a glimpse of the blue-cloaked soldiers of Tirhin's personal bodyguard out in the passageway before the door was closed firmly.

Although Caelan stood tall and straight, Orlo was still bowing. "As you can see, sir, he is ready."

The priest looked Caelan over with open appraisal.

Prince Tirhin barely glanced Caelan's way. "Leave us," he said curtly to the trainer.

Still bowing, keeping his gaze down, Orlo scuttled out in a way unlike him.

Surprised, Caelan stared after his trainer for a moment, then returned his gaze to his master. He was full of curiosity, but questions were not permitted. It was necessary to wait until the prince chose to speak to him.

"He looks fit, even after a grueling season," the priest murmured. He was still studying Caelan in an unpleasant manner.

Caelan kept a wary eye on the man. He had been raised to revile the Vindicants. He would never trust them.

Prince Tirhin turned his gaze full upon Caelan at last and nodded. "Of course. I told you he finished the season without a scratch. He's had two weeks of rest."

"Those two weeks are what worry me," the priest murmured. He circled Caelan. "I know what fighters do between seasons. Drinking, slackness, frolicking with the Haggai."

Caelan frowned in affront while Tirhin raised his hand with a laugh. "None of that," the prince said. "He doesn't care for the witches of ecstasy, do you, Giant?"

Taut with resentment, Caelan found a very thin smile in response and said nothing.

"Our entrant is an ascetic, very strict with his native Traulander ways," Tirhin continued. "He is fit. I depend on his trainer for that."

The priest said nothing.

"You must not worry, Sien," the prince assured him. "I tell you this man will prevail."

The priest shook his head and fixed his gaze intently on Caelan, who stared back with new interest. Lord Sien was the high priest of the Vindicants, a man said to have more power in the empire than anyone save the emperor himself. He outranked even the prince, who had not yet been officially named heir to the empire. What was such a man doing down here below the arena, involving himself in the pitiable life of a gladiator?

"You will fight a Madrun savage," Sien now said directly to Caelan. "The creature understands nothing of the arena, nothing of the rules of combat."

"There are no rules of combat in the arena," Caelan said.

"Silence!" Prince Tirhin said in annoyance. "Listen to Lord Sien."

The rebuke was like a whip crack. Caelan glanced at his master and saw strain in the prince's face. Beneath the handsome looks and the expensive tailoring, his highness was drawn as taut as a bowstring. The corner of his mouth twitched, and there was a certain dark wildness in his gaze, an impatience, an anger that seethed all too near the surface.

Caelan bowed his head in apology and turned his gaze back to Sien.

"The emperor is clever in choosing his entrant," the priest continued. "This prisoner is at his physical prime, very strong and courageous. He fears nothing. He will fight you to the death without a second thought. However, enemies of the empire die well before the people. You will defeat the Madrun. You will prevail until you are victorious."

Puzzlement filled Caelan. Of course he intended to win. He always fought to win.

"There is more," Tirhin said impatiently. "You must fight as you have never fought before. This must be a tremendous spectacle."

Caelan's impatience grew. Any veteran gladiator knew how to play to the crowd. It was a matter of testing the opponent's strengths and weaknesses, then drawing the contest out as long as possible. Why did the rich and powerful think they were authorities in every matter? He didn't need this useless lecture. "I always give the people their money's worth, sir."

"It is more than that!" Tirhin said with a scowl. "You fight my father's choice. The Madrun is an extension of my father, just as you are an extension of me. When you defeat your opponent, in a way you are defeating my father."

Caelan felt alarm. This was treasonous talk. "Sir," he said softly, his voice full of warning, "these walls are honeycombed with listeners."

"We are safe," Tirhin said, but Sien lifted his long hand.

"Perhaps the slave is right," the priest said. "Take care, your highness."

Anger clouded Tirhin's face. Clenching his fists, he swung away. "I am tired of waiting! I am tired of being careful! Swallowing insult after insult. Waiting endlessly on a man who will not die! I—"

He broke off, choking back his emotions, and gestured furiously at Sien.

The priest gripped Caelan by the arm. "Heed your instructions," he said. "You are to win, by any means possible. Is that clear?"

Caelan stared at him. The man was a fool. "Yes, Lord Sien," he said, keeping his voice as neutral as possible. "I understand."

Sien gave him a little shake. "You are as blind as an eyeless man. You understand nothing. There is more at stake here than a mere arena victory."

Caelan glared at him and pulled his arm free. "I will win, if I am the better fighter. I will fight my best for my master, as I always do."

"Not enough," Sien said. "There is no passion here, no loyalty to you, sir." He glanced at Tirhin; then his gaze returned to Caelan. He had yellow eyes, Caelan noticed with an inward shiver. Unpleasant, cold, inhuman eyes. They seemed to bore to Caelan's very heart.

"There is no question of who is better," Sien said. "Do as you are told. Nothing more, nothing less."

The room was suddenly close and still. The air felt hot, stifling. Caelan tried to swallow, but his throat felt constricted. There was a strange roaring in his ears, and through it came Sien's voice:

"You will kill the Madrun."

Caelan bit back a sigh. "Yes, Lord Sien."

"You will tantalize him and play with him as a cat toys with its prey."

"I will, Lord Sien."

"The object is to win the crowd's approval for your master."

"Yes."

There was something heavy and hypnotic about the priest's voice. His statements and Caelan's responses had the solemn cadence of a religious ritual.

"You will rob the emperor of his acclaim."

"I—" Caelan's voice died in his throat.

He stepped back, forcing himself to break Sien's intense stare. Blinking furiously, and sweating as though he'd run a long distance, Caelan scowled.

"Get back from me, priest!" he said, spitting the words in his fury. "Keep your filthy spells to yourself!"

"Caelan, silence!" Prince Tirhin commanded. "Remember your place."

Caelan turned on him. "My place is to serve you. I will fight, sir. I will give my best to this contest, as I do every time I enter the ring. But I need no spells cast on me. I need no one to tell me how to fight. I will not submit to such—"

"You will have your tongue cut out for this insolence," Sien said rapidly. "Speak to your master—or me—in like manner again, and you'll—"

"Beat me, and I cannot fight," Caelan retorted. "Cut out my tongue, and I'll bleed my strength into the sand. You'll have no victory then."

The three of them glared at each other in long silence. Caelan knew well that Sien could carry out his threats, but he was too angry to care. The Vindicants had tried to meddle with him before. He wouldn't submit to their blasphemy. He'd rather die than lose his soul to their brand of darkness.

It was Prince Tirhin who was the first to speak. "My Lord Sien," he said, "I think it best if you step outside."

Sien scowled in outrage.

"Please," Tirhin said. "Your efforts have served to gain the slave's attention. Now let me finish the persuasion."

"You cosset him and spoil him, granting him privileges above his station, allowing him ideas of his own importance."

"He *is* important," Tirhin said, still calmly. "It is not boasting to state a fact. My father surely requires your return by now. Let me have the bag."

Sien hesitated further, but at last he drew a small leather pouch from his robes and put it in Tirhin's hand. "Make very sure," he said, his voice hoarse with anger. "This chance must not be wasted."

Tirhin's handsome face tightened with annoyance. "I know what's at stake, Lord Sien."

Inclining his head slightly to the prince, Sien strode out. The door closed behind him with an echoing thud.

Caelan and the prince faced each other in the small space. Tirhin laid the pouch casually on the table, but to Caelan its presence seemed to throb in the room. He could smell herbs in the compound, mixed with something tainted and unnameable. Swallowing his distaste, Caelan took another step back.

"If that is a potion for me, I won't take it," he said.

Tirhin's mouth tightened for a moment; then he turned to gaze at the wall. "Sien is right," he said. "You have grown full of your own importance. It is not good for a slave, even one as well favored as you, to forget his place."

Fresh anger roared up inside Caelan. Now that they were alone, he knew he could speak freely to this man, who was master, yet almost friend. It had ever been so between them, although such moments of privacy were rare.

"I have never lost a combat in all the time I have worn your colors," he said, his voice tight with hurt. "Why am I treated so today? Why do you doubt me? My loyalty, my strength are yours. When have I failed, that you should distrust me like this?"

Tirhin sighed and tipped back his head for a moment. "I knew you would take this wrong," he muttered, half to himself. He glanced at Caelan. "Why must you always be so damned difficult?"

Caelan knotted his brows, too full of resentment to permit himself a reply.

"We came to help you, you damned, stiff-necked fool. Sien's potion will give you extra strength."

"I am strong enough."

"Against a Madrun?" Tirhin's voice rose with doubt.

Although he made sure nothing showed, something inside Caelan withered and died. To his people, killing for any reason was a horror. Caelan, stolen from his homeland and exiled from his people, had found himself forced to fight if he was to live. Moreover, he had found in himself an unexpected gift for battle. Put a sword in his hand and he became a different man, quick and complete. He was efficient, tireless, ruthless. And all the while he was triumphing in the ring, glorying in the acclaim, it seemed the spilled blood of all his many defeated opponents kept seeping into his very bones, into his heart, into his conscience.

Take him from the arena, take him from the cheers, take the sword from his hand, and he was a man uneasy with his own conscience, never settled one way or the other. His own pride in his fighting ability shamed him, yet why should he hate his skills? When the gods gave a man a certain talent, was he not to use it? Still, what trick of fate was it to grant him exceptional ability in killing others? He could find no peace, although he had formed a shell between himself and his own trampled morals. Only at night, when the nightmares came, did that shell break.

He told himself that to fight to protect one's home, or loved ones, or life, was a different matter. To fight and kill simply to provide entertainment was a stain against mankind. His soul felt black and heavy with it. Yet he belonged to Tirhin, and Tirhin commanded him to serve in the arena. For Tirhin, a man he admired above all others, a man he longed to emulate, he was willing to do anything.

The prince was strong, courageous, and intelligent. Despite his high station, he found time to listen to the people who came to him for help. He was generous to the poor, kind to his slaves, fair to his soldiers. He had served his father loyally and patiently, at least up till now. In all respects, he was someone to admire. Had Caelan been free, he would have sought to be in this man's employ, and he would have longed to be Tirhin's friend.

Now, however, Caelan found himself witnessing a side of this man he had never seen before. A resentful, angry man, barely keeping his emotions in check. Tirhin had lost confidence in Caelan for no explainable reason, unless . . . unless it was because the prince had lost confidence in someone else, his father perhaps, or even himself.

Whatever the reason, it hurt. Hurt terribly to know that Caelan had sacrificed his conscience for someone who now showed how little he cared.

Like a vine scorched by fire, Caelan's trust and admiration curled up inside him. He swallowed, and found himself adrift in bitter disillusionment. Yes, stupidly he had continued to hope that if he kept serving Tirhin faithfully and well, that if he kept winning championships, one day the prince would free him as a reward. Now he saw he had been a blind fool, a fool filled with dreams and fantasies as insubstantial as the air.

"So," Caelan now said in a flat, toneless voice. "You believe I cannot defeat this Madrun."

Apology, or perhaps consternation, appeared in Tirhin's face. He said, "I have fought them in the border skirmishes. They are relentless. They fear nothing. It's terrifying to stand on a plain at dawn and have them come swarming out from the mist in a yelling horde.

"Yes, Caelan, you are strong and relentless. As for fear, you don't know what it is. But champion or not, I cannot afford a gamble of any kind. Too much depends on this victory."

"Such as?"

"You've been told enough," Tirhin said impatiently. "You wouldn't understand the intricacies of our political intrigues."

Caelan's jaw clenched hard. He drew in two deep breaths, fighting to keep his temper. "The priest said I must win the people's favor today. Are they not shouting for me now? Am I not already popular? The people know I belong to you. I came here as the favorite. The betting odds are—"

"There must be more. You must do more. I cannot explain it. This coronation business . . . the insult to me. It is the final straw in—" Breaking off, Tirhin pointed imperiously at the pouch. "Take it. Take the strength it will give you."

Caelan stared at him, not moving. Then finally he walked over to the small table and picked up the pouch. It wasn't necessary to loosen the strings to smell its contents. Revulsion shuddered through him. The very thought of swallowing an infusion made from this choked him.

There was something in it that would give him more than strength. He could feel the taint crawling through the leather into his fingers, searching for him, reaching for him. And a part of him welcomed its horribleness, reached back eagerly, longing to be set free.

Caelan opened his fingers and dropped the pouch

onto the table. Little shivers ran through him. He felt wretched, as though he had been vomiting from stomach grippe. Forcing himself under control, he turned to his master.

"There is another way to make sure I fight beyond all I have ever done before," he said, his voice tight and hollow. "A cleaner way, sir. An honorable way."

Tirhin flinched at that accusation. His face darkened, but he kept his temper. "Take care," he said softly.

Caelan knew the danger he courted, but he would not back down now. Too much was at stake. "May I speak?" he asked.

Tirhin's eyes flashed. "Damn you, *yes!*"

A flicker of triumph went through Caelan then. Whatever Tirhin was plotting, he needed Caelan, and that gave Caelan the advantage.

"I will fight this Madrun in a way that will bring the people to their feet," he said in a low, determined voice. "I will fight in a way you have never seen before. I will give you everything that potion would have dragged from me. But it will be by my will."

Tirhin frowned as though impatient with such narrow distinctions.

"I will defeat the Madrun."

"You cannot promise that! No matter how good you are, or have been, you cannot give me complete assurance."

Caelan looked him right in the eye. "I do. I give you my word."

"You can't, you fool. The word of a slave? Bah!"

Tirhin swung away, but Caelan blocked his path.

"No," he said, his gaze meeting Tirhin's intently, "not the word of a slave. I give you the word of a champion. You will have your victory, but you will pay my price for it."

Tirhin frowned. "You dare bargain with me? You?" he said, his voice rising. "You are my property. You fight because I command it. You serve because you are mine!"

Caelan's own temper flared. "If you believe that, then you are a simpleton, sir. Truly I know different."

Shock spread across Tirhin's face. He stared at Caelan as though he couldn't believe Caelan would dare speak to him in that manner.

Caelan could have said more, but he didn't. Already he had crossed too far over the line. Besides, he was choking with his own tangled emotions. How much did a man have to reveal in order to convince another to trust him?

He backed up a step. "Sir—"

But the fire was already dimming in Tirhin's eyes. He held up his hand to silence Caelan. "You have never been a slave," the prince said softly. "Even wearing shackles, you have never been a slave. You were born a free man, and you have kept that freedom in your heart always. In that sense, you were never gentled. Even Orlo could not break you. You have served me because for some insane reason you wanted my praise."

It was Caelan's turn to grow red. He wanted to look away but didn't.

"From such a desire grows loyalty," Tirhin said. "It is what makes men serve their commander through the worst conditions. They will follow him anywhere and give him their all in battle. This is what you have given me. This is what Lord Sien and I have trampled on today."

He had put his finger on it unerringly. Caelan dropped his gaze and said nothing. There could be no apology from a master to his slave, but there had been an admittance, and that was enough.

"What, then," Tirhin asked wearily, "is your price? What reward do you want? Better quarters? Another servant? More gold to line your pockets? Special privileges to travel? The opportunity to serve me as my protector when I have the throne?"

How casually he said that last, as though it carried no more weight than the other offerings.

Caelan's heart dropped inside him. He felt suddenly hollow and adrift, as though he had ceased to exist. Thoughts spun inside his head until he could not grasp them all.

The emperor's protector . . . sworn to save the emperor's life with no heed for his own . . . constantly at the emperor's side . . . awarded rank and privilege . . . the highest honor for a soldier to attain . . . a lifetime of work that was honorable and true . . . no more torn conscience . . . no more doubts . . . freedom.

He looked into Tirhin's eyes, seeking honest intention, and found it. His voice seemed to have left him, but he managed to gasp out a simple "Yes. That is a sufficient price."

Tirhin's face held a tangle of conflicting emotions, chief of which was worry. Sighing, he pinched the bridge of his nose. "Great Gault, I must be mad to trust you."

"To escape the ring I will fight with all that I have, and more," Caelan said.

His voice rang out too harshly, too forcefully, but he didn't care. His heart was soaring at this chance. The Madrun was doomed. Caelan intended him no mercy.

Tirhin still looked doubtful, but he nodded and headed for the door. Just as he reached it, he glanced back. "Bring me victory, Giant," he tried to say lightly, and failed.

Caelan faced him with shoulders erect and chin high. "I will. It seems, sir, that this time we must trust each other to keep our word."

Tirhin frowned. It was as though the temperature in the room grew icy cold. "There can be no failure," he said harshly. "None. Win a victory for me in the manner I request, or die on the sand. For by all the gods, I swear that I personally will take your life if you fail me today."

With a swirl of his blue cloak, he was gone, leaving his threat hanging heavy on the air.

Chapter Two

ORLO RETURNED, BUSTLING and flustered. "These damned delays," he grumbled. "Your muscles will be tight and cold again."

Rubbing his hands briskly together, he reoiled Caelan's taut shoulders, massaging deeply, then slung a blue cloak around Caelan, tightened his wrist cuffs, and straightened his fighting harness.

Caelan endured these preparations in grim silence, his thoughts on the arena.

Each of his wins had built up a larger and larger reputation that had to be met or surpassed constantly in order to please. After his first championship, it hadn't been enough to kill. No, then he was expected to fight with panache, drama, and flair. With each successive win came the added pressure of sustaining his record. He lived with the small, gnawing fear that someday he would meet his match. Then would come public, humiliating defeat, and probably death. No one remained champion for long; no one had won as many seasons as he.

And now all that he had done wasn't enough for his master. If he did not prevail today against the worst opponent he had ever faced, Tirhin would have him killed.

Caelan's jaw tightened, and he gathered all his determination. He had to succeed. No other option lay before him.

"Now remember," Orlo said, slapping him on the shoulder. "You're in better condition and better trained. You're fit and well prepared. You know the arena; you're used to the crowd. Most of all, you're champion. He is nothing but a foul enemy of the empire. The crowd will be with you every step. And use every dirty trick you know."

Caelan gave him a long look, but said nothing. He felt distracted and tense, off-balance in some way.

The door opened and a guard looked in. "Didn't you hear the summons? Produce your man, Orlo. The crowd is ready to tear down the stands."

"About bloody time," Orlo retorted. He turned his back to the guard and handed Caelan a sword.

Caelan took the weapon and immediately tucked it out of sight beneath his cloak. Orlo was breaking the law to give him this privilege. Already the weight and heft of the wire-wrapped hilt felt good and right in Caelan's hand. He drew in a deep breath and closed his eyes, letting the strength of the steel enter him.

His doubts and inner torment faded. He merged as one entity with the weapon, as though it became a natural extension of his hand. Years of fighting lay inside the blade, which had remained as true as the day it was forged.

"Come," Orlo said.

The guards swung the door completely open, and Caelan strode out.

"You trainers," one of the guards muttered as Caelan and Orlo passed. "Always stretching things out in hopes of keying up the crowd. We'll have a riot on our hands if you don't hurry."

Orlo snorted but did not reply. This delay had been the emperor's fault, or perhaps Tirhin's, no one else's.

Out in the passageway, chaos reigned as usual. A few weary fighters were being dipped in the water vat to clean off the worst of grime, sweat, and blood. Somewhere in the infirmary, a man was screaming over the rasping sound of a bone saw. Armed guards watched everywhere, alert and tense today because of the emperor's presence. Boys ran here and there, carrying bundles of clothing, bandages, and oil jars. Trainers stood in small groups, huddled in conferences that paused as Caelan strode by.

He looked neither right nor left, but he was aware of their eyes, narrowed with speculation and assessment as they watched him pass. Orlo flanked him, glowering fiercely in evident pride.

Ahead of them ran the call: "Make way for the champion! Make way!"

A path was cleared. Conversations halted in mid-sentence as people stared. It was considered bad luck to speak to a fighter on his way into the arena, for at this moment Caelan's life was held in the hands of the gods. But although no one whispered a word, he could feel waves of emotions beating at him. Envy, admiration, hope, frustration, dislike. A tangle of feelings he forced himself to resist.

Severance was one means of keeping himself steady. But experience in the arena had taught him to control himself without that severity of detachment. A man could grow dependent on it. Better to save it until he needed it in combat. Besides, he needed *sevaisin,* the joining, in order to evaluate his opponent in the first moment of confrontation.

So he had grown progressively calmer, colder, unemotional in public, training himself to remain focused and empty of all save his own assigned tasks. His mental toughness had given him an aura of grim purpose, which spoke its own kind of authority to people. They respected him, whether slave or free, and they moved aside as he passed by, only to surge after him in a mob eager to watch the coming contest.

Up the worn stone steps. Past the shadowy walls stained black with smoke from years of torchlight. Then, at the top of the steps, a shout from someone in warning, the outcry flashing on from person to person ahead of him.

"He's coming! Giant is coming! Make way for the champion!"

A flurry broke out ahead of him as men scurried up the ramp to find seats for themselves. Sunlight slanted down the ramp to meet him as he emerged from the darkness.

And the roar of sound, tremendous, overwhelming, deafening. It never stopped, never diminished. It was a force in and of itself, like a living thing, this mighty cheering. He could feel a wave of sheer anticipation hit him like a wall.

He started to sweat lightly. His heart was thumping like mad in his chest. Orlo patted his shoulder and said something Caelan could not hear.

He lost awareness of his trainer. Something in the cheering, stamping crowd mesmerized him and called him forth. Without hesitation he squared his shoulders and strode ahead of Orlo into sunlight and sound, becoming one with both.

The crowd screamed his name, and if possible the cheering grew louder.

Caelan strode across the freshly raked sand to the center of the arena, then turned to face the stands. Halfway up in the prime seating was the emperor's box with its red-striped awning. Imperial flags streamed in the breeze, and the emperor, his son, and their guests sat watching. Caelan lifted his hand high in salute, and saw Prince Tirhin raise his wine cup in return. The emperor was chatting with someone else and paid no attention, but Tirhin's gaze never wavered from Caelan.

His words passed through Caelan's mind, and Caelan felt a shiver inside himself. He wanted this win and what it would bring him. The desire was so strong he could taste it.

Caelan spun around and yanked off his cloak. The winter sunlight fell warm on his shoulders. When he lifted his bared sword to the crowd, they went into fresh frenzy. Many threw coins and flowers onto the sand, while a young boy raced to gather up Caelan's cloak.

A scream of bestial rage came from the holding pen on the south side of the arena. Caelan let his gaze flicker in that direction even as he saluted the crowd again.

A Madrun was only a man, he reminded himself quickly. There was no demon blood, nothing to fear. He had faced lurkers and wind spirits before and survived. He would succeed in this.

Were his opponent a veteran fighter like himself, Caelan would have continued to pose and posture for the crowd. They liked that sort of nonsense. He had once found it embarrassing, but now he did it without thinking. However, he remembered Orlo's words of warning and decided to take no chances. He had never seen a Madrun before, not face to face. But their fighting prowess was legendary, and they reputedly had no fear for their own lives at all. A man who did not fear death had the upper hand in any combat, but Caelan intended that to be the Madrun's only advantage. He vowed he would not be killed at the hands of a dirty savage. Moreover, he was determined to make good his promise to fight as they had never seen him fight before.

Another bellow came from the holding pen. Handlers scurried around, swearing at each other and sliding long, barbed poles between the wide slats to drive the occupant back from the gate.

It was rumored that in some of the more backward provinces, wild animals and lurkers were sometimes loosed in the arenas as opponents. Perhaps it was no Madrun he faced, but instead some beast.

Caelan ran his fingertips lightly along the flat of his blade, gently flexing it. He faced the holding pen, concentrating on it.

The crowd was slowly settling down, although they continued to shriek his name. Normally he would have continued to salute them or flourish his sword about. They loved seeing him execute drills to warm up.

Today, however, was no occasion for playacting, exactly as Orlo had warned him.

Another bellow came from the holding pen, and one of the handlers fell back with a scream. The crowd jeered a bit in impatience, then grew reluctantly quieter. Anticipation rolled down from the top of the stands.

Shivers crawled along Caelan's spine in response to it.

Normally he waited until his opponent appeared before reaching out with *sevaisin,* but now Caelan dared to join early.

A wall of rage hit him, red-hot, and so forceful he felt momentarily stunned.

There was no joining with *that.* It was murderous rage, a blind hatred as impenetrable as a shield.

Caelan's mouth went dry. During his stint as a gladiator, he had relied on his special, secret gifts to give him the winning advantage. He depended on them, and now he realized *sevaisin* would be useless.

How would he anticipate the man's next moves? How could he make sure he outguessed and outmaneuvered him?

Ruthlessly he shoved his rising doubts away. This was no time for alarm. He must rely on what Orlo had taught him. If nothing else, he could *sever* the man's life.

And if he could not cut through that rage with the reverse side of his gift?

Before Caelan could even dare think about that alarming possibility, the solid wood gate to the holding pen burst open. One of the handlers flung a sword onto the ground for the Madrun, and they all fled.

The crowd screamed with glee.

"Giant! Victory! Giant! Victory!" they chanted.

Caelan well remembered his first day in the public arena in what now seemed a lifetime ago. The sight of the stone bleachers rising above him in a towering circle had been overwhelming. The magnitude of the crowd, the noise, the blinding sunlight after such a long time down in the darkness below . . . arena shock was an involuntary reaction in anyone new to the games.

The Madrun who emerged came scuttling outside in a half-crouch, dropped to scoop up the sword, glanced left and right to get his bearings, spied Caelan, and came at him with a shrill war cry that raised the hair on the back of Caelan's neck.

It was as though the Madrun didn't notice the crowd or the noise. It was as though he didn't care.

Surprised in spite of all his preparation and Orlo's warnings, Caelan set himself and waited for the man's rush.

It was his first mistake.

The Madrun was big, nearly as tall as Caelan, and built like a bull. His massive shoulders rippled with muscle as he swung the sword around his head in a circle, running full tilt now through the deep sand. His head was shaven except for a bushy stripe of rust-red hair, and his ears were misshapen with mutilation scars. He was older than Caelan by at least five years, a man in his full fighting prime. The deep sand did not slow him. The sunlight did not blind him. The crowd did not distract him. His fight with his handlers had not tired him.

Still screaming in his own incomprehensible tongue, he was suddenly upon Caelan. Too late, Caelan snapped to attention and realized he should have been moving to meet the man. To wait for the first strike was a tactical mistake made by the greenest recruits. The speed built up by the Madrun would knock him flat, even if he did manage to deflect that shining blade.

Swearing at himself, Caelan drew on his incredible speed and pivoted at the last possible second, dodging his opponent and moving toward him rather than away.

Their swords clashed with a resounding bang of steel against steel that had the crowd back on its feet, cheering. To the crowd, their champion had seemingly waited calmly until the very last minute before moving. To the crowd, their champion looked very courageous against this barbaric enemy of the empire.

To the crowd, Caelan looked daring. To Orlo and Prince Tirhin, he must look like a lunatic.

Grimly Caelan put the prince's threat from his mind yet again. He exchanged a fast series of blows, then backed up, dancing around the Madrun in a circle. He wanted to evaluate this creature's fighting skills before he closed with him again.

The Madrun's red eyes glared at Caelan without wavering. With teeth bared, he rushed again, forcing Caelan to feint and spin without even an attack in return.

Hating being on the defensive, Caelan feinted, then feinted again, but the Madrun was not fooled. He simply attacked, hacking and screaming while the crowd moaned and jeered.

When Caelan had boasted he would fight as Tirhin had never seen him fight before, he had *not* intended this.

Forget that, Caelan told himself. *Concentrate.*

The Madrun slashed, and white-hot pain sliced through Caelan's arm. He struck back in anger, forcing the Madrun to retreat a little, then circled to catch his breath. Blood dripped steadily down his arm, his fighting arm. Already he could feel blood pooling between his palm and the hilt of his sword, making the grip slippery.

Sometimes the game would be halted, if one of the owners wanted a fighter's wound bound up so the contest could continue equally. But Prince Tirhin would never do that, not for his champion, not for the fighter considered the best in the empire, a man who needed no coddling, a man who had not been wounded in over a season.

Every time Caelan flexed his arm, the wound opened and air rushed in, making it burn like fire.

Caelan frowned and *severed* the pain. Stepping into icy detachment, he felt the wound fade from his consciousness. Everything around him seemed a bit slower; the Madrun looked a bit smaller than before. His fear dropped from him, as did his distractions. On one level he laughed at the Vindicant priest's offering him a potion to increase his fighting strength. This was all he needed.

Caelan drank in the coldness, letting confidence increase almost to arrogance. At the edge of his vision he could see the threads of life. How easy it would be to cut those surrounding the Madrun right now.

The temptation grew in him as time seemed to stand still. He held the power of life and death in his grip. It was sweet and exhilarating. The more he drew on it, the more pleasure he derived from using it.

And here, in the void of *severance* where there were no lies and no need for lies, he could admit to himself that this was why he fought. In the arena he could sip from this forbidden pool as much as he wanted.

But it was not right for a mere man to have such knowledge.

He feared the strength of *severance*'s pull; he always had. He knew what he would become if he ever gave way completely to it.

Besides, merely killing the Madrun was not what the prince had requested.

With a wrench, Caelan brought himself away from the edge of danger. *Severance* must always remain his tool, never become his master. He needed only to block the pain of his wound, nothing more.

Meanwhile, in those few split seconds when the world had paused for Caelan, the Madrun continued to circle him, eyeing him steadily. Now, as Caelan met his gaze, the Madrun lifted his sword and licked Caelan's blood off the edge of the blade. Then he laughed.

Caelan rushed him in a swift attack that caught the man unawares. Grunting in surprise, the Madrun stumbled back, defending himself strongly but clumsily. He learned fast. Caelan found the same trick did not work twice with this man, who was a better swordsman than he appeared.

Back and forth they parried, their blades ringing out in a steady crisscross of deadly force. Up and down pumped their arms, fast and furious, attack and counterattack, until suddenly in one shining moment Caelan felt himself riding a surge of sheer, unbridled joy.

He laughed aloud, and the Madrun was caught by surprise a second time. The Madrun stumbled, made a mistake, and barely evaded Caelan's lunge. Scrambling back, the Madrun found himself pressed hard by Caelan, who gave him no quarter. Caelan pushed him across the arena nearly to the wall.

The crowd roared approval.

Caelan's sword was slipping in his hand despite his stranglehold on the hilt, and he didn't know if he was streaming sweat or blood. He knew only that he had this man where he wanted him. The wall loomed just steps away from the Madrun's back. And when the Madrun bumped into it, Caelan would finish him.

But suddenly the Madrun dropped his arm, exposing himself to Caelan's blade. A split second before Caelan could lop the head from his shoulders, the Madrun dove to the ground and rolled toward Caelan's feet.

Caelan leaped over him and sensed more than saw the Madrun's blade coming at his vulnerable lower body. Twisting desperately in midair, Caelan brought his sword around and deflected the blade just in time to save himself from losing a leg.

That was all he could do, however. Caelan fell and rolled blindly, unsure where the Madrun was. He scrambled to his feet at once, but the Madrun was already tackling him, and brought him down with an impact that jolted half the breath from Caelan's lungs. Caelan kicked and squirmed, but he found himself pinned by the man's weight with the Madrun's forearm pressed down across his throat. The Madrun lifted his sword to plunge it into Caelan's side.

However, the swords were too long to fight with at such close quarters. Caelan got one hand free and jabbed his fingers into the Madrun's eyes.

Howling with pain, the Madrun shifted but didn't let go. Caelan chopped him in the throat. The Madrun made a strangling, gasping noise and went slack enough for Caelan to push free. Kicking hard against the man's side, Caelan scrambled away, recovered his sword, and swung it around.

Just before the blade connected, however, the Madrun flung a handful of sand at Caelan's face. Caelan had been caught once long ago by that ancient trick, but never again.

He ducked, closing his eyes, even as he finished his sword swing.

A choked cry of pain coupled with the jolting bite of steel into meat told him he had hit his mark.

Blinking, Caelan saw he had sliced into the man's hip, but the Madrun half hobbled, half crawled away from him and recovered his sword.

Good spectacle demanded that Caelan let the man regain his feet. Good sense told him to finish the Madrun quickly while he had the chance.

Caelan wavered for an instant. Tirhin wanted more than a quick victory; he wanted the crowd in his hand. Even now, half the crowd was shouting for Caelan to finish the kill but the rest were roaring approval as Caelan stepped back and waited for the Madrun to recover. The show was not finished yet, and they loved it.

Forcing a smile, Caelan turned to the crowd and lifted his bloody sword in quick salute. They clapped and cheered all the more.

It was his second mistake.

In that moment of inattention, the Madrun regained his feet and impossibly rushed at Caelan with all the speed and fury of before. Disbelief hit Caelan at the same time as the Madrun did.

Caelan parried the attacking blow clumsily, feeling the jolt travel into his wrist and up his arm. There was no time to wonder how the Madrun could move like this with such a deep wound in his hip. There was no time for Caelan to curse his own stupidity. There was only desperation throttling him now as he fought off the Madrun again. Despite *severance,* he could not ignore the leaden ache creeping through his arm. As he tired from exhaustion and blood loss, he would get slower. He could not continue much longer. Yet what choice had he? The Madrun seemed tireless. Despite the blood coating his leg, the barbarian gave no evidence of pain or distress. His red eyes glared as fiercely as ever.

Perhaps he understood the principles of *severance* too.

That was a disconcerting thought, at a time when it was foolhardy to think too much. Grimly, Caelan forced himself to ignore everything save keeping his blade in motion. No faltering, no mistakes. He had been lucky thus far. He could not depend on fortune to save him a third time.

Back and forth they fought, scrambling and dodging, only to rush at each other again. No trick Caelan tried seemed to work. No amount of skill seemed to be enough to break through the Madrun's guard.

Well matched, Orlo had said. It was true. For the first time, Caelan felt he had met his equal.

He could hear himself gulping air. Little black spots began to dance across his vision. Everything but the Madrun was a blur. Yet Caelan would not give up. Tirhin had promised him his freedom, and for that Caelan would go to the wall.

Caelan felt as though he had fought for hours. It should be enough. Let the crowd be happy this once so he could go home. Let the other man fall down; let him die so Caelan could end this.

But the Madrun would not surrender either. He would not weaken. He would not die.

They fought until both of them were heaving for air, stumbling apart to eye each other, only to attack and clash again.

There had to be some way to outwit this creature, Caelan thought with rising desperation.

What had Orlo said? The barbarian had sheer strength and brute force? How true. Orlo had also warned Caelan not to prance about, but to use every dirty trick he had.

Caelan wearily cast about for something he had not yet tried. He had used everything Orlo had taught him. He had used everything the other gladiators had taught him in barracks. He had used the tactics old veterans tried on each other in combat. He had even watched the Madrun's style of fighting and returned some of that to the man.

The Madrun's eyes widened, but he only bared his teeth anew and fought harder.

Evading him once again, Caelan circled to gain a breather. *Severance* would keep him going until his heart exploded. Then he would drop dead in the sand, and it would be over.

Caelan gritted his teeth. There had to be another way.

There was, of course. He had known it even as he stood in his ready room and boasted to Prince Tirhin that he would fight with everything he had until he prevailed.

He had hoped it would not come to this, but now he knew such a hope was futile. One trick left, something he had never used before, had never seen used in the arena. Only a few of the oldest veterans ever mentioned the Dance of Death, and then in lowered, awe-hushed voices.

Now that the time had come, Caelan felt a coldness that had nothing to do with *severance*.

Of course he could still cut the Madrun's threads of life, but although the barbarian's sudden collapse would look natural enough considering the amount of blood he'd lost, it would be a poor finish to this battle. It would not gain Caelan his freedom.

No, he had to give the crowd the ultimate spectacle. Never mind fear. Never mind his own doubts.

Meanwhile the Madrun still kept pace with him, still circled with him. The Madrun was looking pale from blood loss, but he would fight until he dropped. The stories were true; Madruns did not fear death. Caelan could see nothing in the man's eyes but the desire to kill.

Still, it had to be tried.

Caelan shifted *severance,* sucking in a sharp breath as pain swept him, and reached out with *sevaisin.* Weakened now, the Madrun still throbbed with hatred, but Caelan caught glimmers of what churned beneath.

Withdrawing back to the cold safety of *severance,* Caelan was able to catch his breath and steady himself in time to meet the Madrun's next attack. He had his answer now.

Blades flashing, they fought with a fury and speed nearly equal to when they had begun. Caelan gritted his teeth, forcing himself to hang on, forcing himself to ignore the scream in his muscles, to keep going for as long as it took.

Wait, Caelan kept telling himself. Don't miss the chance.

At last it came. He saw the Madrun tilt his blade for the lunge attempt Caelan had been waiting for. Over and over in drills, Orlo had taught Caelan how to meet such an attack. Catch the opponent's blade with the flat of yours and lift, using the other's impetus to carry his lunge past its target.

Instead, Caelan caught the Madrun's blade and twisted it beneath his. The circular motion of his blade directed the Madrun's sword point straight into Caelan's side.

The Madrun's eyes flew open wide in astonishment, but Caelan twisted even harder, leveraging the Madrun's blade with his hilt guard to pull the blade into himself.

The crowd screamed exactly at the moment it pierced his ribs. He heard himself grunt from the impact, felt the blade invade his body . . . so huge, so horrible. It was worse than he could have imagined. He seemed to have lost his breath, and for a moment he thought he would lose *severance,* which was all that now held him together. He was burning inside from the strain, and yet it all happened in a split second. His own sword arm was still moving, still twisting around the Madrun's blade, which was now trapped in his body and useless. Disengaging from the Madrun's blade, Caelan's sword shifted up to thrust deep into the man's heart.

The Madrun released a thin, high-pitched scream that sounded piercing loud in the sudden silence. Arching his back, he toppled slowly backward, sliding off Caelan's sword. As he fell, his sword pulled from Caelan's side. The agony of that withdrawal was a thousand times more brutal than the entry.

With all his strength and will, Caelan braced his legs apart and managed to stay upright.

The Madrun seemed to fall forever; then his solid body crashed to the sand. Dust puffed up. He lay still, his open, sightless eyes staring into eternity.

The roaring in Caelan's ears remained the only sound. He seemed to stand in a place that did not exist at all.

Once before he had had a vision in the arena, one in which his dead father approached him. Now, feeling death reaching into his body, Caelan was certain Beva would appear before him again. But there was nothing except him and the pain that beat harder and harder. He looked down and saw a crimson river flowing at his feet. If he tried to look in the direction the river was running, he saw only a terrifying blackness as though endless night waited on the other side.

He must dam the river.

Bending down, he reached out until he could plunge his hand into that crimson flood. Spreading his fingers wide, he grimaced against the agony and expended his last ounce of strength on the command to *stop* flowing.

The rapid rush slowed to a trickle, then ceased altogether. Where there had been a river seconds before, there was now only drying sand, marked here and there by steaming puddles.

Caelan straightened, pulling all the life force back into himself and holding it inside by sheer willpower. He felt as though he might break apart from the effort, and yet he held.

His vision cleared and he was back in the arena, standing there with a dead opponent at his feet. Cheering roared from the stands. Streamers, flowers, and other gifts rained down, glittering in the sunlight. Caelan swallowed hard and dragged in a thin, unsteady breath, then a deeper one.

He heard the attendants coming at a run from behind him and forced himself to turn around slowly.

Although it was almost beyond his strength, he lifted his bloody sword to his master, who was actually standing as though in alarm.

Caelan's salute, however, apparently reassured the prince, who waved and resumed his seat.

By then the attendants had reached Caelan. A boy, wide-eyed and pale, carried Caelan's blue victory cloak. He stood there, staring up at Caelan, while the men knelt around the dead Madrun.

The boy's lips were trembling. "You . . . you let him—" His voice broke off, and he could not finish his sentence.

In silence Caelan took his cloak from the boy's arms and shook out the folds one-handed. He swirled the garment around his shoulders, hiding the wound in his side and most of the blood. Someone shoved the boy aside and took the sword carefully from Caelan's hand.

His fingers ached from having gripped it so hard. Grimly he flexed them, but doing so only reminded him of the cut in his arm. Tucking his arm tight against his side beneath the concealment of the cloak, he hesitated only to gather himself, then strode across the arena, waving as he went.

He remained the champion, beyond all doubt, beyond all expectations.

He circled the arena with his head high and his shoulders erect, hiding everything that might mar this moment. The spectators waved back, called out to him, leaned over the walls as though to touch him, threw coins and flowers.

He felt light-headed and strange, as though he might faint, and yet he knew he would not.

By the time he completed his victory walk, the stricken faces had cleared. Everyone was laughing and congratulating each other. He saw some counting their wager tokens, making faces or openly gloating, depending on how much they had risked that day.

The steps leading up to the imperial box looked endless and slightly crooked. But the fire blazing ever hotter in his side gave him strength, and he forced himself up the steps. He would have his freedom today. He had more than earned it. He had more than kept his word.

To his surprise, the prince left the imperial box and came halfway down to meet him.

It was an unheard-of honor. Tirhin's guards—obviously caught unawares—scrambled to follow him, but the prince strode down the steps through the midst of the spectators and met Caelan with a broad smile.

Behind him, up in the imperial box, Caelan saw the emperor sitting with little expression at all. The high priest Sien stood near the emperor's chair, watching Kostimon with a small, evil smile.

The prince smiled and waved to the crowd, accepting the fresh accolades and cheering as though they were for him alone. When he reached Caelan, however, his smile was replaced by a frown of consternation.

"My dear Giant," he said, then stopped himself from saying more. Straightening his shoulders, he withdrew into formality, and his smile reappeared—public, practiced, and false. "Well done," he said, the way he would have praised his best stag hound.

Rebuffed, Caelan met Tirhin's eyes, seeking approval, seeking confirmation that he would receive his reward. But the prince's gaze was unreadable. As he listened to the crowd's shouts, Tirhin's smile widened.

Caelan had no choice but to extend the formalities. With all his strength, Caelan forced himself to speak clearly and without any evidence of his inner strain. "Sir, I bring you this day's victory."

Formal words, demanded by tradition and spoken countless times before. Yet they didn't begin to say all that he meant or all that he yearned for.

Let it be true, he prayed in his weary heart. *Oh, Gault, in thy mercy, let this man keep his word to me as I have kept mine to him.*

"And I accept this victory, fought on this auspicious day in my name," the prince said. His baritone voice rang out loudly, carrying across the hushed stands.

A servant joined him with a silk pillow supporting the victory crown of ivy. As Caelan bowed, the prince set the crown on his head. The leafy vines scratched, as usual.

"You have served us well, champion," the prince said. "You have defeated an enemy of the empire, as our armies will defeat the Madruns and drive them far from our borders."

Cheering surged up, drowning out his words until the prince lifted his hands. With quiet restored, he continued. "We thank you, champion. We admire your strength, courage, and fighting prowess, shown this day as never before. In appreciation of this magnificent effort, which has more than surpassed my expectations, I wish to give you a special reward."

Caelan's gaze snapped up, and his heart surged. Suddenly his ears were roaring. He tried to swallow and couldn't. His eyes filled with tears that he struggled manfully to hold back.

Tirhin smiled, glancing around to be sure the crowd was still watching. "Here is a personal token of my pleasure."

As he spoke, he took a heavy gold chain off the pillow. "Wear it with pride, my champion."

Caelan stood there, stricken and silent. Disappointment crashed through him, and he felt as though he were falling a very long distance.

A frown touched the prince's features momentarily, and he cleared his throat.

Belatedly, Caelan somehow managed to bow his head, although his neck felt so stiff he thought it might snap. Tirhin slipped the chain around Caelan's throat, and a smith appeared from the crowd to close the final link.

Then the prince leaned near and whispered into Caelan's ear in a voice that was low and furious, "You fool, you weren't to take a scratch. If you collapse publicly from this stunt, I shall see your soul damned for all eternity."

With that, he extended his hand to Caelan, who had to kneel and press Tirhin's fingertips to his sweaty brow.

Fresh cheering swelled, but in Caelan's heart there was only fire and bitter disillusionment. What cruel betrayal was this? His master was a fair man. They had bargained squarely. The prince had given his word . . . somehow Caelan choked off the desperate round of thoughts spinning through his brain.

He climbed to his feet, although the effort made him dizzy, and held on. He was too proud now to show any weakness. Nor would he meet the prince's gaze again, fearing he would not be able to conceal his fury.

The prince stepped back and lifted his arms in a cheerful wave to the crowd. He was still smiling. But his eyes were like stones.

With more waves for the crowd, he walked back up the steps.

Caelan stood there, stunned. That was it. That was all. Whatever he had expected, it was not this. As he watched his master's retreating back, Caelan's temper rose. Of all the ungrateful . . .

An attendant prodded his arm, distracting him from his furious disappointment. Recalling where he was, Caelan executed a very small, very stiff bow to the prince's retreating back.

There remained the crowd, chanting his name. Like an endless sea, the faces surrounded him, held back only by the soldiers.

Caelan battled himself, trying to believe there would be more later. He was a fool to expect the prince to free him on the spot.

Yet a little voice in his heart whispered, *He could have.*

Crossing the arena had never been so difficult. It took an eternity, and despite the crisp winter air Caelan was sweating. He could feel himself weakening with every step, yet he kept his chin high and his shoulders erect, forcing one foot ahead of the next as the guards escorted him to the ramp. Behind him, young boys ran across the arena sand with crimson and blue streamers unfurling from their hands while Tirhin's slaves threw coins and favors into the crowd as part of the celebration.

Caelan saluted the crowd one final time before going in.

One of the guards stopped him. "By your rights, you can circle the arena again. As long as they shout for you, enjoy your victory."

Caelan shook his head. His elation was gone. He'd lost the heart for another victory walk. Besides, his knees were growing spongy and he dared not keep up the pretense much longer.

Even now, he could hear voices in the crowd: "He's fine. Look at him! You only thought the Madrun stabbed him."

And others: "Who knew a Traulander could fight like that? If they'd all take up arms like Giant, they could help the emperor defeat the Madruns once and for all."

And someone else: "The prince can pick his fighting men. By the gods, we need a leader like that. I say let him take charge of our army."

Fresh bitterness flooded through Caelan, and he descended into the torchlit gloom of the subcaverns.

Many of the guards left their posts to cluster around him, eager to slap his back and shake his hand.

"I've won a fortune on you today, Giant!" one of them said.

"By the gods, I've never seen such fighting."

"You're a devil, blessed by the dark one, to fight like that."

They wanted to talk it over, describing every move in detail as they relived it again and again. Caelan stood with them a moment, longing for Orlo to come and shoo them away. His head was spinning and he didn't know what he said to anyone. But no one noticed. Finally he brushed past them and went on while they talked and laughed behind him.

With every step, the new gold chain thumped a little against his collarbone. It was a generous gift indeed, heavy, and of extremely fine workmanship.

But to Caelan it was still a chain, put on him by a master who would never let him go.

He felt like he was choking.

Chapter Three

AT THE STEPS leading down to his ready room, Caelan found his strength suddenly deserting him. He paused and sagged against the smoke-blackened wall, trying to catch his breath. Another cluster of guards and workers waylaid him, all talking at once. Caelan felt everything blurring, and he panicked. He could not fall; he must not fall. Questions came at him from all sides, but he found he did not have to answer. They were all too busy congratulating each other to care whether he spoke or not.

Then an insolent voice cut across the chatter. "Giant! Ho, there!"

Blinking hard, Caelan managed to rally. With great care, he turned around to face a lanky man wearing the imperial coat of arms on his sleeve.

It was Nilot, head trainer of the emperor's gladiators.

The others fell silent and stepped back with respectful bows. Many remembered they had work to do and melted away.

"Quite a spectacle you put on," Nilot said. His dark eyes raked Caelan up and down. "Frankly, I didn't think you had so much toughness in you. You've never fought this way before."

Caelan was burning up. His legs trembled with weakness. He struggled to hold himself together, aware that this man's eyes were sharp and unfriendly. Nilot had never spoken to him personally before, but his hostility was plain.

"Who taught you the Dance of Death?" Nilot asked sharply. "That's an old dueling trick, used only by officers in the Crimson Guard."

A sense of danger alerted Caelan. He fought off the gathering mists and forced himself to focus on what the man was saying. Insolence seemed the best defense.

"And as such, is it sacred?" Caelan asked with open mockery. He knew Nilot was an army veteran, supposedly much decorated for bravery. "Does a gladiator slave sully this type of swordplay by using it on an enemy of the people?"

Nilot's thin mouth tightened to a hard line, but he was not deflected. "There's not a gladiator alive who would know such a move, or how to execute it properly. Who taught it to you?"

"I have an excellent trainer."

"Orlo?" Nilot snorted. "Excellent for turning third-rate scabs into second-rate fighters. Has your master been giving you special lessons?"

Caelan saw the trap yawning before him, now when it was too late. Inwardly cursing this man, Caelan sought for a quick answer that would be believed. He found nothing. He could not say the truth, that he had joined with a sword and learned its secrets from all the combats it had known. The secret ways of Trau mysticism were feared here.

Yet how could he answer in a way that would protect Prince Tirhin?

"Masters do not have time to teach their slaves the finer secrets of swordplay," he said as scornfully as possible.

"Oh, that's a loyal answer."

Caelan's gaze snapped to Nilot's. "What would you have me say?"

"The truth. Did Prince Tirhin teach you that move?"

"No."

"Then who?"

If insolence would not work, perhaps arrogance would. "Perhaps you did not know that I was born free and of good birth. I have not always worn chains and served the will of others." Caelan pushed himself forward, praying he would not stagger. "I cannot linger here."

Nilot blocked his path. "I am not done with you."

"Caelan!" came an angry shout. "What are you doing standing in this cold? Are you mad? Your muscles will stiffen."

It was Orlo, coming down the passageway at a furious pace. Caelan had never been so relieved to see the man.

He glanced at Nilot and shrugged. "I must go."

"But—"

"I must go."

Nilot reached across him and gripped Caelan by his injured arm. The pain was like a spear point, impaling him. Caelan sucked in a breath, and felt the world turn gray.

"By the gods, I'll have a straight answer from you yet," Nilot said angrily. "Tell me the truth! Was it his highness who taught you?"

Caelan gritted his teeth. He wanted to scream from the pain. He knew his face must be as white as paper, but *severance* still served him. Coldly, he said, "You speak disrespectfully of my master. Shall I defend him, here and now, with my bare hands?"

Nilot's eyes flickered as though he realized he stood unguarded, face to face with an unchained gladiator. Caelan reeked of sweat and blood. He had just killed in the heat of combat; his temper still ran high enough for him to risk the punishment of death or mutilation for threatening a free man like this. Nilot swallowed, and his grip slackened on Caelan's arm.

At once Caelan yanked free. Glaring, he started to speak but Orlo reached them, hastily interceding.

"Enough, enough," the trainer said, his eyes darting from Nilot to Caelan. "Nilot, what are you doing, keeping him standing here? For Gault's sake, let him clean off the gore first and have his wine. There'll be occasion enough to talk to him tonight."

Nilot scowled and stepped back. "I think not. There is no reason for me to attend the victory party of the emperor's opponent."

Orlo sent him an innocent look. "What a pity. I thought the Madrun was considered everyone's opponent."

Nilot's scowl deepened. Without another word, he turned on his heel and strode away.

Orlo gestured at Caelan to descend the steps. "Get on with you! I thought you'd have enough sense to get to your bath at once. You can reap your glory later."

Sighing, Caelan turned in silence and somehow got himself moving down the steps. Orlo flanked him, grumbling and criticizing all the way. He fended off anyone else who attempted to approach them. "Get back! Let the champion pass!"

Leaning closer, Orlo shot Caelan a sideways glance. "What in Murdeth's name did that snake want with you?"

"Nothing," Caelan said. "He was angry at the loss."

"Angry? Him?" Orlo snorted. "Oh, yes, and how innocent you are. You, looking like you meant to tear out his throat. Don't you have better sense than to threaten a man of his position?"

"He insulted the prince," Caelan said through his teeth.

Orlo shot him another look, then frowned. "You are a slave," he whispered hotly, glancing left and right to make sure no one overheard him. "It's not your place to defend the honor of his imperial highness."

Caelan shrugged. Now that he had a little distance from the incident with Nilot, he was annoyed with himself. Tirhin was not worth the risk he took. "You're right, Orlo," he said meekly. "The prince can defend his own honor. I am a fool.

I have always been a fool. It is likely I will be a fool until I die."

Orlo's frown deepened. "I know Nilot. He never does anything without a purpose. Did he make an offer to buy you?"

Caelan snorted, not bothering to answer. There were always men trying to buy him from the prince. Caelan was supposed to be flattered by such offers, but he always found them demeaning and shameful.

"Yes, I'm sure that's it," Orlo continued. "He will bring an offer from the emperor. Gault, that will be a problem! If the prince refuses to sell you, he runs the risk of offending—"

"Stop worrying," Caelan said tersely. "Nilot didn't come to buy me. He wanted to know who taught me the Dance of Death."

Orlo veered onto that subject immediately like a dog after a bone. "Hah, wouldn't he just! Wouldn't we all? You didn't get it from me."

"No."

"And it was a damned stupid thing to try! You—"

"It worked."

"Oh, yes, it worked, but the risk!"

Caelan's gaze dropped. "Necessary."

"You could have killed him several times before you finished him," Orlo said sternly. "Gods, it was like watching your first season. My heart nearly stopped at the mistakes you made. Besides, have you ever practiced that move? It was invented for bravado by lovelorn officers wanting to duel over their women."

"It was invented for combat," Caelan said stubbornly, concentrating on each step. "Later, it was used in duels."

"Yes, by the officers in the emperor's Crimson Guard. You had no business using it."

Caelan threw him a cynical look. "Because I'm a slave."

"Because you're not in the Crimson Guard. They'll be offended. They hold their traditions as high as their honor."

Caelan frowned. No wonder the prince was displeased with him. Caelan thought he was doing the right thing, but once again he had blundered. It did no good to say he wasn't versed in military traditions. Neither the prince nor the army was interested in his excuses. Some of Caelan's anger returned. He hadn't asked to be involved in this intrigue. He was no good at it. And now he had made things worse.

Someone hailed Orlo from the bottom of the steps, calling out congratulations.

Orlo waved, and swiftly changed the subject with a warning glance at Caelan. "I'll bet you twenty ducats that putting the Madrun in today was Nilot's idea. Stupid. If the brute had won, how could they celebrate the victory of an enemy? If he lost, who would care?"

Caelan nodded, conserving his strength against the mists that were blurring everything. He bumped into the wall and had to bite off a groan.

Orlo's hand gripped his uninjured arm to steady him. "Stiff," he said with pretend anger while he hastened Caelan past the group eager to offer yet more congratulations. "Too much standing around talking. Time for that massage."

The moment they were inside Caelan's ready room, Orlo slammed the door and yelled for the slaves.

Unz appeared. Scrawny and perpetually nervous, he was the youngest.

"Where is everyone?" Orlo demanded, looking around. "Why isn't the massage table ready? Where's the bath water?"

Unz bowed. "I'll get—"

"I'll flog their hides for this. Where are they?"

"Gone to cash in their wager tokens," Unz replied nervously.

Orlo's face turned a dark purple. "Get the water" was all he said, however.

Unz fled.

Orlo kicked a stool over to Caelan. "Sit!"

Caelan dropped heavily onto it. His side began to bleed again; he could feel it warm and wet against his arm. The effort of holding *severance* was too much. He longed to let go, yet he was afraid to.

"Hurting, are you?" Orlo asked. He tossed his club aside and advanced on Caelan. "I thought I'd never get you safely out of sight. You reckless idiot, I told you to stay out of his reach. Let me see that arm."

As he spoke, he pulled the cloak from Caelan's shoulders, then stood there, staring. The cloak slid unnoticed from his fingers. "Merciful Gault," he whispered. "I thought I saw him stick you, but then you seemed unhurt. I couldn't get out of the stands sooner to help you."

"It's all right," Caelan said through his teeth. He had never seen Orlo look this pale, this frightened. "I had to provide . . . spectacle."

"You fool," Orlo said, pressing his fingers gently against Caelan's side where the trickle of blood was beginning to bubble faster. "You great, hulking fool. When I told you to use every dirty trick, I didn't mean *this.*"

Caelan felt suddenly flushed and hotter than ever. He twisted on the stool. "Where's my bath? It's too warm in here. I—"

Orlo gripped his shoulder. "Boy!" he bawled at the top of his lungs. "Unz! Bring bandages, quickly!"

The room started spinning around Caelan. He braced his shoulder against Orlo's side and gripped the bottom of the man's tunic. "Not so loud. They'll hear you."

"Why the devil shouldn't someone hear?" Orlo said in exasperation. But he lowered his voice. When Unz came running with a handful of gauze strips, he grabbed them from the boy's hand, knocking some of them to the floor. "Get more! Idiot! Can't you see he's bleeding to death?"

Unz stared, his face as white as the bandages, and stammered something incomprehensible.

"Get more bandages. And water. And the healer. We need the healer!"

"No," Caelan said.

Orlo pressed the gauze to his side, and he flinched at the pain.

"Steady," Orlo said, but he sounded more desperate than soothing. "Don't talk. Just stay quiet. Boy! Where are you?"

Unz reappeared with more gauze. "This is all—"

"Never mind. Get the cloak. We'll bind it around him. Quick, boy. No, I'll do it. Support him."

Unz timidly grasped Caelan's shoulders while Orlo hacked the cloak into long strips and wrapped them around Caelan's torso. He knotted them with a firmness that made Caelan cry out.

Severance slipped, and he could not hold on any longer. The river of blood escaped him and gushed into the cloth. He could feel his life, his awareness flowing out with it.

"Forget the water. Run for the healer now," Orlo said while the room swirled and eddied. "Go, boy!"

"No," Caelan said. He reached out, his hand groping blindly.

Orlo gripped his fingers hard enough to crush them.

"No one to know," Caelan insisted. "Spoil the victory. Spoil the prince's . . . orders . . ."

He couldn't finish. The room grew white, blurring into

shapeless light, then fading, fading until there was only shadow.

"Get the healer," he heard Orlo say. "Don't say why. Don't say anything. Just get him. *Run!*"

Caelan came drifting back to the pleasant fragrances of balm and honey, herbal scents that reminded him of his childhood safe in E'nonhold. Someone nearby was grinding with a small mortar and pestle, working the old-fashioned way, doing things correctly.

He opened his eyes a fraction, not quite willing to wake up completely yet. There was a fire burning to keep him warm. It cast a ruddy glow across his bed. He listened to the hiss of the embers, a steady singing of flame that seemed to be calling his name.

Wind spirits had called his name once, and nearly killed him when he went to them. There were no wind spirits in Imperia. He wondered if the fire spirits had come here instead.

Restlessly, a little frightened, he turned his head on the pillow, only to have a shadow fall across the firelight. A hand slipped beneath his head and lifted him slightly.

"Drink this," a voice said.

Caelan sipped the potion, finding its taste bittersweet. The effort exhausted him, but once he was lying down again he found his head felt much clearer.

He gazed up at the healer, but the man's face remained hidden in shadow, silhouetted against the firelight. Something about him seemed oddly familiar, yet he wasn't the usual arena healer. Caelan frowned, unable to sort it out.

"These aren't my quarters," he said fretfully. His voice sounded weak and hoarse. "Have I been sold?"

"No," the healer said soothingly. "Rest. Do not talk. Give the potion time to do its work."

Caelan frowned, but the healer moved out of his line of vision. In growing puzzlement, Caelan stared instead at his surroundings. He seemed to be in a spacious chamber, one that extended well past the circles of light cast by the lamps placed around his bed. He could not see into the shadows, but it was evident that he was lying in a very fine bed carved of exotic woods and covered with linens as fine as gossamer. The coverlet beneath his hand felt smooth and strongly woven, like silk.

Caelan was sweating again, and he felt a wave of weakness flow through his body in a sudden tide. Perhaps this was all a fever-ridden fantasy. In reality he must be lying in his narrow room on his hard bunk. Unz would have kindled a small fire in the brazier to ward off the winter chill. Imperia winters were as nothing compared to the deep snows and frozen rivers of Trau, but because of the mildness of the weather, Imperia craftsmen never bothered to make buildings snug and warm. As a result, winters were drafty and miserable indoors.

Sometimes at dawn Caelan would rise and stand outside with his face turned to the north. His nostrils would draw in the scents of frost while his heart ached for the old glacier up beyond the Cascade Mountains. He missed the deep, blanketing silence of the pine forests after a snowfall. He missed the ice coating his eyebrows and eyelashes after a brisk trek out for wood cutting. He missed the rough-coated ponies, sturdy and surefooted, who would toss their white manes and gallop, snorting, across the glacier.

Gentle hands probed his side, and agony speared him, driving back his memories. He stiffened, holding in a cry. Then the pain ebbed quickly, as though it were being drawn from his body.

The healer *severed* him from the wound, and when the

sure hands finally lifted, Caelan felt only a soft tingling sensation in his side. Without looking he knew the wound had closed. His skin there felt too drawn and tight, as though newly grown. The pain did not return. Slowly he let his body sag with relief. He hadn't realized until now how much he had been fighting to control the pain.

"Drink again," the healer said. "Then sleep."

Caelan looked up at him, troubled by something elusive in that soft voice, something he should have recognized. But all of this was like a dream.

"Sleep," the healer said.

Although he meant to ask a question, Caelan instead shut his eyes, and slept.

The next time he awakened, the lamplight was much dimmer around him and the fire had burned down to hissing coals. Several figures stood a short distance from the foot of his bed, arguing in low voices. He recognized the prince's among them; there was no disguising that crisp, distinctive baritone.

Lifting his hand to rub his eyes, Caelan felt refreshed and clearheaded. He gazed at the fine furnishings around him and realized he must have been brought inside the prince's own house. This both gratified and disturbed him. Without bothering to sort it out, he tried to lift himself onto his elbow, and found himself as weak as a newborn.

Orlo reached him first. "What are you doing?" he asked sharply. "You are supposed to be resting, sleeping. What kind of potion wears off after only an hour? Are you in pain? You must lie still."

The discussion between the prince and the healer ended. The prince departed, but the healer came forward, stopping just beyond the lamplight.

From the shadows he spoke: "Have no fear on the champion's behalf. He does not suffer. All he requires is rest."

Caelan frowned, his attention caught once again by the healer's voice. Now, however, he was sufficiently alert to recognize the slightest trace of accent. The healer was a Traulander. Small wonder Caelan had thought he recognized his voice. Now it made sense. It also explained the good, fresh herbs in the healer's potions and how he had *severed* the wound. Caelan probed his side with his fingertips. He felt no tenderness, no soreness. The stab wound was gone, as was the cut to his arm. It was excellent work, as good as something his father would have done.

"You are still in pain," Orlo said in open concern. "Please lie down."

Caelan shook his head, but allowed himself to be pressed down onto his pillow. This was a stupid time to let his emotions gain control of him.

To change the subject, he said, "His highness sounded angry. Have I—"

"You've done nothing wrong," Orlo said.

But he spoke too quickly.

Caelan's eyes narrowed. "I missed the victory party, did I not? How long have I lain here?"

"Not long enough," Orlo said gruffly.

"A day," the healer replied.

Orlo shot him a glare, then swung his gaze back to Caelan. "Never mind the damned party. It wasn't important. Neither is tonight's—"

"The festivities," Caelan said. "I forgot them."

He reached for the coverlet, but Orlo's callused hand gripped his and held it hard.

"No," Orlo said. "You will not go with him, no matter what he wants. You are not well enough."

Caelan stared up at the trainer, then threw back the coverlet and sat up. Swinging his legs over the side of the bed, he shivered lightly in the cool air and wondered if he had the strength to stand.

"Stop this!" Orlo said. "It doesn't matter whether you go with him or not. This is a trivial thing, not worth your life. Not worth—"

He broke off and stood there scowling. His jaw muscles bunched as though he struggled to hold back words.

"My life is not at risk," Caelan said gently, although his temper was beginning to fray. He was tired of Orlo's interference. The trainer was only trying to protect him, but Caelan didn't want protection. He wanted his freedom, and Prince Tirhin was his only means of getting it. "Already I am much better, thanks to the skilled ministrations of my countryman."

As he spoke he glanced at the healer, who still kept to the shadows. "I must thank you," Caelan said. "I—"

The healer bowed and retreated quickly, saying nothing. The door closed silently behind him.

Astonished, Caelan looked at Orlo. "Who was that?" he asked.

Orlo shrugged.

"Why was he in attendance, and not the arena healer?"

"That quack," Orlo said with a contemptuous snap of his fingers. "What could he do but dither and shake his head? The prince asked for one of the palace healers, and this man came."

"A Traulander," Caelan said softly, conscious of a hurt in his heart that had never healed.

"It is said they are the best healers in the empire."

"Yes. I know."

How long had it been since he had heard the accent, the particular inflections of vowel and syllable heard only in the north country? He felt his eyes grow gummy and wet, and sternly he pulled himself together. This weakness must be put behind him.

"You are tired," Orlo said, still watching him. "Please rest. No matter how fancy the healer, it is still old-fashioned rest that makes the best cure."

"There is not time for rest," Caelan said, frowning. "And I am well."

Orlo touched his shoulder gently. "A lie," he said, but the reproof was mild. "Stop the lies, Caelan. You lie to the world. You lie to the prince. You lie to me. Worst of all, you lie to yourself."

"I don't understand."

Orlo's gaze never wavered. "I think you do. You threw yourself on the Madrun's sword as though it was nothing. Stupid or courageous, who can say? But why can't you throw yourself on the truth?"

Caelan's temper slipped. "Speak your mind, Orlo. Not these riddles."

"He won't free you."

It was like having the sword pierce his side all over again. Caelan lost his breath and struggled to regain it.

"You are wrong," he said, his voice weak against the intensity of his emotions. His fist clenched on the coverlet. "Wrong."

"I have made my share of mistakes," Orlo said, "enough to know that it is stupid to walk about in blindness. His highness will never free you as long as you are valuable to him. No matter how many times you guard his back when he goes where he should not. You have served him with all your heart and soul. Yesterday you nearly got yourself killed for him, and none of it will avail you."

"I will be free again," Caelan said grimly, staring into space. "I have his word."

Orlo snorted, his square face branded with cynicism. "Oh? You have the word of our kind, honest master. Soon enough there will be betrayal to balance the honey. I have warned you enough, but you never heed warnings, do you?"

Caelan glared at the trainer, hating everything he said. "Careful, Orlo. You're stepping close to treason."

"No," Orlo said. "He is."

Caelan surged to his feet.

Orlo took two quick steps back, balancing on the balls of his feet, his eyes watchful and wary. "Defend him," he said in what was almost a taunt. "You always do."

"It is my duty to defend him," Caelan said hotly.

"Why? Do you have hopes of becoming his protector when he takes the throne?"

The accusation hit Caelan like a glove of challenge. Caelan's eyes widened. How much did Orlo know? How much had he overheard? Or was this only speculation?

He was not quick enough to keep his reaction from his face. It was Orlo's turn to stare with widened eyes.

"Great Gault," he breathed, taking yet another step back from Caelan. "So he has promised you that."

Caelan felt stripped and vulnerable. To deny it would be useless, yet he could not confirm it either without condemning himself. He said nothing.

Orlo frowned and slowly shook his head. "You great fool," he said at last, pity in his voice. "Can't you see he is—"

"He does not use me," Caelan broke in hotly. "You understand nothing of this matter. Nothing!"

"No wonder you pulled the Madrun's sword into your side. With that incentive, what man would not take tremendous risks?" Orlo glanced sharply at Caelan. "But can't you see that he is jealous of you?"

Caelan's mouth fell open in astonishment. "Jealous!"

"Whose name were they screaming yesterday?"

"But he is the prince."

"And you have the popularity," Orlo said with scorn. Glancing at the door, he kept his voice low. "When you ride through the streets at the prince's side, cheers from the populace are guaranteed. He can pretend the cheers are for him. It sends a message to the emperor, does it not? But inside, the prince knows the truth. His popularity is purchased, and at the crux it will not hold."

"Take care, Orlo," Caelan said in warning.

"No, *you* take care. Prince Tirhin is a desperate man, and I tell you to watch yourself. When you cease to be of use, he will discard you as he does all his worn-out possessions."

Caelan's chin lifted with dignity. "I have his word."

Without warning Orlo closed the distance between them and gripped Caelan's shoulder hard. "And what is the worth of a promise made to a slave?" he snarled. "Nothing! Nothing at all." He gave Caelan a shake and released him. "He doesn't see you as a man. You belong to him as his dog belongs to him. As that chair over there belongs to him. He owes you nothing, do you hear? No matter what you do for him, there is no obligation from him in return."

Caelan sighed and stopped listening. Orlo held some ancient grudge against Tirhin that he never discussed. For Caelan's sake, he had returned to the prince's employ, but he was never comfortable in Tirhin's presence. And when the prince was out of earshot, Orlo could be full of venom and paranoia, just as he was now. Caelan felt too tired to pay attention to any of it.

"Let me relay this to you, although Gault knows why I bother," Orlo said. "Since yesterday, has the prince been a man happy and carefree? You won a tremendous victory on his behalf. He has every reason to celebrate, yet beneath the smiles and the charm there is anger. All the anger that was present before the contest. Did you not see it?"

"Yes," Caelan said reluctantly. "Angry, but hiding it."

"Do you know why he's so angry? Why he's ridden three horses into the ground and broken their wind in the last week? Why he's taken to staying out all hours of the night? Why he's so often in the company of that creature Sien?"

Caelan thought of the bizarre meeting he'd had with the prince and Lord Sien. Hiding a shiver, he said nothing.

"It is the coronation," Orlo said, looking at Caelan as though he had just failed an examination. "His temper gets more foul with every passing day of the festivities. The empress threatens his position, and if you're wise you'll avoid getting caught up the middle of this family's conflicts. No matter what he promises you."

Caelan hated politics. He hated court intrigue. He hated all the gossip conducted by people who weren't directly involved.

"The imperial family's problems are none of your business," he said coldly.

Orlo flushed, and he glared at Caelan with his eyes narrowed. "Let me tell you something. Years ago, when Tirhin was much younger, and much more impetuous, he tried to rally the imperial army around him. He intended to bring off a coup d'etat. And I was at his side."

Caelan rolled his eyes and turned away. "I don't want to hear this."

Orlo gripped his arm and pulled him back. "You *will* listen," he said angrily. "You must!"

Caelan shook him off, and found himself swaying weakly with the effort. "Why?" he shouted. "Why should I listen to this parable of yours? I have no need of lessons—"

"I committed treason for his highness," Orlo said bleakly, his eyes pinpoints of cold.

"What?" Caelan said in disbelief. "When?"

"Years ago. I was young and hotheaded. I was impatient for change. I had just been passed over for promotion into the Imperial Guard for the second time." His mouth twisted with old bitterness. "My family wasn't good enough. Simple country farmers, with the stink of manure on their shoes. It didn't matter how good a soldier I was or how ably I served. I wasn't the right sort for the elite Crimson."

Caelan looked at him, at his stocky shoulders and bullish neck and square face, and knew all about class and status. He thought of his own birth and how he had been raised in Trau. He had resented being the son of a famous and esteemed father. How spoiled he had been. How disdainfully he had taken so much for granted.

For the first time, Orlo was baring his soul. Caelan glanced at the door, wishing he could escape this. He had no desire to hear Orlo's secrets, not now, not like this. But when he met Orlo's eyes, he knew there was no leaving.

"What treason did you commit?" Caelan asked.

Orlo's eyes were on fire. His face contorted with old memories and his hand groped instinctively for the dagger in his belt. "I killed General Solon, the Lord Commander of the army," he said in a hoarse whisper. "At Tirhin's order, and in cold blood. The man was defenseless, asleep in his own quarters. I crept in, and stabbed him in the heart."

Orlo's eyes flinched, and a tide of red colored his face. "I stood over him in the lamplight, this general who had denied me my dream because of tradition. I had never met him before, never spoken to him, never been addressed by him. Had he been awake, he would not have recognized me. He did not know of my existence, and I took his life."

Orlo drew his dagger and held it aloft so that its blade reflected the ruddy dance of firelight. "This is the weapon. I carry it as my conscience, that I may never forget the thud of impact, the heat of his blood, or the soft sigh of death that issued from his lips. This knife is my mark of shame."

He fell silent, lost in his own tormented thoughts, turning the knife over and over in his big, callused hands. No sound disturbed the quiet.

Watching him, Caelan had no words. He understood revenge. And although he had never killed in cold blood, he had thought of it. There had been many sleepless nights in his bunk, thinking of Thyzarene raiders and how to torture them into hell.

Finally Orlo seemed to come to himself. Still staring at the dagger in his hands, he said, "I might have burned over the injustice for years, without acting, but the prince gave me the means. He bribed the door guards and obtained a way for me to enter the man's house. He promised me leadership in the army he would reorganize."

Orlo snorted and sheathed the dagger. "For fledgling conspirators, we were lucky. The only part of the plan to succeed was mine. No one else carried out their orders. In the hue and cry over the unsolved murder of the Lord Commander, the prince's plans fell apart. His supporters lost courage, and he departed for the border to fight the Madruns."

"And you?" Caelan prompted.

"I barely escaped with my life and hid for days, terrified of arrest. His highness abandoned me."

"But he—"

"Don't defend him!" Orlo snapped. "By the gods, you will not find excuses for him in this."

"You weren't caught," Caelan pointed out. "Did he not have you protected?"

"No. He was long gone by then, anxious to cover his trail. I spent a year in hiding, skulking around the provinces, until I was caught for army desertion and flogged. I spun a believable tale. I wasn't connected to the murder. At the end of my term, I didn't reenlist. Instead, I took employment in a run-down gladiatorial arena out in Sarmina. That led to a better job in a bigger town with a bigger arena. Finally I returned to Imperia."

"And the prince made you one of his trainers."

Orlo's expression filled with contempt. "The prince had nothing to do with it. I gained the job on my own."

"But you trained me. You trained his other fighters."

"I worked for the public arena," Orlo said coldly. "When the prince was informed of my skills, he came to interview me for his service."

"And he had forgotten you," Caelan guessed.

Orlo's mouth twisted. "You love a tale, don't you, boy? No, he had not forgotten me. Recognition lay in his eyes the moment we looked at each other. He was shocked and cautious, but he knew I could never denounce him without destroying myself. I took his money to train occasional fighters for him, but I did not reenter his service until you came."

Caelan stared at this man, who had once been his enemy and who had slowly become a friend. To see Orlo so vulnerable, so open, disturbed Caelan. He understood now the cynicism and bitterness, and most of all, the distrust.

"Why did you help me?" he asked now. He had tried to ask before, but Orlo would never give him an answer. "Why do this for me? Why trust me now with your secret?"

Orlo frowned and finally looked away. Something

helpless and bewildered lay in his face. "I—I don't know," he said at last. "I cannot explain why I should care what befalls you. But . . . Ah, gods, what lies in a man, that he can convince others to help him? Why do the gods give one man qualities that they deny to others? Why have you succeeded in the arena beyond anyone else? How have you survived, and how have you kept your spirit that will not be tamed? What makes you different and unique?"

His expression deepened into a scowl. Suddenly he looked angry and embarrassed. "I'm a fool," he said gruffly.

Caelan was touched. He reached out, but Orlo flinched away from his hand.

"Why," Orlo asked heavily, "did you have me train you?"

"Because you're the best trainer in Imperia. You could keep me alive."

"No. I meant, why ask for me when you have never heeded anything I've said to you?"

"I heed you when what you say is useful," Caelan retorted, annoyed again. "Otherwise, I follow my own judgment."

Orlo's gaze dropped to Caelan's wounded side. To the side that was now healed by a mysterious process that Orlo, in his fear of foreign religions and ways, probably didn't understand.

"Thank you for your trust," Caelan said. "I will not betray your confidence."

Orlo shot him a look of despair mingled with exasperation. "You will not learn from it either."

Caelan had no answer.

"You will continue to follow him," Orlo said bitterly. "You great, stubborn lout. You cannot be taught. You cannot be shown. You cannot be warned. Always you will do things your own way."

"My way works best for me," Caelan said softly. "All my life others have tried to shape me to their will. I cannot do that."

"Then he *will* destroy you," Orlo said. "Perhaps he will even get you killed. Be damned, then," he muttered, and flung himself out.

Chapter Four

CAELAN TURNED AROUND too fast, nearly lost his balance as his knees went wobbly on him, and sat heavily on the bed to save himself from falling. For a few seconds he was so dizzy he had to grip the side of the bed; then his head cleared again. Breathing hard, he wiped sweat from his face.

The door opened quietly. Inwardly Caelan groaned, and he forced himself to lift his head. "Orlo, I—"

It was not Orlo who returned, but the healer. For the first time the man stepped into the light where Caelan could see him clearly. It was Agel. His cousin and boyhood friend, whom Caelan had not seen since being expelled from Rieschelhold, the school of healing arts.

Agel . . . the steady, dependable one . . . grown to manhood now . . . more gaunt and austere than handsome. His face had the etched clarity of an ascetic. He stood tall and still, his hands folded out of sight in the wide sleeves of his white robe.

Caelan lost his breath. Thoughts tumbled through his mind without making sense. He had believed he would never see any of his family again, yet now he had found Agel. It was a miracle, a return of hope.

Consumed with happiness, Caelan smiled and tried to speak. But his throat choked up, and unmanly tears blurred his vision. Caelan averted his face sharply, struggling to master himself.

Agel's hand settled gently on his shoulder. "You are overwrought," he said. "Rest and let the healing finish."

Caelan gripped Agel's hand in both of his. "I cannot believe you are here," he said in Trau, his words running eagerly over each other. "I have often thought of you, wondered how you did and where you were. And now, to find you here, in Imperia, is—"

"Rest," Agel said. His voice remained calm and serene. He continued to speak in Lingua, and his hand lay slack in Caelan's grip. "Loss of temper destroys the balance of harmony, and healing cannot finish. I should have denied you all visitors until you were stronger."

Caelan stared at him. There was no joy, no recognition in Agel's face. When Caelan's fingers loosened, Agel withdrew his hand and tucked it back inside his sleeve. Caelan's happiness faded, to be replaced by sharp hurt.

"Don't you know me?" he whispered. "Cousin, I am—"

"Yes, Caelan, I know you."

Caelan waited, yearning for more, but Agel said nothing. His eyes betrayed nothing. It was as though Beva had returned—cold, detached, unfeeling. Agel was living in *severance,* too distant to touch.

"Is there nothing you will say?" Caelan asked hoarsely.

"You should lie down and sleep."

"Damn you!" Caelan shouted. He shoved himself furiously to his feet.

Agel blinked and took an involuntary step back.

That angered Caelan more. "How in Gault's name can you do this to me? We were friends, the closest. We grew up together. We were—Is there nothing left between us? Nothing? You are all the family I have left. Can you not even say 'well met' to me? Can you not give me something?"

Agel's expression did not change. He met Caelan's eyes steadily. "What would you have me say?"

"Oh, something like 'Caelan, I'm relieved to find you alive. Caelan, I'm glad to see you. Caelan, let us sit a while and talk of old times.' Something along those lines. Nothing too emotional. I wouldn't want you to lose harmony."

Agel might have been a stone. He watched Caelan lurch to the foot of the bed and grab a bedpost for support. He did not move.

"Discussing the past is unproductive," he said. "The events have occurred. They cannot be undone. As for regrets, they are a waste of time. You chose the course of your life, as I have chosen mine."

"I did *not* choose this!" Caelan said violently. "Gods, do you think I crawled into the city and begged them to make a slave of me?"

Agel turned his head and gazed about the luxurious room. Compared to a Trau home, the place looked too full of furniture, too gaudy; it would be considered excessive and wasteful. Caelan frowned, but it was Agel who spoke next:

"Slavery seems to have its rewards. You have done well for yourself here."

Caelan gasped, but even as memories of floggings, nights spent crouched in filthy straw, long hours of brutal drills, and the grim realities of arena combat flashed through his mind, he realized he could not explain anything to Agel. His cousin had already judged him by these surroundings, and would never believe anything else.

Pride lifted Caelan's chin. "Yes," he said tightly. "I have done well. I have a master who rewards me when I please him. I have a roof over my head. I have the security of knowing I will be fed and clothed. Even my slave chain is made of gold. Isn't it pretty?"

"You have the gifts of healing," Agel said in a stern voice. "So much talent and potential, and you wasted it all. Worse, you have put your gifts into the hands of evil. You use *severance* to kill, do you not?"

The unexpected attack left Caelan silent.

"To do so is an abomination," Agel said. "An abhorrence to all life. The citizens of Imperia worship you. They throw coins and flowers at you in tribute. 'The mighty warrior Caelan,' they cry. How greatly would they cheer you if they knew the truth? That it is not with the sword that you slay your victims, but with your talent?"

Agel's unjust accusations stung Caelan. Years ago, when they were young boys, Agel had been fair and open-minded, but the teachers at Rieschelhold had obviously erased those qualities from him. Now he was petty and prejudiced. He had prejudged Caelan, and his disapproval hurt.

Before Caelan could say anything, Agel continued in that same soft, relentless voice:

"The deaths of your many victims is like a dirty cloak over you. When I look at you from *severance,* I see you in shadow, vague and obscured. You are tainted and foul." He paused a moment, his lips tight as he assessed Caelan. "You even use *sevaisin,* do you not? I can tell it is entwined about you."

Repulsion filled his eyes. "It has always been forbidden. Where did you come by it? Who taught you such evil? In the memory of your father and all he stood for, how *can* you?"

Caelan sighed. All his life he had struggled between the two extremes of his unwanted gifts. *Severance,* the cold isolation, and *sevaisin,* the joining of life to life. No man should be able to do both, yet he could. The struggle to keep them balanced, the struggle to keep himself from going mad between them at times, seemed harder and harder. He feared himself, feared what might befall him if he ever gave way. Which side of him would eventually win? Yet, for now, he had no means of saving himself except to practice the very principles of balance so revered in Trau. He often felt like a man walking the crumbling edge of a precipice, with no solid ground ahead of him.

No one had ever known his secret, except his father,

who had called him a monster. And now Agel knew also. His condemnation showed plainly in his face.

"Please," Caelan said softly. "Try to understand . . . "

"*Sevaisin* is forbidden!" Agel snapped. "Why did you seek such a thing? Why did you study it?"

"I didn't—"

"Was it to dishonor your father's memory? Was it to stain his accomplishments, all he stood for? Has this been your purpose?"

Caelan's temper slipped. "You said to let the past lie. My father is dead. Why should I seek to dishonor a dead man?"

"What other reason could you have to willingly pursue such a course of study?"

"I didn't study *sevaisin!*" Caelan shouted. "I was born with it, just as I was born with *severance.*"

"No one has both!"

"I do!"

They glared at each other, both tight-lipped and pale. Agel's eyes slowly widened. He looked increasingly alarmed.

At last, Caelan thought in satisfaction. He had managed to break through his cousin's icy reserve. There was nothing like shock to destroy the harmony.

Agel's gaze flickered toward the door.

"You can't run and tell the elders," Caelan said. "Traulanders are scarce in this city. There is no one to *scourge* me because of your accusations. There is no one to *sever* me or to put me out in the wilderness to wander. No one in Imperia cares. Half the citizens don't believe in either *sevaisin* or *severance.* The rest follow observances that truly are abominations. The city is a melting pot of cultures and beliefs. You will have to get used to that."

"What is to be done with you?" Agel said despairingly.

"Nothing. I am what I am."

Agel frowned. He seemed to be trying to regain his composure, although he still looked shaken. "You are much changed in the years since we last saw each other. You have grown harsh and cynical. You jest about evil with an air of worldly sophistication. You commit unspeakable acts, then ask me to accept you. I used to think you would grow out of your rebelliousness and settle into a useful life. Instead, you kill for the amusement of others. You are an entertainer of the vilest kind. I cannot begin to comprehend what you are."

Now it was Caelan's turn to be made of stone. He stared at his cousin and felt only coldness. "It is time for you to go."

Agel looked jolted. "My work is unfinished."

"I don't want you. Go."

Agel's expression smoothed into something tight and unreadable. "It is not a question of your choice. Your master has requested my services on your behalf. The fact that you are so difficult to heal is—"

"Tell him I'm too difficult. You've done all you can. Get out."

"I will not lie. And I am not finished."

"You are if I refuse you," Caelan said, clenching his fists. His head was throbbing, and he was beginning to feel faintly nauseous. The pain came seeping back. "Go back to wherever you came from and stand there looking wise, mysterious, and foreign. I'll take my chances with the arena physician."

His harsh, sarcastic tone slid off Agel without effect. "I am newly appointed to the imperial court," Agel said with a trace of pride. "The emperor gave his gracious permission that I should attend you. However undeserving, you have been honored, and I will not shirk my responsibilities no matter what private opinions I hold."

Caelan frowned. He thought Agel had hurt him all that was possible. He realized how wrong he was. As long as he still cared for his cousin, he would go on being hurt again and again. "You really hate me, don't you?"

"Hatred is the antithesis of balance," Agel replied.

"All right, then. You've made yourself clear enough. You consider me a monster and an abomination. Not original, but then you always wanted to imitate my father. What do you feel, if not hatred?" He leaned forward and glared at Agel. "Fear?"

"Disappointment," Agel said without flinching.

Caelan's frown deepened. The anger in him deflated, leaving him hollow and tired. As a reunion, this was a nightmare. Lectures . . . disapproval . . . disappointment. It never changed. He'd been a fool to want to return to Trau. He told himself now he would never go back. As for Agel, there would be no future meetings with him if Caelan could help it.

Lifting his chin, Caelan squared himself and faced his cousin. "I, too, am disappointed," he said, holding his voice hard to avoid giving away his emotions. "I thought, despite everything that has befallen us, we could still hold our friendship."

Agel met his gaze. "You are the one who turned away from our friendship. We had everything planned together, but you ran away from Rieschelhold, putting yourself and everyone in jeopardy that night. You did all that you could to get yourself expelled. You even broke our bond. I wept for you as you walked through the gates, turning your back on the greatest calling a man can follow. But I have not wept for you since. And I will not forgive you now. I see you clearly, Caelan E'non, for what you represent. I do not like it, and I will not keep friendship with you, not even for the sake of the blood we share."

Caelan felt frozen. Every word was like a blow, and despite his anger and disappointment he had no defenses with which to shield himself.

"The road of life has turns we do not always foresee," he said. "I am glad your road has always been so simple and straight. Mine has not been, and probably will never be. All I know is that I must stay true to myself, not to what other people planned for me. I have only one final statement for you, and then we will be finished with our candor. We need never speak to each other again.

"After the bone-breaking labor and the whippings and the insubstantial food . . . after the sweating nightmares and the shakes . . . I used to lie awake at night and think of my loved ones. I would think of Lea and the servants . . . and even Father. I would think of their deaths, my grief burning a hole in me. And I would comfort myself that you were alive and well. I would tell myself that I wasn't completely lost in this nightmare, that someday I would regain my freedom. Someday I would return to Trau and find you, my remaining kinsman. My family. I told myself I hadn't lost quite everything. You were a small, precious part of my hope." Caelan managed a twisted grimace of a smile and shrugged. "I never imagined you would be like this. Still condemning me after all these years because I rejected what you wanted for yourself. Can't the jealousy and envy have an end?"

"I see no reason for jealousy here." Appearing unmoved by what Caelan had said, Agel made a slight gesture at the room. "The things you value have no interest for me."

"Envy, then," Caelan said harshly. "Every time Beva spoke to me, you were green with it."

"I wanted what he gave you."

"You have it," Caelan said. "You're the healer, not me. You wear the white robe. I don't. You are good at the art, as good as my father was. You have his skills, his abilities. You took the court appointment he refused. You have succeeded in emulating him. You will be even more famous than he. Let the envy go, Agel. Accept me for what I am. Please."

"A killer? How can I accept that?"

Caelan shut his eyes and gave up. He'd bared his soul to this man and been spurned. It was pointless to keep trying.

"You are as foolhardy and reckless as ever," Agel was saying. "I saw yesterday's contest—"

Startled, Caelan opened his eyes wide. *"You?* I don't believe it."

"You were too stubborn yesterday to give up, and you are as stubborn as ever in refusing to cooperate today in what is good for you."

"Oh, so you do remember a few things about me." Caelan said sarcastically.

Agel did not flinch. "I remember everything."

"And you don't care, do you? You're so perfect now, so *severed.* You can remain detached despite what happened at E'nonhold. Everyone was slaughtered in the raid. My home was burned to the ground. You used to wish it could be your home too. Now you don't care."

"To grieve for the hold does not bring it back," Agel said. "To grieve for Uncle Beva does not restore him to life. Do you wish me to join the inner confusion you live in? What purpose would that serve? I have my work, which is to heal. It is enough for me."

"You're just like Father," Caelan said bitterly.

"Thank you. That is high praise."

"No, it's insult!" Caelan screamed at him. "You *fool.* My father and his stupid philosophy opened the hold to destruction. He let his own servants die. He stood like a stupid moag and let Thyzarenes slit his throat. It could have all been prevented, and he would not act!"

"Uncle Beva lived by his beliefs. If he also died by his beliefs, then he did so with dignity and honor. I will not debate the principles of harmony and balance with you," Agel said sternly.

"Why did you have to stop being human? Why can't you be a healer and still care?"

"I care that you have undone my work," Agel said. "Has the pain returned?"

Agony throbbed in Caelan's side. He frowned, certain he would rather die than let Agel near him again.

"Lie down," Agel told him. "We must begin again."

Caelan shook his head. "Please," he said. "Please be the Agel I once knew."

"Let the past lie where it is," Agel said. "I live in the present. My task is to tend your hurts."

"I can tend my own hurts," Caelan retorted. "I—"

Pain covered him in a sheet of grayness. He sagged against the bedpost, robbed of breath and sense for a moment.

When he regained awareness, he found Agel gripping his elbow and steering him back to bed. Caelan did not want him, but had nothing left with which to drive his cousin away. He found himself suddenly spent by his emotions.

Agel was gentle and ministering, but the icy barrier remained between them. Caelan let Agel work, but nothing could heal the wound inside. For all his principles regarding peace and tranquility, Agel had inflicted the harshest blow. No mere stab would could surpass it.

It was as though his father had come to life again. If pride had not choked him so, Caelan would have wept.

Chapter Five

At twilight the summons came, brought by a timid servant who also carried new clothing and bathing water. Thankful at last for something to do, Caelan put on the finery. Admiring his reflection in the looking glass, he smoothed the tunic of pale brown silk. It fit him perfectly. Tirhin's coat of arms was embroidered on the left sleeve; otherwise, Caelan might have passed for a courtier. He sleeked back his blond hair into a neat braid and spent a moment fingering his amulet bag concealed at his throat.

He desperately needed consolation, and he sent a little prayer to the memory of his dead sister Lea to help him find some inner peace. She had been little and sweet, her wealth of golden curls as bright as sunshine, her heart pure goodness. He still grieved for her, more than for any of the others. After his encounter with Agel today, Caelan missed her even more intensely.

And Orlo still had not returned, not even to check on his health. It was possible the trainer would not come back at all. He was a free man, and if he chose to leave the prince's service, he could. Caelan sighed. He did not even know what terms he stood on with the prince at present. He had sent word to his master that he was well enough to resume his duties of attendance. His highness had not replied, other than to give him this curt summons.

There came a soft tapping on the door. "It is time," the servant said.

Anxious not to keep the prince waiting, Caelan gathered up his cloak and hurried out. The hours of rest following Agel's departure had done wonders. Caelan felt

physically strong and complete once more. His side gave
him no more than an occasional twinge, provided he did not
overexert himself. Yet despite that, he felt grim and old inside. He tried telling himself that depression was useless and
that he must not let these people affect him so profoundly,
yet it was hard to feel positive when his emotions had been
ruthlessly pounded. He kept asking himself if he could have
done better, if he could have done differently. Would it have
mattered?

The sun was melting into a golden stain on the horizon
as he emerged through the main entry of the prince's house,
descended a flight of grand steps flanked by life-sized stone
dragons, and halted under the portico. Grooms stood nearby
with saddled horses. Caelan counted them, recognizing
coats of arms on many of the saddle cloths. The prince and
his entourage had not yet appeared.

Catching his breath, Caelan was glad to be here ahead
of his master. He swore to himself that Tirhin would find no
fault with him tonight.

Caelan gazed out toward the sunset and inhaled the fra-
grant air. Prince Tirhin's house was a miniature palace, and
the gardens around it had been expertly designed to please
the senses. Normally had Caelan found himself standing
here at ease, he would have let himself pretend he was the
master of his surroundings. The sidelong glances of respect
and awe from the house servants as they hurried past on
myriad tasks could also be woven into the fantasy. Suppose
they were his servants. Suppose the grooms were holding
his horses saddled and ready. Suppose he were a free man,
master of himself, successful, and at ease.

But tonight the fantasy did not come readily. He was
not in the mood for make-believe.

A bargain was a bargain. The prince had ordered Caelan to win, and Caelan had. The prince wanted Caelan to ap-

pear at tonight's parties, healthy and whole. Caelan was here.

But he had done enough. He was tired, tired to his very bones and beyond, of slaying men for no purpose. As a boy he had dreamed of being a soldier who fought for the glory of the empire. Never in his wildest imagining had he believed he would ever end up in exotic, decadent Imperia, killing efficiently and ruthlessly almost daily to provide public entertainment. Agel was right to call it a moral violation, and whenever he allowed himself to think of it as such, Caelan felt sickened to his core. But even worse, he feared his own skills. He feared how good he had become, how attuned he was to his weapons, how easily his body quickened to the task before him. He *liked* the risk and challenge of combat. He thrived on it, and that—more than anything else—frightened him.

Laughter from within the house made the grooms put away their dice game and straighten to attention. The horses snorted and pawed. Caelan smoothed a wrinkle from his tunic and flung his cloak over one shoulder.

Emerging from the house, the prince came down the steps with about six of his friends in tow. All were dressed in sumptuous velvet tunics that were padded and lined with rich silks. Tirhin wore his distinctive blue, with a fashionable velvet cap set at a jaunty angle on his dark head. He was adjusting the belt of his dueling sword as he came. To Caelan's eyes, the sword was a strange-looking weapon, quite long but scarcely thicker than a knitting needle. It was designed for thrusting only, no edge to it at all. One stroke of a broadsword would shatter it. Caelan considered it an overly dainty weapon, useless and silly. Still, all the fashionable courtiers wore them now.

"Caelan, there you are," the prince called out. "Attend me."

Startled from his thoughts, Caelan realized he was staring like a half-wit. The prince had stopped partway down
the steps and stood waiting. Caelan hastened to him and
bowed low.

The prince gestured for his friends to go on, and waited
until they were under the portico at the foot of the steps before he returned his attention to Caelan.

Only then did the prince allow his pleasant expression
to become grim. He looked Caelan up and down. "That will
do. The clothes fit better than I expected."

"They are very fine, sir. Thank you."

"Heed me. I have your instructions for the evening,"
the prince said in a low, curt tone.

Caelan knew his moods well. This was a dark one.
With his heart sinking, he bowed his head. "Yes, sir."

"We shall attend several parties, but Lady Sivee's is the
important one. When we arrive there, do not stay close to
my side. Circulate among the guests. Go and come as you
please."

Caelan blinked in surprise. This was indeed a treat and
a privilege, but he did not understand why the prince looked
so somber. "Thank you, sir."

"I want you to be visible among the guests. Don't go
off and hide yourself the way you usually do. Stand about
and talk to whoever will give you permission."

Caelan frowned slightly. "Usually those are men wanting to make offers to buy me."

"I don't care what you discuss or what you do, as long
as it's within permissible bounds."

"No, sir." Caelan hesitated a moment, then seized his
courage. "Sir, I wish to—"

"No questions now. We're late already." The prince
swung away, pulling on his gloves. Then he paused and sent
Caelan a hard look. "You are well? Up to this excursion?"

"Quite well, sir."

The prince nodded. "The emperor's healer is new at his post, I understand. A stiff-necked Traulander like yourself. Still, they are the best healers in the empire. I trust he was satisfactory?"

Caelan felt his face go stiff. "Yes, sir. Quite satisfactory. Also, may I please ask forgiveness for not being able to attend your highness last night?"

The prince frowned. "The last thing I want from you is phony courtier pleasantries. You could not attend me because you were near death. All because of your exhibition of audacity and bravado which has offended the Imperial Guard, and possibly alienated some I may need to rely on most."

The rebuke stung. Caelan dropped his gaze in humiliation. "Yes, sir."

Tirhin's eyes were dark and stony. "I did not order you to kill yourself, or to let yourself be killed."

Caelan swallowed. "No, sir."

"You are a reckless fool. You could have cost me—" The prince broke off and slapped his palm with his gloves. "But you did not. It has worked, I think. Thus far, at least. And because there is a rumor that you are dead, your appearance tonight should be precisely the type of distraction I want."

"Distraction?"

"Enjoy yourself, Giant," the prince said, ignoring his puzzled question. "Take pride in the accolades that will be thrown your way. You've earned the attention."

As praise it was much less than usual, hardly anything. Yet it seemed odd coming after the prince's sharp reprimand. More puzzled than ever, Caelan wondered at the manipulative game his master was playing. Only one thing seemed clear; the reward Caelan had hoped for would apparently not be forthcoming.

Anger surged into his throat like hot bile. Furiously, Caelan struggled to block it. If he forgot himself and lost his temper now, he would find his head on a wall spike before morning. With all his might, he fought back resentment. He had made a mistake, and this was his master's way of punishing him.

Orlo had been right. A promise made to a slave wasn't binding.

Trembling started in the pit of Caelan's stomach and traveled up. Clenching his fists at his side, he swallowed hard and knew he had to control himself. He mustn't think about it now. If he was to get through this evening, then he could not feel and he could not think. There would be time later tonight, after he was finally dismissed from his duties, when he could decide what to do.

A shout from the courtiers at the bottom of the steps caught Tirhin's attention. A smile of acknowledgment appeared on his face, but there was nothing jovial in it.

"Come, then," the prince said and walked on.

Silently, Caelan followed. His eyes felt hot in the coldness of his face. His gaze burned into the prince's spine. How he would like to seize this handsome, privileged man by the neck and shake him the way a weasel shakes a rat. How he would like to say, "You cannot toy with lives. You are not a god. There are consequences for what you do, and someday you will pay them."

Over his shoulder Tirhin added, "Mind that you understand me. This is to be your night. Do not tag at my heels. Do not attend me. I need no protection. I need no service. Am I clear?"

Scorn filled Caelan like lava. The prince was still playing his game, still taking Caelan's loyalty for granted. Let him lay his mysterious intrigues, for all the good they would do him.

This evening the prince looked keyed up and bright-eyed, his outward gaiety a thin, brittle layer over irritation. He looked as though he was up to mischief. Anyone who knew him well could see it.

The prince snapped another look at Caelan. "I asked you a question. Are you paying heed to me?"

"Yes, sir," Caelan replied at once, his tone flat. "Forgive me. Your highness has been quite clear."

"Good. I want no more trouble from you. No straying from your instructions. No surprises. Do only what you are told. No more. No less."

"I shall obey your instructions precisely, sir," Caelan said, and his voice was flatter than ever.

The prince did not seem to notice. He strode down the steps to join his friends and resumed his strange, thin smile. He quickly added a quip of his own to their jokes and merriment, and everyone laughed. All were sons of the finest families in Imperia. Well-born, well-dressed, wealthy, they might have simply been a group of comrades ready for an evening of festivities. Yet there was a faintly dangerous air about them, an air of bravado and defiance that indicated trouble to come. *You will make a good distraction,* the prince had said. Caelan frowned to himself. Distraction for what?

Servants came down the steps with tray of tall silver cups. Caelan could already smell the sweetness of honeyed mead on the men's breath, but they drank deeply and with gusto, then climbed onto their mounts. There was a momentary milling about with horses prancing and men flinging back fur-trimmed cloaks over their shoulders; then they were off at a gallop.

Caelan rode as one of them, galloping down the mountain road that wound through the hills overlooking the western crescent of the city. There were no servants along, and no soldiers for protection. The prince and his friends feared no brigands.

It was a sweet night, crisp and still in the way of Imperia winters. The hills stretched and rolled down toward the sea that was inky black in the indigo twilight. Stars began to glitter in the sky, except to the north, where a black cloud spread dark fingers across the horizon. A storm must be coming in, although it was strange to see one approach from that direction. Just looking at it gave Caelan an involuntary shiver he could not explain.

Owls flew on silent wings, eerie hunters among the trees.

Something in all the quiet stillness unsettled Caelan. He had the feeling of being followed, of being watched, a niggling uneasiness that he could not dismiss. He glanced back several times, but nothing came behind them. He gazed into the sky, wondering what seemed amiss. Were he in Trau, he could dismiss his fears as simple nervousness about the wind spirits that hunted at night. But there were none here. Men came and went freely in the darkness. During the blistering Imperia summers, residents left the windows of their houses open all night long with a fearlessness that left him amazed.

He told himself to stop imagining things. They were unlikely to be set upon by robbers. They were not being followed. Yet his fingers itched for a dagger hilt. And his heart beat faster with every passing minute. It was forbidden for a slave to carry weapons, but if necessary he would appropriate arms from one of the men around him.

Yet his worries proved groundless. Without incident, they rode past quince trees marking the property boundaries of expensive villas. Here and there lights glimmered in the distance, and the distant strains of lute music or merrymaking could be heard.

Caelan glanced back yet again, and one of the others looked his way.

"Is something following us?"

"No," Caelan said. "I see nothing."

The other man shrugged, and Caelan told himself to stop imagining things.

Every gate and every house they passed flew the red imperial banner tonight in honor of the empress. Red could be seen everywhere, fluttering from rooftops, windows, gates, and walls. A full week of festivities was still to come; then the coronation would conclude the celebrations.

Caelan had noticed when they left tonight that no imperial banner flew at the prince's gate. Only Tirhin's banner hung over his house. It was a deliberate slight, a deliberate defiance. It was bound to cause trouble.

Tirhin had always seemed to be an easygoing prince, apparently content to let nature take its course with his long-lived father. If he desired the throne, he seemed patient about it. He defied the emperor in small ways, typical of any son with fire in his veins, but politically he had always been loyal.

But since what was obviously to be the last marriage of Emperor Kostimon barely a year past, the prince's mood had grown progressively darker, his temper more brittle. The announcement that the lady would be crowned empress sovereign instead of merely empress consort had snapped something in the prince. In recent days he had been showing his disgruntlement openly. His conversations were impatient and not always discreet.

Tonight, Tirhin went forth beautifully dressed, and his friends were select companions of high birth and respectability, but he was making less than minimal effort to honor his young stepmother. And according to servants' gossip, he had not yet attended any of the palace functions. That in itself was a plain insult.

Caelan whistled silently to himself. The prince played with fire. Would the emperor let his son get away with such behavior? Would he send Tirhin off to the war as he had done before? Would he banish his one and only heir for a time to teach him better manners? Kostimon was infamous for not tolerating any disrespect. He had killed sons before. He could again.

In honor of the empress, every house in Imperia looked alight with guests and merriment. High in the western hills rimming the city, the villas of the nobility stood secluded and separate within their own gardens and groves. It was to one of these exclusive homes that the prince rode now. He was welcomed by his hosts, and the prince and his friends spent an hour among staid surroundings with mostly middle-aged guests of eminent respectability. Having been left in the hall under the sharp eye of the porter, Caelan saw nothing of the house except a few pieces of statuary and a hard bench to sit on. He could hear the sedate strains of lute music, and well-modulated laughter. It was not Tirhin's usual sort of party, but in the past year Caelan had learned that a prince with ambition did not always seek pleasure but instead worked to purposes unexplained to mere gladiators.

The porter had nothing to say to Caelan. Presumably he had no interest in betting on the arena games. Or perhaps his owner did not permit him to gamble. If he even knew who Caelan was, he looked completely unimpressed. It was a long, silent hour of boredom. Caelan had never been one to stand much inactivity.

Just before he rose to his feet to go outside and prowl about in the darkness, the prince emerged with the well wishes of his host, a gray-haired man looking much gratified by the honor that had been conferred on him by Tirhin's visit.

They rode to another villa, staying only a short time before leaving again. The prince did this twice more until at last they arrived at the exquisite home of Lady Sivee.

Caelan had been here before, and he found himself grinning with anticipation. Now that social obligations had been satisfied, they could enjoy themselves. The lady was a youngish widow of considerable beauty and fortune. She spent her money on lavish entertainments, and threw the best parties in Imperia. Her personal notoriety did not keep people away, and she delighted in mixing people of different social classes and standing. As a champion gladiator, even Caelan was welcome in her home, for he provided additional entertainment for her guests, especially the female ones who invariably clustered about to admire his muscles. It was rumored the lady had hopes of marrying Prince Tirhin, but while the prince dallied, he did not propose. Politically, he could do better.

The rooms were crowded with guests, but Lady Sivee came fluttering through to greet the prince warmly.

"Sir, we are honored indeed by your graciousness," she said with a radiant smile.

The prince kissed her hand. "My lady, how could I even think of forgoing your invitation? You knew I would come."

"I could only hope," she replied.

Her gaze swept to the others, and when they had been suitably greeted and directed onward to the tables of food and drink, she turned to Caelan.

"Welcome, champion," she said with kindness. "There were rumors that you had suffered grievous wounds. I am glad to see them false. You look particularly well."

"Thank you, my lady," he said, pleased by the courtesy she extended to him. "Your hospitality shines above the rest."

Her brows arched, and she seemed surprised by his gallantry. "Well, well," she said. "You are gaining polish. Soon you will have a charm equal to your master's."

"Never, if I may contradict a lady's pronouncement," he said, drawing on his boyhood lessons in etiquette. Gladiator or not, he wasn't a barbarian and he didn't intend to be taken for one. "My master surpasses most men in ability, wit, and graciousness. Together, those qualities create a charm I could never approach."

Lady Sivee laughed. "Truly I am amazed by this speech. You sound like a courtier instead of a gladiator."

Caelan bowed, accepting the compliment.

"But I must question you," she continued. "You say the prince surpasses *most* men. Are you not at risk with this opinion? Who possibly could surpass such a man whom the gods have favored so completely?"

As she spoke, her gaze followed the prince, who had reached the opposite side of the room. Everyone was vying for a chance to speak to him or to attract his notice. Prince Tirhin acted graciously, nodding to some, speaking to others.

Caelan watched him too, aware of the ears listening to his conversation with the hostess, aware of those who stared at him as though they could not believe him capable of opening his mouth intelligently. He was not going to fall into any trap. Yet here was one small chance for a dig at the prince's expense, a temptation impossible to resist.

"Who?" Lady Sivee persisted, her eyes shining merrily. "Who is his better? Who? I would know this paragon, this man without peer."

"Only the emperor, my lady," Caelan said in a mild

voice. "I meant no disparagement of my esteemed master; only the truth do I speak."

Someone laughed, and Lady Sivee flushed.

"Very clever," she said, and tossed her head. Turning her back on Caelan, she walked away to link arms with a friend.

The man who laughed gave Caelan a mock salute. "Well done," he said. "An articulate fighter is a curiosity indeed. A witty one is a rarity. Who taught you repartee?"

Another man joined the first, saving Caelan from having to answer. This one leaned forward, his cheeks bulging with honeyed dates.

"Didn't expect to see Giant here," he said, poking at Caelan's tunic with his forefinger. "Word on the streets was that he died."

"Obviously he didn't," the first man replied.

While they were busy talking to each other, Caelan bowed to them and seized the chance to melt away into the crowd. He towered over most of the other men, and his broad shoulders were constantly colliding with others in the general crush. Caelan disliked such close quarters. Living a life of constant combat, he had difficulty switching off his alert instincts. To be crowded like this meant anyone could attack with little or no warning. Caelan tried to tell himself no one had such intentions, but every brush of a sleeve against him made his muscles tense.

Remembering his instructions, Caelan wandered into other rooms away from the eye of his master. He found himself recognized and greeted by some, and stared at by others who seemed insulted by the unfettered presence of a thug in their midst.

Deeply tanned from constant exposure to the outdoors and considered exotic because of his blue eyes, light hair, and height, Caelan found himself ogled and watched by both

men and women. Many asked him to discuss his victory
over the Madrun. Giggling maidens approached him, begging to feel his biceps. Grinning house servants with admiration in their eyes offered him spiced wine and honeyed
smiles. Caelan did his best to be gracious; there was always
another room to escape to.

He strolled through sumptuously appointed rooms
filled with priceless art. He stood in the company of lords
and ladies. He watched; he sampled delectable sweetmeats
and pastries; he drank as he willed. Normally, he would have
spent the time pretending he was a free man. After all, with
the prince's leash so loose tonight this was in one way a
mark of his trust in his champion. In another way it was
Tirhin's silent boast to his friends. His champion could not
only kill the strongest, fiercest fighters owned by anyone in
the empire, but his champion was also civilized, educated,
and trustworthy.

But tonight, fantasy held no appeal.

Eventually Caelan found himself in a quiet enclave
where a poet stood reciting his literary creations. The room
was dramatically lit. A few women sighed over the phrases;
the men looked half-asleep. It was dull indeed, but Caelan
picked up a ewer of wine and helped himself to a cupful
while no one was looking.

He sipped his drink, standing in the back where no one
need notice his presence. The poetry was well crafted, but
staid and unimaginative.

Here, Caelan felt his bitterness return. With a grimace
he lowered his cup. Yes, he could walk about his house as he
willed, but he was not a guest. He could reply if someone
spoke to him, but he could not initiate conversation. He
could watch, smile, and pretend, but he did not belong
among these people. His clothes were made of fine and
costly fabric, but the garments were plain compared to the

tailoring of the others. He wore a gold chain worth a small fortune, but it was still a *chain*.

To a man who had been born free, slavery—no matter how privileged—remained a galling sore that could not heal. What good were possessions, money, and finery when they were only a substitution for civil rights and a free will?

Worse, he had admired his master enough to serve him with honor and complete loyalty. Now he felt like a fool. How many times had Orlo warned him? But he hadn't listened. From his own stubbornness, he had let himself be used and manipulated. When the Madrun's sword and pierced his side, he had felt a fierce satisfaction—almost joy—at having succeeded in serving his master so well. Now he understood just how deluded he had been.

It was not easy to look into one's own heart and realize one was a fool.

As though magically sensing Caelan's dark thoughts, a man robed in green and brown turned his head sharply away from the droning poet and stared hard at Caelan.

At once Caelan put down his cup and retreated from the room.

The man followed, emerging into the passageway with Caelan's cup in his hand.

"Wait a moment," he said. "You left your wine behind. Here."

Reluctantly Caelan took the cup from his fingers. He had left it nearly empty. Now it had been refilled. Out of politeness Caelan took a token sip, but in his present mood the wine tasted as sour as vinegar.

The man sipped from his own cup and smacked his lips appreciatively. "Delicious, is it not?"

"Very fine."

"You appreciate a good vintage?"

Caelan felt as though he'd been trapped in a mad play where he did not know the lines. "I have not the training of a connoisseur," he replied politely. "If it tastes good, I drink it."

"Ah. A simple man, with simple tastes."

As he spoke, the aristocrat smiled toothily. He was not a member of Prince Tirhin's circle, and Caelan did not recognize him. The man had perhaps been good-looking in his youth, but now his square face had jowls and his body was going soft. He was sweating in the heat, and his expensive clothes looked stiff, too new, and uncomfortable.

"I am Fuesel," he said.

It was the plain, unadorned way in which true aristocrats introduced themselves, although there could be only one reason such a man would speak to a slave.

Even as Caelan bowed, inwardly he sighed. The man would make an offer to buy him, which he would then ask Caelan to take to Prince Tirhin. The prince would be displeased by the interruption and would send Caelan back with a curt refusal. It happened all the time, no matter how emphatically the prince said he would never sell his champion, and Caelan found it an embarrassment. Only tonight he did not think he would carry an accurate offer to his master. Tonight he did not think he would cooperate at all.

He sipped more of his wine to avoid the intense way Lord Fuesel was staring at him.

"You're the famous arena champion . . . Caelan, aren't you?"

"Yes, my lord."

"I thought so." Fuesel's eyes were small and dark. They gleamed. "I saw you fight yesterday. Masterful. It was thrilling."

"Thank you."

"Tell me something. Do you enjoy the act of killing?"

Frowning, Caelan tried not to recoil. It wasn't the first time he'd been asked such a distasteful question, but he never got used to it. Fuesel was obviously one of the ghoulish supporters of the games, addicted to the perversions of watching death. There were cults in the city of these people—called Expirants—who were said to raid brothels and poor districts in search of victims to torture and study. Expirants always wanted blow-by-blow descriptions, graphic details and some kind of indication that Caelan shared their own twisted excitement.

"The fatal blow. The moment when life fades . . . you feel it the moment you inflict it, do you not?" Fuesel asked intensely. "You *know*."

"Yes."

"Ah." Fuesel inched closer so that his sleeve brushed Caelan's. "And when it happens, you feel that indescribable thrill. It is like joy, I think. Am I correct?"

Holding back a sigh, Caelan said, "No, my lord. I do not enjoy killing."

Fuesel's smile only widened. "You lie. Success in any endeavor is based on enjoyment."

And sometimes fear, Caelan thought to himself. Refusing to reply, he kept a respectful stance, his gaze focused slightly to the left of the man's shoulder. He was suddenly very thirsty, and he finished his wine in a quick gulp.

"Well," Fuesel said when Caelan remained silent. "Like many successful men, you maintain your greatness by keeping mysteries within yourself. Too much chatter destroys the mystique, does it not? Yes. But everyone has chattered about you. To actually execute the Dance of Death with such boldness, such courage . . . even now, it steals my breath to remember the sight." He shivered ecstatically and gripped Caelan's wrist with clammy fingers. "You have seen death. You have felt it within yourself. *That* I would love to discuss with you."

"I must go," Caelan said. He felt uneasy and overly warm. The passageway seemed dark and stuffy. He needed air.

Fuesel released his arm but did not move aside. "Ah, of course. This is not the time. This is a party, is it not? Not a time to discuss the dark sides of death and savagery. No. And I have kept you from the poetry reading. Will you return?" He gestured at the room they had both exited.

Caelan shook his head.

"Ah," Fuesel said. "Then perhaps we might find something more entertaining to occupy our time. If your master does not request your presence elsewhere?"

Strange as he was, this man seemed genuinely interested in talking to Caelan as a human being. Although Caelan tried to remain aloof, a part of him felt flattered.

"I have no commands to serve at this time," he said formally.

Fuesel smiled. "Splendid. Let us walk in this direction." As he spoke, he started down the passageway, and Caelan fell into step beside him.

"Now," Fuesel said. "You are a natural competitor. I have won many wagers because of you."

Caelan nodded. He still felt too warm. Perhaps the wine had been stronger than he thought. He said with a touch of arrogance, "Bet on me to win, and you take money home in your pockets."

Fuesel laughed and slapped him on the back. "Yes, indeed! Well spoken, my tall friend. Tell me, do you enjoy other kinds of competitions?"

"It depends."

"Such a cautious answer!" Fuesel reached into his

pocket to produce a pair of dice. "I, like yourself, am a lover of risk. But my arena does not shed blood. Interested?"

Caelan's suspicions relaxed. He returned the man's smile, aware that he had money of his own through his master's generosity. And although no one of Fuesel's rank had ever asked him to play before, Caelan knew how to dice. He had learned from Old Farns, the gatekeeper of E'nonhold, on lazy afternoons when Caelan's father was away and could not frown on such pursuits. The gladiators in the barracks were keen on dicing—everyone in Imperia was—and would play for hours, betting anything in their possession, even straws from their pallets.

Fuesel smiled and rattled the dice enticingly in his fist. "Yes?"

Caelan's pride soared. A lord had sought him out for a game, as one equal to another. Even if Lord Fuesel was planning to fleece Caelan of his money, it hardly mattered. It was a gesture of social acceptance that warmed Caelan inside as nothing else could.

"I am delighted to play with your lordship," he said, and he didn't care if his eagerness showed.

"Good. Let us freshen our drinks and seek out a friend of mine."

Thus at midnight, Caelan found himself facing two professional gamblers—Lord Fuesel and his roguish friend Thole—over the felt dicing board. A pile of gold ducats spilled over the painted crimson edges of the stakes square. It was enough gold to sustain a modest Trau household for a year, enough gold to sustain a lord of the empire for a month, enough gold to keep the prince in pocket money for a week.

It was more gold than Caelan had ever seen before, more than his father's strongbox had ever held. From his modest initial stake, his winnings had grown steadily. For

the past two hours the stakes had increased even more as
ducats were tossed onto the pile. Now the croupier rang a
tiny brass bell, its sound barely heard against the backdrop
of reveling going on in other rooms of the villa. The small
bell signaled the final throw of the game—high throw champion, winner take all.

The other two men had already thrown. Now it was
Caelan's turn. Sweating in the room's excessive warmth,
feeling a little dizzy and breathless, he leaned over the felt-
covered board and scooped the ivory cubes into his palm.

"Bell's rung!" someone called out, and more spectators
crowded into the already packed room to watch.

The audience shouted encouragement and advice in a
din that rang off the stone columns at the doorway and
echoed down from the ceiling.

Caelan tried to ignore the noise. He was used to people
cheering his name in the arena. Yet this was somehow different.

In the arena he had the open air, plenty of space, and
only the eyes of his opponent to watch.

Here, he could feel the oppressive closeness of too
many people, their perspiration and perfumes intermingling
with lamp smoke in a cloying fugue. Garbed in silks and
velvets of bold colors, they clapped and chattered. Their
painted faces loomed grotesquely from the shadows. They
shouted his name, all right, but as many called drunkenly for
his failure as for his victory. And laughed when they said it.

With the dice in his hand, Caelan swallowed and suddenly found himself unable to breathe. What was he doing
here among these strangers? How long had he been here?
He could not recall the hours. How many cups of wine had
he drunk? How many strange dishes had he sampled? How
had he come to find himself in this room, far from the dancing

girls and poetry readings, caught up in the spell of these gamesters?

Why were they staring at him so narrowly, sitting so still and tense? What was this particular eagerness in the pair of them? He could see it radiating from their skin.

His thoughts spun, and everything seemed to slow down as though a magical net had been thrown over time to hold it still.

Suspicion entered him, and it was as though he suddenly inhaled the crisp clean scent of fir needles on a snowy day. His mind cleared of the strange mist that had engulfed it, and he frowned. The stack of ducats gleamed softly in the lamplight; their excessive amount staggered him anew. How repugnant so many coins were, how obscene. Before him lay his own future, the gold coins with which Prince Tirhin had rewarded him earlier that day.

No . . . his master had not given him money.

Caelan blinked and rubbed sweat from his eyes. He struggled to remember. It had been yesterday when he fought. Tirhin often gave him gold for winning championships.

But he had not won yesterday; he had died.

A shiver passed over Caelan. Suddenly he felt wild and panicked. He did not know who he was or where he was. Perhaps this was a fevered dream, and in truth he lay in his bed, sweating with delirium and madness.

But he remembered Agel, the block of granite that was his cousin. Kinsman Agel, who cured him, so that he could come tonight with his master.

"We are waiting," Lord Fuesel said. "Please throw."

Caelan drew a deep breath. For wielding death so successfully, for killing to amuse his patron, he had been dressed in finery, brought to this social function among the elite of Imperia, and invited to play dice with lords. It was a mockery of death to accept such rewards. Now—worse—he was about to fritter away his money, this mysterious, ghostly money, about to waste it gambling. Agel's sour face hung before him like a vision, mouthing accusations.

Clenching the dice harder in his hand, Caelan stood up so abruptly his stool turned over.

Both of his opponents glanced up. Lord Fuesel looked flustered, even momentarily panicked. Thole, a swarthy man with a thin mustache adorning his lip, raised his brows at Caelan.

"Running away?" he asked with a sneer.

"You can't quit now," Fuesel said.

Thole brushed Fuesel's hand in warning, and the lord subsided with a nervous rat-a-tat of his fingers on the board.

"How long have I been playing?" Caelan asked in confusion, brushing his face with the back of his hand. His thoughts were full of holes. He could not make sense of anything except the overwhelming need to throw the dice. "My master may require me—"

"Nonsense. No need to worry about that just yet," Thole said. "You will forfeit all that you have bet up till now."

"Giant! Don't quit!" shouted a buxom woman from the crowd. "Keep your courage. Don't rob us of the end."

Frowning, Caelan edged back from the board. Thole leaned over and gripped his wrist. His hand was soft and supple, lacking the calluses of physical labor. The touch of his warm, moist palm made Caelan's skin crawl.

"They want their spectacle," Thole said, tightening his grip. "Don't you want this fortune?"

Something seemed to lie beneath his words, as though another language had been spoken, with a different meaning. The mists were swirling anew in Caelan's brain. He was so very thirsty, and he looked around for his cup.

Everyone seemed to be shouting now. The din increased in volume, making Caelan's head ring. He blinked off a sudden feeling of dizziness, and felt the internal shift of *sevaisin* taking hold.

Not here, he thought in panic. *Not with so many.*

But something inside him surged to connect with Thole, before he hastily yanked free of the man's grip. Just as hastily the gambler shielded himself from any empathic link.

But Caelan had gained one impression from that fleeting connection.

Trap.

He swallowed hard, hearing anger in the voices shouting at him now. Disappointment and derision came in open jeers.

"Why doesn't he throw?" someone asked in bewilderment. "All he has to do is throw."

"Take the sword from his hand, and he's just another stupid gladiator."

"Maybe his victories are as fake as his dice game."

The croupier leaned forward. "You are delaying the game. Take your turn, or forfeit."

Caelan uncurled his fingers and stared at the yellowed ivory dice lying on his palm. *Sevaisin* shifted within him again, and he knew the elephant from faraway Gialta that had died and left its tusks to be crafted into ornaments and baubles. He knew the craftsman who had carved these dice from the ivory. He knew how the slivers of lead had been cleverly worked into the interiors of the cubes.

These were not the same dice he had been playing with before. They had been skillfully switched since the last throw, and they would roll up a high number.

If he threw, he would win.

That large mound of ducats would be his. He would be a very rich man.

Caelan frowned. He would be a very rich slave, he corrected himself.

But one rich enough to purchase his freedom?

Even as the thought crossed his mind, he shoved it derisively away. If the prince would not free him in honor, he would not accept a price either.

What, then, did a slave need with so much money?

Even more puzzling, why did these men want him to win?

Why had they let him win until his stake rivaled theirs?

Why had they lured him here and kept him so long? Why were they so interested in him?

Trap. But what kind? What did it mean?

"You must play or forfeit," the croupier said sternly. "Follow the rules of the game before we have a riot in here."

"The barbarian doesn't know the game!" someone shouted.

"Throw the damned dice," Lord Fuesel said. "Where is your nerve now? Show us the courage you exhibited in the arena."

He was too vehement, too desperate. Fuesel's thick fingers were gripping the edge of the board so hard they turned white.

Thole watched Caelan with the unwavering gaze of a serpent.

Meeting that gaze directly was a mistake. Caelan felt mesmerized, unable to look away. His heart started thumping hard, and once again he felt he could not breathe. The compulsion to throw the dice grew inside him as though the collective wills of everyone in the room had merged into a compelling force. Caelan could feel himself being drawn into it, being absorbed by it as though his own consciousness were melting.

The dice themselves grew warm in his palm, pulsing against his skin, almost purring as though they had come alive. Strange whispers floated through his mind: *wealth, please us, fortune, obey us, treasures incomparable, obey us, obey.*

His eyes fell half shut, and he swayed. His blood still pounded dizzily in his ears, and he felt boneless and adrift. Why fight it? What harm could there be in winning?

Something icy cold seemed to pierce his breastbone. The pain touched him directly beneath where his small amulet bag swung on its leather cord beneath his tunic. New visions filled his mind, overlapping the mist and heat with swirling snow, icy blasts of cold wind, the scents of fir mingled with glacial ice. And Lea's small face, her blue eyes bright, her mouth open as though she called to him.

He strained to hear her, and as he did so something snapped inside him. He slipped into *severance*. It was as though a knife sliced through the spell that had engulfed him. He stood apart, detached and separate in the cold wind. He saw the plan in its entirety. Fuesel and Thole were paid agents, intending to accuse Caelan of cheating as soon as he made the winning throw. Such a charge was serious. He could be imprisoned, and his hands cut off. He would never fight in the arena again. The competition could then step in with new contenders and new champions. The betting odds would once again be more even.

Caelan set the dice on the edge of the gaming board and stepped back with a shake of his head.

"I forfeit the game," he said.

Fuesel's mouth fell open, and Thole looked furious. The spectators roared with disappointment.

Avoiding everyone's gaze, Caelan turned his back on the money that was spellcast and not his. He shoved his way through the crowd. People growled and swore at him. A women even struck his chest with her fist. Wrapped in his cloak of icy detachment, Caelan ignored them all and pushed his way clear.

The moment he exited the room, he felt another tug of resistance, then a final snap as though the last tendrils of the spell had broken. He hurried away, and every step brought a cool, refreshing sense of relief and freedom.

Finally, he let *severance* drop from him. He paused behind a column in the passageway. Drawing in several deep breaths, he pressed his hand against his chest, feeling the small, reassuring lump of the amulet bag beneath his silk tunic. Even now it still felt cold to his touch, as though a chunk of ice swung inside the leather pouch. His emeralds, gifts from the ice spirits of Trau that had favored him long ago, had protected him many times before. No ordinary gems, they looked like plain, ordinary pebbles whenever anyone else examined them, and they revealed their true shape only to him. He had never understood why the ice spirits had chosen to give him such magical stones; he had never understood what purpose they might be intended to serve. Never had they intervened as directly as they had tonight.

He realized he was still sweating. He felt trembly and a little sick. The wine, of course, had been drugged. Tipping his head back against the wall, he struggled to compose himself, then wiped his face with his sleeve and sent a small prayer of thanks to whatever benevolence existed within the stones.

Painful memories of his sister flooded his heart. He choked a moment before he pushed such thoughts away. He had loved her with all his heart, and he had failed her utterly. He had failed other people as well, including his father, but it was only Lea he felt the sharpest guilt for. She had been sweet, innocent, special—a tiny, golden-haired child beloved by nature, people, and the gods.

And he must stop thinking about her now, must drive her from his mind once more, knowing he could not return to the past and undo his mistakes, knowing he could not go back and save her.

Wiping his eyes, Caelan repressed a shudder and walked on in an effort to pull himself together. Forcing his mind back to Fuesel and Thole, he found his anger growing. It had been a vile plot to remove him from the games. Rivalry among the owners was fierce, and sometimes fighters were stolen and sold illegally. Sometimes they were poisoned or hamstrung. The prince must be told without delay. He had the authority to order these agents questioned. Tirhin could find out who hired them, then plan his own retaliation.

Yet the prince was not to be found. Searching discreetly, Caelan drifted from room to room, yet did not find his master. Occasionally he made an inquiry, only to be told, "His highness was last seen with Lady Sivee."

Yet Lady Sivee sat in the main reception chamber, surrounded by all her male admirers except Prince Tirhin. The group chattered wittily and nibbled on delicacies while dancing girls whirled seductively to erotic music. When Lady Sivee saw Caelan lurking in the doorway, she beckoned to him.

"Tell your master I miss him dreadfully," she said with a pretty pout. Drink had softened her eyes and her mouth. "Must he talk politics in the garden all night?"

Caelan barely concealed his reaction. In that moment he had a sudden vision of Tirhin on horseback, galloping away into the darkness, alone.

Somehow Caelan found a smile for the lady. "He is returned to the house, my lady. He sent me to ask you to meet him."

"Where?" she asked, too eagerly.

Some of her male friends scowled. Others nudged each other.

Caelan said nothing, and she gave him a quick nod and a sudden, dimpling smile.

"I *know*," she said and put her finger to her lips.

Caelan smiled back, although he could be flogged for playing such a prank. But the lady would never guess. He left the room and slipped outside into the cold air. As soon as the shadows engulfed him, he lengthened his stride, cursing to himself with every step.

Every action of the prince's made sense now. Bringing Caelan and his wealthy young friends to the party as distractions, chatting freely and moving about from room to room until everyone had seen him and everyone thought he must be nearby, ordering Caelan not to stay close to his side. Yes, it had been perfectly planned for the prince to slip away unnoticed. Even Lady Sivee would now contribute to the deception by going to wait for a rendezvous. Her tipsy departure would be noticed by her guests. Alone in her chambers, she would disrobe and wait. The prince would not come to her, but to save herself humiliation she would not rejoin her guests. They would never know he stood her up, because she would never tell.

But the prince had no business going out unescorted and unprotected. Not late at night, not with strangers casting spells on his slaves for dastardly reasons, not with the land restless and unsettled as it was.

"Fool," Caelan said under his breath and quickened his pace.

Twice he nearly ran into couples entwined in the dark shrubbery. There were almost as many people in the gardens as in the house. Torchlights blazed everywhere, but the noise and general confusion was a blessing. Finding a dark wool cloak lying across a bench, Caelan put it on, drawing up the hood to disguise himself. Joining a group of guests who were leaving, he was able to get his horse and mount up, unnoticed by the harried grooms and stableboys. He also casually drew a sword from a saddle scabbard as he rode by. His heart was thumping hard, for if he were caught it would mean his death.

But the gods favored him, and he was able to conceal the weapon under his cloak.

Leaving the gates, he wheeled his horse around uncertainly and set off at a trot. The moon was too thin to provide much light. It was hard to see the road, and he had no idea which direction the prince had gone.

Again he cursed his master, then he cursed himself for caring. What had happened to his anger and resentment? The prince could risk his foolish neck if he wanted.

But if anything happened to the prince, Caelan knew he would be sold to a new master. Better to stick with the master he had than risk the unknown.

He tried to calm down, although impatience and worry made it hard.

He sought, extending *sevaisin* farther than he had ever tried before. A flicker of the prince came to him, but it was clouded by something else, something evil and horrifying.

Caelan's mouth went dry, and he cut off the contact with a shudder. He did not know what he had sensed, but it was of the darkness. And it was on the prince's trail.

Praying he would not be too late, Caelan turned his horse north and spurred it to a gallop.

Chapter Six

THE NORTH ROAD climbed steadily through the hills rimming Imperia, its broad, unpaved expanse twisting lazily through the inclines, then crossed a narrow plain and began to ascend to the mountains. Highest of all of them stood the ancient and forbidding *Sidraigh-hal*, its jagged peak shooting up a pale curl of smoke against the night sky.

Ever questing with his senses, Caelan kept his horse at a gallop until the animal foamed with lather. The prince was not that far ahead, but he must be setting a blistering pace, for Caelan never got within sight of him. Caelan had to ride on faith, the amulet bag bouncing against his chest as though to urge him on.

And if he was wrong? If the prince had remained at the party? Then eventually bounty hunters would come after Caelan. He would be dragged back to the city in chains, and without trial or the chance to offer explanation, he would have sentence read over him. When the floggings and other punishments were done, his broken, mutilated body would be thrown into an iron cage, and he would be suspended from one of the city gates, given no food or water, and left there to die and rot.

It was the kind of risk to make a man sweat with fear.

But Caelan didn't draw rein. Danger rode on the prince's trail, and if Caelan could save him, then perhaps he would be made Tirhin's protector after all.

Cresting a low rise, Caelan spotted a glimmer of light below, far down inside a valley. He let his winded horse slow while he glanced about and took his bearings.

This land lay empty of dwellings. The hills were not

farmed. There were no villages. The light that winked briefly through the darkness, then vanished, had to be connected with whomever the prince was meeting.

Caelan frowned. More conspiracies. He wanted no part of them, no knowledge of them. The prince could lay plots all night, for all Caelan cared. But as for the creatures on Tirhin's trail . . . that was different. Stripping off his cloak and tying it to the saddle, Caelan drew the sword he'd stolen.

Using his knee, he nudged his mount forward cautiously.

He was halfway down the hill, still on the road, when a sudden flurry of wings above him gave him a split second of warning.

His horse screamed in fear and reared. Caelan had a confused impression of something large and black descending on him from the sky before sharp talons ripped across his shoulder. Crying out, he stabbed up with the sword and caught the creature deep in its vitals. Inky blood gushed forth, running down his sword arm and splattering across his face. The stench that accompanied it was of something putrefied.

The creature made no death cry, but simply plummeted past him to land in a dark heap on the ground. Caelan's horse shied and bucked away from it, and by the time he was able to regain control of his mount and move closer, the creature was crumbling rapidly into dust. A breath of wind scattered it away, and he never got a good look at what it had been.

Breathing hard, Caelan wiped off the stinking blood as best he could. Inside, he was shaken more than he wanted to admit. What, in all the names of the gods, was that thing? It had very nearly killed him, and he still could not quite believe his luck.

After a moment he forced himself to ride on, but he kept his senses attuned to the sky as well as to the shadows around him. Even so, he nearly missed the small trail branching off from the road. It led down the hillside that was rough with boulders and thickets of stunted trees.

Caelan hesitated a moment, then turned his mount that way. His horse's ears pricked forward alertly. The animal seemed more nervous and reluctant than ever, and he had to force it to take the trail. Step by step, the horse picked its way along, while Caelan's unease grew.

He had the same eerie feeling of being watched as he had earlier that evening when he'd ridden with the prince and his friends. Yet though Caelan's eyes were never still, he saw nothing.

The glimmer of light he'd spied before now reappeared in a brief wink, then was gone as though a door had been opened and closed. It was not far ahead.

But the land itself grew increasingly desolate. The trees were either stunted and deformed, or they stood as burned skeletons leaning over the progressively steeper trail. The air had grown strangely warm and oppressive, smelling strongly of cinders, ash, and smoke. Yet he saw no fire. Sweating, Caelan loosened the throat of his tunic and slicked back a strand of hair from his eyes. His horse pranced and minced along as though walking on eggs, snorting with every uncertain step.

Caelan realized he had come to the forbidden mountain of *Sidraigh-hal,* once sacred ground of the shadow gods. Across the narrow valley, it rose above him, black and forbidding, its fiery top wreathed in yellow, sulfur-laden mists.

Drawing rein in dismay, Caelan knew he should turn back before he found himself in worse trouble. This was no place for him. Even the simple awareness of where he was sent goosebumps crawling up his spine.

Breathing an old childhood prayer, he edged forward.

Here and there, frozen tongues of black lava scored the hillside. Lava canyons fell away sharply, their razor precipices offering death without warning.

The trail crossed a tiny stream, and the horse balked at first, refusing to cross it. Glancing around warily, Caelan dismounted and knelt at the edge. He was thirsty, and he wanted to wash off the creature's blood that still stank loathsomely. But when he put his hand into the water, he found it strangely warm as though it had been heated.

Caelan cupped water in his palm and tasted it. It was foul. He spat, shuddering, and splashed some of the water quickly onto his arm and shoulder.

A faint rumble passed through the earth.

Uneasily Caelan scrambled to his feet. His horse broke away and ran off. Caelan swore silently, but he did not go after it. The panicky animal could elude him easily, and he dared not waste time chasing it.

Feeling isolated and more vulnerable than before, he stepped over the stream and continued, keeping to cover as best he could. The farther he went, the hotter it became. The air smelled of ashes, and the ground grew unpleasantly warm beneath his feet. Here and there, the earth broke open to let steaming mud bubble out.

Something screamed in the distance, and Caelan jerked himself up tight against a tree. He stood there, tense and listening, his mouth open to gulp air, his heart pounding out of control. The outcry had been too brief for him to guess whether it belonged to a man or wild animal. But something out there in the darkness was hunting.

Hunting . . . *him.*

His hand grew sweaty and tight on the sword hilt. Again, he cursed himself for having come to this godless place. But he could not retreat now. Caelan pushed himself forward, his breath coming short and fast.

Ahead, past a stand of charred trees and new saplings, a hut loomed in the shadows. Its windows were shuttered tight, permitting no light to escape. Yet Caelan could hear the restless snorts and shifting about of horses, as though the animals were inside. His keen ears picked up low murmurs of voices, punctuated occasionally by a sharper exclamation.

Caelan circled about in search of a sentry, and found none. Only then did he approach the hut, from the back, and with great care. His feet moved soundlessly over the hot ground until he could press himself against the wall. Back here, there was only one window. Its shutter was warped, and Caelan could peer inside through the crack.

He saw a single room littered with straw and rat trash. The walls were crude daub and wattle. A fire burned on the hearth, smoking as though the chimney was blocked. In one corner the horses stood tied. Weapons, including Tirhin's fashionable rapier and jeweled dagger, lay in a small stack near a water pail. In the opposite corner Prince Tirhin, Lord Sien, and two other men stood clustered about a tiny, crude altar. Warding fires burned in tiny bronze cups, emitting green smoke as protection against whatever spirits lurked in this place of ancient evil.

The prince looked very pale, angry, and uncertain. Sien spoke and Tirhin shook his head violently. He broke away and began to pace. Doing so gave Caelan his first clear look at the other two men.

One stood in worn battle armor, tall and grizzled, missing one ear and badly scarred across the face. He was Madrun, no mistaking it. The other man, younger and well dressed in a foreign style, was also Madrun.

He spoke Lingua persuasively: "Please listen to the rest of our proposal, Lord Tirhin."

"No!" the prince said, casting a furious glare at Sien, who stood impassively with the green smoke floating across his face. "I will not betray my own people, not for gain, not for anything!"

"It is not a question of betrayal," the civilian Madrun said. "It is a question of helping each other. This war has drained us severely. We are an exhausted people. We are a starving people. Our men die in the battlefields, and who is left to raise crops and father children? Help us, Lord Tirhin, by giving us a way to end this war. And we shall help you to take your father's throne."

The prince barely seemed to hear. He was still glaring at the priest. "You brought me here to listen to this? What were you thinking?"

Sien's yellow eyes gleamed in the torchlight. "I was thinking your highness needs allies and support."

Tirhin clenched his fists. He was white about the mouth, and his eyes were blazing. "I have support—"

"From the army?" Sien said softly. "The way you had its support before?"

Red stained Tirhin's cheeks. "That was—"

"Need real army," interrupted the Madrun soldier, his voice gruff and guttural. "Need fighters to tear throne from dying emperor. Wait too long already."

"I see," Tirhin said, clipping off his words. "I am to let you into Imperia, let you pillage and destroy my city. And what assurances do I have that you will leave when your work is done?"

"Our word," the civilian began.

Tirhin uttered a short, ugly laugh. "The word of a Madrun? No."

The soldier bristled, but Sien lifted his hands. Gowned in saffron with a leopard hide worn across his shoulders, his shaved head gleaming with oil, he stepped between the Madruns and the prince.

"Let us speak openly of our needs and how we may help each other. Sir," he said first to Tirhin, "you have need of armed support, substantial enough to subdue civil unrest. Without an army, you cannot hold the empire together. We have already seen enough evidence to warn us that the provinces will split from each other if given the chance."

He frowned slightly at Tirhin, as though conveying an unspoken message, and turned to the Madruns. "And you, sirs, have need of peace."

The soldier growled.

"An alliance between our empire and yours would allow you a chance to recover. Once your resources were rebuilt, perhaps with the help of advantageous trade agreements between us, you could then wage new wars on your other enemies." Sien lifted his hands. "It is such a simple solution, and satisfies so many things for both sides. Come, sirs, put aside old grievances and traditions. Consider the future and new ways."

"We are willing," the civilian Madrun said.

All of them stared at Tirhin, who still looked pale and tense.

His eyes sought only Sien's. "There has to be another way."

"You have been loyal to your father," Sien said persuasively. "No one could argue that. You care about your people. Yes, they are yours, by right! You are the true heir to the throne, not that woman. What will become of you, of your steadfastness all these years, of your work, of your service when he gives his empire to *her?* She cannot rule this land. She lacks the strength of will, the knowledge, the ability. She is only a woman, foolish and weak. Her training comes from the Penestrican witches, and you can imagine what they have implanted in her mind. She will lose the empire. She will let it crumble into anarchy. She cannot hold it. You know that."

"Yes," Tirhin whispered. His face held bleak bitterness and resentment. "I know."

"Be bold. Seize what belongs to you now, while the chance is in your hand. At least listen to what the Madruns propose. They are not the first enemy to be turned into friends. Let them help you, and then help them in return."

Tirhin frowned and turned his back on the priest. In doing so he faced the back wall, and Caelan could see his face clearly. There was torment in the prince's eyes, torment overladen with anger and a dawning look of purpose. Caelan could see the decision in his master's face long before Tirhin drew a deep breath and squared his shoulders.

The prince swung around and faced the other men. "Very well. I agree."

The Madruns grinned and slapped each other on the back. Even Sien permitted himself a faint smile of intense satisfaction.

"Now," he said in his deep voice, "you become the ruler you were born to be."

Tirhin shrugged angrily, still visibly tense as he accepted the assurances of the Madruns. The civilian crossed to the horses and took down two bulging saddlebags. He flung these on the altar, and gold coins spilled from beneath the flap of one.

"Here is our first way of giving you support," he said eagerly. "Bribes for officials. Bribes for officers. Bribes for the palace guards and those who protect the woman. Our army will stand ready. Prepare an order for those who man the post towers at our border—"

"My priests can persuade the soldiers to let you cross the border," Sien said.

Tirhin threw him a sharp look, but the Madruns smiled.

The soldier leaned forward. "Give us that, and army will stand at Imperia's walls in these days." He held up his hand, all five fingers spread wide. "We help you take city."

Tirhin gestured in repudiation. "You move too fast. If you think I will let you through the city gates, you—"

"There have been too many delays already!" the civilian Madrun said fiercely. "Had you accepted our proposal last year, there would be no empress in the way now."

"A mere detail," Tirhin retorted hotly. "First you want the border, and our strategy plans, then the palace, now the city. What next will you demand from me?"

"Gently, gently," Sien said in quiet warning.

Tirhin looked as though he might choke, but he silenced himself.

"We do not beg you," the soldier said with gruff dignity. "We offer deal. You take it. Or you not take it. You decide now."

Tirhin looked ill. "I have already given you my decision."

The soldier shoved the saddlebag at him so that the coins spilled in a heavy golden stream to the floor. "Then take! And give what we ask. Do not wring your hands like woman, moaning about honor. In war, there is no honor. Only victory, or defeat."

Cocking his head to one side, he glared at the prince.

Tirhin drew a folded piece of parchment from inside his tunic and handed it over. The Madruns fell on it eagerly, and Tirhin turned away. He walked over the coins unheedingly, his face bleak and empty.

Sien spoke very quietly to the Madruns, who laughed, but took their horses and weapons and left.

Caelan grimaced to himself and stole to the corner of

the hut. Watching unseen, he saw the two men mount up and ride away into the darkness.

Torn, Caelan wondered whether to run after them. With luck and the element of surprise, he might be able to slay them and recover the plans the prince had given away. But the Madruns galloped away, too fast to catch.

That left his master the traitor.

Caelan's frown deepened. He felt sickened by what he'd witnessed. His former admiration for Tirhin now felt like cheap delusion.

To betray Imperia to its direst enemies, out of spite and ambition . . .

Disgust filled Caelan. He vowed to put a stop to Tirhin's plots, but how?

Uncertain of what to do, Caelan returned to his spyhole and peered in just as Sien lifted a smoking pot from the fire and poured its dark liquid contents into a cup. He proffered this to Tirhin, who was sitting dejectedly on a stool.

"Here," the priest said. "It is time to finish what you have begun."

The prince waved it away without glancing up. "Do I poison her or merely stab her in the throat? Do I bribe my way into her chambers and smother her in her sleep? Any suggestions for how this infamy should be conducted?"

"You are tired," the priest said soothingly. "Do not think of those details now. There are other matters that should come first. Drink this."

"One of your potions?" the prince said. "No."

Anger crossed Sien's face. "This is a gift. Not from my hands, but from he whom I serve. It will give you strength. It will make you greater than any other man. It will start you on the path to immortality."

Reverence filled his voice. He held the smoking cup between his hands as though it were something to be worshipped. "The cup of Beloth," he intoned, his face radiant. "The gift of life."

Tirhin glanced up, his interest caught at last. "My father's drink," he said. "What my father bargained with the shadow god for, and won."

Sien smiled. "Yes."

Tirhin's face hardened. "Once again I walk in my father's footsteps. Am I only to follow? Never to forge my own path?"

"You have begun your own path tonight," Sien assured him. "Your father's road is ending."

"And all I have to do to live for a thousand years is drink this?" the prince asked, his voice harsh with disbelief. "Don't I have to go before the god and make my own bargain?"

Sien put down the cup and frowned. "You fool! You jeer at what you do not understand."

"I am not an idiot. I know nothing is that easy."

"You are mistaken," Sien said angrily. "The path to Beloth is very easy. Once fear is put aside—"

"So I am afraid, am I?" Tirhin said with equal heat. "Why? Because I am a skeptic? I am not of the same superstitious, primitive era as my father. What did he do to awaken the shadow god?"

"That, you may not know," Sien said. "But I brought him the first cup, as I have brought it to you tonight. If you spurn this, then you are not worthy of—"

Tirhin jerked to his feet, knocking over his stool. "It is not for you to decide that!" he shouted. "You are no king-maker, for all your power. You do not rule the empire. You never will. Get that clear, for I will not be your puppet."

"Events are already set in motion," Sien said. "You cannot undo them now."

"No, but I shall control them as I wish. Not as you

wish."ⁿ As he spoke, Tirhin took the cup and dashed it to the floor.

The dark contents splashed out, hissing before the tamped earth absorbed them.

Sien cried something, but it was lost in a loud rumble that shook the earth.

Caelan scrambled upright and clung to the outer wall of the hut for support. This sudden violence from the ground was terrifying. Caelan found his heart slamming against his ribs. If Beloth did indeed live inside this mountain, then the prince's defiance had angered him.

Ash and smoke belched from the top of the mountain. The ground went on shaking violently, as though it would split open. Part of the hut's roof began to fall in. Caelan could hear the horses neighing in terror.

Racing around to the front of the hut, he shouldered open the door with a slam that nearly broke it off its hinges.

"Get out!" he shouted. "If you don't want all of it coming down on your head, get out now!"

Seeing freedom, the horses bolted past him. Caelan grabbed at one's bridle, but it knocked him spinning. Winded and stunned, Caelan struggled upright. By the time he regained his feet, the ground had stopped shaking, but the prince was standing over him.

"Sir—" Caelan began.

Without warning, the prince struck Caelan a harsh blow across the face.

Caelan went staggering back, and managed to catch himself against the hut. He straightened slowly, his cheek throbbing with pain. He could feel a hot trickle of blood down his jaw, and guessed he had been cut by the prince's signet ring.

Tirhin advanced on him and struck him again. "You followed me. You deliberately disobeyed my orders."

He lifted his hand a third time, but Caelan brought up his sword and held the point between them.

Caelan's own temper was running hot now, and he let it show in his eyes. "I came to help you. To protect you from what has followed you tonight."

Illuminated by the torchlight spilling outside through the open door, the prince kept a wary, furious eye on the sword in Caelan's hand. "The only one who has followed me is you, you filthy spy. This is the end of you!"

Caelan refused to back down. He intended to drag Tirhin back to the palace and denounce him before the emperor for his crimes. But if he said so, Tirhin would fight him. Better to lie and be crafty for now.

"Your highness promised me I should be your protector," Caelan said. "That is why I am here."

"Stop being so damned noble. I am sick of your honor. Sick of your loyalty. You are like a dog that is kicked but still comes cringing back for more."

"Where is the priest?" Caelan asked, interrupting. "We must go, and quickly. There is danger here. It—"

A shriek, similar to the one he had heard before, but much closer, cut across his sentence. The hair on the back of Caelan's neck stood up. For an instant his bowels were water. He did not know what it was, but it was not of the earth.

The prince whirled around, his eyes bulging. *"Shyrieas!"* he said in a strangled voice. He made a clumsy sign of warding and stumbled back into the hut. "Sien!" he shouted. "Sien!"

Caelan followed him, and stood blinking on the threshold. The priest was gone as though he had never been there. Even the cup that Tirhin had thrown on the floor had vanished. The fire on the hearth had been put out. Only the torches still burned.

The prince was buckling on his sword with a wild look in his eyes. "Damn him," he muttered, thrusting his dagger into his belt sheath. "This is his way of punishing me."

Caelan barely listened. He was eyeing the hole in the roof where the earthquake had broken it. Kicking the debris across the floor, he circled, feeling edgy and trapped. "This could have been a refuge. Better than taking our chances outside. But with that hole, I don't think we should stay here."

Prince Tirhin nodded grimly. He glanced at the door and swallowed. "They hunt in packs. The blood on you will draw them." As he spoke, he gave Caelan a second look and blinked. "In fact, you're covered with blood. What is all that?"

"I killed something," Caelan said shortly, picking up a torch. "I don't know what it was."

"Something that was following me?" Tirhin asked.

Nodding, Caelan tossed the torch to Tirhin, who caught it deftly, and picked up the other. "Ready?" Caelan asked.

"These torches will help, but they won't last long."

"It's less than an hour till dawn," Caelan replied grimly. "That is our hope."

Shoulder to shoulder, armed with torches and drawn swords, they left the hut and began to run.

It was crazy, running like this, struggling up the steep hill, stumbling over the sharp, cold lava that sliced through footgear. Ducking tree branches and avoiding puddles of hot bubbling mud, Caelan ran until his lungs began to heave, until his stomach felt as though it would spew the evening's rich dinner, until his freshly healed side ached. He ran, hearing the prince's breath sounding harsher and more ragged. He wondered if he was a fool to fear so much, when as yet he had seen nothing.

Yet they were coming, the dreaded guardians of the Forbidden Mountain, and all his instincts knew it. Fear filled him, clouding his mind. He remembered the night he'd been caught by the wind spirits, and knew the *shyrieas* would be somehow worse.

They splashed through the warm stream, and a little ray of hope lifted in Caelan. Better than halfway to the main road now. He did not think reaching it would save them, but at least it meant they would be off the mountain, in the clear, and on better defended ground. They would make it to the road, he told himself, and there they would fight.

The scream rent the air, right on top of them, so startling, so unworldly that Caelan cried out with it. His heart was pounding as though it would burst. He was out of breath, out of strength. Sweat poured off him in a river. His sword weighed a thousand pounds, and he was too weak, too spent from running to lift it.

Caelan *severed*, leaving his weariness behind. A part of him knew he was taking a risk, *severing* so close to the prince. Tirhin might suspect his secret, yet what did it matter right now? Surviving was more important than anything else.

Whirling with all the speed he was famous for, Caelan lifted his torch aloft, just in time to ward off the creature rushing at him.

It *was* a wind spirit, he thought, feeling fear return. Yet the detachment and heightened awareness of *severance* was already telling him differently. The *shyrieas* swirled and circled about them, long misty entities half seen in the darkness. Some seemed to have the faces of women; others were too fearsome to describe. They shrieked, and the sound was horrible enough to drive a man mad. Caelan heard Tirhin scream.

The prince dropped to his knees, and in a flash the *shyrieas* were on him, swarming in silent flight, rending with claws and teeth.

Caelan waded into them, feeling as though his skin was being sanded away. His clothes billowed in the wind of their passing. He felt the cloth tearing into shreds. His sword passed through them without effect, but everywhere the torch touched, a *shyriea* screamed and shied back.

Grimly Caelan could think of only one thing to do. He focused on his torch flame and shifted to *sevaisin*, joining himself to the flame, becoming flame, becoming heat.

Fire shot down the length of the torch and along his arms. He screamed in the flames as they consumed him, yet when he opened his mouth, fire burst from him and blazed across the *shyrieas*. They parted in a frenzy, melting and dissolving as the flames drove them back.

Caelan's hair and clothes were on fire. Flames shot from his fingertips, from his eyes, from his open mouth. He could not stop it, could not control it. He was burning in the fire, dying in it even as the spirits were dying.

He felt the earth scorching his feet as though he were drawing fire from what seethed below its surface. From far away, he heard a rumble that grew in volume as though the whole mountain stirred.

Then from the top of *Sidraigh-hal* behind them, molten lava spewed forth a shower of red and gold. The rumbling grew more violent, shaking Caelan off his feet.

The fire in him went out, and somehow he was able to reach for *severance*. It snapped the last connection, and he was free, blessedly free, back in the icy safety of nowhere at all.

"The void," he mumbled, and lost consciousness.

*   *   *

He awakened in the cold grayness of dawn to find himself sprawled on the ground while a fine mist of rain fell on him. His clothing was sodden and plastered to his skin. Across the canyon, the mountain still belched smoke, indistinguishable from the mist at this distance. The air smelled of sulfur and wet ashes.

Caelan groaned and managed to roll over until he could sit up. His clothes hung on him in filthy tatters. His hands were streaked black with soot and grime. His hair smelled as though it had been singed. Still, as bad as he felt, he could have been dead. He *should* have been dead.

His amulet pouch swung heavily against his chest. He held it a moment for comfort, then frowned. It felt wrong. With sudden foreboding, he shook the contents onto his palm. Before, he had had two small emeralds. Now they were fused together into a larger whole, as though somehow they had grown. He did not understand what had happened. His memories of fighting the *shyrieas* were unclear. Yet clearly there had been much magic wrought.

He ran his fingertips over the gem and frowned. It worried him that the emeralds had changed. It was as though he was losing a piece of his last memories of Lea.

Finally he put the emerald back in the pouch. It barely fit there now. He secured the top of the pouch tightly and frowned, still disconcerted.

His sword was a melted lump of metal, useless. He climbed stiffly to his feet and stamped around unsteadily, observing the ring of charred grass around him. What had he done this time, he wondered dazedly. He could barely think, much less remember.

Then he saw a crumpled figure a short distance away. Caelan's breath caught in his throat. He stumbled over and dropped to his knees beside the prince.

Tirhin lay on his side, unmoving. His clothes were as

torn as Caelan's. The rain had streaked the bloody stains, washing them to pink. Cautiously Caelan touched Tirhin's shoulder and turned him onto his back.

The prince's face was pale and drawn with pain. He was unconscious, but not dead. Caelan did not waste time trying to rouse him. He remembered that men attacked by spirits often went mad. It would be easier to handle Tirhin this way.

Kneeling, Caelan pulled the prince's weight over his shoulder, then stood up, staggering a little. His feet sank into the mud, and he found it hard to get his balance, but little by little he made it up the hill to the main road.

There, the mire was deeper than ever, but Caelan trudged steadily southward. *Sidraigh-hal* grumbled and belched threats behind him. Caelan was glad to turn his back on this evil place. He hoped he never saw it again.

It would be a very long walk back to the city. If the gods were kind, Tirhin would not die on the way. To live was not what the prince deserved, but Caelan might as well run for his own life as bring home a dead master.

"Traitor," Caelan said aloud, grimly ignoring the ache in his muscles and the prince's heavy weight. He forced himself to walk steadily and slowly. He had a long way to go. "Master traitor, what will I say about you when I get you home? What will I do with you? Bargain for my freedom in exchange for silence? Pit my feeble word against your exalted one? Hope to gain an audience with the emperor, which is as likely as learning how to fly? What am I to do? Who will believe me? As a slave and a foreigner, I am nothing, and you are all. There is no one who will believe me, for I have no proof of your infamy."

Every word he spoke aloud depressed his spirits. Would the prince be grateful for having his life saved? Caelan no longer believed in fairness, not from the man slung across his shoulder.

"All my life I have believed in the wrong things," he said aloud, speaking to the sky that was slowly brightening despite the rain. "I should be running for my life. I think I would be safer trying to hide in the wilderness than going back to resume my chains." He sighed. "A fool who serves a traitor. The gods help me."

Chapter Seven

A LOUD NOISE awakened Elandra from sleep.

Groggy and confused, she sat bolt upright and brushed back her long heavy tangle of auburn hair from her face. She listened, even drawing back the velvet bed curtains, but all lay silent around her. Not even the palace servants were stirring yet.

It was that cold, still time just before daybreak, when the night reluctantly released its dark grip on the world. Elandra had been dreaming—strange, unpleasant dreams mingled with intense anxiety about some task she had to perform.

Sighing, she gripped her head in her hands. She felt tired. Sleep came fitfully these days, if at all. She could not stop worrying about the coronation and all it entailed. Since Kostimon had told her last month that she was not to be crowned consort but instead sovereign, she had suffered a sense of gnawing dread.

Everything had been changing so quickly since the announcement. She had already been moved from the women's wing of the palace to new state chambers near the throne room. She had her own guards now, the members drawn from the elite Imperial Guard. All were strangers to her. They had been brought before her yesterday in a brief, private ceremony, wearing tunics emblazoned with her new coat of arms. One by one, each man had knelt before her and sworn to serve her with his life. Afterward, she had been informed that this ceremony of fealty would be repeated following her coronation. She was asked to choose a color for her guardsmen. One of the chancellors also muttered that a protector should be chosen. The protocol involved seemed unclear; there had been no empress sovereign since Fauvina some nine hundred years before. Many ancient tomes in rotting leather bindings were pulled down from the palace archives and consulted with much head-shaking and lip-pulling.

Even the coronation ceremony itself had to be conducted differently. There was some problem with the Vindicant priesthood over the matter of the wording. Elandra, beset with seamstresses fitting her for her coronation robes, had not yet learned the words of her own oaths because she kept getting revisions. Her political tutor, Miles Milgard, stamped in and out of her chambers regularly, trying to teach her history or inform her of the current state of alliances and trade agreements while she stood on a cushioned stool like a mannequin, with four seamstresses surrounding her, pinning and stitching as fast as they could.

Her gown was fashioned entirely from cloth of gold, its stiff heavy folds reaching to the floor and extending behind her in a train that pulled at her shoulders. Over it she would wear the robes, so heavily embroidered with gold thread and trimmed with rare white sable from Trau that they were too stiff for her to sit in. The robes and gown combined weighed almost as much as she. Every morning she had to don a bulky contraption fashion of thin plate metal and practice walking back and forth in it. It was crucial that she be able to move gracefully in her first and most important public appearance. She had to be able to curtsy in the robes without falling, and she would have to kneel and rise to her feet without assistance. Then there was the crown to manage as well, and she would be given a scepter to hold aloft—without wavering—as she recited her oath.

At night, too weary for restful sleep, she often dreamed that she was climbing a thousand steps with a tremendous burden on her back. She climbed and climbed forever, until her legs and back were aching, yet the steps never ended.

How amazing it was to think that just over a year ago, she was an insignificant girl in her father's household, working as a menial in her half-sister's service, assigned to run errands and do stitchery.

Even now, when she tried to think back to her wedding day, the memory was clouded in a haze. She had been so nervous she thought she would faint. Heavily veiled and richly gowned, she had gone into the temple on the arm of her beaming father. Vindicant priests had chanted over her and the emperor. She and Kostimon held hands, and the high priest tied a silk cord around their wrists. Then had come the blessing, and the drink of sacramental wine. Past that, she had only vague recollections of sitting for hours under the suffocating veil while the feasting went on. She'd been too terrified to eat or drink all day, but Kostimon had been kind to her.

He had come to her chamber and unveiled her. For a long time he had stood gazing at her, as though to drink in her beauty. He had been old and strange in his festive clothes of imperial purple, a tasseled cap on his head. His skin was creased and weathered, but not as much as she expected. He looked no older than a man of seventy, instead of nine hundred years more. His eyes were yellow and very wise. They twinkled at her before he smiled. Only then did she relax and begin to feel that she would survive.

"You are very lovely my dear," he had said to her. "Exquisite, in an unusual way, and a little like someone I loved long, long ago. If the gods are kind to us, perhaps I will come to love you too. And perhaps you will love me. But we will not rush it. There is plenty of time to get acquainted first. You look exhausted. Your day has been long, and so has mine. We will talk again tomorrow."

Approaching her, he gave her a gentle little kiss on the forehead, the way her father might have kissed her good-night. "Sleep well, little one."

And that was their beginning, a slowly evolving friendship based on courtesy and respect. She could not have been more grateful.

In this year, she understood she was on trial. She could make no public appearances. She had to keep to her own private quarters in the women's wing, confined to a suite of rooms and her own small garden. This was chafing. Sometimes she thought she would go mad from all the restrictions. But her Penestrican training helped her.

She read all she could, and her request for tutoring was granted with amusement. Finally, Elandra could have the education she'd always wanted. She took to her studies with zest.

After a while the emperor began to drop by to talk to her. He would quiz her about her studies, and when he found her to be both intelligent and conversant, his visits became regular and longer. They played chess, and he taught her military strategy in the process. Sometimes he would conceal her behind a panel in his audience room while he conducted business. Then he would question her afterward for her reactions and judgments.

With his encouragement, she grew less timid and learned how to state her opinions and even defend them without growing uncertain or confused.

He acted more like a parent than a husband, and began to take pride in her. He showed her off to his chancellors. He deferred some decisions to her. He watched.

And last month he had come to her one afternoon when she was playing the lute in her garden. He dismissed her attendants and took her hand in his rough ones. His yellow eyes had never been so serious.

It frightened her suddenly. She found herself lost in his eyes, in their age, wisdom, and coldness. He was looking at her as though they were strangers, and her heart stopped beating.

Perhaps it was over, she told herself. He had tired of her. She was not feminine enough for him. He had never consummated their union. That alone should have warned her. Now he had come to tell her he was putting her aside. Perhaps she would go to the prisons, or perhaps her father would take her home to Gialta. Her very life depended on the whim of this man.

She tried to meet his gaze bravely, but she found herself trembling.

Kostimon bent over her and kissed her full on the lips, something he had never done before. As a caress it was exploratory and expert, but she felt no spark between them, nothing in him.

Straightening, he stroked her face with his fingers. "Our year is nearly over," he said.

She struggled to hide her fear, to show nothing except attentiveness. "Yes," she whispered, her voice not quite steady.

"I have had you all to myself. Now that is ending as the bridal year draws to a close." He smiled briefly. "In a month you will be crowned."

She started breathing again, with such a sudden gulp of air she found herself coughing. Reaching for a handkerchief, she pressed it to her lips.

"Forgive me," she gasped, trying to stop the coughs without success. "I am not heeding you with much composure."

He laughed at that and touched her hair. "So I see. Did you think I would cast you out?"

"I—" To her mortification, she felt her face burning. She tried to meet his eyes and couldn't. "I have failed to be a —wife."

He laughed again, while her embarrassment grew hotter. She longed to throw herself in the reflecting pool.

"Ela," he said fondly, using his pet name for her. "You silly child, I have no need for a bed companion. There are plenty of those, disposable pretties with no thought in their heads."

Still staring hard at her hands, Elandra frowned and began pulling her delicate handkerchief to pieces.

"You are so much more," he said, pride evident in his voice. He put his knuckle under her chin and tilted up her head. "Look at me."

Her gaze shifted away.

"Look at me," he commanded.

She obeyed him, still upset although she wasn't sure why. It took effort to meet his eyes, but she saw no anger or disappointment there. She bit her lip to stop it from trembling and tried to listen.

"You are spirited and courageous," he said. "Better than that, you are pure of heart and true of conviction. I have been neither for centuries. You would go to the wall for what you believe in. Imperia needs that."

Her eyes filled with tears. "Let me give you sons," she whispered.

He shook his head. "I have a son. I do not need more. They have always disappointed me."

"Then—"

"Hear me," he said, putting his finger across his lips. "I believe in nothing anymore. I have lived too long. Seen too much. Been disillusioned too many times. But you have brought hope back into my heart. You, and you alone. I have tested you, and found you worthy. I have had discussions with your father. I have even talked to the Penestrican witches about you."

She frowned at that, but before she could speak, he

continued, "I am going to crown you sovereign empress, Ela."

She looked at him, stunned.

He smiled. "Do you understand what that means?"

Her wits were scattered, yet this was no time to be undone. She struggled to find her voice. "I—you want me—I am to—"

"You will rule with me, as me, for me."

She swallowed, choking a little, and had nothing to say. The magnitude of it overwhelmed her.

"I am getting old," he said, then grimaced wryly at his own understatement. "Let me rephrase that. I am coming to the end of my time. I have cheated death a long, long while. But that is over. The augurs have cast no prophecy after me. There has been no one named who will follow me."

She knew that. It made her feel slightly faint.

"Some say the world will end," she said softly, and by sheer strength of will managed not to glance at the black cloud that had lain across the northern horizon for several days now. "Some say we are facing the end of time."

"Some say that," he agreed. "Fools. I do not believe such superstitions. I am emperor, but I remain a man. To the gods, I am not important enough for them to end the world they play with. But neither will I go peaceably; neither will I go without putting my stamp on who is to follow me."

She was feeling stronger now. Her thoughts were more coherent. "Will it be the prince?"

"Probably. If he is man enough to seize control without destroying the empire in the process." The emperor shrugged. "I do not worry about Tirhin. If it should be someone else, then that is for the gods to decide. But I want my final days to be easy. I am tired, Ela. I am bored at last with my power, and that tells me my time is near."

"No—"

"Hush! Don't start any foolishness now, not when I've decided to depend on you. Be strong. You are to rule in my final days, leaving me free to be as idle as I wish. Fauvina ruled at my side in the early part of my reign. She had a mind much like yours, tough and quick, resourceful and clever. She aided me much when we were forging the empire. You will aid me now in preserving it."

For a moment he looked into the distance, very much lost in his thoughts.

Elandra dropped her ruined handkerchief on the ground and drew in several deep breaths. To rule . . . to sit at council and make decisions . . . excitement burst inside her, then she swiftly quelled it, afraid to believe it could be true. It was a monumental responsibility. No one had prepared her for this. Even the Penestricians, with their visions, had not foreseen such a turning. They had taught her to please, had taught her to be patient, had advised her to bear children quickly in order to secure her influence. She had realized months ago that the Penestricians—for all their wisdom— had no real understanding of what went on in the palace or how the mind of the emperor worked. How could they, when they had been banished from Imperia for centuries?

But to rule as empress . . . what would her father say? Would he be proud, or would he be horrified? After all, who would accept her in such a role? Why, all the lords of the provinces would have to come and bow to her in fealty, even her own father. They wouldn't do it. Not those men. They were warriors, and she was a woman.

"I understand," she said quietly, lifting her chin. "I am to hold the empire together until Tirhin takes over. I am to make a stable transition of power."

The emperor turned back to her with a look of approval. "Excellent! I knew you would grasp it without tedious explanation. But hear this: hold it for the boy, or hold it for yourself. I care not. I am done with it, if I can be left alone. If you want this empire for yourself, then hold it, girl! Hold it hard in your fist, and never let it go! Never stand back for another, do you hear? Not unless that is truly what you wish."

He glared at her, clenching his square hands into fists that were still powerful. "If there is any tiny part of you that wants to keep the throne for yourself, then do what is necessary to hold it. Choose your own consort and found your own dynasty. Make it what you want. That is my gift to you . . . this chance to shape the world to your liking."

As quickly as it had come, his vehemence faded. He blinked his yellow eyes and tilted his head to one side to look at her quizzically. "Well, that's enough for now. You'll have time to chew it over, see if you like it. Tirhin has no more claim to the throne than you or anyone off the street. I earned my throne, and by the gods I do not relish handing it over to any young pup who thinks he can demand it by some ridiculous right of birth. Fight him, marry him, or depose him. I do not care. Just bring me peace in my final days. That is all I ask of you."

She rose to her feet, gripping his rough hands in her slender ones. "You have my promise," she said earnestly. "All I can do, I will."

"I know," he said with a smile, and left her.

From that day, the news had spread through the palace like wildfire. Peace became a laughable word, for it was not to be found. All was chaos and preparations. And now that the event was finally close at hand, there were endless feastings and celebrations that exhausted her and certainly must be exhausting the emperor.

She hadn't spoken to him privately for nearly two weeks. Meanwhile, Tirhin sulked in his own house, complained to his friends, and declined all invitations from his father. He was acting like a spoiled child, which perhaps he was. Only he was too old for such behavior. He was making the emperor angry with his petty defiance, and Elandra had lost patience with him also.

Although she had met the prince publicly, in her veil, she had never really talked to him. After her coronation, however, she would be able to come and go as she pleased. She could attend public functions, and she could leave off her veil. She could do anything she liked, and that aspect as yet seemed like a dream. It was exciting, but frightening as well.

The world, after a year of living cloistered in her quarters, seemed to be growing too large too suddenly.

But she had no time to brood about it. Today she would go to the temple for fasting and the purification ceremony. Tomorrow she would be crowned. That meant this was her final day to be simply a woman. Tomorrow she would become something else. Would power corrupt her? What would she be expected to do first? Would the emperor truly relinquish the reins to her, an untried girl?

She drew up her knees and hugged them, rocking herself. Everything was unknown, yet she had faced other tests and survived them. She could survive this too.

As a child, she used to dream of living life boldly, of having adventures, of taking journeys, of gathering knowledge and ideas. She used to question why women should be shut away and cloistered from the world, ripened like conservatory fruit for the pleasure and disposal of men. She wanted to follow at her father's heels when he inspected his troops. She loved to hear his stories of the battles when he came home after long absences, grown crude and harsh and louder than usual. His armor would have new dents in it. He would be restless and tense at first, then gradually he would soften and relax. Never would he tell her everything; his stories would have odd gaps in them, gaps that her imagination struggled to fill.

But dreams were easy for a girl without prospects. Illegitimate and hard-working, uncertain of her status in a household too busy, Elandra had never imagined she would find herself here in the imperial palace. Childhood dreams were not supposed to come true. That was what her cruel Aunt Hecati used to say. Elandra had never imagined she would find herself at the edge of a destiny such as this. She kept waiting for reality to bump her harshly from this fantasy. She kept waiting for Aunt Hecati to strike her with a switch and order her to get back to work. Sometimes she sat up in the night, breathless and choking, and believed she was back in the Penestrician stronghold, blind and imprisoned in her tiny stone cell while ancient chanting rose and fell in the distance.

Was that a rumble she heard?

For an instant she believed she felt the room tremble around her.

She leaned over the edge of the bed, but already the faint sensation had stopped. Perhaps it was only her imagination at work again. The night was a strange place, and dreams were not safe from intruders. She sometimes felt afraid here, as though the shadows held things unseen that watched her. If she could have had a *jinja* to guard her from magic, she would have slept deeply and peacefully, but the emperor did not like the useful little creatures and would not allow her to have one.

Moaning a little, Elandra threw herself back on her pillows. It was barely dawn. Her new room was dark and shadowy, the outlines of the furniture still unfamiliar to her. She needed more sleep, but she was too excited to drift off now that she was awake.

What had that noise been? She was certain now that she had heard a noise.

Loud and sharp, as though something had broken. Like the mortal snap of a large tree when loggers bring it down.

Sliding from her bed, she picked up the long hem of her silk nightgown and crossed the cold floor in her bare feet. One of her ladies in waiting snored gently on a cot by the door. Elandra slipped past her like a ghost.

In the anteroom, however, she could hear low voices talking outside her door. Her guards were alert and on duty. They did not usually talk, though. Something *was* amiss.

She opened the door a crack, only to find her way barred by a strong chest plated in armor.

"What is it?" she asked, squinting against the lamplight in the passageway.

"A noise, Majesty," the guard replied. "In the throne room. Men have gone to investigate."

Her puzzlement grew. "The throne room? Is it the emperor?"

"Nay, Majesty. Wait within until the investigation is complete."

The guard shut the door firmly against her. Elandra stepped back, but she was more alarmed than reassured. If something was wrong, she did not intend to sit here in the darkness like a mouse.

Some ladies might say that courting servants' gossip was common, but Elandra had survived her difficult childhood by gleaning every rumor, report, and speculation from her father's servants that she could. Since coming to the palace, she had tried to build a discreet network, and with her new status, information was easier to acquire.

Thus, she knew why Tirhin was flaunting his father's wishes. She knew Tirhin was furious with her. He resented her. He felt betrayed by his father. He had been laying plots and sounding out men's loyalties. Kostimon chose to over-look his son's activities, but she could not afford to be so generous. Tirhin was rapidly becoming her enemy, and per-haps a coup was being struck right now.

With her heart beating fast, she hurried back to her bed-chamber. She was grateful now that she had taken certain precautions. Pulling on a heavy robe and fur-lined slippers, she opened a box of ebony and took out a dagger. It was a large knife, heavy and curved near the tip. A man's weapon, not a dainty, feminine stiletto. It filled her hand, and her fingers closed around it gratefully. She felt marginally safer now.

Gripping it, she went to the wall and ran her fingers impatiently along its shadowy surface. Finally she touched a narrow crack. She found the depression and pressed it, and a section of the wall sprang silently open. She slipped through, taking care to close it quietly after her, and felt along a small table just inside the dark passage. She lit a lamp, and its yellow light drove back the darkness, showing her a cramped, crude passage filled with dust and cobwebs. It smelled of age and damp, but she did not care. It was her own private passage to the throne room, and she hurried along it with the lamp in one hand and her dagger in the other.

Years ago, when she was a young child, she had listened to her father talking about another warlord who had lost his life and his property to the hands of a rival. The warlord had just hired a new contingent of warriors to replenish his army. He felt secure from his enemies. But the new soldiers felt no loyalty to their lord and were bribed into turning against him. They let the enemy into the palace, and the warlord was slaughtered in his own chamber.

Elandra thought of the new guards who had sworn an oath to her with their lips but not yet with their hearts. She thought of her stepson, who was her enemy, and as yet an unknown quantity. She thought of what lay at stake in this affair.

She had no intention of being a fool. Better to be over-prepared than taken unawares.

Reaching the door that would open behind the curtains at the rear of Kostimon's ruby throne, Elandra paused a moment, holding her breath as she listened. She decided then and there that she would choose her own protector following the coronation. If she had to, she would ask her father to provide her with a Gialtan candidate of unimpeachable loyalty.

Voices echoed in the throne room, rising in consternation. She heard no sounds of battle, no shouts, no evidence of danger. Only a hysterical babble.

Frowning, she opened the door and emerged cautiously behind the curtains. From their concealment, she could recognize not only the voice of some of her guardsmen but also that of Chancellor Wilst.

"What is to be done?" he moaned, wringing his hands. "What a terrible omen. It is the end of the world. We are finished. The gods have struck us a mortal blow. They mean for all men to die."

Suddenly impatient, Elandra emerged from her hiding place, still holding lamp and dagger, her auburn hair spilling unbound down her back.

"Cease this commotion at once!" she cried. Her voice rang out over the others, and everyone grew silent.

As one they turned to stare at her, their eyes wide with fear.

Her frown deepened. "What in the name of the gods is the matter?"

Then her gaze took in the throne. It had always been a marvel to her since the first time she had seen it. Carved of a single gigantic ruby, it sparkled and glowed as though alive in the torchlight. No one knew how it had been fashioned. Its origins were a mystery. Where such a tremendous gemstone could have been mined was impossible to guess. Kostimon claimed it was given to him by the tribes of Choven, famous throughout the empire for their spell-forged metals. The throne had to have been spell-carved. According to legend, shortly after Kostimon proclaimed himself emperor, the Choven had entered the crude beginnings of his city. They bore the throne, swathed in cloths, upon the shoulders of ten bearers. Chanting in their eerie tongue, they had come before the emperor and unveiled their gift of tribute. The throne had caught the sunlight and turned to fire, dazzling the eyes of all who beheld it.

It was the seal of Kostimon's reign, the very symbol of his power.

And now, within the vaulted throne room at the center of the palace, the ruby throne lay broken in half.

Elandra stared, her mouth dropping open before she recovered herself. Unable to tear her eyes away from the sight, she walked forward, right up to the shattered ruins. Her slippers crunched lightly over some of the tiniest fragments, and she stopped in her tracks.

She could see where it had cracked cleanly down the center, the fissure marks bold on either half.

"What does it mean?" someone asked. "What is to become of us?"

Was the emperor dead? The thought nearly stopped Elandra's heart. She looked up wildly. "The emperor! Quickly, someone go to him and see if he is well—"

"I am well," Kostimon's deep voice replied from the other side of the room.

Elandra saw him coming, robed in crimson and wearing a tasseled cap. His protector Hovet, looking old and grim in plain steel armor, stalked along behind him with a drawn sword.

People scattered out of the emperor's way until only Elandra stood there by the ruined throne.

Hovet snarled something, and with a start she realized she was holding a drawn weapon in the emperor's presence. Hastily she bent and placed her dagger on the floor, then retreated respectfully with her eyes lowered.

Kostimon's face might have been carved from granite, but as he reached the throne, his shoulders sagged. He touched the polished side of one half, and it was as though he physically shrank. Suddenly he looked old and defeated.

Pitying him, Elandra would have given anything to see that look erased from his eyes.

He sighed. "Then it is finished," he whispered. "All is over. The gods have spoken—"

She moved before she realized what she was doing, rushing up to stand between him and the ruined throne. Fiercely she glared at him. "It is *not* finished!" she said, keeping her voice low, but letting all her anger show. "You are not finished. Not yet. Oh yes, Majesty, it was a rare work of art, a thing of surpassing beauty. But you were not born with it. It came to you, to serve *you*. Had it been otherwise, you would be dead now, at the same time as its breaking."

Kostimon's expression did not change. He shrugged. "I am tired, little one. Let it rest."

"No!" she said, daring to defy him for the first time. "I will not let it rest."

Anger stirred in his eyes. He glared at her. "Keep your place. This has nothing to do with you."

All the breath seemed to leave her body. It was as she feared. In one second he had forgotten all his promises to her. Everything was swept aside, and she might as well be one of his empty-headed concubines. Fear filled her, but she knew that if she backed down now she was truly lost.

"I *am* keeping my place," she said fiercely. "And this has everything to do with me. Have you not charged me with new responsibilities?"

A shuffle from the people nearby caught the corner of her eye. Without waiting for the emperor's reply, she turned her head to glare at them.

"Leave us!" she commanded. Her voice rang out across the room. "All of you. And you, Hovet," she said, turning on the protector who glowered at her, "go with them to see that they wait in a group outside. I will not have anyone running off to spread the word about this. Guard them!"

Hovet did not move. Nor did anyone else. In dismay, she saw she had no authority at all. It was all a sham. An empty promise.

Then Kostimon gave the protector an all but imperceptible nod. Hovet wheeled around and brandished his sword at the others, even the guards.

"You heard the Lady Elandra," he said, still stubbornly using her old title.

They obeyed, although her guards looked outraged at being put outside. Elandra did not care. Alone with Kostimon, she prayed for the strength of her father and the iron will of her mother. The emperor was a capricious man. She had seen him turn on others with little provocation. Right now, in his present mood, he could have her destroyed without a moment's hesitation. But if she gave way, if she backed down now and sought to save herself, she would lose everything, possibly even her life. She saw that clearly, although what she has to do terrified her.

"The throne can be bolted back together," she began, trying to keep desperation from her voice. "It can be mended."

Contempt crossed his face. He turned away from her. "Ah, the mind of a woman. Always mending."

"What, then?" she shouted at his back. "Would you throw it away? Will you let this tiny flicker of adversity defeat you? Have you ceased to be a man?"

He swung around, livid now, and raised clenched fists. "I shall have your tongue cut out for that. You impertinent little hellcat—"

"Yes, I am impertinent, because I speak to you tonight as your equal. Is that not what you wanted from me? Is that not what you assigned me?"

"Not yet!" he roared. "Not until tomorrow—"

She chopped across this impatiently. "What do these niceties matter in a crisis? Only a few days past you spoke to me of holding the empire together. If you panic, what choice do the people have?"

"How dare you?" he whispered, his yellow eyes blazing. "How dare you accuse me of panicking?"

"Haven't you?"

They glared at each other in tense silence. It was the emperor who dropped his gaze first.

"I have never panicked in my life. I see how greedy you are for power, how swiftly you grab for it at the first opportunity—"

"You threw it at me!" she shouted, truly furious now. He was unfair, stupidly unfair. She had liked him, believed in him, but in reality he was just a wicked old man who would turn on even the people who loved him. "Did I caress you and whisper to you, begging to be crowned a sovereign? Did I? Did I ever ask for it? Did I ever scheme for it? No! If nothing else, at least admit the truth!"

"I make my own truth!"

"Then it is good your throne has broken! Has the weight of your own caprice and injustice shattered it? How can you think only of yourself at such a time? How can you be so selfish?"

"I am the only one who matters," he told her. "I am the center of the world. Everything revolves around me. You were a fool to forget that. Hovet!"

The door opened, and the protector entered. He saw in a glance their flushed, angry faces. He drew his sword, advancing slowly.

She was too angry at this shortsighted, arrogant man to care about the danger she was in.

"If you were not so conceited and vain," she said sharply, "you would understand that I agree with you! Of course you are the center of our world, the center of the empire. It *does* depend on you. It needs you to stand firm and calm, to look unconcerned by this omen. It needs you to mend the throne so that the people need not know what has happened. It needs you to sit on it and to dispense your justice as you have always done. Sweet Gault, man, send to the Choven to come and repair it, or ask them to make you another, but do not crumple before your own servants and say you are finished. If you believe it, they will also. Then the empire *will* begin to die. And it will be your fault."

By the end of her speech, Hovet had reached her. Grimly, he held his sword ready, awaiting the order to strike her down.

Breathing hard, spent from her emotions, Elandra raised her chin and glared at the emperor like a true Albain. Inside, her heart was hammering, but she was glad to die in a fight, glad to die with her blood hot and her last words the truth. Kostimon would not see her quail, she assured herself, trying to maintain her courage. He would not see her back down.

The emperor raised his hand, only to let his fingers curl weakly. Lowering his hand, he shook his head at Hovet, who looked almost disappointed. The emperor snapped his fingers in dismissal, and Hovet trudged out again, sheathing his sword as he did so.

Elandra thought she might faint with relief. Barely she held herself together and went on standing there, proud and straight, her chin still high.

"By the gods," the emperor said quietly. He still looked angry, but he was calmer now. Reason had returned to his eyes. "It is true, my assessment. I said you would go to the wall for what you believe in, and you have."

Her anger came back, a flash of white heat in her face. "Was this another test?"

"No." He gestured at his broken throne. "Even I would not go to these lengths to test you."

She turned her back on him, filled with disappointment so sharp it was like a pain through her ribs. "I believed you," she whispered. "I thought you meant all the things you said. But it was only a cloud, fluffy and bright, meant to amuse us, nothing more."

He did not pretend to misunderstand her. "Yes, I talked to you about ruling for me. I have trained you, raised your expectations. I admit that." He sighed. "But when you seized the reins just now, I—" He broke off and frowned. "I did not like it."

She remained with her back to him, unable to face him now. It was impossible to keep her broken illusions from her face, and she did not want him to see how deeply he had hurt her. "Of course you did not like it," she agreed softly.

Silence fell between them. She understood. He had clawed his way to power, then fought fiercely to maintain it. For a thousand years he had fended off every foe, and there had been many. He could not relinquish his throne now, not even to a regent. Not even to her. She had known it in her heart all along, had known it was too incredible to be true.

What she had not known, had not suspected, was how much she wanted it.

It was as though only in the loss did she see the truth of her own ambitions. She was shocked, and as angry at herself as at him.

"Will you have me moved back to the women's wing, Majesty?" she asked finally to break the silence. She even forced herself to turn around as she said it. "Will you send me into exile?"

He frowned in instant scorn. "Don't be stupid," he said sharply. "There will be a coronation, even if it's only to name you consort. The imperial family always moves forward. We never step back." He eyed her long and hard, his mouth set in a thin line. "Go and get your rest. You have a long and arduous day ahead of you."

Her mouth was equally set. Formally, she gave him a deep curtsy, then collected her lamp and dagger. Clinging to the tatters of her dignity, she stepped back behind the curtains and took her private passageway back to her chambers. Just before she went in, she left her weapon on the table and extinguished her lamp.

Inside her rooms, she found her ladies in waiting awake now and flustered in their nightrobes.

"My lady!" one of them cried. "What has come about? We could not find you. We have heard such terrible rumors. We were afraid and nearly sent the guardsmen to search for you."

Elandra eyed them coldly. "I was with his Imperial Majesty," she said in a voice like ice.

"Oh."

Her attendants faltered. Some of them exchanged glances. She saw all of it in an instant, read their minds as clearly as though they spoke their thoughts aloud. A fresh sense of failure twisted in Elandra's heart. If they wanted to think she had been in her husband's bed, so be it. That would at least start other rumors that might distract them from the truth.

After dismissing her ladies, she did not return to bed. Instead, she paced back and forth in front of her window, shivering and clutching her robes around her. Visions of the shattered throne haunted her. It and the dark cloud on the horizon were clear omens. The gods had spoken plainly. The end was near. At least for Kostimon, if not for them all. Swallowing hard, she kept telling herself she should be grateful she wasn't dead or cast out. But she wasn't grateful. She found herself growing angrier with every step.

What was her place now? Kostimon had admitted that he could not support his own intentions. At the first crisis, his kindness had fallen away to reveal the true man beneath. A cruel, manipulative man, with a mind from the dark ages, who asked her to help him yet would not let her try. He had humiliated her, and believed to do so was his right.

There could be no apology from the emperor. Probably he believed that letting her live was amends enough.

Be grateful, she told herself.

But she could not be grateful. She would rather choke.

Be humble, she told herself.

Her pride was thundering out of control. Humility could not even be approached.

Go through with it and wait for another chance.

But that thought appalled her. She was no schemer. She was not like Tirhin, with his plots and intrigues.

She thought of her oaths to be spoken tomorrow. Hot tears sprang to her eyes. How could she go through with any of it? A vow had to be honest and heartfelt, if it was to mean anything. Her integrity would not let her mumble empty words, simply for personal gain.

She could defy him. She could refuse to proceed further. She could ruin her father, destroy the long-range plans of the Penestricians, walk away from an empire teetering on the edge of civil war and chaos. She could retreat to a Penestrican stronghold and live out her days in silence.

And wasn't that what the Vindicants were praying for? Wouldn't that hand everything to Tirhin on a platter?

She frowned, feeling more confused than ever. She did not know the prince, did not know if he was a good man or a bad one. He was handsome, certainly, but that did not mark a man's worth. How could she judge his merits, or decide the course of his future? Who had given her the right to decide anything? She was alone, with no one to advise her. At least no one she trusted.

She went on pacing, feeling pinned under the direct scrutiny of the gods, and could not determine what she should do.

Chapter Eight

ALL DURING THE morning her entourage surrounded her like magpies, coming and going in excitement, chattering constantly. There was an atmosphere of great expectancy among her ladies, who knew nothing of the truth. Rumors flew in all directions, but the throne room had been locked—even her private passage was now barred—with guards at the door. The people who had witnessed the scene in the throne room had all vanished, including Chancellor Wilst, without explanation.

Elandra knew what had happened to them. Or at least she guessed.

It angered her that her husband would silence people, even good, useful people like the chancellor, with such un-toward finality. While she would have commanded their promise to not speak of what they had witnessed, Kostimon simply used execution to silence them. Like a barbarian, he treated death and mutilation casually. People were com-pletely expendable, in his view. It was the side of his per-sonality that terrified her.

She said little while her ladies chattered. She had a headache, and she felt nervous and tired. Then her tutor came in, with yet another version of her coronation oath.

"At last!" he said in excitement, waving the sheaf of papers. "There has been an agreement within the priesthood. Lord Sien has graciously conceded one point which the em-peror wanted most particularly. All can proceed now."

Elandra looked at Milgard coldly. It was tempting to tell him that his efforts were for naught. She was only to be a consort after all. Everything would have to be changed back to the original ceremonies and protocol. She wondered when the emperor would deign to inform his chancellors. Probably at the last moment, just to watch them sweat and bustle.

Then her own bitterness dismayed her anew. She tried to shake herself into a better frame of mind.

"Now, Majesty," Milgard said eagerly. He pulled over a footstool and stood on it beside her. She stood on her cushion like a statue, arms extended while the seamstresses made finite adjustments to the fitting gown she wore over her clothing. "Let us begin. It will occupy your mind while you stand here being stuck with pins. Repeat after me—"

"No," Elandra said suddenly.

Her head was splitting. The room was too hot and too full of people. She could bear no more of this.

Gesturing the seamstresses aside, she stepped down off her cushion and shrugged off the fitting gown.

"I wish my cloak and veil," she said.

Looks of consternation flashed about her. "Majesty," Milgard stammered, "there is little time to learn what you must say. Tomorrow the eyes of the empire will be upon you. It is important that you speak well. Rehearsal is—"

Elandra snapped her fingers, and one of the ladies hastened to throw her fur-lined cloak about her shoulders. Elandra pulled up the hood and fastened her veil into place.

"Majesty, please," Milgard said, looking distraught. He ran his long, ink-stained fingers through his graying hair.

"Not now," she said tonelessly. "I wish to go for a walk."

The ladies put down needlework and other activities in immediate compliance. They went to get their cloaks, but Elandra raised her hand.

"Stop. I will walk alone. I wish no accompaniment."

They protested, but she left her chambers and walked rapidly outside into the frosty air of midday. The winter sun-

shine looked pale and blighted today. Even inside the protected walls of her garden, her flowers had been nipped by
frost. They drooped, the edges of their leaves rimmed in
black. Two guardsmen trailed after her, keeping a respectful
distance.

Elandra glanced over her shoulder at them once, and
quickened her step. Her garden walls loomed high, and she
felt enclosed inside a topless box. This was a prison, no matter how comfortable. She felt confined and frustrated. Why
must she be watched over constantly? What harm could befall her here within the palace? Why, for once, could she not
be alone?

Her head ached more fiercely. Stopping a moment to
rub her temples with her gloved fingers, she drew in several
breaths of frosty air. Nothing helped. The tension knotting
her neck did not slacken. And it was too cold for her to
linger out here.

Yet she did not want to return to her chambers to be
fussed over endlessly, suffocated with attention. Abruptly
she made a decision and veered from her garden. Indoors,
she headed toward another section of the palace, walking
with swift determination. Her guards moved closer. Unob-
trusive, yet there in her wake. She reminded herself they followed to protect her, yet she did not feel safe.

She walked quickly along the galleries and passageways, keeping her hood up and her veil in place for concealment. Each time she met a courtier or a servant or a
chancellor, she was conscious of the swift flick of their eyes,
followed by a little gasp of recognition. It irked her. Why
should she maintain this pretense of being hidden away
when anyone who saw her knew who she was? Or maybe it
was the fact that she'd left her chambers to stroll through the
palace at large that shocked everyone she met. She must be
violating another rule and another set of protocols. For once

she did not care. She felt restless and edgy, rebellious and daring.

Finally she reached a section where she did not know her way. She stopped and gestured. One of her guards stepped forward and bowed.

"The new healer," she said impatiently. "Where is his workroom?"

The guard frowned, looking shocked. "But, Majesty, if you are ill he will be brought to you. You must not go to him. It is not—"

"Do not tell me what is and is not permitted," she said sharply enough to make the man blanch. "Direct me to his workroom."

The guard bowed again. "If your Majesty will follow me . . ."

He led her into a modest area of pokey passageways, dark, ill-lit rooms, and storerooms stocked with provisions. Women on their knees scrubbed steps and floors with brushes. The men were all carrying items or hurrying somewhere. Elandra saw no idleness, no slacking.

Unconsciously she gave a nod at the activity. It looked well supervised, but she would very much like to check the inventories someday to see how much waste and graft were going on.

Then, for the first time all day, she nearly smiled at herself. The steward would die of horror if he found her in his storerooms, counting barrels herself. No, no, he would expect her to sit in her audience room while he laid carefully penned lists before her and assured her all was as it should be.

She passed an open door where cold air was pouring in along with servants busily unloading laden carts. More feast day provisions. So much work toward an event that might be canceled.

Stop it, she told herself sharply. The emperor had said there would still be a coronation. She might as well shake herself out of this dark mood.

They climbed a long series of steps, leaving the bustle of the storerooms behind. Here, there was no heat and no activity. Despite the warmth of her cloak, Elandra shivered. Ahead she could smell the unpleasant scents of a sickroom mingled with the aroma of herbs and bracing tea.

The guard leading her stopped. "Wait here, Majesty."

He walked alone to the infirmary door and knocked, while the other guard stood close to Elandra.

The door opened, and the new healer peered out. He and the guard spoke softly a moment, and the healer shook his head. He pointed and closed the door.

The guard returned to Elandra. "Healer Agel is honored by your visit, Majesty. He begs you to enter his study. He will attend you shortly."

Already half regretting her impulse, she nodded. The guards led her a short distance down the shadowy hall and opened a door.

She was shown into a small, austere room. Almost entirely bare of furnishings, it contained only a writing table, a stool, and a simple chair. There was a case to hold parchment scrolls, and everything looked neat and utterly clean. Even the table was swept clear, and the medicine cabinet stood open to show orderly rows of small jars.

No fire burned on the cold grate. A single lamp struggled to supplement the inadequate light streaming through the window.

Elandra gazed about her with keen disappointment. "Is this all?" she asked.

"We Traulanders require little in the way of material possessions," said a deep, faintly accented voice behind her.

Elandra turned as the healer stepped into the room. He

wore the plain white wool robe of his calling, and his hands were tucked inside his sleeves. His face was gaunt and pale. His eyes were calm, dispassionate, uninvolved.

Seeing him, she relaxed at once. "You are Healer Agel," she said, "newly appointed to the court of my husband."

His eyes widened at this hint. He bowed deeply to her. "Majesty," he said, less calmly than before. "Forgive me. Had you but summoned me, I would have come to your assistance at once."

Her eyes narrowed in annoyance. So, when the guard had first spoken to him, the healer had thought her one of the concubines. Presumably they came often to his infirmary. "Had I desired you to attend me in public," she said through her teeth, "I would have done so. I prefer privacy for this consultation. Without my ladies in waiting, without my tutors, without my guards." She gestured at her guards in dismissal. "Leave us. This room is too small."

"Majesty—"

She glared at them over her veil. Reluctantly they left the tiny study and shut the door.

Closing her eyes a moment, she released a sigh.

"May I see your hand?" the healer asked.

Shivering and wishing he would light a fire, she extended her left hand.

He supported it carefully on the tips of his fingers, taking care to touch her as little as possible. When he massaged the web between her thumb and forefinger, she winced at the tenderness.

"You suffer the affliction of a headache," he said.

"Yes."

Releasing her hand, he studied her a moment. His eyes were so serious. She wondered if he ever laughed.

"May I reach beneath your veil and touch the back of your neck?"

"Yes."

Again his touch was impersonal, professional. He moved around her with exaggerated care until she longed to scream at him to simply take down her veil and handle her as he would any other patient. She resisted this, knowing it was foolish and self-indulgent.

Finally he stepped back. "Your Majesty is very tense," he said. "You have not been sleeping well, and you are overly fatigued. My advisement is rest."

She looked at him directly. "I do not have that luxury. I will be involved in ceremonial activities this afternoon, all evening, and all day tomorrow."

"The coronation, yes." He frowned. "I can remove the headache. I can induce calm, if your Majesty wishes. However, without rest the headache is likely to return in a few hours. I can also mix you a very mild sedative to help you sleep."

She knew nothing of Traulanders, except that they were cold, characterless giants who lived in a country of snow and ice. They were said to be incorruptible and trustworthy, clannish, and hard to like. Suspicious of strangers, old-fashioned, and nonprogressive, they rarely traveled beyond their own province. It was strange to meet this man from a land that sounded like a tale for children. She did not think he would poison her.

"The potion is acceptable," she said at last. "You may also treat me."

Bowing, he said, "If your Majesty would remove your veil and hood."

She could not hesitate, could not betray any nervousness. It was said that healers from Trau possessed extraordinary powers. They could remove all kinds of hurts with a

simple touch. She marveled at such abilities, but she was not
sure she believed. Kostimon had an old man's desperation to
try anything that would ease his aches and pains.

Lowering her veil, she pushed back her hood and faced
the healer. Gravely he seemed to gather his concentration;
then, with a frown, he pressed his fingertips against her forehead.

"No," he murmured and shifted his touch around to her
left temple.

The pain flared harder inside her skull, throbbing
wildly for a moment, then it eased. Suddenly it was gone, as
though it had never been.

Elandra's eyes widened. She drew in her breath
sharply. "It's gone."

The healer stepped back and bowed again. "Yes. But
your Majesty must heed my advice to rest. Also, you should
avoid salt in your diet for a few days. These simple precautions will insure that the pain does not return."

"Thank you," she said with a smile. Impressed by him,
she marveled at his skills. Kostimon was wise to bring this
man to court. He should have done so years ago.

Nodding, the healer moved to his cabinet and began
taking down bottles. "I will make an infusion which you
might drink later with tea, just before you retire. It will help
you sleep."

"Yes. That would be helpful," she said, keeping her
tone as formal as his.

"Your Majesty should not wait," he said. "It will not
take long to make the infusion, but I shall be happy to see it
delivered—"

"No," she said sharply, fearing poison and interference.
Anyone might meddle with it on the way. "I shall wait."

"My humble study is not comfortable."

"No," she agreed, putting up her hood and veil again for warmth. "But I shall wait."

He did not protest further. Gathering his materials, he walked out into the passageway and shut the door quietly, leaving her alone.

Sighing with relief, she sat down and massaged her temples. Miraculously, the pain was still gone. She felt restored, and some of her edginess was fading. Even this dreadful, icy room was better than her own quarters. At least it was quiet and utterly private. She shut her eyes a moment, sinking into the tranquility.

The window slid open with a scrape, startling her. She looked up at a man's head and shoulders framed within the window's opening. He was climbing inside.

Even as she scrambled to her feet, he pulled himself the rest of the way through and dropped to the floor like a cat.

He was immensely tall, taller even than the healer, with broad, muscular shoulders and a tangled mane of golden hair. Dressed in filthy rags, he was covered in grime from head to foot. His blue eyes glared fiercely, darting here and there in feral distrust.

Elandra regained her startled wits immediately. "A thief," she breathed, and gathered herself to scream.

Faster than thought, he was across the small room and on her. Her cry was cut off by his hand pressing roughly against her mouth. He pushed her back against the wall and pinned her there with his body, holding her fast despite her struggles. He stared at the door, but her guards had not heard her. They did not come to her aid.

"Be quiet, or I will choke the life from you," he whispered harshly.

She heaved against him, but he might as well have been a rock. His hand was crushing her lips. She drew them back from her teeth and bit him.

Sucking in a breath of pain, he shifted himself slightly and gripped her throat with his other hand. The pain was immediate and terrifying. She couldn't breathe at all.

Then his crushing fingers lifted from her throat, and she sagged weakly, struggling to draw in air.

"Now be quiet, and I will not hurt you more," he said.

She started coughing. Her throat burned like fire.

He seemed to take her coughing for assent, for he released her slowly and cautiously. Lifting his hand from her mouth, he held up his forefinger in warning.

"Remember, not a sound," he whispered. "Who is out there?"

"My guards," she replied, her voice a strangle. She was thinking desperately, trying to devise a plan to escape. All the while a derisive voice in the back of her head jeered at her: *Oh, yes, how safe it is inside the palace. You may roam anywhere you please. Why not dismiss your guards entirely?* But telling herself how stupid and naive she'd been did not help. This seemed to be a day of hard lessons.

He was eyeing her in a speculative way she did not like, obviously taking in the richness of her velvet gown and fur-lined cloak. Her veil had come loose in the struggle. She tried to pull it back in place, but it would not stay.

"Where is the healer, my lady?" he asked with a little more respect in his voice. "Is this his room?"

She nodded. "He went to make a potion for me."

The thief pushed himself away from her with a scowl. He crossed the room in two long strides and came back again. "Agel, Agel, where are you?" he muttered, shoving back his tangled hair from his face. "How long has he been gone?"

"Only a few minutes," she answered.

The thief, if he was a thief, grimaced impatiently. He seemed very nervous, and he was limping. She noticed his footgear was worn through as though he had walked a long distance. He looked half frozen as well. He had no cloak, and what remained of his tattered tunic was silk. One of his hands looked burned; the flesh across the back was puffed an angry red.

"This was the only window," he said. "Tell me, is there more than one entrance into the infirmary? Or must I reach it by the passage outside?"

"I do not know," Elandra replied calmly. She had revised her original estimate of him. By his speech, he was provincial but not lowborn. He looked worried rather than insane. A thief did not refer to his intended victim by name and fret because he had stepped out for a few minutes. She decided he meant her no real harm.

"My guards are outside in the passage. You must wait until the healer returns."

He pulled at the back of his neck, tipping back his head in a weary motion. "There is no time," he said.

Without further hesitation he went to the medicine cabinet and started picking through the bottles there, examining one after the other as though he could read the arcane symbols on the labels.

"Ah," he said finally, lifting one to the light. "That will do for a start."

Tucking it in his pocket, he started for the window.

"Wait!" she said. "What is your need, stranger? Why do you come here in this clandestine way, asking for our healer by name? Why do you hurry away, when you need care for your hurts?"

With one hand on the open windowsill, he hesitated. The thin sunlight slanted across his face, picking up the molded angles of cheekbone and jaw. His nostrils were etched fine, and there was a hint of tender fullness about his mouth.

The door opened without warning, and the healer walked in.

Startled, Elandra whirled with a gasp and pulled her veil across her face. The stranger dropped to a quick crouch, looking as though he would attack.

Only Agel kept his composure, although he stared very hard at the stranger for a moment. Then he shut the door as though his were an ordinary visitor. He glanced once at Elandra with a frown, then held back what he had intended to say.

"Well," he said at last. "This is unexpected."

"Agel! At last." The stranger hurried to him and gripped his sleeve. "You must help me at once."

"I am with a patient."

"Gault above, don't be an ass." The stranger didn't even throw Elandra a look, although Agel kept glancing at her. "Put her out, and listen to me. There can be no delay."

"I will *not* dismiss her Maj—the lady," Agel said severely. Red crept into his face, and Elandra could have throttled him herself. The idiot would give her away yet. "Her well-being is of the utmost importance."

"Nothing is more important than what I need you to do."

But Agel was drawing back with a stern shake of his head. He looked angry, embarrassed, and disappointed. They obviously knew each other. In fact, there was a similarity to the shape of their heads and the cast of their eyes. They might be kinsmen. Watching, Elandra let her curiosity grow.

"Get out," Agel said coldly. "You are clearly up to no good. I will not get involved with—"

"It concerns my master," the strange said impatiently. He cast Elandra a worried look, as though she might know whom he referred to. "There is trouble."

"You are always in trouble," Agel said with asperity. "Have you run away?"

"Only you can help me. I need an audience—"

"If you have run away, or done something even worse, I cannot help you," Agel said. "I have no influence in that quarter."

"You have the ear of the emperor," the stranger said. "I must speak to him."

Agel's gaze shifted nervously to Elandra. "Impossible," he said.

"May Faure burn your ears!" the stranger said. "Don't say 'impossible' in that pompous tone. It must be done. Every moment is vital. Give me your spare set of clothes and some wash water. While you ask for an audience, I will get cleaned up."

The healer looked exasperated, and Elandra had to smile behind her veil. This filthy stranger clearly had no idea of how the emperor was approached.

"Well?" he demanded.

Agel sighed. "You are mad to come here like this. Why didn't you send for me in the normal way?"

Even Elandra lost patience with him. He was stodgy and stupid, for all his professional skill. She could see the stranger was rapidly losing the scant shreds of temper he had left.

"Healer Agel," she said imperiously, stepping forward.

Both men glared at her as though they wanted no interference.

"If this man is known to you, why do you deny him your assistance?"

Agel's mouth dropped open before he hastily closed it. "But I cannot—"

She gestured to silence him. "The man is hurt, and cold, and has obviously walked many miles to come here. He is in trouble and has need of you. Will you refuse him care?"

"No, of course not, my lady," Agel said, looking confused and frustrated. "But I must attend you first."

"If you will give me the potion I came for, I will consider myself satisfied." She reached out her hand, and he reluctantly gave her the bottle.

"Thank you," she said. "Now care for this man."

"I don't want that," the stranger said, interrupting. "The emperor must be warned."

"Of what?" she asked. "What news do you bring?"

He glared at her.

"Answer her, you fool," Agel said.

The stranger whipped his head around suspiciously. "Why?" he asked the healer. "It's no concern of hers."

Agel's face went red again. "You lout. You have no manners. A savage would be better than—"

"You can correct his manners later," Elandra said, losing patience with both of them. She pinned the stranger's gaze with her own. "What would you tell the emperor?"

His blue eyes were stubborn. He made no answer.

"See?" Agel said to her. "He is hopeless, no one for your Maj—for you to concern yourself about. Just a stupid, troublemaking slave who has run away from his master and wants protection."

"The law forbids harboring a runaway," she said severely. However, when she looked into this man's fierce blue eyes, she had difficulty believing he could belong to anyone. He looked like the hunting eagles of Gialta. Even with tresses on their legs, their talons blunted, and their wings clipped for training, their eyes remained untamed. "Have you run away?" she asked gently.

His eyes did not flinch from hers. "Not yet," he said.

There was darkness in his voice, a tangle of undercurrents and emotions she did not wish to unravel. As interesting as this was, she could not tarry here for long.

"Take care," she said in warning to the healer. "Your oath is to help the sick, the injured, and the helpless, but you may not extend that to sheltering runaways or those who have broken the law."

Agel's eyes narrowed. His face remained red. "I shall not break the law for this man, my lady. I shall not harbor him, and I cannot give him what he asks for." He turned on the stranger with open resentment. "Always you cause trouble. Go! Whatever you have done, I want no part of it."

The stranger looked frustrated. "Yes, you have always been more interested in preserving yourself than in doing what is right. What hope have I of reaching the emperor, if you will not help me? Would you at least carry a message to him?"

"No," Agel said without hesitation.

The stranger turned on Elandra so suddenly she jumped. "And you, lady?" he asked desperately. "Could you do it?"

She found herself unaccountably flustered. "Do what?"

"Carry a message to him."

"I—I—"

"If I wrote it down, would you give the paper to him?"

"Stop it!" Agel said before she could reply. "Leave her alone. She is no one you may address, much less command."

The stranger glared at him. "In this matter, I would crawl on my belly if it would get me to the throne room. I have asked you, begged you. But you cannot dismiss the past long enough to think of the empire. Now I ask this woman. I beg her."

"Stop!" Agel cried.

"For once, will you not listen to me? I must speak to the emperor, and as soon as possible. It is vital—"

"Vital for the preservation of your own hide," Agel said spitefully. "You have finally gone too far. I know how you are. You have ruined your relationship with your master—defied him, insulted him, or attacked him. And now you think you will run to the emperor for clemency. As though the emperor cares one jot for who you are."

"You're wrong," the stranger said. "It isn't like that. It isn't—" Breaking off, he put out his hand and braced himself against the wall. He looked suddenly white and spent.

Agel hesitated long enough to make Elandra angry again, but before she could urge him he took the stranger by the arm and steadied him. Gently he probed here and there, checking pulse points, examining more burn marks beneath the mud and soot.

"What has happened?" he asked, his voice softer now.

The stranger winced. "Trouble. Terrible trouble. He brought it on himself."

"You were with him?" the healer asked cautiously. "At his side, as usual?"

Wearily the stranger nodded. He dropped onto the stool and sat there with his head down. "*Sidraigh-hal*," he muttered. "Brought him back. I carried him . . . I don't know how many miles. We lost the horses."

Agel gripped his arm. "Where is he now? Is he hurt?"

"Yes."

"Then I must attend him at once. Where is he? Did you bring him here?"

"Gault, no," the stranger said, horrified. "I left him on the doorstep of his house, for his damned servants to find. He can rot in his bed, for all I care. I've done enough—"

"No, you haven't done enough," Agel said. He strode to his cabinet and began filling a leather pouch with items. "Why didn't you inform me of this immediately? To what extent is he injured?"

The stranger glanced at Elandra, and his face grew tight and distrustful. He said nothing.

Agel sighed and came hurrying over to her. "My lady, please," he said softly. "I think it best if you go."

She stood her ground. "And I think it better if I understand more of this intrigue, healer. Who is this man who has come to you for help? And who is his master?"

Agel might have a stony face, but his eyes flinched at her questions. Seeing that, she knew she was right to be suspicious.

"Answer me," she commanded.

"Lady, I dare not." Frowning, he glanced at the man who had come to him for help. "Until I understand what has happened, I can give you no—"

"Who are these men?" she demanded more loudly.

The blond man rose to his feet and advanced on her. "Put her out, Agel. Already she has heard too much."

"I cannot put her out, you fool!" Agel said to him. "Have a care."

"A simpering courtier's wife? She's in the way. Already she knows more than is good for her."

Elandra glared at him and let her veil fall. She'd had enough of this overgrown lout who was clearly up to no good. "You will tell me now who you are," she said in a voice of steel. "I command it."

The man glared back, crossing his muscular arms over his chest. His face was mulish with defiance. "Go to—"

"Caelan, *don't*!" Agel said with a gasp. "If you value your miserable life . . . if you value mine . . . go no further."

The man named Caelan turned white, then a dull shade of red. He turned on the healer with unmistakable menace and gripped him by the front of his robe.

"You fool!" he snarled. "You had courage once. Now you quail and quiver even before a woman—"

"She's not just a woman," Agel retorted, pulling free. "She is the empress!"

Caelan jerked back from him, and looked from the healer to her and back again in plain disbelief. Then his gaze returned to her, standing there haughty, angry, and unafraid. Consternation filled his face.

He went to one knee, bowing low, and said nothing.

The instant obeisance and humility in a man so fierce, so masculine, so rough absurdly pleased her. She hid that, however, and turned her gaze on the healer.

He looked as though he wished the floor would swallow him whole.

For her part, Elandra was busy thinking. The name Caelan sounded familiar to her. She had heard it before, in passing, perhaps from the guards or some of the servants. A wager . . . ah, that was it. He was a gladiator, the champion of the seasonal games. A participant in a hideous, blood-thirsty sport she was not permitted to view. He belonged to Prince Tirhin.

Both men were watching her. They read her face as she reached her conclusions, and they exchanged a swift glance of dismay. Caelan, unbidden, rose to his feet once more.

"I see," she said coldly, putting it all together. She turned her gaze on Caelan. "You are known to me, by reputation and through my knowledge of your master. Tell me now, with no evasion, of what has occurred."

He swallowed, his throat working convulsively, but he met her gaze steadily enough. "Forgive me, my lady, but I can speak only to the emperor."

The refusal, mild though it was, was like a slap. She realized again that she had no real authority. Even a slave such as this—arena meat, her guards would call him—knew that.

"Mind your stupid tongue," Agel said to him sharply. "You have done enough harm to yourself already without adding defiance to it." He turned to Elandra with a bow.

"Your Majesty, I ask forgiveness on his behalf. My cousin is a coarse knave, untrained in—"

Caelan tipped back his head and laughed. Only then did the healer seem to realize what he had said. Looking confused and embarrassed, he broke off his sentence and stood there.

"Agel of the big mouth," Caelan said, his face still alight with derision. "First you betrayed who I was, then you betrayed who she was, and now you have betrayed yourself. As an intriguer, you are hopeless."

Agel pushed away from him in outrage. "I am *not* an intriguer!" he said vehemently, glancing at Elandra as though to see if she believed his denial.

She gazed at him with disgust. He had pretty manners for her, but question his authority even the slightest, or even thwart him, and he grew petty and arrogant. He was a toady, ready to flatter but equally quick to check everyone's reaction before he committed himself to any opinion. If she ever acquired any influence at court, he would not rise far.

He stepped toward Elandra, his face filled with consternation. "I swear to you that I had no knowledge of these events. Our relationship is a coincidence. Whatever has occurred—"

"Yes, healer," she said without interest in his continued denials. "Why don't you confine yourself to your duties?"

"Yes, Majesty," he said in visible relief. "If I may be permitted to excuse myself, I think I should go to his highness and attend him if he will receive me."

She looked at this man, so eager to rush to the aid of the emperor's son while remaining impervious to his own kinsman who stood here injured and pushed to the limits of his strength.

She could not resist saying "But the prince has not sent for you."

Agel's eager expression faltered.

Did he not realize the mistake he made before her? Suddenly she was weary of the man.

She made a gesture of dismissal. "Go. Do what you feel is necessary. Certainly the prince must stand in need of your skill at this time."

The healer smiled. "Majesty, forgive my haste," he said. "Is there any other way in which I can serve you?"

"No."

"May I have leave to attend you later, Majesty? To inquire about your headache?"

"Yes."

He bowed to her, frowned dreadfully at Caelan, and vanished, closing the door with a firm snap.

She found herself alone with the gladiator. He eyed her like a predator, wary and dangerous. For a moment she felt afraid again, but she refused to show it.

"As for you—"

"My lady, let me speak," he said urgently. "What I have asked from my cousin, now do I ask you. Have mercy and help me reach the emperor. This is important."

"I'm sure you think it is, but I cannot do as you ask."

His face hardened. "You mean you will not."

"Do not censure me!" she snapped. "There are protocols and procedures. I cannot rush up to the emperor and demand he give you audience."

"Not even when the safety of the empire is at stake?"

She refused to be flustered and eyed him coolly. "How would a slave know whether the empire is in jeopardy?"

He went pale, and for the first time his eyes seemed to show realization of what he faced.

"You have pushed your way into the palace in a clandestine manner, like a thief. That is a grave offense," she said, making her voice curt and harsh. "You have come here without the permission of your master. That is another offense. You have dared attack my person. Now you make demands that cannot be met. How do you answer for yourself?"

"My lady—"

"Address me as Majesty," she snapped.

He bowed his head, chastened. "Majesty," he said in a low voice.

She did not like his deplorable manners. He had been too much indulged. It often happened to slaves who acquired fame. They found it difficult to remember how unimportant they really were. Yet he was an uncommon man, with uncommon qualities. It must be hard for him to mute that with deference and humility.

"What was your master doing on the Forbidden Mountain?" she asked.

Caelan's head snapped up, his eyes wary once again.

"Answer me!" she commanded. "What was he doing there?"

"Indeed, my lady—Majesty"—he corrected himself—"I cannot say without betraying him."

"Is that not your purpose? Haven't you come seeking audience with the emperor in order to betray and denounce your master?"

Again his eyes widened. She felt her irritation rise. Did he think her incapable of guessing the truth?"

"Majesty, I stand before you a condemned man," he said finally, his voice low with pleading. "I have attacked you, insulted you, acted in all ways wrong. I will die for it. I have no defense to offer, save these circumstances."

She stared at him. This was a man of rare courage, far more pragmatic than she'd expected. His qualities had held her from calling her guards. They intrigued her enough now to give him a nod.

"Speak," she said. "And tell me the truth of this matter."

His blue eyes were grave. He hesitated.

"If I judge it sufficiently serious, then perhaps I will go to the emperor on your behalf," she said. "Mind, I make no promise. But in the interests of the empire, I will listen to what you know."

"No," he said wearily and turned away.

She stared at him in disbelief, unable to comprehend that he was refusing the opportunity she had just granted him. Was he mad?

"Will you die in silence?" she asked him in open exasperation.

In return he shot her a look that made her flush. "Majesty, if I may speak freely, to denounce the prince is a punishable offense. Why should I confide my knowledge in you, expecting you to then denounce him for me? Why should I request that you endanger yourself on my behalf? Can a slave ask this of his . . . queen?"

She felt both hot and cold. Her feet were rooted in place. Her heart was suddenly pounding in embarrassment. She had completely misjudged this man, from his first appearance at her throat, to the brutal accusations Agel had hurled at him, to his stubbornness in not obeying her commands.

Only now did she understand that he was trying to protect her. Not to gain her favor, but because doing so was natural to him. What kind of man was this, to think of others beyond his own terrible predicament? It was obvious that Tirhin had been plotting treason, and that this man, this gladiator champion in his possession, had witnessed everything. Was Caelan so honorable that he could not withdraw into the blindness and deafness that every slave acquired for self-protection? Was he truly willing to risk his life in order to carry a warning to the emperor?

She saw that he was, and understood his frustration all too well. Here was a man trying to help, and hindered at every turn.

"I am sorry," he said now, spreading out his hands. "I am a man of action and the sword, not of polished words. I cannot go back to my master's service, even if he orders me killed for my disobedience. I cannot take back what I have done and said in this room. I can only ask for pardon, and your help."

His appeal moved her deeply. She believed his sincerity now.

"If you truly want my help, you must be forthright in your answers," she said. "Speak to me about your master. Is he badly hurt?"

"Yes."

"Is he dying?"

"He could be. I do not know." Caelan hesitated. "The *shyrieas* got to him."

"*Shyrieas?*" she echoed amazed and fearful. "In the city?"

"No. Beyond." He gestured vaguely.

"Ah, on *Sidraigh-hal*," she said, remembering what he had said earlier. "What were you doing there? Plotting treason against the emperor? Was that how the two of you were caught by the demons which protect the mountain?"

Caelan's mouth opened.

She went on. "The mountain was active last night. We felt tremors, even here in the city."

As she spoke, she thought, *Yes, even a tremor that broke the ruby throne. Did Beloth plan that? Can the shadow god reach so far now into our world?*

Driving such thoughts away, she continued.

"Yes, you were there by your own admission. That is how you got your burns. And you carried his highness back?

All that way? That indicates deep devotion to your master. Why are you now so eager to denounce him?"

He frowned. "I—"

"Are you guilty as his accomplice? Have you also committed treasonous acts? By his order or by your own free will? Have you listened to treasonous talk and not reported it? Today is not the first time surely that Prince Tirhin has acted against his emperor, yet why haven't you spoken up before now? Why wait? Is it for revenge against your master that you speak now? Why did you not come forward at the first incident? Do you understand that if you speak, you will come under blame?"

His chin lifted. "I am prepared for that."

"How proudly you say it. Have you realized that if you lay such a charge, you must be questioned? Do you understand that slaves are questioned by torture, and must make confessions in order for their evidence to be admissible in court?"

Her scorn was coming out into her words. How big and foolish he was, standing there with his mouth open. He looked at her as though he could not imagine a woman would know about such matters, much less understand them. He was like an ox, too big and docile to comprehend that he was being led to slaughter. She wished she could tell him that Kostimon knew his son was plotting, but that was privileged information, not for disclosure.

Caelan sighed. "I would not be risking this if I did not believe the emperor should be warned without delay. Will you now keep your promise, Majesty, and tell him?"

"I made no promise."

He scowled. "You—"

Her hand flashed up to silence him. "I said I would judge your message and then decide whether I could help you. It is quite impossible."

His shoulders sagged, and despair filled his face. It was as though he was too weary to be angry anymore.

"The emperor grants few audiences," she found herself explaining out of pity. "Those are set weeks in advance. He will see no one on whim or demand."

"But for this—"

"No. It is by his will," she said. "It cannot be changed."

"But how—"

"There is another way," she said.

Hope dawned in his face. Eagerly he nodded. "Tell me, and I shall do it."

"You offered to write your message. Do that, and I will see that it reaches the hands of Lord Sien."

Everything in his face crashed. He drew back, shaking his head. "No."

"Why?"

"It is impossible."

Elandra's patience crumbled. She had made more explanations and offers of assistance than he had any right to expect. Suggesting Lord Sien's help was the only avenue of seeing that his message got to the emperor, for the high priest alone had unlimited access to the emperor's ear. But this man was indeed an ignorant knave. If he did not understand how far she had been willing to go on his behalf, then she would not explain further.

"Very well," she said coldly, and walked to the door.

Caelan came after her. "Majesty, please!"

"I must go."

He reached around her and held the door shut with his palm when she would have opened it.

Outraged, she whirled to face him and found him far too close. "How dare you keep me here against my will!"

"What is one more offense among so many?" he retorted. "Will you help me if I tell you the Madruns are coming?"

"The Madruns are always coming," she said, unimpressed. "It is a threat spoken to frighten children. They cannot break through our defenses."

His face was intense. "But if they could?"

"They cannot!"

"But if they could!"

She stared at him, wondering for a moment if it could be true. The very idea chilled her. "Is this the terrible warning you bring?" she asked, putting a slight hint of laughter in her voice.

He met her gaze, emotions at war in his face. Finally he took his hand from the door and stepped back.

"It is impossible for them to reach Imperia," she went on derisively. "Our defenses are very strong."

He said nothing. His eyes held defeat, and it was as though he refused to plead or argue further.

She watched him a moment, wanting to believe him, but unable to. With a sigh, she replaced her veil and straightened her cloak. Her obligations could not be put off any longer. She had tarried here too long already. Elandra's curiosity was stronger than ever regarding what Tirhin had been up to. But if the slave would not talk openly, she could waste no more time trying to draw it from him.

"My advice for you is that you run," she said. "The healer will tell Prince Tirhin what you have done here. You are lost. No one at the palace will grant you sanctuary, and you cannot return to your master with any hope of his mercy now that you have attempted to denounce him. Run. It is your only hope."

"I can't live with bounty hunters on my trail," he said quietly.

It was not the answer she expected from him. She cast him one final look of amazement, then gathered her potion from the table and left the small study, taking care to close the door after her.

In the passageway the guards snapped to attention and fell into step behind her. Elandra walked quickly, moving with purpose but not unseemly haste. She was late; she had been gone too long. There would be an uproar to face in her chamber.

It did not matter. She had much to think about regarding this chance encounter.

Was it chance or fate? whispered a voice in the back of her mind. The Penestrican sisterhood did not believe in chance, only in connections.

What had Tirhin done?

He had plotted treason unsuccessfully in the past, and Kostimon had overlooked his transgression. Lately the prince had been surly and rebellious, but more toward her than toward his father.

But now he had done something wrong enough to shock a slave still loyal enough to carry his master bodily all the way back from *Sidraigh-hal*. As for how the slave had escaped the *shyrieas* himself, that had not been explained. She was inclined to think there had been no encounter with demons.

What, then, had Tirhin done? What was this wild talk of Madruns overtaking the city? It was unthinkable that Tirhin would join in some unholy alliance with the enemy, and yet it made sense. It explained what had made this slave claw his way through an unguarded palace window, risking everything for a chance to warn the emperor.

She had barely managed to pretend that she didn't believe the slave's hint about the Madruns. But inside, her heart raced at the possibility. Yet they couldn't take the city. They couldn't.

Even with help?

She dismissed the thought, telling herself not to become fearful and foolish. Her own father considered fear a contagion. He despised anyone who was governed by it. Elandra told herself she must think on this matter with her coolest reason.

But what if the slave was right? What if there was little time? What if her indecision and delay cost the city dearly?

What if she broke protocol and risked demanding an audience with the emperor? Even she had not the right to go to him unbidden. What if Kostimon heard her secondhand tale of supposition and hearsay and disbelieved it?

After the events of this morning, her ground had become very shaky. She did not think Kostimon would receive her at all, much less listen.

Besides, if she took the risk and Kostimon did believe her, that would mean Tirhin's arrest. An investigation would be carried out. Possibly he would be tortured. If the charges were proved true, Tirhin might be executed.

Elandra frowned to herself as she hurried along. She held a man's future in her hand, and she was not certain she liked it.

But if she kept quiet, deliberately suppressing the knowledge she had been given. How could she live with her own conscience? Would her silence not make her a coconspirator against her husband?

What was she to do? What was the wise course? The right course? They did not seem to be the same.

Did not Kostimon genuinely want his son to succeed him? Had he not hinted as much to her earlier? If she accused his son, would that not enrage him? The relationship between father and son was clearly a troubled and complex one. She would be foolish to step between them in any way. Besides, Kostimon had been laying many secret plans lately. His network of spies informed him of everything, and he

had Tirhin watched constantly. Was he not already informed
of where his son had been last night?

The easiest course would be to consult with Lord Sien.
He would know how to handle this news and whether it
should be mentioned to the emperor.

Such thoughts brought her no relief. She did not like
Sien, or his priesthood. Something about the man chilled
her. In his presence she always longed for the protection of
a *jinja*, and until now she had avoided him as much as possible. He did not approve of her, nor did he approve of the
emperor's recent decision to make her a sovereign.

To approach him for his advice might be the avenue toward making peace. However much she disliked him, it
would be better to have him for an ally than an enemy.

Her chin lifted, and by the time she reached her chambers her difficult decision had been made.

Her ladies clustered around her, fussing and scolding,
and hastening to remove her cloak and veil. She was terribly
late. Where had she lingered so long? Was she not frozen
from being outdoors for nearly an hour? The delegation of
Penestricans had arrived. She had kept them waiting. No,
there was no time now for anything except her preparations.
No, she was very late, too late to think of writing notes to
people. She had no time for discussions with priests and
chancellors. Everything must now wait.

Resignedly, Elandra allowed herself to be led into her
bedroom, where she was undressed and bathed in warm
water scented with rose petals and fine oils. Then the preparations began, with each lady in waiting standing in line
with the one article of clothing she was responsible for. Each
lady walked up to Elandra in turn, curtsied low, handed over
the item of clothing to Elandra's dresser, and curtsied again
before retreating. It took an inordinate amount of time, but
it was the customary ceremony of dressing the empress and

it occurred several times a day, for every separate function. Late or not, protocol must be maintained.

Today, she was not impatient with it. Her mind busily turned over every aspect of what she intended to do. And she decided against putting herself under an obligation to the high priest. It was too risky. Elandra stilled her uneasy conscience. If Tirhin had done serious wrong, the emperor's own spies would bring word to him soon enough.

"Keep your place," Kostimon had shouted at her this morning.

Elandra's eyes narrowed as her gown was slowly lowered over her head and fastened at the back. Her place was remaining the empress, remaining alive. She would do whatever was necessary to keep that. Even if it meant not passing on a warning to her husband.

Chapter Nine

DRUMS ROLLED LIKE thunder across the vast expanse of parade ground; then the beat became a steady cadence, like the fast throbbing of her heart.

Borne in a swaying litter whose leather curtains were tightly closed, and surrounded by a solid phalanx of armored soldiers, Elandra was carried down the lengthy steps of the palace and across the parade ground past endless rows of men and horses, all at perfect attention. Swathed in furs and heavily veiled, Elandra peered out through a crack in the curtains, curious to see the army turned out so smartly in her honor.

Divisions from every province in the empire had arrived. She knew the barracks were crowded to bursting, that the city was swollen with citizens pouring in from the countryside, that every inn was full and people were camping illegally in the streets, hoping to see her tomorrow. Ambassadors and delegations from outside the empire had even sent gifts of all kinds, some of them said to be truly magnificent, although it was considered bad luck for her to see them yet.

So much attention and tribute was overwhelming, yet she felt isolated from most of it by the restrictions surrounding her. In a way, it almost seemed to be happening to someone else.

She wished she could see her father. Homesickness filled her suddenly, and she found herself missing the river and humid jungles of Gialta. If only she could talk to her father, tell him of the events that were happening, and ask his advice. But when he had given her hand in marriage, she had been cut off from him. Until her bridal year was finished, she could seek no one outside the palace without the emperor's express permission. And to ask Kostimon's permission meant she would have to explain.

Elandra sighed. There were no easy answers or solutions. She must find strength inside herself, somehow.

Tucked in her glove was a folded paper that Miles Milgard had slipped to her at the last moment. She was supposed to be studying her oath right now while she was being taken to the temple. But how could she concentrate when her nerves were keyed up? All she could do was wonder what the purification rites entailed.

They were part of the mysteries . . . no one would tell her more.

Although the Penestricans had been banished from court for centuries, due to some ancient feud between them and the Vindicants, the sisterhood had been permitted to return for this occasion. They were to conduct the final rites tonight.

And although Elandra feared the Vindicants and their strange ceremonies, she could not feel relieved to be in the hands of the sisterhood either. She had endured their lessons before. They were always unpleasant experiences.

Elandra had been dreading the purification more than anything else. Gripping her hands together in her lap, she tried to shore up her faltering courage. But her nervousness kept growing. She drew in deep breaths, telling herself she must stay calm.

If only there was something to distract her. But there came no cheering from the silent ranks of the cavalry and foot soldiers lined up at attention. They did not move. They did not salute. They did not shout her name. All she could hear was the ominous beating of the drums and the rapid thump of her own heartbeat. It was alarming, this great silence.

Then, with a slight bump, her litter stopped and was lowered to the ground. She heard stamping and the thud of fists against armored chests in salute.

Hastily Elandra secured her veil just as the curtains of the litter parted.

A very stern officer wearing armor polished to a blinding sheen reached in and took her hand to assist her out. Still holding her hand in a ceremonial clasp, he led her up a crimson strip of carpet laid over the steps of the small temple. A man in the black mask of an executioner followed them with an axe.

On either side of the crimson carpet stood an unmoving line of veiled women robed in black. Each woman held a burning candle in her hands. Seeing this, Elandra shivered.

Once before she had entered the Penestrican stronghold between rows of women holding candles. That time, she had been attacked by a Maelite witch and blinded. It had been weeks before she regained her sight, and then she had been told her true destiny.

With a sinking feeling, Elandra could not help wondering if yet more surprises awaited her inside this small, shabby temple.

It was the ancient Penestrican temple, a place closed and deconsecrated centuries before during the purge. The Vindicants had wanted it torn down, but Kostimon refused because Fauvina's remains were buried there.

At the top of the steps, Elandra's escort halted before the small, plain altar fashioned of stone. A wreath of flowers lay on it, along with a clod of earth and a simple clay vessel of water. The sisters began to chant, and with deep bows both the officer and the executioner backed away, moving down the steps with care.

Elandra was left alone.

She stood facing the altar, gripping her cloak to her throat with both hands to conceal their trembling.

The chanting grew louder. It was an elemental, primitive sound that sent shivers up her spine.

Beyond the altar hung a curtain the color of the sky. It was drawn open by an unseen hand.

Dry-mouthed, Elandra walked around the altar and ducked beneath the fold of curtain. She passed into the gloom beyond.

She found herself in a tiny room, very dark after the daylight outside. Candles burned in numerous niches around the walls. The air was dry, musty, and cold, overlaid with incense.

Before her a hole yawned in the floor. Steps of crumbling stone led down into a shadowy unknown. Removing her veil, Elandra pushed back the fur-lined hood of her cloak and gathered up her long skirts. Slowly and cautiously she descended the steps, her hem dragging behind her with a soft rustle.

Candles burned at the foot of the steps. Thus, she descended into light, blinking as the illumination grew stronger.

At the bottom of the steps, she found herself in a circular chamber lined with stone. The tamped earthen floor was decorated with a five-sided star drawn with red sand. The serpent box stood in the center of the star, its lid firmly closed.

The chamber was very warm, although she saw no fires burning. Only the candle flames, flickering steadily, reflected in the somber eyes of the sisterhood gathered around her.

Elandra swallowed, but her mouth remained dry. The silence was daunting, and she lacked instructions in how to proceed. Yet the time she had spent with the Penestricans had taught her to exhibit patience and calm in the face of uncertainty. She tried to do so now, waiting without speaking or moving, gazing back at this group of impassive women with an assurance she did not feel.

After what seemed like an eternity, the women parted before her to reveal a doorway. Elandra walked toward it.

When she stepped through, she found herself in total darkness. Startled, she turned around, but it was as though a door had been closed behind her. She had heard nothing, but she could not retreat. Nor could she go forward. When she turned about again, she bumped into a wall. She was enclosed in a tiny cylindrical prison that was barely big enough for her to turn around in, nothing more.

The darkness was the most frightening aspect. She tried to stay calm and not panic. She did not want to be blind again. It was cruel of them to do this to her, knowing what had happened to her in the past. They could have at least given her a candle to hold for illumination and comfort.

But already she guessed that comfort was hardly a factor in what was about to befall her.

The floor moved beneath her. To her surprise, she realized she was being lowered yet deeper into the bowels of the earth. By what means she did not understand, but when she stretched out her hands to the walls she could feel them scraping against her gloves as she went down.

Then her progress stopped with an abruptness that made her stagger. Without warning, she was flooded with light.

Dazzled by it, she shielded her eyes with her hands and came stumbling out into a sand pit.

It was very hot, so hot her clothes were suddenly stifling her. The sand burned through the thin soles of her slippers, making it difficult to stand still.

She hurried across the sand to the other side, and went up three shallow steps to a stone landing.

This chamber lay in a natural cavern of rough walls and a ceiling hung with strange formations of translucent stone. On the far side a niche had been carved high in the wall for the goddess.

"Elandra," said a woman's voice.

Elandra turned and saw Anas walking toward her.

The deputy had not changed in the past year. Slim and straight, her long hair hanging unbound down her back, she approached Elandra with her hands outstretched in welcome.

They clasped hands quickly, then stood apart.

"The Magria is well?" Elandra asked.

"She is well," Anas replied.

"And you?"

A remote glimmer of a smile touched Anas's lips for a moment. "I also am well."

"My sister?"

Anas shook her head. "Bixia left us. She was . . . unwilling to accept our training."

Old guilt rose in Elandra. She knew she was not to blame, yet she still felt responsible for having ruined Bixia's hopes. Her half-sister had been raised from the cradle to think herself betrothed to the emperor, yet destiny had decreed that Elandra should marry him instead.

"Where has she gone? Back to Gialta?"

"No. We do not know."

Elandra bit her lip. "She cannot wander the countryside. What will befall her? Someone must inform my father—"

"Lord Albain knows," Anas said coldly.

"But—"

"Our purpose today is not to discuss your sister, but you."

"She needs help," Elandra said stubbornly.

"If she has gone to the Maelites, we cannot help her."

The rebuke was as harsh as a slap. Elandra frowned and fell silent, while inside she wanted to cry out denials. Bixia couldn't be foolish enough to go into that darkness. To follow Mael was an unthinkable blasphemy against all that was of the light and good. Yet Aunt Hecati had been a Maelite witch, skilled enough to conceal her evilness from all the safeguards in the Albain palace for years. It made sense that Bixia would return to the woman who had raised her. Still, Elandra hated to think it.

"Come," Anas said, with that sharpness still in her voice. "Put your mind on the future, not on the past. There is much to do."

She turned and went back the way she had come. Elandra followed her in silence.

Anas took her through a short passageway into another chamber. A small, round dais stood in the center. Elandra was told to stand on it.

As soon as she complied, Anas left her. Five women entered the chamber and began to undress Elandra, beginning with her gloves and fur-lined cloak.

The paper Miles had given her fell from her right glove and drifted to the floor.

One of the women paused and picked it up.

"Forgive me," Elandra said, embarrassed. "I forgot that was there. Put it back in my glove, please, and I'll—"

But the woman holding the paper suddenly hissed as though in pain and dropped it. The candles lighting the room guttered, and several went out.

Looking alarmed, the sisters backed up rapidly. "Anas!" one cried.

The deputy came running into the chamber just as the paper on the floor burst into flames.

Yet it was no ordinary fire, for the flames were a sickly green and emitted a strange odor.

Inhaling made Elandra feel dizzy and faint.

"Protect her!" Anas commanded.

Two of the women ran to Elandra and pulled her off the dais away from the weird fire. She wanted to cooperate, but her legs felt spongy and strange. She stumbled and fell to her knees. She felt horrible, so sick she thought she might vomit.

Anas grabbed a candle from its wall niche and hurled it at the green fire. Golden flames burst against green. For an instant both blazed high; then the golden flames were gone and only the unearthly fire remained, larger than ever. Ugly green smoke spewed from it, filling the chamber.

Coughing, Elandra tried to get to her feet. She must not breathe this. None of them must breathe this. Across the room she thought she saw fear in Anas's face. All the sisters were shouting. More came, some of them carrying staffs that glowed with a nimbus of yellow light. These women struck at the green flames with the staffs, but the fire seemed to grow stronger from everything used to fight it.

"Silence!" commanded a voice above the commotion. "Trust in the mother. Do not feed evil with your fears."

The Magria appeared in their midst, naked and grim. Her gray tresses hung unbound down her back, and the terrible mutilation scars looked old and white on her skin. She was carrying a basin of dirt, and her face looked as bleak as death.

The fire blazed very high as she approached it, belching the evil, poisonous smoke more than ever.

Coughing and gasping, the sisters backed away. One of them fainted. Elandra herself lay flat on the ground, pressing her face to it in an effort to breathe air as yet untainted.

Undaunted, the Magria dumped the basin of dirt on the fire, shouting an ancient word that jolted through Elandra although she did not understand its meaning.

The fire died, and the green smoke vanished except for a few lingering wisps.

For a moment there was only the sound of coughing and retching. The Magria glared at all of them, especially Anas.

"Bring the serpents," she commanded. "Let them finish cleaning this chamber. Search for any other traps that may await us. Use earth, not fire in this place. None of you are novices, to fall for such obvious tricks!" Her glare raked all of them. "You and you, bring the girl to me as soon as she is able. Anas, I will speak to you now."

She turned and strode out. Anas, wearing an unreadable expression, hurried after her. The others exchanged glances of shame and embarrassment. Most faded away until only the two assigned to care for Elandra remained with her.

"Can you breathe better now?" One of them asked. She had a soft, kindly face. "Are you able to stand?"

Still nauseated, Elandra shook her head. Her eyes were streaming, and her throat burned from the smoke she had swallowed. She wanted to crawl into a corner and die.

Probably that was what someone had wanted her to do.

Her near escape had shaken her badly. Here among the Penestricans she had always felt safe.

They brought her water, which she didn't want, but it made her feel much better and soothed her upset stomach. After a few minutes she could sit up. By the time the snakes were brought in, she was able to stand unsteadily.

Flanking her on either side, the two sisters supported her from the chamber and took her to a room fitted with a chair, a table, and a cot. A scroll-box stood opened on the floor beside a small chest of cedar wood.

The Magria sat there with a fearsome expression. Anas stood near her, looking tense and unhappy.

They brought a stool for Elandra, who sat down feeling as though she was made of glass.

"This will be explained," the Magria said in a voice like iron. She turned her formidable gaze on Elandra. "You said the paper was yours. You brought it here deliberately concealed in your glove."

Elandra stared at her in surprise. Was she being accused? Indignation replaced her astonishment. "How can you—"

"Silence!"

Elandra cut off her sentence abruptly.

The Magria leaned forward. "You said it was yours. You told the sister to replace it in your glove."

There was menace in this room, combined with considerable anger. Elandra fought back her sense of injustice and struggled to present what she knew in a matter-of-fact voice. If she let herself get too emotional, they would truly think her guilty.

"I thought the paper was the oath I must learn for tomorrow," she said in a quiet, controlled voice. Her hands were shaking in her lap. She curled them into fists. "It was given me as I set out. I was supposed to study it in my litter, but I didn't bother."

As she spoke, a horrified corner of her mind was refusing to believe her tutor Miles could have done such a thing. She had always liked him, trusted him. Why should he want to harm her?

"Who gave you this paper?" the Magria asked.

"A man named Miles Milgard. He is my political tutor."

"You trust this man?"

Elandra's eyes filled with tears. She fought to hold them back. "Yes. I—I thought I did. Was I meant to die?"

"Yes. The smoke could have killed you. Had you been closer to it, you would be gravely ill now. Had you handled it in your litter, you would be dead."

Elandra felt icy cold. She shivered, hugging herself. "Why would he do this to me? I cannot believe he would turn against me."

"The Vindicants have many ways of turning people. How well do you know him?"

Elandra frowned, struggling to concentrate. She must be objective, she told herself. She must put aside her memories of this man, must put aside her emotions. "I have spent an hour with him daily for nearly a year," she replied slowly. "I have found him patient, a good teacher, always kind, and considerate. He is from good family, if undistinguished. He has spent his life earning a living from teaching."

"Perhaps he did not know," Anas said slowly. "Perhaps he was used as a tool."

"Perhaps. Perhaps." The Magria brought her fist down on the arm of her chair. "This was a serious attack. Whoever lay behind it is desperate enough to risk using magic openly. Now, girl. It would seem you have more resourceful enemies than we thought."

Elandra stared at her. "Who else?"

"Don't be a fool! Anyone with a stake at getting the throne for themselves. The prince. The Vindicants. The Maelites. The Madruns. Choose one or several. There could be more." She scowled. "You were to marry and bear children. You were not intended to be at the center of a political storm."

"It was Kostimon's decision," Elandra said defensively. "He told me he consulted with you and—"

"Hah! A lie!" the Magria said with a fierceness that silenced Elandra. "He would rather cut off his right hand than consult with me on anything." She shook her head. "The visions did not show your sovereignty. None of them showed this. Has he learned to confound not only the augurs, but me?"

"Excellency," Anas began, but was gestured to be silent.

"It is foolish to disregard Kostimon. He has more resources than we," the Magria said as though to herself. "He did this for a purpose. Perhaps he has more than one strategy in mind."

"His time must be drawing near," Elandra said. "The ruby throne has broken."

She did not know why she blurted out what the emperor had decreed must be kept secret. It seemed to come of its own accord. Besides, she trusted these women more than she trusted anyone else. She needed their help.

Neither Anas nor the Magria seemed surprised.

"It's a terrible omen," Elandra said.

They nodded without concern.

"He was furious and a little frightened," Elandra continued. She looked at them in growing puzzlement. "I do not think he will crown me as more than a consort now."

That got their attention.

A cool, unreadable smile appeared on Anas's face. "What brings you to that conclusion? Did you have something to do with the throne breaking?"

Upset, Elandra started to deny it; then her sentence died in her throat. She looked at them in suspicion. "No," she said, "but you did. Yes! You did, didn't you? How—"

"Hush," the Magria said quietly. "The breaking of the throne was foretold at least a century ago. It can hardly be a surprise to him now."

"I don't understand," Elandra said.

"You are not meant to," Anas told her coldly.

Elandra's temper flared. She stood up, facing them both. "If I am to be empress, then I cannot be ignored and I will not be toyed with. I am not your puppet, Anas, to be manipulated as you please. You did not foresee me as having any true power, but if the throne comes to me by the will of Kostimon, then you must deal with me as you have dealt with him. With respect."

Anas stared at her with widened eyes.

The Magria smiled. "Well spoken, girl. You are growing up a little."

Angered by this patronizing remark, Elandra turned on her, but the Magria raised her hand.

"Careful," she said in soft warning. "Your rebuke was well delivered, but do not go too far. There is much to sort through, and in the meantime you have not begun your purification. If you feel recovered, I suggest you commence."

Elandra frowned. "We are to continue, as though nothing happened? Is the emperor not to be informed? There must be an investigation."

"I prefer my own investigation," the Magria said. "And, no, I do not think the emperor should be informed. Not yet."

Elandra shook her head. "I do not believe he is behind this attack on me."

"You have failed to make him love you; how can you be sure?" Anas said tartly.

It hurt, exactly as she intended it to hurt.

"Anas," the Magria said in displeasure. "You go too far. Events have turned, and we must reevaluate their meaning." She turned her gaze on Elandra. "The important thing is to let nothing deflect you from the events of tomorrow. You have done well thus far. You must continued to be courageous. If your enemies stop you, then they have won. Do you understand?"

Elandra nodded slowly.

"We will be more careful now. There must be more safeguards taken," the Magria said sternly.

"Excellency," Elandra said, choosing her words with care, "in your visions, have you foreseen the Madruns invading Imperia?"

The Magria's eyes widened. "What question is this?"

"Have you?"

"I have not."

Elandra frowned and told herself her fears were groundless. The army was strong. There could be no invasion.

The Magria watched her closely for a moment, then said with unexpected patience, "We have naught to do with the wars of men. The goddess guides our attention elsewhere."

Elandra asked no further questions.

Finally the Magria said, "Anas, resume the ceremony."

Anas sighed. She walked past Elandra. "Come, then."

"Anas," the Magria said.

Both Elandra and the deputy looked back.

The Magria's gaze was for Anas alone. "Be kind," she said.

Flushing, Anas inclined her head and walked out, stiff-backed, leaving Elandra to follow.

Whatever Elandra expected, it was not the gentleness of the sisters as they finished undressing her and led her to a stone cistern filled with warm, steaming water. Chanting, they pushed her completely under, then sprinkled dried rosemary and rue on her as she emerged, dripping. The purification chamber was small and cramped. Sand covered the floor, and besides the cistern there was only a stone bench. Elandra sat on it, shivering and dripping water.

The sisters carried in braziers of red-hot rocks. Placing these around Elandra, they poured small dippers of water on the rocks to create steam. Soon she was warm again. Then she was sweating. They scraped her skin, wrapped her in a robe, and led her into an adjoining room to be plunged into a cistern of fresh water.

The water was so cold it had pieces of ice floating on it. The shock of immersion in it robbed her of breath, and she could not even scream.

Then she was out, teeth chattering, hugging herself. They took her back to the steam and warmth, sweating her again.

And thus it alternated until her body was pliant and relaxed. She felt sleepy but marvelous. How could she have been afraid? she wondered. Even the aftereffects of the poisoning attempt had vanished.

When an elderly sister rubbed scented oil on her hands and began to massage Elandra, she closed her eyes and sank deep into luxuriant sensations. The sister's strong fingers dug into all the sore spots and melted away Elandra's tensions. She felt boneless, utterly at peace. Fears and worries about tomorrow faded from her mind. Even the chanting about her sounded lighter now, more like singing. Smiling, Elandra sighed and floated into sleep.

Only it was not sleep. She had the sudden sensation of falling, and although she threw out her hands to catch herself, she could grasp nothing. Faster and faster she hurtled down through a darkness that terrified her. Then the darkness changed to light, and she was falling through images. Faces loomed at her, huge and confusing, only to dissolve and vanish as she fell through them. Dreams . . . no, memories. She saw her father shouting at a hapless servant. She saw the emperor place his hand on a fragment of his magnificent throne. She saw Lord Sien sneering down at her during her wedding ceremony.

Then with a jolt she ceased falling and found herself in a featureless hallway. The walls were very narrow. She could barely squeeze through, but she felt the urgent need to run.

She did so, her feet flying faster and faster. She wanted out of this place, wanted this strange dream to end. But as she ran, a hand reached out from nowhere to grab her arm.

Glancing down, she saw the hand projecting from the wall. She screamed, but heard no sound. Somehow she wrenched free and hurried on.

But there were other hands brushing her, grabbing at her clothing and hair. Ahead of her stood the healer Agel, arms outstretched. She veered around him and collided with Caelan, who seized her by the throat. Pulling free, she stumbled on around a turn in the passageway. And now Hecati followed her, beating her with a switch until her back and legs stung.

Then, without warning, she found herself in the grip of a woman tall and warm, smelling of ambergris and henna. This person held her fast when she would have torn free.

"I must go," Elandra sobbed. "I must run."

Abruptly the loving hands were gone, and she found herself standing alone in the darkness.

From far in the distance came a whisper: "Elandra, my daughter. Do not run. Do not heed them. Find your own way. Walk to your destiny at your own pace. Do not be forced."

Elandra spun around, searching for the voice with a sudden yearning. "Mother?" she called. "Oh, Mother, please help me!"

"Help yourself," came the reply, fainter than ever. "You

are stronger than they know. Trust your own heart. Heed nothing else."

Elandra ran toward the voice, wishing now she had not pushed her mother away. She had so many questions, so much need for this woman she had never known. "Mother—"

But she could not find her. The voice spoke no more to her.

Finally Elandra stopped running. Anguished tears streaked her face. She had never understood why her mother sent her away when she was so young. She had never understood why her mother did not want her.

A feral snarl from behind her scattered her thoughts. Whipping her head over her shoulder, Elandra saw a huge black game cat leaping toward her from a thicket. Without warning she found herself in the jungle, sunlight barely filtering down through the upper canopy. The panther came at her fast. With fangs bared, it was intent on bringing her down.

And she was ten years old. Foolish and headstrong, she had wandered away from the safety of the camp against orders, and now found herself terrified, the intended victim of this predator.

Before she could turn to run, its paws hit her chest with a jolt that knocked the wind from her. She was falling, falling, her scream entwined with that of the cat. Its hot breath scorched her face as its fangs tore into her exposed throat.

"Stop!" Elandra cried.

She struck the panther, and her hand passed right through it as though it were only mist. The beast dissolved, and she was no longer lying on her back in the rotting humus, but instead standing on a desolate mesa, all bare rock and scrubby weeds, overlooking a sharp drop to the open plains below.

The air was cold, and it blew constantly at her back with a mournful howl.

The jungle cat's attack was not a true memory. Elandra frowned, still feeling shaken by how close it had come to killing her. But she had not wandered away from camp. Someone else had—a bearer. He had been brought down and killed before the soldiers could drive the animal away. And it had been tawny, not black.

And had her mother ever spoken to her? Was that a true memory, or just a hope?

She felt angry now. She had been toyed with enough. The sisters had no right to put her through this nightmare.

"Stop this!" she said aloud. "I will participate no further. Bring me back and have done with your games."

But nothing changed or responded. She stood alone on the mesa, the precipice at her feet. There was not another living creature within miles of her.

Suspiciously she turned around, gazing in all directions, but she did not even spy a dream walker standing at the fringes of her vision as they so often did. She no longer chased dream walkers as she had at first. Right now, however, she would have chased anything, if it meant a way of getting out of this dream.

The sky was overcast and very dark, as though a storm was coming. The clouds roiled, and now and then lightning flashed in their bellies, although none struck at the earth. On the plains below she glimpsed movement.

Turning to give it her full attention, she watched until she saw an army coming over the horizon. Soon she could hear its approach, like thunder that grew ever louder. It was huge—black, distant figures that stretched as far as the eye could see, an endless mass that came and came. And as the army marched in perfect rows, spear points gleaming with green fire, she saw dragons flying over, wheeling in the sky and belching fire as they bellowed.

Every creature in the army was black. The soldiers' armor was black, as were their helmets, cloaks, and gloves. Their swords were fashioned from black metal. Their horses, dogs, and dragons were all black.

As the army came closer, her vision improved. Suddenly she could see them clearly, although they were truly too far away for such clarity to be real. She realized the cavalry was not riding horses, but scaly four-footed beasts with vicious, barbed tails and nostrils that breathed fire. Those were not dogs that bounded ahead of the foot soldiers, but hellhounds with eyes of flame and teeth like razors. The dragons were ridden by demons who screamed with laughter.

The sound was so insane, so awful, she clapped her hands over her ears and tried to back away from the precipice. She did not want to see the faces of the soldiers beneath their helmets.

Yet she found herself frozen, unable to move or look away. With the army came a dreadful stench of death and decay. And at the head of the army rode a figure as large as a giant, with armor that threw off sparks at every movement and a winged helmet that caught bolts of lightning in its span, yet never burned. This figure's cloak was darkness. Wherever it looked, scrub crumbled to ash and the rocks melted into lava. It carried a quiver of fire, and flames danced at the tips of its spurs.

Terrified, Elandra found herself consumed with recognition. The god's dire name trembled on her lips, demanding to be spoken. With all her might, she fought to hold it back, knowing that if she said the name Beloth aloud, she would somehow chain herself forever to his darkness.

The god looked up as though he saw her standing on

the rocky cliff high above him. He raised one arm as though to launch a hunting falcon, but the creature clinging in chains to his wrist was not a bird but a man, a man square and powerful of body, a man with white curly hair and yellow eyes.

"Kost—"

She bit back his name also, fearing to say anything.

The emperor waved his arm in supplication. "Ela!" he cried, his voice a thin wail against the howling wind. "Ela, help me!"

"Do not say my name," she whispered, pressing her fists against her lips.

The god looked in her direction again, but his terrible eyes went on scanning as though he could not see her.

She had the terrible urge to kneel before him, to hurl herself over the cliff and fall to her death screaming his name. She felt pierced with a thousand red-hot needles, until she was writhing in agony, and yet she knew there was far worse to come if she succumbed.

Sobbing, she crouched down and plunged her fingers into the thin, stony soil. "Oh, goddess mother, help me," she prayed. "Give me the strength I need. Take me unto thy bosom and shelter me."

Suddenly she felt as though invisible shackles had been removed. She whirled about and ran for her life, full tilt away from the horrors behind her.

Then the ground that should have been flat dipped down into a low place that was sheltered and hidden. The cold wind ceased blowing. She found herself stumbling and slowing, sobbing for air.

Ahead, her path was blocked by a low altar of stone. Four thumb-sized jewels lay on top of it, each of a different color, each square-cut and perfect.

An enormous serpent, perhaps eight or ten feet long,

lay coiled on the other side of the altar. As Elandra approached reluctantly, the serpent lifted itself into the air until its head was at her eye level. It swayed there, its forked tongue flickering, with the altar between them.

"Choose a stone," the serpent commanded.

Shivering in fear, Elandra closed her eyes a moment. She was still too close to the dreadful army. She wanted to keep on running and never stop. She had no time for this.

"Choose!" the serpent commanded.

She tried to go around the altar, but her feet were frozen again.

"I don't want to choose!" she cried furiously. "I must run and warn the others. There is no time."

"Choose!" the serpent commanded. "You will not pass by me until you have chosen."

Impatiently she swept her gaze across the gems again.

Ruby. Sapphire. Topaz. Emerald.

Each was beautiful. Each was flawless, worth a king's ransom.

"Only one may you take," the serpent told her.

She felt hurried and flustered. This was some sort of test, but she could not reason it out. There was no time. She had to run and warn the others of what was coming.

"I don't want any," she said.

"Then you will stand here forever."

An unearthly howl lifted behind her. The hairs on her arms prickled, and she felt herself shrink inside with fear. The armies of hell were coming closer. She dared not glance back.

"Choose!" the serpent said. "Quickly."

The ruby she did not want. She hesitated over the others, not understanding the significance they represented.

The howl came again, louder and closer. One of the

dragons swept over her, and she felt the hot scorch of its flaming breath.

Without further hesitation, she reached out and plucked up the topaz.

There was a tremendous explosive sound around her—blinding light and deafening noise. The world went white, then black, and once again she was falling.

Chapter Ten

IN THE HONEYCOMB of chambers beneath the temple of the Penestricans, the night had passed and dawn lay near. The candles were burning low with tired flickers. The chanting had stopped hours ago. All was silent, and in that silence anxiety stretched so strong it nearly became a sound itself.

The Lady Elandra lay on a slab of stone, straight and stiff, with her hands folded across her stomach. Robed in simple white, her unbound hair spread out beneath her, she remained unconscious and still. Her breathing was so slight she might have been dead. Her pale face was drawn, and a frown knotted her brows.

On one side of her stood two of the sisters, looking frightened and anxious. On the other side stood Anas, almost as pale as Elandra. And at Elandra's feet stood the Magria, her old face very grim indeed.

With angry eyes, she swept the faces of the others. "This has been badly handled from the start," she said, her gaze stopping on Anas. "I told you to be kind to her. Have you grown so efficient, so cold, so brutal, Anas, that you have forgotten how to be gentle? Have you forgotten the meaning of kindness?"

Anas looked mulish and upset. "You blame me for this?"

Denial was always a clumsy line of defense. It showed how rattled Anas was.

"You pushed her into the memories," the Magria said. "You pushed her too far."

"The memories are an important part of the cleansing

process," Anas said half angrily, defending herself like a child. "I did not know she would go past them. We screened her before, when she was with us. She exhibited no abilities to have visions then."

"But she has had one now," the Magria said. She sighed, feeling every year of her age. It had taken all her strength to pull Elandra back. Even now, as she thought of what she had seen through Elandra's vision, she shuddered. It was fearsome indeed, as clear and vivid as any of Magria's own visions, and all too likely to come true.

"The child was not prepared for this. She has had no training. She could not protect herself."

"But you brought her back," Anas said, insisting as though she wanted comfort.

But there was no comfort to be handed out. The Magria looked at her deputy unsparingly. "Yes," she said. "But whether she has returned with her reason intact is something we do not yet know. Whether she can survive the shock is another question beyond it."

"The coronation is in three hours," Anas said. "The guard of escort is already waiting outside the temple."

"Do not speak to me of time!" the Magria snapped. "Do you think I can simply put my hand on her forehead and revive her to her senses? Do you think she is likely to recover in time to be crowned?"

"But—"

"I told you not to do this, and you disobeyed me," the Magria said, too angry now to soften her tone.

"The purification ceremony must be difficult—"

"Why? The girl did not require it. She is no threat to us."

"She will be if he gives her the throne," Anas said sharply. "You saw how much she has changed already. She must be taught to need us."

Disappointment caught the Magria in the throat like a knife. She had trained Anas with such hopes, but Anas continued to fall short. Another candidate to succeed her must be sought, and there was no time for that now either. Not with events shaping themselves so quickly.

"You are wrong," the Magria said flatly.

For the first time Anas looked uncertain. She opened her mouth to say more, but the Magria lifted her hand.

"You are no longer deputy," she said in a harsh, toneless voice. "If you cannot realize what your mistake has cost us in terms of time and trust, then you are incapable of judging what needs to be done to salvage this situation. We have lost this child."

"She still lives," Anas said, white-faced and shaken.

"Go."

Anas started to protest again, but the Magria glared at her and curled her fists. She was angry, so angry she could barely trust herself not to strike.

As though finally seeing this, Anas bowed her head and crept from the room.

The other two sisters exchanged frightened glances. "Excellency," one said, "may we assist you in—"

"No. I must do this myself. There can be no more mistakes."

The Magria steeled her heart, although already she was grieving for Anas, whom she had loved like a daughter. *I was proud of her*, she thought wearily to herself. *I indulged her too much, overlooked too much. I have myself to blame as much as her.*

"Go with Anas," the Magria said. "Do not talk of this to the others. I must guide Anas later when this matter is back under control. For now, stay with her. Do not let her out of your sight. Comfort her if she will permit it."

Reluctantly, the two sisters filed out.

Alone with the empress, the Magria sighed and buried her face in her hands for an unguarded moment of despair.

The sisterhood had grown so weak, and the Vindicants seemed stronger than ever. It had been Vindicant poison that had gotten past their safeguards to strike at this girl. There would be other attempts, and the Magria did not know if the sisters would be vigilant enough to thwart them.

And now this precious child had been seriously mishandled. It was an appalling blunder, but even worse was the vision of a released Beloth marching across the world again. The Magria herself had not foreseen that.

In her earlier visions she had seen that Elandra would marry the emperor but that she would turn to the man who would succeed Kostimon. One of the choices had been Tirhin. The other man was unknown. These men would war against each other, and Elandra would go to the victor to help found a new dynasty. Now it seemed the Magria's interpretation had been wrong. Elandra had not chosen either Tirhin or the unknown.

Gently the Magria pried the topaz gem from Elandra's fingers. The girl—so stubborn, so headstrong, so surprising—had chosen herself. Just as Kostimon—in an astonishing twist of contrariness—had chosen her.

None of this had lain in the visions.

The girl could not rule alone. The idea was impossible. Kostimon must know that. He must have some ploy in mind, but what? Did he realize that this child with her long eyelashes, mahogany hair, and Albain chin had the steel of kings in her? Did he understand what he had unleashed? Did he care? Or was he simply planning to create as much chaos as possible in his final days?

The Magria shook her head. Truly she had never felt as blind and helpless as she did now, with no inkling of how to judge the events taking place.

She took Elandra's cold, still hand between hers. "We are falling into darkness," she whispered. "Kostimon has given the shadow gods the means to unchain themselves. You have foreseen their return. You alone have divined our way of escape. What is it, little one? What is it?"

But Elandra lay still and wan, lost as yet to all of them.

Chapter Eleven

IN AGEL'S STUDY, Caelan stood a moment longer after the woman left, his mind awash with her beauty. He had never seen anyone like her before. She was exotic, unusual. Slanting cheekbones, almond eyes fringed with incredibly long lashes, a voluptuous mouth, hair like darkened copper. She smelled of sandalwood and cinnabar, clean and inviting. Tall and slender, richly gowned beneath her cloak, she came from another world far from his, a forbidden world he would never enter. He felt a little stunned by her, like a man who had stood too long in the sun.

She had been quick and clever, too slippery to convince. He did not believe she was truly the empress as she had claimed. Despite Agel's collaboration, Caelan thought she was probably an attendant, a lady highborn and very adept at deception. But she was too young to be empress; she was younger than he. Besides, for all her cleverness, she had not acted like a wife. She seemed confused whenever the emperor was mentioned. She had stammered stupid things about rules that kept her from seeing the man.

Wives were not kept from their husbands. That was nonsense.

But if she was only a lady of the court, then no matter what she had said or half promised, she could not really help him.

Hopelessness swept over Caelan. He sighed and felt weariness sink through his bones.

"Run," the woman had advised him.

He could barely walk, and yet he knew her suggestion came from genuine concern. He had no future here. Even if the prince still lay deeply unconscious and knew nothing of Caelan's attempt to betray him, Caelan could not return. He had taken the prince home, but that ended his service. Already he had torn the prince's coat of arms from his sleeve and hurled it into a roadside ditch.

Where, then, did he go? Did he slip out again through the side gate of the palace, winked on his way by the sentry who had won such a fortune on him? Did he hide himself in the city, waiting for the bounty hunters to sniff him out? Did he set out along a road? Did he take passage on a ship? No sea captain would allow him aboard as a passenger, looking like he did.

Could he admit defeat and give up when he was this close to the emperor? Or should he try again?

Aching and tired, he limped to the door and eased it open a crack.

The passageway seemed clear. He stepped out, holding his breath, and headed down it. There had to be a way to reach the emperor. He would find it.

As he passed the door to the infirmary, however, it swung open and Agel stepped out.

Astonished, Caelan stopped in his tracks. "You! What are you doing here? I thought you left."

Agel shook his head and pointed to the bulging pouch he carried over one shoulder. "I had preparations to make. And I could not leave you here in such terrible condition."

Caelan was not ready to forgive him. Kinsmen should stand together, no matter what their private differences were. He had seen behavior in Agel today that shamed him.

"All I need is a meal," Caelan said, knowing that what he really wanted was a soaking bath, a massage, and several hours of sleep.

Agel nodded. "Let me tend you first. It won't take a moment, and then I will go to the prince."

Agel walked back into the study, and Caelan followed. His mind was too blurred with fatigue for him to wonder much why Agel had delayed leaving. In a way, Caelan found himself relieved. He needed his cousin's help. Perhaps Agel had finally calmed down enough to offer it.

"Sit there," Agel said, pointing at the stool.

Caelan obeyed and Agel took a small vial from his pouch. He handed it to Caelan.

"Drink this," he ordered.

Caelan sniffed it but detected nothing repulsive. "What is it?"

"Who is the healer here?" Agel said, as prickly as ever. Then he smiled. "A restorative, you idiot. Drink it, and you will feel strong enough to eat the meal I have sent for."

Caelan swallowed the liquid in a swift gulp. It had no bitter aftertaste. Relieved, he handed over the empty vial.

"Thank you for waiting," he said. "I got nowhere with the woman."

"Can't you speak of her respectfully?" Agel said with irritation. "You are fortunate to still have your tongue. She was too lenient with you."

"Oh, come, I know she isn't the real empress, but only a handmaid," Caelan replied. "Enough pretense. I must have your help, if only to—"

An involuntary shudder passed through him. He broke off his sentence and passed his hand across his brow. It felt clammy.

Agel stepped closer to him, staring down at him as though from a very great height.

Alarmed, Caelan wondered why Agel was suddenly so tall and he was suddenly so very short, so very tiny, shrinking and shrinking, until he was only a speck, and then nothing at all.

*   *   *

When he awakened, he was lying on a braided run in the antechamber of Prince Tirhin's personal suite of rooms. Puzzled, Caelan took a while to sort through it. He did not understand what he was doing here, or why he was lying on the floor.

When he tried to sit up, every muscle in his body protested with a level of soreness that made him groan.

At once Agel appeared in the doorway that led to the bedchamber. "So you're finally awake," he said coldly. "It's about time. Get up and come in here."

Caelan opened his mouth to ask questions, but Agel had already vanished.

Frowning, Caelan slowly sat up, finding his wits by slow degrees, then levered himself to his feet. He had slept deeply, but he still felt muddled and groggy. A glance at the small window told him night had fallen outside, but how many hours had passed? And how did he come to be back here in the prince's house?

Memories sifted back to him in pieces. He realized he had been drugged.

Agel's meddling angered him, but he wasn't ready to face the implications yet.

Limping with one hand pressed to his aching side, Caelan went first to the door that led outside. It was locked, and he could not budge the latch. Grimly he turned around and walked to the bedchamber.

He paused in the doorway, looking inside.

A single lamp burned near the bed, leaving most of the room in shadow.

Within the circle of light, the prince lay beneath a blanket, asleep or unconscious Caelan did not know. His face had a waxy sheen, far too pale. Agel stood beside him, holding the prince's wrist in his long fingers.

Disappointed and worried, Caelan drew in a sharp breath and walked on into the room.

Agel released his grip on Tirhin's wrist and turned to face Caelan.

"Is he better?" Caelan asked.

"Not much," Agel said bluntly. "His physical hurts are minor. Those I have dealt with. But it is his reason that concerns me."

Caelan frowned at the man who was now his master in name only. "Yes," he said very softly.

Agel's gaze narrowed. "It is time that you told me exactly what happened. I can do nothing if I do not have information."

Caelan's frown deepened. "Why did you bring me back here to him? Why drug me? What is your intention?"

"It should be obvious," Agel said coldly. "You are intent on self-destruction, as usual. But this time I will stop you."

"Why?"

"Because we are kinsmen," Agel said sharply. "What happens to you will affect me. If you betray this great man who is your master, will I not also be looked on with suspicion? Treachery is said to run in families."

Caelan stared at him in amazement tinged with disgust. "You are thinking only of yourself."

"I am being prudent."

"You hypocrite—"

Agel lifted his hand. "I will not argue further with you. You are the property of his highness. If you do not stay where you belong, you will be branded a runaway. It is shameful enough to have a cousin who is a slave. Worse to have a cousin who kills for sport. But to have a cousin who attacks his master and then runs from his crime is—"

"Wait!" Caelan said in bewilderment. "What twisting of truth is this? I didn't attack him."

"Didn't you?" Agel said, his gaze never wavering. "Didn't he reprimand you, and didn't you turn on him violently? Your temper has always been unreliable. And now you are afraid, too afraid to confess what you have done."

Caelan was horrified. He realized immediately what the implications would be if Agel spread this lie. "You can't do this," he said, his voice choked. "You mustn't."

"Then cease this stupid insistence that the prince is a traitor," Agel said.

Caelan stared at him, his mind whirling. He felt stunned with disgust at what his cousin was attempting to do.

"Who has set you to do this?" he asked finally. He was shaking inside, from rage and fear both. He wanted to throttle Agel, but he dared not move until he had answers. "Who?"

Agel would not meet his gaze. "Our purpose is to save this man. Tell me what you can."

"Why should I?"

Agel looked suddenly fierce. "I have worked long and hard to secure my appointment to the imperial court. I won't let you jeopardize that."

"Tirhin is a traitor," Caelan said in a hard voice. "You cannot coerce me into saying otherwise. My loyalty to him has ended. Don't serve him, Agel. He is not worth your concern."

"That is not for you to say!" Agel said sharply. "You are not this man's judge."

Anger leaped in Caelan, but he crossed his arms over his chest and said, "If his mind has gone, there is no reclaiming it."

"I did not say his mind is gone. But he is far away, deeply *severed*."

"That is justice," Caelan said.

Agel's eyes grew even colder. "And I have said you are not his judge! This man is a prince, and you are a slave. You are dust beneath his feet, unworthy in rank even to lick them."

Caelan snorted. "I do not need a lecture about rank and standing. I have been taught my place at the end of a whip. But I am well born, and there is nothing in my lineage to make me ashamed. Never will I forget that."

"If you are a slave, it is because you threw away all the advantages you were born to. You wasted everything. You deserve to be here, abased and wearing a chain of possession."

Caelan's fists clenched. He wanted to choked those pompous, lying words from his cousin. He wanted to hit Agel, to hurt him. He wished with all his heart to see Agel facing a Thyzarene attack, with the dragons screaming and belching fire, and the laughing riders spearing their victims. Oh, to see Agel in shackles, naked and covered with welts from a scourging, lying in filthy straw and grateful for a crust of molded bread.

All Agel knew about slavery was what he saw in Imperia's most fashionable circles—the sleek, pampered house slaves, the groundskeeping workers, the champion gladiators who wore fine clothing and had servants of their own. He would never understand the debasement and degradation. He would never know the shame or the mental torment.

Agel already lived in a cage, one of his own making. His bars were prejudice and narrow thinking. How could he understand anything, much less the desperate need to be free? How could he understand honor, when he had thrown his own away? How far had the cruel elders at Rieschelhold twisted his thinking?

Caelan's anger faded to pity. His fists uncurled, and he drew in a deep, ragged breath. Agel was not worth his hatred. Agel was not worth anything.

He turned in silence to walk out.

"You can't go," Agel said to his back.

Caelan kept walking.

"You can't! I will say that you attacked the prince and injured him. I will accuse you, and you will go to the dungeons a condemned man."

Caelan drew in a breath. He felt cold with contempt.

Turning around, he sent Agel a steely glare, but it was met by the ice of Agel's gaze.

"You don't want to die, do you?" Agel asked him. "You still care about your own life."

Caelan said nothing. His jaw was clamped too tightly.

Agel took his silence for assent. "Now. You will answer my questions and give me the assistance I need."

"If you condemn me," Caelan said hoarsely, "will you not also condemn yourself, as my kinsman?"

"Treachery and murderous assault are two different things," Agel said in a calm voice. "I cannot be blamed for the latter. You are well known to be a violent man, of unreliable temper and savage fighting skills. And it is also known that you expected his highness to free you for your successes in the arena. He has not done so. Are these not sufficient provocations for a man of your ilk?"

Caelan frowned, wondering how Agel could be so ruthless. "Why are you doing this?"

"I told you. It was very difficult to get this appointment. Now that I have it, I intend to keep it. How better to impress the emperor than by healing his beloved son of these injuries? Do you think I came to Imperia merely to

treat wounded gladiators, favorite slaves, and imperial concubines? No, I came to treat the emperor himself, and I will
not let your stupidity keep me from that."

Understanding dawned on Caelan. "You haven't been
received yet," he said slowly. "The emperor has not yet permitted you to examine him."

It was Agel's turn to stand silent and tight-lipped.

"You are here on a trial basis. You can be dismissed if
you fail to please."

Agel's chin lifted. "Already I have been called on by
the empress. That was a great step forward, at least until you
broke in and interrupted the consultation."

Caelan shook his head. "She wasn't the empress, you
fool. Her Imperial Majesty wouldn't come to your shabby
infirmary in person."

"But she did."

"I have been here longer than you," Caelan said scornfully. "I know palace protocol. The empress would send for
you, by messenger and escort."

"But the guard said she was . . . she herself said she
was—"

Agel's confusion made Caelan laugh. "People lie," he
said. "Especially do aristocrats lie to their servants and infe-
riors."

A tide of red crept up Agel's throat into his face.

"She was *not* the empress," Caelan said emphatically.
"Perhaps she came to you on her Majesty's behalf, to ob-
serve you and your methods, to see how clean you are, to see
whether you are suitable. That's all."

"But . . . but still, the empress has expressed interest,"
Agel said finally, trying to rally. "It changes little. As re-
gards you, it changes nothing."

Caelan's amusement died. He looked at Agel stonily.

"Now, back to the matter at hand," Agel said, gesturing

at the unconscious prince. "Does he know anything about *severance*? Can he return by himself? Has he had any training?"

"No."

"Of course. *Severance* is not practiced here." Agel compressed his lips and stared at Caelan very hard. "You were on the Forbidden Mountain. You encountered wind spirits—"

"No, *shyrieas*."

Agel waited, but when Caelan said nothing further he walked to the far side of the room and motioned for Caelan to follow him. "Am I to wrest every word from you like drawing teeth?" he asked angrily. "Must I threaten you again to elicit your cooperation?"

"No, I think you have threatened me sufficiently," Caelan said.

"Then answer my questions, that I may do my work."

It occurred to Caelan that if he was to accuse the prince with any hope of being believed, then Tirhin should be conscious. It was possible that Tirhin might confess or reveal his guilt in some way if questioned. Unconscious and half-dead, he would have the benefit of his father's sympathy, and only Agel's lies would be believed.

Sighing, Caelan nodded. "Very well."

He went back to Tirhin's bedside with Agel and stood there looking down at the man he had once respected.

"You know what *shyrieas* are," Caelan said before Agel could prompt him. "Demons of this land. I cannot describe their appearance. They—they feed on a man's thoughts, his fears. All that is dark inside you draws them like honey. All your sins, all your evil intentions are food for them. They come at you half seen, like wind spirits. They scream until you go mad, and then they are upon you . . . in you."

His voice grew ragged, and he fell quiet. His memories were unwelcome, bringing back the horror of that attack. They had fed on him as well, and he still felt shaken and not quite whole. He wondered if he ever would. Worse, he kept thinking back to the night he had been attacked by the wind spirits at E'nonhold. Old Farns had tried to save him, and had died for the effort. The memory of the old man's dear face, so drawn and still on the pillow, came back vividly. Prince Tirhin's face had a similar look. Caelan could feel himself knotting even tighter inside. The prince was not likely to recover. And if he did not, Caelan's warning would never be heard.

He needed Tirhin on his feet and sane, to betray guilt when questioned so that the council would believe Caelan's accusations.

"If the demons have indeed taken his reason," Agel said in his somber way, "then I cannot restore it."

Caelan drew in a sharp breath but did not speak.

"If he is simply hiding deep within himself from shock, then he has a chance to eventual recovery," Agel said. "But it will be slow and difficult."

Caelan looked at him. "Can you determine which it is?"

"I will try."

Agel leaned over Tirhin and placed his palms on the prince's face. Uttering the *severance* mantra under his breath, Agel closed his eyes. After a moment his own expression grew still, then went slack. He began to sway rhythmically at first, then more jerkily, then convulsively as though he were trying to hurl himself back but could not break the contact.

His mouth opened, and he made wordless, gasping sounds.

Alarmed, Caelan reached out, then stopped himself at

the last moment from touching his cousin. Even without actual physical contact, *sevaisin* was stirring in him. He could feel a force of evil reaching forth, something that sent chills racing through him. The evil was centered in Tirhin's body, but now it was twisting and entwining through Agel as though the healer's touch had brought it forth. As Caelan stood beside his cousin, he sensed this evil wanted him too.

Repulsion filled him, but Caelan had no time to delay if he was to destroy this thing.

Sweat was pouring off Agel. Still standing there with his eyes closed and his mouth screaming silently, he went on twisting from side to side, unable to break free.

Pressing his fingertips together, Caelan closed his own eyes and plunged deep into *severance*. At once its icy walls closed around him, buffering him from the black, writhing, indescribable thing that coiled and twisted around Tirhin and Agel. It turned its wedge-shaped head and opened its mouth to display dripping fangs. Hissing, it struck at Caelan, but *severance* shielded him. He forced himself to look on this evil, to look into it. He saw its threads of life and where they stretched back to the source that governed it.

Caelan *severed* the threads. The creature screamed with a shriek so piercing it brought Caelan pain. Both Tirhin and Agel screamed too.

In that one brief second of contact, Caelan felt a flood of black hatred and viciousness flow over him. He felt one touch from what lay beyond the creature, and it was clammy and rotted and utterly horrifying.

Then he was free, and the link was broken. The creature faded from black to gray, then to nothing at all. It was gone, as though it had never existed.

Breathing hard, Caelan released himself from *severance* and stood blinking and shivering in a room that was suddenly too cold for comfort. Even now he could still feel a lingering foulness that made him shudder. But whatever had been planted inside Tirhin was gone.

Leaning over, Caelan rubbed his eyes with the backs of his hands and gulped in more air. He felt spent and winded, as though he'd run miles.

Then he pulled himself together and straightened. Almost afraid to know, he turned to the others. Tirhin looked gray-faced and dead. Agel lay slumped over him.

Anxiously Caelan pulled his cousin upright and gripped him by both arms to shake him.

Agel flopped in his grasp, semiconscious, knees buckling.

Caelan sank with him to the floor. "Agel! Agel, wake up!" he said urgently. "Come on. Wake up. You must wake up."

Agel moaned and opened his eyes. His face was still beaded with sweat. He looked as though he had been dragged through a place no man should ever have to enter.

Caelan patted his cheek, still talking to him, urging him.

Finally Agel grabbed his hand and pulled it down. He blinked in an effort to focus, and scowled at Caelan. "I *am* awake," he said acidly. "Stop trying to revive me."

Relief swept Caelan. He grinned and almost laughed as he helped Agel sit up. "Thank Gault," he said. "I thought you were lost to us."

Agel leaned over again, bracing his hands on the floor as though he was going to be sick. But he was not. After a moment, he pushed himself to his feet and stood swaying unsteadily.

His eyes met Caelan's and held them. "What, in the name of all purity, have you brought here with you?" he asked.

Caelan sobered instantly. "I don't know. It's gone."

Agel closed his eyes a moment, then opened them to glare at Caelan. "How do you know?"

"I sent it away."

"You have authority over it?"

Caelan heard accusation in his voice. He could see fear in Agel's eyes, along with a dawning look of horror.

"You can make it come, and go, at your bidding?" the healer asked, his voice rising. "What *are* you?"

"You misunderstand!" Caelan said sharply. "I do not govern it. Murdeth and Fury, why must you always leap to the wrong conclusions? Anyone else would be relieved that I was able to destroy it."

"Only evil can destroy evil," Agel said, his eyes still wide with shock. "Only evil knows the secrets within itself."

"All I did was *sever* it from its source," Caelan said impatiently.

Agel flinched away from him, bumping into Tirhin's bed as he did so. "*Severance* cannot be used that way. It is not possible."

"Of course it is. Beva taught me—"

"Don't even mention your father's name in connection with this! It's unspeakable."

"Shut up," Caelan snapped, trying to stem Agel's hysteria. "You are still using a mantra to *sever*, like a novice."

Agel was tight-lipped. "Not everyone is as talented as you."

"To *sever* is to take away. You see the source of disease, and you simply cut the link. You see the threads of life, and you simply cut them. You see the source of a demon or whatever in Gault's name that thing was, and you—"

"What simplistic nonsense is this?" Agel said angrily. "You—"

"Simplistic?" Caelan retorted. "Is not all truth simplicity? That's how you recognize it. Are you angry because I saved your life, or are you angry because I can do what you cannot?"

"You are evil. I felt you join with it."

"I didn't—" Caelan cut off the denial. He could not explain the difference. "*Sevaisin* exists everywhere. It calls constantly. Sometimes it is difficult not to use it."

"Exactly why it is forbidden."

"It is not forbidden here. No one condemns the joining."

"No one has ever considered Imperia the center of purity or balance either," Agel replied. "Hedonistic, all-embracing, indulgent of every vice—"

"Why don't you calm down?" Caelan interrupted. "It was a trap, a bad one, but you survived it. What about the prince?"

Agel glared at him, then turned resentfully to examine Tirhin.

"He is alive," Agel said at last. "Weaker than before. The rest . . . I do not know. I am not fit enough to work as I should."

"You should sit down," Caelan said. "Let me bring you a cup of water."

"A cup of poison, more likely," Agel snapped.

Caelan had been about to offer him a steadying hand, but now he stepped back. He was hurt and furious by Agel's attitude. Agel was badly frightened, clinging to blind prejudice and superstition rather than reason. Caelan tried to keep his own temper, tried to be compassionate, but he was losing patience rapidly.

"If you were well, I would hit you for your insult."

Agel made a gesture of repudiation. "Spoken like a true believer in peace and harmony."

"Damn you, Agel!"

"You are *casna*," Agel retorted. "You must be."

"Don't say that! I am not a devil. I am not of the darkness."

"Then what are you?" Agel shouted back. His detachment and trained calm had deserted him. With his hair matted with sweat and his eyes wide and fearful, he looked like
a boy in over his head instead of a master healer with a pres-
tigious appointment to the imperial court. "You cannot be
my uncle's son. You are no kinsman of mine. Not with the
things you do, with the knowledge you have. I've heard the
stories," he went on before Caelan could interrupt. "I heard
about warding keys. Even Papa used to say that Uncle Beva
was mad to take on a son like you. He never should have
struck that bargain with the Choven."

"What do you mean?" Caelan said, desperately trying
to follow Agel's angry spate of words. "What are you saying? What bargain with the Choven?"

"Pretend all you like. But I *know*, Caelan. You are
not . . . the elders were right to drive you from school. In
their wisdom, they saw the makings of evil."

"I just saved your life, you fool," Caelan said furiously.

"And what will you demand for it?"

Rage and intense hurt battled inside Caelan. He could
not believe Agel was saying such things. What had turned
his cousin into this petty, fearful, small-minded man?

"I loved you like a brother," Caelan said softly. "I came
to you for help and your sage council. Instead, you have insulted and slandered me. Now, after I just saved your life, it
is not thanks you give me but harshness. Why, Agel? Is it
only jealousy that has made you so small?"

Agel's face turned white. He glared at Caelan, his jaw
tight, his lips thin. "Always you are the injured one, the innocent one," he said in a harsh voice. "But why did the evil

lurking in the prince's body not touch you? You carried him for hours, or so you claim. Yet it did not strike at you."

Caelan's mouth dropped open. "I did not seek to heal him. That must be what triggered the trap and unleashed it."

"Yes, and who suggested that I examine him?"

"I didn't want him treated!" Caelan said in disbelief. "You insisted. You want my master to be grateful to you."

"Master?" Agel snorted. "You do not know the meaning of the word. Rebellion is your name. Yes! Rebellion and disorder."

There was no getting through Agel's fear. It shielded him from reason and logic. It closed out all truth. He had no intention of listening to anything Caelan said.

Yet still Caelan tried. "If I had known a demon lingered inside the prince, I would have warned you."

"Not if you wanted to entrap me and turn me to your darkness."

"I—" Caelan threw up his hands. "What is the use?"

Agel stared at him, eyes glittering with condemnation. "This all begins to make sense."

"Finally!"

"There has been no treason. You lured the prince out into danger. You did this to him."

Caelan blinked in disbelief. "What are you saying? Why should I?"

"*Casna*! Devil! You are aptly named. You—"

"Are you blaming me for the attack of *shyrieas*?" Caelan shook his head. "Why not claim next that I commanded them?"

"Do you?"

"No."

Agel nodded, but his expression did not change. "No, you do not command them. No, you do not run with them. Yet you emerged from their attack unscathed."

"Hardly—"

"You were not hurt by the wind spirits either."

"Yes, I was."

"You survived," Agel said, his voice cutting and hard.

"Would you rather I died?" Caelan retorted bitterly. "Am I to be condemned for living?"

"There is something about you that is unlike other men," Agel said. "Something inside you that makes you different."

Caelan wanted to laugh. "And therefore I am evil?"

"The elders of Rieschelhold thought you were."

"They were secret followers of the Vindicant sect," Caelan said. "Or something worse."

Agel took a quick step toward him. "Don't you dare slander them!"

Now Caelan did laugh, throwing back his head to crow with derision. "How long have you been in Imperia, cousin?"

Agel blinked at the sudden change of subject. "Two months."

"Oh, only two months? Then you've scarcely had time to learn your way around the city."

"What has this to do with—"

"And when did you graduate from the school? A year past? Two?"

"Five months past."

"Five months," Caelan said with false heartiness. "Imagine. You have been in training all this time—"

"I spent extra time there," Agel broke in defensively. "Since I was denied my apprenticeship with Uncle Beva—"

"And now you are newly arrived in Imperia, a wise man, a trained man, a man used to the ways of the world."

Agel was growing wary now. He watched Caelan and said nothing.

"Therefore, with all your tremendous travel and experience, the wide range of your encounters, the expansion of your innate wisdom, you are able to make judgments about all manner of things, whether you know aught of them or not."

Agel drew himself erect and tucked his hands inside his sleeves. "I have *severance* to guide me."

"And harmony?" Caelan asked.

Agel nodded. "Yes, the ways of harmony."

"And balance?"

"Yes."

"No!" Caelan shouted. "You lie! You denounce *sevaisin*, and without it there is no balance. You live in a one-sided world, cousin. You see through one eye. You understand so very little, and as long as you live in fear, denouncing everything that is strange to you, you will understand less and less."

The prince shifted his head and moaned.

At once Agel turned to him, but instead of touching the prince with a reassuring hand, Agel eyed him a moment, then backed away.

Caelan hurried to the other side of the prince's bed. "He is coming around. He is better. Help him!"

Agel backed even farther and shook his head.

Annoyance swelled inside Caelan. "You fool. He won't hurt you. The evil is gone from him."

"You are the wise one," Agel said in a tight, spiteful voice. "You are the one who can *sever* without using a mantra. Why don't you heal him? Just reach in and *sever* him from his illness."

"Please," Caelan said.

The prince moaned again, and Caelan gripped the man's hand tightly to offer comfort. It was an action done without thinking, and Caelan realized that even if he had lost respect for Tirhin he had not yet lost his compassion.

"Agel, help him."

"You have the gifts. You have the goodness. I am only a second-rate healer from a school of evil blasphemers." Agel shrugged. "What can I do?"

"This is unnecessary," Caelan said, his frustration rising. "You were the one who insisted on coming here to attend the man. Why don't you help him now?"

"I have done all I can."

"No, you haven't!"

"And I say I have." As he spoke, Agel looked past Caelan at the doorway. An unreadable expression flickered in his face; then he smiled very slightly at Caelan. "What his highness needs now is rest . . . and perhaps some water. There is a ewer in the other room. Fetch it, please."

Puzzled by his sudden switch of mood, Caelan turned and walked into the antechamber. There was a ewer on a stand, but it was empty. Even as Caelan picked it up, Agel slammed and bolted the door behind him.

Whirling, Caelan realized he had been neatly trapped. He hurled the ewer at the door, where it clanged loudly.

He tried both doors, pushing against them with all his strength, but they remained firmly bolted. Swearing to himself, Caelan paced rapidly back and forth.

The window was too small for him to climb through. He went back to the door that led to Tirhin's chamber and pounded on it with his fist.

"Agel!" he shouted. "Agel!"

But his cousin did not respond.

Chapter Twelve

ENRAGED, KNOWING HIS arrest was imminent, Caelan went on a rampage in the tiny room, smashing and destroying. When at last he heard a commotion of voices outside and the tramping of boots, he straightened and faced the door. Breathing hard, he held a broken chair leg in his hand for a club. Slaves could not offer a defense when accused of crimes, however falsely. He would be considered guilty as charged. So he had nothing to lose by fighting. By Gault, he would not go tamely to his doom.

The outer door opened with a bang.

Caelan expected a pair of common foot soldiers under the command of an arrest sergeant. Instead, five armored men in the helmets and red cloaks of the Imperial Guard rushed inside with drawn swords and war clubs. Yelling, Caelan swung his club, only to see it splintered by a sword. Caelan dived at the guardsman's knees, bringing him down. Throwing himself bodily against the struggling guardsman, who was hindered by his own armor, Caelan caught his wrist and wrenched his sword away.

A club thudded into his shoulder, knocking him sideways. Caelan struggled up, but before he could completely turn around, another blow drove him down. Surrounding him, the guardsmen bludgeoned him to his knees.

Stunned and knowing he was in trouble, Caelan slashed with his sword and cut a man in the leg. That guardsman stumbled back, yelling in pain as blood splashed across the floor. Caelan grinned to himself and tried again to regain his feet.

They closed in on him. A numbing blow crashed into his forearm, and he dropped his sword from nerveless fingers. He scrambled to pick it up with his right hand, but a guardsman kicked it out of reach. Caelan lunged after it, but he was kicked back.

Black stars danced across his vision. Shaking his head to clear it, he struggled up only to be slapped by a heavy net that settled over his head and shoulders.

"No!" he shouted furiously, but the net was already over him.

A swift jerk pulled him over onto his side. They had him then, trussing him expertly with thick ropes before he could scramble free.

Struggling still, consumed with rage and intense fear, Caelan cursed them in Trau. Sweat and blood were running into his left eye, half blinding him. He heaved himself up, despite his bound arms, and rolled to his knees.

The guardsman working the net jerked again, expertly, and sent Caelan crashing onto his side again. The world grew dark and blurred, and by the time he managed to blink things back into focus the officer had come up and planted his boot on Caelan's neck.

"Have done, man. You're caught," he said.

Caelan lay there with his sweat and blood smearing across the polished floor. Shame flooded him, and he would have wept in humiliation had his pride not burned all his tears away.

Around him the guardsmen put up their weapons and wiped their perspiring faces with looks of relief.

"Murdeth, what a fighter," one said.

The man whose leg was still bleeding freely looked up from his efforts to staunch the wound. "What do you expect? He's a gladiator."

"Still, five against one—"

"Silence," the officer said sharply. "You, see to the wagon. You, get that wound bound up quickly."

Saluting, the men assigned moved to obey. The rest stood alert, as though aware that Caelan would fight again at the first opportunity.

The household servants crowded into the doorway. Craning their necks, they chattered among themselves. Caelan saw Orlo among them with his blocky shoulders and shaven head, looking like a thundercloud.

"Orlo!" Caelan called out, but the trainer only glared at him and shook his head in pity.

"Orlo, for Gault's sake—"

"Silence!" The officer ground his foot harder into Caelan's neck, almost choking him. His gold rank stripes glittered on the shoulders of his crimson cloak. His eyes were as brutal as the desert. "Caelan E'non—slave and property of his imperial highness, Prince Tirhin—you are arrested on charges of willfully turning upon your master with intent to harm, on charges of striking your master's face and person, and on charges of—"

"No!" Caelan shouted. Wildly he looked around, but he saw condemnation on every face. "Who makes these charges?" he demanded. "Who claims these lies?"

"As a slave you have no rights, not even the right to know who has accused you," the officer said.

"If it was not my lawful master, I demand to know," Caelan insisted defiantly. "You cannot arrest me without the knowledge and consent of the prince."

But Agel's voice rose over his. "I laid the charge," he said, appearing at the doorway. He looked composed and stern as he stood there in his white robes. His eyes held nothing at all. "His highness lies unconscious, grievously injured. The servants will testify that this slave brought the prince home in such a state. It proves his guilt."

"No!" Caelan said, the denial bursting from him. "I did

not hurt his highness, as he will tell you once he is recovered. Orlo, speak for me. Tell the officer the truth."

But Orlo did not come forward, and the officer ignored Caelan's protests.

His gaze locked on Agel. "Your name?"

"I am Agel, a healer newly appointed to the imperial court." Agel spoke calmly and with dignity.

"You are prepared to swear to the extent of Prince Tirhin's injuries?" the officer asked.

"I am prepared to swear."

"No!" Caelan said, horrified. "He was—"

He broke off, aware of how fantastic the truth would sound. The prince's reputation was impeccable. Who would believe he had gone to *Sidraigh-hal* to strike an evil bargain with representatives from Madrun? Who would believe he had been attacked by *shyrieas* on his way home?

Caelan realized he had been foolish to bring the prince back. He should have left him on the scorched hillside, perhaps to die. By bringing the prince home, he had left himself open to misinterpretation and outright lie.

Caelan's desperate gaze collided with Agel's cold one, and Agel's eyes did not waver. Caelan knew he had been a fool, an utter fool, to trust Agel at all. There had been plenty of warning signs, and he'd ignored them all.

This, he thought bitterly, was the result of his ambition. He'd wanted to be named protector of a future emperor, and so he'd tagged after Tirhin, willingly involving himself as a witness to treason. And now he lay here accused himself, the reward of having served an unworthy master, the reward of having trusted his own kinsman. As a slave, he would not even get a trial.

Even as cold fear washed through him, the guardsmen dragged him bodily out into the spacious atrium. Bile rose in Caelan's throat. He remembered lying rolled in a net while the Thyzarenes burned and looted his home. He couldn't submit to this again. He would rather fight and be killed than submit.

Panicking, he kicked and struggled, but he was helpless and the guardsmen were experienced. One of them gave a vicious twist to the ropes binding him, and another kicked him hard in the kidney.

The world tilted a moment, and Caelan's only fight was against blacking out. He coughed a little, trying to regain the air that had been knocked out of him.

"There'll be no trouble from you, gladiator."

Biting back a moan, Caelan sagged against the stone floor. Nothing to lose, he told himself. But he must fight with his wits to have any chance at all. He must not panic, must not lose his temper. He must think if he was to have any hope of getting out of this. Besides, the more he fought, the more guilty he would appear.

They loosened the net and put shackles on his hands and feet. Shame burned Caelan. He hadn't worn chains since before he won his first season championship.

The servants watched in silence. Their eyes reflected the lamplight like mirrors. Not one spoke up for him.

He was pulled to his feet. "Walk," a guardsman commanded him, prodding him with a dagger. "And remember, I know every trick you do, so don't try anything."

Caelan stumbled out past Prince Tirhin's collection of priceless statuary and busts. Tapestries and fine paintings hung on the walls. His feet trod priceless carpets.

The officer waited by the doorway leading outside. His gaze took in the fine furnishings, the beauty of the house, without expression. He was all business, alert and watchful as though he fully understood how dangerous Caelan could be.

Caelan drew a deep breath, well aware of the dagger pressed to his ribs. "Lieutenant," he said quietly, trying to sound educated and civilized. "My master has not laid these charges. Take care you do not make a mistake tonight."

The guardsman at his side struck him hard, nearly knocking him down the steps outside. Stumbling, Caelan caught himself against one of the dragon statues. As he straightened, he thought he glimpsed a flicker of something in the lieutenant's eyes.

"I am valuable property," he said quickly. "Too valuable for quick disposal or illegal sale on the block."

"Silence!" The guardsman shoved him down the steps.

The lieutenant watched Caelan go by and said nothing.

Despair rose in Caelan. He had done all he could. Now his life hung in the balance. If these men had been bribed to dispose of him, they would do it.

The servants followed, coming outside to stand between the stone dragons. Caelan could hear their murmurs, both sad and condemning. Even they believed his guilt.

Glancing back over his shoulder, Caelan saw Orlo. He wanted to call out to the man, wanted to tell him he was sorry. Orlo had been right, while he was wrong. He wanted to ask Orlo to believe in his innocence. But he held his tongue, aware that no appeal would help him now.

Under the portico, a wagon supporting an iron cage stood waiting next to the guardsmen's horses.

Caelan's spirits sank. Yesterday he had been a champion. His name had been on everyone's lips. They had cheered him and praised him. Now—on the lie of one unscrupulous man—he was considered a villain. Condemned already, he would die unheard and unseen.

Agel came down the steps, his robe moth-pale in the moonlight. "Where are you taking him?" he asked.

Caelan knew the options. He could be sold directly to

the galleys, where he'd been once before. He could be taken to the city executioner, who would behead him. His head would be placed on a spike above the city walls to warn other slaves of the penalties for rebellion.

The guardsman laughed, and one of them spat on the steps.

"Why, to the dungeons of the palace, of course. This man has an appointment with the torturer, who is very interested in taking his confession."

Caelan's blood ran cold, but Agel turned pale. "The palace?" he said. "A confession?"

The lieutenant stepped between him and Caelan, whom the guards prodded into the cage. The barred gate was slammed shut and locked.

"But he is not a political figure," Agel protested. "He is merely a slave."

"He's the most famous slave in this city," the lieutenant said impatiently. "And he belongs to the prince. Until his highness is recovered enough to lay blame against his own property, no one has the authority to dispose of this wretch. No, he'll rot in the prison, and he'll make his confession or go mad from the instruments."

"But—"

"Get back now," the lieutenant said. "This matter is no longer in your hands."

Turning from Agel, he shouted an order. The wagon lurched forward, rolling through the gates and out onto the road.

Clutching the bars of his cage, Caelan pressed his face against them and glared at the diminishing figure of Agel for as long as he could. Inside he knew the cold satisfaction of having thwarted his cousin's attempt to silence him quickly. He'd give his warning now. He'd bray it for the confession, and it would have to be believed.

But under the bleakness of his satisfaction lay raw fear.

Gault help him, but he knew of the dungeons. He knew that once a man entered them, he did not emerge alive. Only Prince Tirhin could order his release, but once his confession was made Caelan would have no help from that quarter. Truly, his doom was being spun around him like a shroud.

In the temple of the Vindicants, the air lay thick with incense. Crimson smoke curled from the flared nostrils of two enormous bronze dogs flanking the stone altar. Lamplight flickered about the circular chamber, and oppressive silence hung like a shroud.

The bronze doors leading into the sanctuary were bolted from the inside. No one could disturb the lone occupant of the chamber.

Lord Sien, high priest of the Vindicant order, knelt on the floor before the altar with his head bowed and his hands pressed tightly together.

He was stripped to the waist, and although the sanctuary was chilly a light coating of perspiration covered his skin. He was breathing hard, as though he had been running a long distance. His eyes were closed.

On the floor beside him stood an emptied cup. The flat taste of blood, ashes, and wine still lingered on his tongue.

The air around him felt charged with gathering energy. Opening his eyes, Sien faced the altar with his arms spread wide. Above him on the wall hung the dread visage of the shadow god. Empty eyes stared down at him, but he knew he was watched. He knew that Beloth sensed him from far away, and stirred, and was aware.

Some day, when Beloth was free, the shadow god would remember his loyal servant. Reward would be great.

Sien shivered and closed his eyes to regain his concentration. His arms were leaden with exhaustion. His body swayed, but he held onto the threads he had sent forth. It was almost time, almost time. He must not falter.

A whisper touched his hearing, faint yet unmistakable.

He turned his head slightly, acknowledging the sound with a slight curl of his lips.

Ah, they came.

The first shadow appeared, sliding under the doors and racing across the floor. It was a man's shadow, short and square, but it came alone. When it overlapped Sien's own elongated shadow, he shuddered and felt a moment of elemental pain before the joining.

"Speak," he commanded.

The shadow belonged to Hovet, protector of the emperor. "He has gone to bed. I am free to roam a short time."

"Tell me," Sien commanded.

"The wasting sickness returns. The emperor will send soon for his new healer. He is unhappy tonight. He is lonely and afraid. He counts the number of his years. He feels the weight of his sins. He mourns the destruction of his throne. He fears tomorrow, when he must put the crown on the woman's head."

"Will he name her sovereign?" Sien asked impatiently. That was the only important bit. Sien had no interest in the aches and tremblings of an old man who had lived too long. "What is his decision?"

"He wavers first one way, then the other. He schemes and forgets. He schemes and forgives. He is angry at Tirhin. He is angry at the woman."

"Tell me more," Sien commanded.

The shadow writhed across Sien's. "Let me go," it wailed. "I am too far. I will die alone."

It had nothing more to tell him. Disappointed, Sien released it.

The shadow sailed across the floor and vanished beneath the door as though it had never been.

But already another appeared to take its place. Petite and slender, it flitted back and forth, darting about the sanctuary as though reluctant to join. Finally, however, it came to Sien and merged into him.

"Tell me," he commanded.

"She survived the poisoned smoke."

Rage scorched the edges of Sien's concentration. He held it away, however, refusing to let the spell disintegrate at this stage.

"Was she injured?"

"No."

"Tell me more."

"The women have begun the purification ceremony. It goes ill."

His interest quickened. "How ill? Why? What has happened?"

"She has visions."

"That is the purpose of the ceremony."

"Visions beyond her ability. She sees too far."

Sien smiled to himself. He liked this. "Can they bring her back?"

"She must come of her own accord."

"Has she the strength?"

"They worry, master. Anas is blamed. She is no longer deputy."

Sien had little interest in Anas. If the Magria lost her second-in-command it might be useful in the future, but on the whole it was of little significance to him.

"Can you ensure the girl does not return from purification?"

"I promise nothing, master."

"Try!" he urged.

"I will try."

The shadow fled him then, darting all around frantically before it finally found the way out.

Sien moaned aloud. His strength was waning. Great droplets of sweat poured from his forehead, but he was not yet finished. He struggled to hold the spell.

The third shadow came to him, lean and cold. It flowed into the room and sprawled long across the floor until it joined with his.

This time the pain made him grunt. Sien pressed his lips hard together to maintain his control.

"Speak!" he gasped out.

But the shadow said nothing.

Sien could feel its invasive coldness, its strength. He struggled to maintain mastery. To command Tirhin's shadow was far from easy. It possessed a will of its own, colored by the personality of its owner. It fought him every time.

"Speak! I command it."

The shadow said, "The healer has come, but he fears the taint of the *shyrieas*. He fears many things."

"Does he foresee?"

"No. He has no visions. He is busy making mischief."

"As I bade him?"

"Yes."

Sien almost smiled. He was pleased, but he could not indulge in his emotions now while he fought to hold this shadow.

"Stay," he commanded. "Tell me."

"The slave has been accused and taken away. He will be silenced."

"Good. No one believed him?"

"He made his accusations only to the healer," the shadow said, and tugged against him.

Sien grunted, straining to hold it. "Stay. Tell me more."

"The servants are afraid. They will send word soon to the palace, asking for help."

"Will Tirhin recover?"

"Unknown. Without him, I shall die."

"Will the healer treat him?"

"No. The healer is afraid."

"Then I must take action."

"Free me," the shadow said.

"Not while you are useful."

"I must return," the shadow said, and wrenched away.

It vanished quicker than thought, and Sien was left in a huddle on the floor, chilled and clammy from his efforts.

Slowly, breathing hard, he let the spell dissolve. His strength seemed to ebb with it, but he finally forced himself to his feet.

Swaying and shivering, he wiped the sweat from his face and pulled on his robes. He had done enough for now, he thought in satisfaction. Everything was proceeding to plan.

The prince had been too arrogant, too headstrong before. Now, after this lesson the *shyrieas* had taught him, he would be more malleable. It was a hard lesson to learn, but Sien had been patient enough with him. It was time Tirhin learned who truly ruled this empire.

As for the girl . . . he was displeased that she had escaped the poison attempt, but it was designed more to frighten and warn the witches than to do serious harm. He planned far more serious damage to the Penestricans before he was finished.

Sien rubbed his hands briskly together. All was going well. Even the Madrun hordes were on schedule, already massing at the border. Soon they would come pouring through.

He lifted his empty cup in a mock salute to Kostimon,

the man who had once depended on him, the man who had used him as a bridge to Beloth and the bargain of a thousand years. Kostimon had discarded his old friend Sien of late, however. The emperor preferred to keep his own council, wanted to plot his own schemes alone. He would regret that. Soon he would regret everything.

Sien laughed softly to himself, and poured himself another serving of blooded wine. Kostimon's days were numbered. It was time to pay the shadow god's price.

And what a steep price that was. Sien laughed again and drained his cup with a smack of satisfaction. Kostimon had no idea.

Part Two

Chapter Thirteen

THE BELLS OF Imperia began ringing at sunrise, filling the air with joyous peals as the new light gilded the rooftops of the city. Already revelers from the countryside thronged the gates; some had spent the night on the road in order to be here in time. The city gates, normally massive and grim, had been cleared of the rotting heads of offenders and festooned instead with garlands of greenery. Just behind the sentries stood wooden tubs filled with tiny muslin bags of dried flower petals. Each person entering was to have a sachet, in order to toss flowers at the empress during her processional. A burly sergeant, his face impassive between the chin straps of his helmet, tossed sachets to eager recipients the way he tossed grain rations to foot soldiers.

The sentries were alert, but not actively checking anyone. Mainly they shouted to keep people in an orderly line, but the gates remained thronged. Women exclaimed over the sachets, and children milled about heedlessly, constantly in danger of being trampled.

Every street was choked with carts, people on foot, people on horseback. There were whole families in their finery, ribbons fluttering in the frosty air, scrubbed children wide-eyed with wonder. Keyed up with excitement, they cheered each time a squadron in burnished armor and crimson cloaks trotted past, forcing them up against the buildings to make way.

Red imperial banners flew from every rooftop and hung from the windows along the coronation route. People were already clustered at second-floor windows, clutching red scarves in their hands, laughing and chattering.

The coronation would be at mid-morning, followed by the swearing of allegiance, then the processional through the city. Feasting would come afterward.

Within the immense granite walls of the palace, servants worked frantically to put the finishing touches on decorations. Normally the buildings were impressive enough with their massive scale and walls of gleaming marble, but everything had been gilded so that in the sunlight all the buildings and statuary blazed in dazzling grandeur. The imperial banners, vast sheets of silk so heavily embroidered with gold that the breeze could not lift their folds, hung from gilded poles. Streamers in the lady's golden colors fluttered gaily, however. White doves—imported at great cost—were released at regular intervals into the sky.

On the parade ground, sergeants bawled orders as horses and elephants were lined up in proper order for the processional. Arguments over precedence flared among warlords from different provinces, and heralds scurried about to soothe and placate, intent on keeping peace.

Inside the palace itself, musicians in palace livery were already tuning up. Majordomos strode along the passageways and galleries with fierce eyes, making the final inspection for any omission. Within the vast banqueting hall, sweating servants hauled the new banners up to the vaulted ceiling on ropes and secured them. The table stood in the shape of a T, extending the full length of the hall to accommodate all the dignitaries and aristocrats in good standing. Stewards walked the length of the table, measuring the distance of gold wine cups from the edge, so that the entire lengthy row of them stood absolutely straight from one end to the other.

Exotic flowers grown in the conservatory for this occasion were laid in place. The heavy fragrance of the lilies and roses filled the air, which was already redolent of roasting meats and baking pastries.

The servants wore new livery, very stiff and fine. All the men had new haircuts and were clean-shaven. The women wore their hair in looped braids, and their stiff skirts rustled as they moved. Again and again, they were lined up and inspected, fussed over and reprimanded by their nervous superiors. Every detail, no matter how minor, had to be perfect.

Within the state chambers of the emperor, Kostimon had risen early, as was his custom. He received his morning reports on the status of the empire and read his dispatches. The barber had shaved him, and he had bathed. Whispered gossip among the servants was that he was behaving as though this were an ordinary day. Only the fact that he still wore his dressing robes indicated any deviation from his usual routine.

Outside his bedchamber, the lords in waiting stood yawning and chatting in their finery. They watched as the imperial breakfast tray was carried in, under gold covers so no one could tell what his diet would be. A few minutes later, there was a bustle and the cadenced clatter of armed soldiers marching in.

"Make way!" cried the Master of the Bedchamber, and the lords scattered in confusion.

The soldiers, their breastplates polished to blinding brilliance, hands on their swords hilts, marched through the long antechamber with a heavy tread, completely surrounding the trio of men bearing locked caskets of exotic woods.

"The emperor's jewels," said one, and the murmur ran around the room. Everyone craned to look.

Next came a group of tailors, swelled with importance and looking very serious, who rolled in huge trunks containing his new coronation garments.

The doors to the bedchamber opened, and all these individuals emerged again. Following on their heels came old Hovet, the protector, looking as sour as ever. Hovet's grizzled hair had been cropped short to his skull, and he wore only a crimson tunic and leggings. It was rare that the man appeared without his armor, and murmurs circled the room again.

Glaring at everyone, Hovet muttered a question to the Master of the Bedchamber, who frowned as he replied. Hovet stumped back into the bedchamber with a slam of the door. Five minutes later he reemerged with his breastplate, elbow spikes, and greaves buckled on, his sword hanging from his hip, and his helmet tucked correctly under his left arm. His gauntlets were clutched in his left hand. All his armor was new and beautifully embossed.

The murmurs began again. No one could recall any occasion, no matter how magnificent, when Hovet had worn new armor. The lords stared at him in astonishment, making Hovet red-faced and more short-tempered than usual.

Snapping at the Master of the Bedchamber, he gestured impatiently and disappeared again.

The Master of the Bedchamber clapped his hands for attention. "My lords, please take your places for the robing of his Majesty."

The courtiers shuffled about. Some could never remember their places and had to be assisted by patient servants. When the line had been correctly reformed, the footmen opened the tall double doors, and the guards on duty saluted and stepped aside.

One by one, the lords in waiting filed into the imperial bedchamber.

In the chambers of state belonging to the empress, the level of anticipation was even higher. Wearing their finest gowns, the ladies in waiting inspected each other's hair and adjusted lace and necklines, smoothed out wrinkles in the folds of their skirts, complained of how much their new shoes pinched, and laid wagers on how well the coronation robes would look on the empress.

Inside the bedchamber, inside the closed velvet hangings of the bed, Elandra lay curled up beneath the heavy duvet and tried to find her courage. Her dreams still haunted her, vivid and real in her mind. Horrible dreams that she would never forget. They had been forced on her by the Penestricans, and she did not think she would ever forgive them. She did not believe purification involved meeting Beloth, the shadow god of all destruction. She did not believe she was supposed to be hunted down like bait by things so dreadful her mind could not recall them without shuddering.

While she had been still locked inside her vision, the Magria had walked into her dreams and confronted her.

"Take my hand, Elandra," she had said, fiercely insistent.

Instead Elandra fled to a dark place, full of gloom and mystery and silence. She crawled into a small crevice hewn from the stone walls. Pressing her back to it, she crouched there, holding her breath to make no sound. The dark god must not find her. She knew he was still hunting, sending his dire creatures questing for her trail. Now and then, although they were far away, she could hear the wailing howl of his hounds. Fear shivered through her, and she curled her knees tight against her chest, pressing her face against them.

But the Magria came after her and bent down. "Take my hand, Elandra," she said. "Take it!"

Elandra shivered. "No," she whispered.

"Take it, girl! I have come to help you."

Elandra did not believe her. The Penestricans gave no one help in their tests. They did not interfere. They only stood aside and judged. Angrily she shook her head.

"Elandra, trust me. I offer you help. I know the way out."

"Go away," Elandra said.

"I will help you."

Again the Magria extended her hand, old and knotted with mutilation scars.

Elandra struck it away. "You will lead him to me. Go away! I am safe here."

"You cannot stay," the Magria said. "Those who search can find you here. Come with me, to true safety."

"No."

"Elandra, I know the only way out."

"No, I must find it myself."

The Magria sighed, and her eyes were sad. "Sometimes, child, you must accept the help of others whether you want it or not. It will be easier if you come with me of your own accord."

Defiance flared in Elandra, fueled by her fear. "Easier?" she said sharply. "Then it cannot be right. You have taught me that yourself."

"This is a time of exception to what I have taught you."

"No!"

"Then I have no choice."

The Magria lifted her hands to the gloom overhead in silence. When she lowered them a moment later, two more Penestrican dream walkers stood on either side of her.

They closed in on Elandra, who screamed.

The Magria gripped Elandra's hands in hers, using surprising strength. No matter how much she struggled, Elandra could not pull free. The other dream walkers also took hold of her, and the three of them drew her from her hiding place.

Crying and struggling, she could not escape them. She planted her feet, but the three women were stronger, pushing and propelling her along the stony path.

Ahead, the path lay obscured in mist. Pale light glowed from beyond two looming stone pillars.

Seeing the upright stones, knowing instinctively that they were some kind of gateway, Elandra struggled even harder. "No," she gasped, managing to get one hand free only to be gripped again. "No, I can't. I'm not finished."

Behind her, the hellhounds howled. Chills clawed up her spine. She looked back, and could see the creatures coursing in the distance, closing rapidly. Their eyes glowed red, and their flanks shone with green fire.

"Come!" the Magria said sharply. "There is little time! Do not let them follow us through the gate."

At the last moment, Elandra could no longer stand against the others. Her fear was too great. Ashamed of her own cowardice, she leaped between the stone pillars . . . and found herself sprawled in the sand pit on the Penestrican temple, drenched with sweat and sobbing.

Shivering now in her bed, Elandra curled up tighter. They were only dreams, she told herself, but she did not believe it. The object clutched in her hand told her otherwise.

Uncurling her hand, she forced herself to look at the large topaz. In the gloom within her enclosed bed, it looked dull and lifeless, but she remembered how it had flashed radiantly in the torchlight of the temple. Since Elandra had awakened, it had not left her possession. It had been given to her by a mysterious force, and it symbolized a future she could not as yet claim. In a strange way, to hold it gave her comfort.

She had nothing else to reassure her. Until now, she had believed the Penestricans to be her friends. She no longer trusted them.

The bed hangings were pulled back with an abrupt scrape of the rings across the rod. The Mistress of the Bedchamber stood peering in at her.

"Majesty, it is morning," she said.

Elandra frowned. Of course it was. Did the woman not understand that Elandra had returned from the temple less than an hour ago?

Dragged forth from the sand pit and hastily revived. Sponged down and comforted with empty words. Given something sweet to drink that had cleared her head and put strength back into her limbs.

And how long would that potion last? Elandra had no faith in it either. For all their work, she still felt hollow and strange inside, displaced as though she had traveled too fast from too far away.

Sunlight blazed in through the windows, bringing life to the silk and velvet gowns worn by the ladies in waiting. They came in, giggling and staring at her, looking eager and giddy.

She stared back in dismay, feeling unready to deal with any of them.

The Mistress of the Bedchamber curtsied low. "Majesty, the delegation from Mahira has arrived. They await an audience with you."

Elandra's frown deepened. Pushing back her tangle of long hair, she sat up on one elbow. "I don't understand. I cannot have visitors now."

"But these are *Mahirans*," the woman said insistently. Her eyes were large with excitement. "It is a great honor, to wear garments sewn and blessed by—"

"Yes, I know," Elandra said. She knew all too well how

fine and costly such raiment was. Her bridal robe had been Mahiran and exquisite. It had never been worn.

A superstitious shiver passed through her. If the Mahirans had brought her a new gown, would that mean she would never be crowned?

Immediately she forced such thoughts away. She could not go on like this, afraid even of her own shadow.

Lifting her chin, she sat up in bed. "Let them enter."

But first the ladies crowded around her, pulling her hair back into braided order. One draped a dressing robe of costly silk around her shoulders. Another brought her a gossamer-thin veil.

Only then did the doors open, and the women from Mahira enter. They came in a procession, solemn and formal. Dark-skinned and liquid-eyed, they wore vestments of plain, undyed flax and raw silk. Their ebony curls were braided through with little ropes of gold beads. Gold rings adorned their ears and noses. Although female, they wore loose-fitting trousers and tight-fitting vests over their tunics. The elderly members of their contingent walked at the front of the line, straight-backed and proud, their eyes flashing as they looked here and there. The younger women walked at the rear, bearing the sealed boxes that contained their gifts. With every step, their gold ankle bracelets tinkled a soft melody.

Halting at the foot of Elandra's bed, the women bowed deeply in unison. The oldest one, her hair liberally streaked with white although her dark skin remained smooth and youthful, stepped forward as spokeswoman. She made a graceful gesture of obeisance.

"You may speak," Elandra said.

"Gracious one, we come to make a gift in honor of this rare occasion." The woman spoke slowly, as though Lingua was difficult for her. Her voice was a melodious contralto, her accent exotic and rich. "May it please thee to gaze upon our humble offering. And then perhaps to accept it."

Elandra inclined her head.

The woman stepped aside with a gesture at the others, who came forward with the boxes. With eager chatter, the ladies in waiting also surged forward to see.

The Mahirans stopped and stared at them.

Elandra snapped her fingers, and the chatter stopped. She glanced at the Mistress of the Bedchamber. "I will see these gifts alone. Dismiss the ladies for now."

The mistress curtsied and shooed the others out quickly, her expression giving away nothing. With the doors closed after the last one, the Mahirans seemed to relax.

They turned back to Elandra and bowed.

"Proceed," she said.

One by one the boxes were opened, giving off a slight fragrance of sweet lavender and something unidentifiable. Elandra could feel little currents of energy released as each seal was broken. Magic filled the room. For a moment she was afraid, but the air turned warm and gentle. She could smell more scents rising to combine with the lavender: frangipani, roses, jasmine—the fragrances of home. Inhaling deeply, she let her eyes close briefly, and her fear melted away. In her hand, the topaz grew warm, and, drawing strength and comfort from it, she relaxed.

Opening her eyes, she sat forward with anticipation. These garments, whatever they were, would be exquisite.

The first gift was a long scarf of delicate lace, the pattern intricate and lovely. Holding it up to the light, Elandra spread it across her fingers and knew immediately how it would look draped over her hair. She smiled, and the women smiled back.

"*Chiara kula na*," they said softly.

It sounded like a benediction. Elandra inclined her head.

One by one, the other offerings were brought forth. Undergarments of the finest silk, embroidered with white silk thread in intricate patterns. An undergown of silk gauze so light and sheer that in the sunlight it almost seemed to disappear. A cloak of amber-colored wool, spun so soft and fine it draped fluidly in her hands. She could put her thumb and forefinger together to form an O and draw the cloak through it, yet when she put it around her shoulders she could feel its warmth. She felt safe and protected in it, and was loathe to pull it off again.

They gave her gloves of the same material to match, and perfectly fitted to her hands. Drawing one on, she flexed and turned her hand, marveling at how strong she felt. When she pulled the glove off, the illusion of strength faded. Her skin tingled lightly, and she frowned. Magic gloves. A magic cloak.

She put the lace scarf on her head, wrapping the ends beneath her chin, and at once her vague headache cleared. She felt alert, brilliant, decisive. When she took it off, she could tell a difference. Would wearing the undergarments make her feel invigorated and tireless?

The women from Mahira watched her, their dark eyes wise and patient.

"I give you my thanks," Elandra said slowly. "These are precious gifts indeed. I am honored by your kindness."

The spokeswoman bowed. "They will never wear. They will never soil, although they may be washed," she said. "They are to assist thee in thy hour of need."

During the ordeal of the coronation? Or during something else? Elandra wondered, but she did not ask.

"We ask thee to accept our gifts of protection," the woman continued. "We are but women. Our weapons are only needle and thread, but what we have we give to thee. To help thee in all that is to come."

"What is to come?" Elandra asked, feeling suddenly cold.

"The emperor wears his armor, spell-forged by the Choven. The empress wears her armor, sewn by the Mahirans. Alike, and yet not."

Gratitude flooded Elandra. She smiled. "Your concern honors me. I shall not forget the kindness of the women of Mahira. Thank you."

The women bowed; then the spokeswoman brought forth a small box of cedar and proffered it. "Then, if we have pleased thee, may it also please thee to accept this final token of our respect."

The topaz grew suddenly hot, too hot to hold. With a gasp, Elandra dropped it, and the gem went tumbling across the bedclothes like a nugget of fire, flashing brightly in the sunlight.

At the foot of her bed, the Mahiran stood holding the small box and ignored the topaz winking brilliantly atop the coverlet.

Nursing her scorched hand, Elandra took the box and broke its seal. As she opened the wooden lid, a heady fragrance of cedar mingled with roses filled her nostrils. The touch of magic drifted against her face, caressing her cheekbones. With wonder, Elandra took out a small pouch sewn of dark green moire silk, lined with velvet the same color. It had a drawstring top and a long cord of braided silk. Her coat of arms had been embroidered on the side with gold thread.

She knew at once what it was for, and drew in her breath sharply. Forgetting dignity, she crawled forward until she could reach the topaz, then slipped it inside the pouch. It was a perfect fit. Delighted, she closed the top, and slipped the looped cord over her head.

She smiled warmly at the Mahirans, feeling more than a little astonished. "How did you know?"

They smiled back.

"*Chiara kula na*," the spokeswoman said softly, with reverence. "You were foretold in our legends. Woman of fire."

Elandra stared at her, thinking of her destiny and wondering why it had not mentioned any of this. "I was foretold?" she echoed in puzzlement. "But—"

The women bowed, putting their fingertips to their foreheads in obeisance. They retreated, backing away from her with a series of deep bows.

"Wait!" Elandra said, scattering gifts in all directions as she scooted out of the tall bed. "I have questions. Please wait."

"*Chiara kula na*," they said in unison, still bowing.

The double doors opened behind them, and they left.

Elandra stood there in her nightgown, her hair flowing down her back, the green jewel pouch hanging from her neck. She felt she stood at the window of some great understanding, only to have a curtain drawn closed, shutting her out.

Frustrated, she tried to make sense of it even as the Mistress of the Bedchamber peeked inside.

"Majesty?" she said hesitantly. "It is time for the preparations."

The ladies in waiting poured back into the room, and in moments Elandra was surrounded by eager hands pulling and pushing at her in all directions.

"I shall wear those," she said sharply as some of them examined the gifts. "The cloak, scarf, and gloves should be put away carefully."

Her attendants curtsied. "Yes, Majesty."

Already the hairdresser was knocking for admittance, a woman and her assistants had arrived with jewel cases, and the head seamstress rushed in, wringing her hands with an anxiety that cleared from her face as soon she saw that the Mahirans had not brought a coronation gown that would rival hers.

In an hour, Elandra had bathed and nibbled at a breakfast she found tasteless. She was powdered and dressed. Her fingertips and the soles of her feet were anointed with oil of myrrh. The Mahiran underthings were so light and filmy she almost felt as though she were wearing nothing, yet new energy flowed through her. She felt refreshed and calmer. After her ordeal last night, she was grateful indeed for this assistance.

Her hair was smoothed down and coiled in a heavy, intricate knot at the base of her neck. Curly tendrils escaped to frame her face. The simple styling was to complement the crown that she would wear later.

Thinking of it, Elandra found her mouth dry and her heart suddenly pounding. She tried to think of something else, anything else in order to quell her rising anxiety.

They made her stand while they carefully lowered the gown over her head. It was made high to the throat, and she could wear her jewel pouch concealed without difficulty. She wished there was time to have the topaz secured to a chain so she could wear it as a pendant, but instinct told her this was a jewel to hide, not to flaunt.

The dress, made of cloth of gold, had always been extremely heavy, especially with its train that swept the floor. But today its weight did not seem so great. She stood patiently while the seamstress pulled at the long sleeves, making sure the wrist points reached Elandra's knuckles and were not twisted. Then the full sweep of skirts had to be smoothed and the hem checked once again to be sure she could walk without tripping, yet would show no unseemly expanse of ankle.

Next came the jewels she was to wear. A new necklace of rubies had been created in her honor. Elandra examined it without much favor. It looked gaudy and overdone.

"Did the emperor order this made?" she asked.

The woman in charge of the jewels looked suddenly nervous. "Not exactly, Majesty."

Elandra's brows lifted. "What *exactly* do you mean?"

"It is a very fine piece of work," the woman said, staring at the floor. "The jewels are beautifully matched."

"Perhaps," Elandra replied. "Answer my question. Did the emperor order this to be made for me?"

"No, not this necklace. The jeweler thought your Majesty would admire it."

"I don't," Elandra said curtly. She had seen this trick pulled before at her father's court. A jeweler would fashion something extra and send it in among the rest of the order. If it was accepted, he would then pad the bill accordingly. And he would use its acceptance to solicit more orders. "I do not like it at all," she said. "I do not wish to wear it. If the emperor did not order it for me, then it may be returned to its maker."

"But—but, Majesty!" the woman protested nervously. "It's design was chosen by the emperor."

"What do you mean?" Elandra demanded. "You speak in riddles. Either he ordered it, or he did not. Are you saying he chose this design, then changed his mind and did not request it to be made?"

"No. It was made to his order. I mean, another was made to his order."

Elandra looked at the woman in silence. By now, the woman was perspiring and knotting her fingers together.

She looked as though she wished to be swallowed by the floor.

When Elandra said nothing, she gulped and began wringing her hands.

"I'm sorry, Majesty. We thought it would please you. It was made up in garnets first, simple, inexpensive stones, but see how much finer it is with rubies?"

Elandra refused to look at it when the woman held it up. "For whom was the garnet necklace made?" she asked coldly, although already she guessed.

The woman's face looked bloodless. "The emperor wished to give it as a gift. He often—"

"I see," Elandra said, her voice like ice. The ladies in waiting watched in bright anticipation. "He often gives baubles such as this to his concubines."

The woman licked her lips and nodded. "Well, not exactly like it. I mean, the rubies are very fine stones. The jeweler thought that since the emperor had commissioned the design, it could be used—"

"This jeweler thought that her Imperial Majesty the Empress Elandra would be happy wearing the same necklace as a mere concubine," Elandra said stonily. "This jeweler is a fool."

"Majesty, forgive—"

"No. Why should I forgive what is a blatant insult?" Elandra said. "Who is this jeweler? What is his name?"

The woman's eyes darted this way and that, but there was no escape for her. "P-Pelton, of Fountain Street. He does very fine work. He always pleases the—"

"He does not please me. How much did he bribe you to bring this to me?"

The woman gasped, but Elandra held her pinned with a stony gaze.

"No more than the others—" The woman broke off what she was saying and began to cry."

"Get out," Elandra said, and turned her back.

Guards took the woman away. Elandra refused to look at her or listen to her pleas for mercy. She stood, opening the other jewel cases and picking through the offerings. Everything was new. She realized they were all from jewelers like Pelton, eager to establish custom with her by making these gifts.

Elandra knew that any or all of them could have pitfalls such as the one she'd just avoided. How was she to know whether these designs were submitted in honor to please her or to trick her or to insult her? The wisest course was to avoid all of them, yet she could not go forth without jewelry. Although she preferred simple adornment, she must not look like anything less than an empress today. She was still on trial. There were still innumerable mistakes she could make.

"Is this all?" she asked finally.

One of the assistants crept forward, eyes down, standing hunched as though in a permanent half-bow. "Yes, Majesty."

"But all of this is new."

"All the jewelers in the city have sent their wares for your selection."

"I don't want these," Elandra said.

Everyone gaped at her, but her mind was already shooting over the possibilities. There was only one way to be safe.

"Bring me Fauvina's jewels," she said.

Someone gasped; she could not tell who it was. Consternation broke out.

The Mistress of the Bedchamber approached Elandra worriedly. "Majesty, there is not time to send to the vaults for them, even if they could be found."

Elandra's head came up. She glared. "There is time, if you do not dally making objections."

The woman curtsied. "Majesty, forgive me. I do not object. But what if they cannot be found?"

"Why shouldn't they be found?" Elandra retorted. "The jewels of the first empress? Are they not honored? Are they not revered? Are they not kept in a special place by the order of the emperor, as all of Fauvina's things have been preserved? Have them brought at once."

"Yes, Majesty. But the emperor must give permission—"

"Why?"

"I don't know. I—I—"

"Do as I command," Elandra said, looking the woman in the eye. The mistress curtsied again, giving way, and turned to snap her fingers.

A half-hour ground slowly by before hastening footsteps could be heard outside. Everyone looked up, but it was only a messenger who came to inform the empress that her presence was awaited.

Elandra met everyone's anxious eyes, and her stubbornness kicked in. When she wanted, she could be as obstinate as her father, who had once stood alone and undaunted against an entire war council's wishes to attempt a peace treaty. Albain had refused to cooperate, had refused to withdraw his troops, and had single-handedly driven back the invaders without the support of the allied forces. It was this action that had earned him his reputation of loyalty and valor and brought him to the attention of a grateful emperor.

"Majesty," the Mistress of the Bedchamber said, "your presence is required."

Elandra's chin lifted higher. She sat regally in her chair,

unable to do much else in her formidable gown. "The empress is not yet ready."

The messenger left, and everyone sighed. Elandra sat there, refusing to budge no matter how nervous they got, and waited.

Finally they heard footsteps again outside the door. This time it was a chancellor who came to inquire how much longer the empress might be.

Murmurs at the door; nervous explanations. The mistress glanced over her shoulder at Elandra and murmured further.

Then she came to Elandra's side and curtsied. "Majesty, the chancellor would like to know—"

"Tell him the empress is not yet ready."

"But, Majesty, any of these pieces would be most handsome and most suitable. If we had known earlier, we could have had the old jewelry ready. It may be tarnished or too brittle. If it needs a repair, that will surely not please—"

Elandra raised her hand, and the woman fell silent.

No one dared speak after that. They waited, the minutes dragging by. The coronation robes, heavily embroidered and trimmed in white sable, waited on their stand. She might never wear them.

"No one has ever done this," someone whispered. "To keep him waiting . . . who would dare?"

Elandra knew the risk she was taking. The emperor's temper was always uncertain. He was displeased enough with her already. By now his irritation must be explosive. He could call the whole thing off. She would be dismissed in disgrace, set aside as an abandoned wife, her reputation ruined, no prospect of future marriage to someone else possible.

Her nerve almost failed her. She found herself looking at some of the jewelry spilling from the opened cases. There were some very fine emeralds glowing richly at her. They were of a pleasing cut. The earrings would flatter her. How easy to give in. Why had she started this in the first place? A little fit of pique could cost her everything.

But she had started it, and she would finish it. If she did anything less, she would be branded as weak. Her authority, what little she possessed now, would crumble entirely. She would never be taken seriously again. She had been insulted, whether through some scheme of the jeweler or whether through someone at the palace or whether through the desires of Kostimon himself she did not know, but she would not let an insult go unchallenged. No one of Albain blood could.

Again, footsteps came to the door. This time it was one of her guardsmen, a trifle breathless as though he had been running. He handed the Mistress of the Bedchamber a leather box, bowed, and retreated.

The mistress, looking stern with disapproval, carried the box to Elandra. It was dusty and spotted with age. The leather had rotted away in places. Elandra was shocked, for she had truly expected Fauvina's things to be better cared for than this.

As the box was unlocked and opened, Elandra swallowed hard. She supposed the mistress was right about the jewels being brittle and tarnished. She would look tawdry wearing them. She didn't even know if they were beautiful or horrid. She should have never backed herself into a corner like this.

In silence the mistress turned the box around so that Elandra might see the contents for herself.

A muted glitter came from the depths of the box.

"Draw back the curtains," Elandra commanded.

The ladies did so, letting more sunlight into the room. Elandra reached in and pulled out a bracelet. It was heavy and dark.

As she turned it over, the sunlight filled the gems with life so that they blazed in her hand. Elandra gasped.

Rows and rows of small, square-cut gemstones filled the wide bracelet. Rubies, emeralds, sapphires, diamonds, topazes, amethysts, spinels, citrines, and peridots all flashed together in a radiance of color. Dropping the bracelet in her lap, she drew out the heavy necklace with both hands. It was a large collar, studded with the same array of stones as the bracelet, that stretched from shoulder to shoulder and dropped to a wide V in the center. The settings were gold and very ancient, but nothing had broken. Normally she would never have chosen pieces with so many colors, but they did not clash, and they would look magnificent against her cloth-of-gold dress.

These, she knew without being told, were the true imperial jewels. No empress since Fauvina had worn them. But their diversity clearly symbolized the many provinces that had forged the empire. Elandra felt a shiver pass through her, as though she felt the dead woman's approval pass through the jewelry to her. She had been right to insist on this. She knew it in her bones.

There was silence around her. Elandra stopped admiring the jewelry long enough to glance at her ladies with an open challenge in her eyes.

"I am late," she said. "Attend me with these final touches."

Her command galvanized them into action. The necklace was fastened for her, as was the bracelet. She found rings to match. They were slightly too large for her tapering fingers, but she slipped them on anyway. The long earrings swayed heavily against her neck.

Elandra rose to her feet, and they brought her a mirror. She saw herself, pale-faced, a little shadowed beneath the eyes, but a glittering, magnificent stranger. She had feared the clothes and the jewelry would overwhelm her, but instead for the first time she saw her own beauty, saw how perfectly these colors and the richness of these clothes brought her looks to life. Even her hair subdued much more than usual, and coiled at her neck so that the crown would fit easily on her head, made her look different—more mature, more intelligent, more lovely than she could have ever guessed.

Startled, she stared at herself in wonder. While she was still gazing, the ladies brought forth the coronation robes and settled them on her slim shoulders. The heavy gold embroidery on the robes glittered in the sunlight. The fur trim looked regal.

She saw all the power and privilege of her position represented tangibly for her. Elandra felt stunned, light-headed, almost foolish. Then she rallied, thinking of her father, thinking of her mother, whom she had never known, yet who had somehow reached out through the visions of last night to help her.

Mother, give me strength this day, she prayed. *Guide my steps. Help me to act and live with honor, as befits this responsibility I have been awarded.*

A rustle around her brought her from her thoughts. She saw the ladies-in-waiting dropping one by one into deep curtsies around her. Elandra's heart quickened, and her eyes suddenly blurred with tears. She wanted to tell them of her gratitude; she wanted to promise them that she would strive never to abuse her position. She wanted to say so many things, yet she could say nothing.

She was an empress. She must get used to people kneeling before her.

Turning with a slow, perfect sweep as she had been taught to manage the tremendous weight of her garments, Elandra accepted her gloves and a small parchment scroll containing the blessings of Gault. She started forward, walking against the drag of her train and robes behind her.

The double doors were thrown open, and a herald's cry went before her into the passageway, echoed again and again by each herald on station within the palace. In the distance, she heard a long drumroll begin.

Chancellors in their fur-trimmed robes, carrying their staffs of office, hovered about, bowing deeply to her, then gesturing which direction for her to turn. Looking neither right nor left, her unveiled face solemn as she met the stares, Elandra walked through another set of open doors into a small chamber containing two gilded chairs and nothing else.

The doors were closed behind her, and she stood there in unexpected solitude.

She recalled that Miles Milgard was supposed to wait here with her. He had promised to give her some final coaching with her vows. Now he was gone forever. She frowned, thinking of his unexpected treachery. Never would she have suspected him capable of such villainy. She had trusted him, admired his mind, appreciated his patience. How could he have tried to kill her?

She told herself she must be wary of everyone. Trust was a precious commodity, to be handed out sparingly. Whether she wished it or not, she had enemies. She must always be on her guard, and she must never take anyone for granted again.

A piece of paper lay folded on one of the chairs. Elandra stared at it a moment, wondering if it was another trap. Finally she picked it up and unfolded it.

The writing was Kostimon's:

Ela,

Have courage this day, little one. Remember always that you are a queen. You must believe it in your heart before others will believe it. You must set the example if they are to follow.

I await you in the temple.

                                                        Kostimon

Reading the brief note, Elandra felt her eyes fill with tears. Even now, he was kind. Even if he was displeased with her for being late, he had taken the trouble to leave her a few words of encouragement. She smiled to herself, folding the little note away as though it were precious. In that moment she loved him.

The doors ahead of her swung open without warning, making her start.

"Majesty?" a chancellor said, peering in.

At that moment she could not recall his name.

"All is well?" he asked.

She found herself consumed with nervousness. Wordlessly she nodded her head.

He smiled and bowed to her. "It is time."

Before her, standing over near the head of the stairs, a small herald filled his lungs and bawled, "Her Imperial Majesty, the Empress Elandra!"

Trumpets flourished, and Elandra walked forward to the head of the stairs.

The dignitaries stood below her, arranged in order of rank at the foot of the white marble stairs and beyond. A crimson carpet ran down the exact center of the stairs, like a stain of blood. It blurred before her, and Elandra wondered how she would ever walk down so many steps in these cumbersome robes without losing her balance.

Then to her left came a slight commotion. Elandra turned her head and saw Kostimon walking toward her.

He was resplendent in gold armor, embossed with a scene from his most famous battle. His long-sleeved tunic worn under the breastplate was of cloth of gold, and he wore a ruby earring in his left ear. A ruby and gold diadem glittered from among his white curls, and his rings flashed as he stretched out his hand to her.

Breathless at this honor, especially when she thought she would have to walk alone to the temple like a mere consort, Elandra reached out and let him grip her hand hard in his. She was trembling as she sank into a deep curtsy at his feet.

"Rise, little one," he said, his voice thick with emotion.

She gazed up at him through her tears and wanted to fling her arms around his neck in joy and relief. He was treating her as a wife. In this, her first public appearance, Kostimon had chosen to honor her in full standing. She was forgiven.

"Rise," he said, sounding amused. "This is your day. You cannot spend it at my feet."

But her emotional reaction had pleased him. She heard it in his voice.

Gracefully she rose to her feet, her hand still clasped in his, and watched his eyes widen as he took in the sight of her. She saw admiration and—for the first time—a stirring of desire.

He smiled. "Magnificent."

There was no time for her to answer, even if she could have spoken.

The emperor tucked her hand inside his arm and led her down the staircase with the ease of a man who had done this countless times before. The trumpets resounded around them. The drums rolled on and on. Sunlight was shining down fully on the staircase through a window in the domed roof. Elandra felt as though she was descending through music and light, a magical creature without a body.

She had never been so happy.

The courtiers and dignitaries, resplendent in native dress from every province, bowed and curtsied as they passed. Elandra wished desperately to see her father's craggy face among the throng, but the sea of faces blurred together. She could not concentrate, could not focus. Her only solid piece of reality was Kostimon's shoulder brushing against hers and the firm grip of his hand.

Outside, the frosty air struck her face, and she found it exhilarating. Kostimon frowned and suddenly looked like an old man as he waited for an attendant to fit a cloak around his shoulders and fuss with the folds.

"It's a damnably long walk," he grumbled.

She gazed out across the endless parade ground where the lines of soldiers and cavalry stood at perfect attention. The crimson carpet stretched the entire distance across it, leading all the way to the Temple of Gault at the far end. She could have floated the distance, but Kostimon was an old man.

Concern touched her. She turned to him, but he was frowning and paid her no attention.

A chariot of gold festooned with flowers and drawn by four white horses rolled up at the foot of the palace steps. It looked old-fashioned and quaint. Seeing it, Elandra had to smile.

Kostimon glared at her, and just in time she managed not to laugh.

"How delightful," she said, and he relaxed.

"Come," he said, and led her to it.

Every time the restive horses shifted, the chariot rolled.

Moreover, it was supported by only two wheels and looked very unstable. Elandra did not think she could climb onto it with what she was wearing. If she fell flat on her face, it would be a poor omen indeed.

Grooms struggled to hold the horses still. The officials and dignitaries stood solemnly nearby, and the very woodenness of their faces told Elandra that they considered this as poor an idea as she did. The emperor stepped aboard, making the chariot dip and roll slightly. He spoke to the driver, then waved to her.

Elandra's heart sank. She still did not understand how she was to get on, much less where she was supposed to stand with her voluminous skirts. The driver and the emperor filled the chariot.

But then another one rolled up before her, and she understood that she was to ride by herself.

"If it please your Majesty," a man said to her.

Elandra turned and saw a young man with dark hair and beautiful eyes bowing to her. He was dressed in dark blue velvet, with a jaunty cap atop his head. She recognized him at once.

"Prince Tirhin," she said in acknowledgement, wary of him. She curtsied very slightly, and her mind flashed back to that tall, bedraggled slave who belonged to this man. What had become of his attempts to lay charges of treason against his highness?

Nothing, apparently, for the prince was here and the slave was not to be seen.

"I am glad to see you looking well," she said politely.

But the prince looked far from well. He was terribly pale, with a strained, exhausted cast to his features. His eyes were haunted, bearing a burden that made her glance away. He moved stiffly, as though his body ached, but with extreme courtesy he held the chariot steady and handed her into it.

She managed, barely avoiding losing her balance by grabbing onto the side. The prince stepped up beside her, his legs crushing her full skirts as he took the reins.

They drove forward, following the emperor's chariot at a slow trot, flowered garlands swinging from the sides and trailing out behind them. The prince concentrated on his driving, and said nothing to her at all.

Glancing at his grim profile, Elandra felt pity for him. What must he feel, this man who had spent his life expecting to inherit the throne and who now was forced to attend her, the unexpected usurper?

Kostimon had dropped hints that she might marry Tirhin some day. Elandra glanced at him again, wondering. He was older than she by several years, but not too old. He was very handsome, giving her an idea of what Kostimon had looked like when he was young. Tirhin dressed better than his father, had more polished manners, seemed more broadly educated. He was a modern man, while Kostimon clung to so many strange and old-fashioned ideas. When Kostimon was gone, a marriage between her and Tirhin would make a good alliance, would seal the throne and the empire for both of them.

But there was a coldness about Tirhin, something hidden or lacking, that she could not define.

She tried to imagine herself in his arms, and could not.

The next time she glanced at the prince, she caught him eyeing her in return. She looked away at once and thereafter gazed only at the long rows of soldiers saluting her with flashing swords.

When they reached the temple steps, she stepped off the chariot with a graceful ease that was due more to luck than her own agility, and rejoined the emperor.

Kostimon glanced past her at the prince with steel in his eyes. For an instant his expression indicated displeasure with Tirhin, and Elandra caught her breath. So he did know about the plot.

She wondered if she dared mention the slave, but this was not the time.

To the fanfare of trumpets, she set her hand on Kostimon's arm, and both of them turned their backs on Prince Tirhin to climb the steps into the sanctum for her holy vows and investiture.

Chapter Fourteen

BY NIGHTFALL, THE ceremonies were at last finished, and the feasting could begin. As the processional returned from its long circuit through the city, Elandra forced herself to keep waving to the cheering citizens although her arms were aching. The crown was nearly as heavy as her dress, and her neck felt stiff from having supported it all day. But she could not complain. She had been cheered everywhere, and all the warlords of the provinces had knelt to swear allegiance to her, even her father—looking both gruff and intensely proud. The processional had taken her down the Street of Triumph, a broad avenue paved with white marble that gleamed radiantly in the sunshine and even at dusk still glowed pale and softly white.

The street ran straight through the heart of the city, all the way out to the harbor. On either side of it stood the famed Arches of Kostimon, mighty stone edifices carved with descriptions of the emperor's many triumphs over his enemies. Statues of the emperor on horseback stood atop the arches, a double row of bronze figures that stretched on endlessly, symbolizing the infinite reign of this incredible man.

Coming back up the avenue in her open litter, Elandra looked at its breadth and its beauty, all extolling the achievements of her husband. Beside her, Kostimon looked tired but still bright-eyed. He clearly reveled in the cheers and adulation. She saw how much energy he drew from the crowds and the noise. Above all things, Kostimon loved being emperor.

Ahead rose the towering granite walls of the palace compound. Enormous bronze gates with great embossed spikes on their panels creaked open, and the processional streamed back inside with the cheers of the people still resounding.

Turning her head to see everything, Elandra considered the palace to be a city within a city, for it was filled with temples as well as a complex of meeting halls, council chambers, storehouses, granaries, and treasuries. This was the very heart of the empire, the center of the power and might of Kostimon's reign.

Involuntarily she glanced at her husband's profile. He had created all this from nothing. He had held it against those who would wrest it from him. He had truly wrought a profound achievement.

Kostimon tipped his crown to the back of his head and scratched his curls. "It's cold when the sun goes down."

She smiled at his complaints and dared give his arm an excited squeeze. "I am constantly filled with renewed admiration and pride at what you have done in your lifetime."

Surprise crossed his face. "What is this? Praise from my newly exalted wife?"

"Yes."

"And what favor are you trying to wheedle from me in exchange for these compliments?"

His sudden cynicism dimmed her happiness. More quietly, she said, "There is no favor. I meant what I said sincerely."

"Ah. There will be too many compliments tonight, too many flowery speeches, too much hot air. If I leave the banqueting early tonight, my dear, don't be put out." He gave her a twisted smile. "You see, I have done this sort of thing too many times to find it quite as exciting as you do."

She drew back to her side of the litter. Her face felt stiff. Proudly she forced her voice to be composed and even. "Yes, of course," she replied. "I understand perfectly."

The boundaries had been clearly drawn for her. She might be sovereign, but she was not his equal and never would be. And for all his smiles and little acts of kindness, he had only been humoring her today. She could not expect such treatment to continue. She could not expect anything to change.

Except that she was empress in her own right. And as long as she did not cross wills with him, she could do what she pleased and command what she pleased.

She held that to her, and refused to let his mood spoil hers.

"I am sorry you are so fatigued," she said formally. "Thank you for this day. It has been wonderful. I shall never forget it."

"The golden riches of my empire are yours," he replied.

Pretty words, but his tone was absentminded. She wondered if he meant any part of what he had just said.

At the imposing palace steps, their litter was lowered to the ground by the sweating bearers. Elandra rose to her feet, shaking off the dried flower petals that had been flung over her by the populace. She stood while her ladies straightened her skirts and smoothed the heavy folds of her robes; then, with her hand on Kostimon's arm, she ascended the steps of the palace, where light glowed through the open doors in warm welcome.

They parted inside, their attendants whisking them away to private chambers for freshening up. The coronation robes were finally lifted from Elandra's aching shoulders. She sighed in relief, then sat in a chair while her hair was restyled around the crown. For the few minutes that her long tresses were brushed, she could look at the tall crown sitting on the dressing table and know the blessed relief of being free of its weight.

An armed guard came in with a small man wearing the sash of a palace official. With a bow, this individual put the crown inside a locked box and in exchange produced a diadem radiant with diamonds and rubies.

He noticed the magnificent necklace displayed across Elandra's cloth-of-gold bodice, and his eyes widened.

"Ah!" he said in wordless admiration. "It will do very well."

She did not know who he was, or why he thought he could give his opinions. Gazing at him in the mirror, she lifted her brows.

"Why do you bring me a different crown to wear?"

He almost smiled. Short and balding, he seemed very self-assured without being officious. "There are several reasons, Majesty. The first is that this is a gift from the emperor in honor of the occasion."

Her heart quickened, and she smiled in instant pleasure. "A gift?"

"Yes, Majesty." He handed it to her on a little silk pillow. "Commissioned by the emperor and of original design."

It was beautiful, delicately wrought and of a design like none of the other jewelry she had rejected earlier today. She took the narrow crown in her hands and turned it over, marveling at the fine gold filigree and the high quality of the jewels. The diamonds were particularly fiery, flashing against the dark bloodred rubies.

"How lovely," she said. "I have never seen finer work. Who made it?"

"Ah," he said, and rubbed the side of his nose with his forefinger. "I believe the, um, Choven."

She nearly dropped it, and her widened eyes flashed to meet his in the mirror. "The Choven! Is this spell-forged?"

He smiled. "I think, um, not, Majesty."

She relaxed. "Oh. Still, it is very beautiful."

"It is unsurpassed in quality and workmanship, as are all things made by the Choven."

She nodded and handed it to the woman dressing her hair. The diadem was fitted into place atop her head, and thick locks of her hair were twisted about it and artfully pinned.

"And it complements the imperial jewels of the Empress Fauvina very well," the man continued.

"You know these jewels?" she asked in surprise. "They are very old."

"They were also Choven-made."

"How do you know?"

His smile broadened, and he gave a small bow. "I am the Keeper of the Imperial Jewels, Majesty. It is my business to know."

She drew in her breath, but did not allow her expression to change. "And as the keeper," she said pleasantly, "I suppose you are aware of what transpired this morning?"

"Yes, Majesty. A regrettable occurrence. The woman is not a member of my staff. The individuals she bribed in order to gain access to your chambers have been dealt with."

"Is this all your explanation?"

He allowed himself a very small frown. "In my defense, I will only say that I received no instructions regarding the jewels your Majesty was to wear. Therefore, I sent no member of my staff to await your Majesty's pleasure. Had I known of your Majesty's intention to wear the Empress Fauvina's jewels, they would have been cleaned and presented at the appropriate hour."

"I see."

She spoke tersely, aware of the meaning that lay beneath his words. Kostimon had not given his permission for her to be arrayed in jewels. As a consequence, she had been deliberately overlooked by this man. Anger flashed inside her, but she restrained it. This man owed her no loyalty yet. Her supporters comprised a very small circle right now, but she intended to change that. Time and patience were all she required.

The Keeper of the Imperial Jewels stood watching her with a pleasant expression belied by the wariness in his eyes. She knew she was being judged for her reaction. It was important that she not make an enemy of him, but neither must she appear weak.

Her gaze met his levelly. "I will not be overlooked again," she said.

"No, Majesty."

"While the Empress Fauvina's jewels are admirable, they were suited for today's occasion only. I will not continue to wear them."

He bowed. "A prudent decision, Majesty."

"I will acquire my own collection, fashioned from my jewel of choice." As she spoke, she thought of the topaz concealed between her breasts. "As Keeper of the Imperial Jewels, will you be my adviser, or do you serve the emperor only?"

A protocol question was always safe. The man's expression relaxed slightly, and he smiled. "I should be honored to advise your Majesty. Establishing your own collection is an eminently wise course of action. It prohibits certain interpretations."

She frowned. Was that a warning?

He continued. "As for selecting designs and commissioning a maker . . ."

"Yes? The jewelers of Imperia do not seem particularly inspired." As she spoke, her mind considered the possibility of sending business to Gialta. The Albain family jewels were very fine.

The keeper allowed himself a small chuckle. "Majesty, may I say that the imperial jewels are always fashioned by the Choven? Imperia jewelers must make do with occasional trinkets, baubles for gifts, and the like. They principally serve the aristocrats of the empire, but not the imperial family."

Elandra grew very still. Mentally she sent forth a quick prayer of gratitude that she had not made a serious error this morning. Collecting herself, she gave the man a gracious nod. "You have been most helpful. My jewel of choice is the topaz."

"Ah," he said. "The golden hues. Splendid."

"You will see to this at once?"

He bowed. "Tomorrow I will send forth a message to the Choven. They cannot be rushed or commanded, but their craftsmanship is unsurpassed."

She nodded, catching a glimpse in the mirror of a gesturing attendant. It was time for her to go. "Thank you."

She rose to her feet, elegant and graceful in her imposing gown. The diadem flashed brilliantly from her auburn curls with every movement of her head.

The keeper bowed deeply and departed with his attendant guard and the locked box containing the larger crown of state. Elandra watched him go. She did not know if she had made an ally of him, but at least he was not her enemy. In the maze of palace politics, even that might be counted as a small victory.

Head high, she swept out to go to the banquet, aware that if Kostimon did not attend there would be talk and speculation. For a moment she felt daunted, but then she steadied herself. One step at a time. She must remember that and not allow herself to be overwhelmed by the challenges that still lay ahead.

At the doorway to the banqueting hall, however, she

found her path blocked by Prince Tirhin. He bowed to her, his eyes shadowed, his expression far from welcoming.

Every eye was watching them. Elandra swept a swift glance around at the sea of faces, then forced herself to face him.

"Are you once again my escort?" she asked.

Tirhin's teeth were clenched, but he gave her his arm with an outward show of gallantry. "If the empress commands it."

She did not know if once again he was following his father's orders, or if he had some other intention in mind. They walked up the length of the vaulted hall together while the guests bowed and curtsied. At the head of the table, servants seated them with one empty chair between them—Kostimon's.

Lord Sien appeared, a gaunt, enigmatic figure in his saffron robes and leopardskin stole. He bowed before taking his seat on Elandra's other side. Having him next to her made her profoundly uneasy, but she refused to show this. The man had always frightened her, especially in what he stood for, and she knew he was extremely powerful. Kostimon was said to listen to his council more than anyone else's. The high priest was firmly entrenched in palace politics, and seemed to know everything almost before it occurred.

Could he read minds? She met his yellow, deep-set eyes briefly and managed a small smile of courtesy. He did not smile back, and his eyes seemed to glow at her, probing deeper than she liked.

Tirhin patted the emperor's empty seat. "It seems his Majesty has already retired."

She wished she could do the same. "It has been a long day," she said neutrally.

Tirhin emitted a short bark of laughter and reached for his wine cup. "Gault, so it has."

She noticed his hands were unsteady when he put down his cup. From his continued pallor, she guessed he was ill instead of drunk. But there was the banquet to open, and the guests were still standing at their places, awaiting her signal.

She gave it, and with a general scraping of chairs they settled themselves. An enormous roasted swan was carried in on a round silver platter by four sweating footmen. This was presented to her, and Elandra praised it.

At once a majordomo appeared at her elbow with a bow. "If I may carve for your Majesty."

She smiled. "Take the most tender portion, please, and convey it to Lord Albain with my compliments."

The man obeyed. Settling back in her chair, Elandra risked a quick glance at Tirhin and saw his face set like granite. Had the emperor been seated beside her, she would have given him the best portion; then he would have returned the favor. But since the emperor was not present, she would honor her father as was only fitting. Tirhin could not expect her to honor him for any reason.

When the laden plate of succulent meat had been carried to Albain, he rose from his place halfway down the table and raised his cup in a toast.

"To the empress!" he said gruffly, squinting through his one eye. "May Gault preserve her."

The guests rose to their feet, echoing the toast as they raised their cups.

Then followed a long succession of toasts and compliments while the meats grew cold and Elandra's face ached from so much smiling. She could feel fatigue around the edges of her consciousness, and knew that without the magic of the Mahirans she would have collapsed long ago.

At last the eating could begin. She nibbled at the delicacies, finding most of them too rich for her taste. Lord Sien ate in silence, ignoring everyone. Like Elandra, Tirhin barely touched his food, but he continued to drink steadily.

She marveled at his capacity. "You seem to have a deep thirst, sir."

His dark head tilted toward her. "Call me Tirhin, mama. We are a family, are we not?"

Heat touched her face, and she bit her lip. "I do not think family is the best term for it."

His eyes mocked her. "Then what would you call us? A gaggle of unhappy relics?"

"You may be unhappy. I am not."

"Oh, ho," he said, sitting up straighter with a sardonic smile. "I suppose you are not. All of Imperia lies at your feet. Or so you think."

Again she thought of this man's slave, distraught and torn between loyalties. She was suddenly tired of Tirhin's petty jealousy, tired of his sulking face, tired of the subtle ways in which he mocked and defied his father.

"I understand you are a devotee of the gladiatorial games," she said, changing the subject without warning.

The prince blinked, and a faint wash of color tinted his cheeks. "Why, madam," he said, signaling for his cup to be refilled, "do you intend to become a spectator now that you are released from your bridal confinement? I had supposed you would instead be busy breeding a new heir for the empire."

Her mouth tightened. He was skating dangerously close to insult. "This sport may begin to fascinate me," she replied, conscious of Lord Sien listening at her other shoulder. "I understand you own the champion."

This time unmistakable color darkened Tirhin's cheeks. He glared into the depths of his cup, and his fingers gripped it so hard they turned white. "Yes," he said at last, flinging a look at her. "I do."

"Is that not gratifying?"

"Of course."

"I understand also that you often take the fellow with you to functions and parties. Is he here tonight?"

"No."

"What a pity."

Tirhin gave her a twisted smile. "Now that you have been raised to such exalted standing, do you intend to sample—"

"Tirhin," Lord Sien said sharply in warning.

The prince frowned and knocked over his cup. Wine spilled like blood across the table linens, and a servant rushed to blot it up.

Caught between them, Elandra looked from one man to the other. The lamplight seemed to fade near her chair, letting the shadows crowd closer; then all was bright and merry again. She blinked, alarmed, and wondered what had just occurred. It felt as thought a spell had been formed and sent, but she was unaffected.

In her lap, her hand clenched hard on her napkin. She wanted to run from this place, but she couldn't. Fear burned in her throat, but she held it back until her breathing returned to normal. Swallowing hard, she looked at Tirhin, who sat as though frozen, his face bleak with unhappiness.

"You were saying?" she prompted.

He blinked and seemed to rouse himself. His eyes, dark with resentment, gazed past her at Sien. "I only meant to ask if you intend to sample the many public events and amusements of the city, now that you are released from your bridal confinement."

She replied with inconsequential chatter, but in her mind she was turning over the true meaning of what he had been about to say before Lord Sien interrupted him. It had been meant as an insult, she was certain.

Elandra sighed. If only she could talk in private with this man and convince him she was not his rival, but such an opportunity had not yet presented itself. She was not certain how to arrange it without causing trouble and talk. She did not want Kostimon to get the idea that she and Tirhin were conspiring against him.

"Your highness looks tired," Lord Sien now said to the prince across her. "Perhaps you wish to retire."

Tirhin's fingers tightened around his wine cup; then he nodded without meeting the priest's gaze. "Yes. If I may have the permission of the empress to withdraw early? I am a little fatigued."

"You look unwell," she said in sympathy, aware that his pallor had intensified. He looked like a ghost above the vibrant hue of his tunic. "Of course you may withdraw."

Tirhin stood up immediately, swaying against the table as he did so. He bowed to her, graceful, debonair, and tense. With one final glance of resentment, he exited the hall.

Now there was only Lord Sien to talk to. Elandra accepted a pastry filled with almond-flavored cream and toyed with the flaky layers, wishing she also could withdraw.

"Take care, Majesty," Lord Sien said in a low voice.

She glanced at him in startlement. "In what way?" she asked more sharply than she intended.

Her nervousness made him smile toothily. She felt pinned by his gaze, like a little animal frozen before a predator.

"Do not underestimate the prince."

Elandra swallowed. "I do not," she said carefully.

"He has not behaved . . . wisely of late. But chagrin can lead to darker motivations if it is not checked."

This cat-and-mouse conversation annoyed her. She took a chance on being direct. "You mean, it can lead to treason?"

Lord Sien blinked; then amusement glimmered in his hooded eyes. "So you know of that, do you?" he asked.

She glanced around, but the servants had momentarily retreated out of earshot. Although in the full view of hundreds of people, she was effectively alone with this man. He spoke softly beneath the general noise of the banquet, and they were in little danger of being overheard.

A cold chill ran through her, but she sat erect in her chair and faced him without flinching. "I do know of a plot," she said. "Has the emperor also been informed?"

A snort of laughter, quickly checked, came from the priest. "Did you not run to him with the news?"

She went on looking at him, although inside she found herself shaking with nerves. "Did you?"

He smiled without amusement. "It seems, Majesty, that we both have a strong degree of caution."

"Meanwhile, Tirhin makes his mischief unchecked."

"Oh, not exactly," Lord Sien assured her. "The prince is learning the price of certain actions."

She did not like the satisfied way in which he said that. She thought of the tremor in the prince's hands, and felt more afraid. Tirhin had never struck her before as a man easily subdued. What had happened to him on the Forbidden Mountain? What had he done? What had he seen?

The priest selected a pear from a dish and began to cut it into small pieces, spearing each with the tip of his dagger, and eating them with relish.

"Might I ask your Majesty's sources?" he asked between bites. "You are better informed than I expected."

"My sources should remain unidentified at present," she replied. "I will only say that my father taught me that information always plays a vital role in any situation."

"Ah, Lord Albain." Lord Sien turned his gaze down the long table, where her father sat shoved back from the table,

picking his teeth and making jests with the man beside him.
"A formidable warrior."

"Yes."

"And your mother, Majesty? What did she teach you?"

Elandra's teeth gritted together. How smoothly and
subtly he reminded her of her own illegitimacy. Temper enabled her to lift her eyes and meet his proudly. "My mother
taught me how to survive, Lord Sien."

Again he blinked, as though he had not expected that
sort of answer from her. He considered her a long moment,
then slowly nodded. "I see."

She frowned, longing to terminate this conversation.
But with him, she did not quite dare.

At the other end of the hall, the musicians were tuning up. There was to be dancing after the feast, but Elandra
did not feel up to that. She sat there, willing this man to go
away.

Instead, he cut up a second pear, his hands quick and
deft with the knife. "You have had fair warning," he said
now. "Your own informants can supply the rest. Take heed
of it, Majesty."

"Yes." She knew not what else to say.

"Your guardsmen are wearing their new colors
tonight," he went on. "I advise you to choose a protector as
soon as possible. It is your right as sovereign."

She nodded. "Yes, I have considered it."

"And will you do more than consider it?"

"Tell me, Lord Sien. In the matter of a protector, must
he be from my guard?"

Sien's deep-set eyes quickened with interest. "No.
While customary, it is not required."

"Then I could choose a warrior from, say, Gialta."

"You could, although it is inadvisable."

"Why?"

"It points a direction."

"I do not understand you."

He laid down his knife. "It indicates a favoritism to your home province. The empire, Majesty, consists of many provinces all joined together under Kostimon's banner. That union took a long time to form. It can be broken apart much more easily."

Again, she had the feeling he was warning her, obliquely, and watching to see if she had the intelligence to understand. Her dislike of him grew.

Sien continued, "That is why the protector is generally chosen from among the guardsmen. Politically neutral."

"But if I wanted to make my selection elsewhere, I could."

Sien's brows lifted. "Yes."

"If, perhaps, I wanted to choose a Traulander, I could."

Sudden comprehension leaped in his eyes. "That is unwise, Majesty."

She had surprised him. She liked that. "Is it? Why?"

"Trau has its own brand of mysticism apart from the rest of the empire. The people are clannish. They seldom venture beyond their own borders. They abhor violence. Few, if any, of them are trained in the high weapons skills required for this position."

"But if there should be an exception—"

"You mean the games champion, the one who belongs to his highness."

There it was, out in the open, like a glove of challenge between them. Elandra did not truly intend to select another man's slave for her protector. The idea was absurd, and would cause unnecessary trouble, yet she wanted to see how far she could push the matter.

"I have heard this man has incredible fighting skills."

"Have you seen him fight?"

She lowered her gaze modestly. "I am sure you realize, Lord Sien, that I have not been permitted to attend the games."

"Of course. Naturally his reputation as a swordsman is formidable. But he is only a—"

"Is it not true that he defeated a Madrun savage in combat this week?" she asked.

"I—yes."

"Is it not true that he is said to fight like a trained member of the Imperial Guard?"

"Yes."

She shrugged as if to say, Why not?

Lord Sien frowned at her. "The man is a slave, a gladiator, a ruffian. He could not be trusted in the palace. Certainly he could not be trusted with the life of the empress sovereign."

She thought of Caelan, with his intense blue eyes. She thought of his steely fingers closed about her throat. She thought of his rudeness, his impatience, his stubbornness. No, he was not suitable at all.

"Still," she persisted, enjoying her game, "he is said to have an unnaturally strong loyalty to his master. Is that his quality, or perhaps it is the prince himself who inspires such dedication in his men."

Sien studied her a moment, then allowed himself a very faint smile. "Interesting," he said softly. "I think the empress will make her choice with great prudence according to precedent. The slave is, after all, a condemned man, and not available for the position, even if Prince Tirhin could be persuaded to sell him."

She was not certain she heard him correctly. "Condemned?" she echoed.

"Yes, Majesty. In the dungeon at this very moment, being tortured for his confession."

She was appalled. Had the fool tried to denounce Tirhin after all? Was this his reward? "Why?" she asked. "Only a day or so ago, he was being praised by everyone. Half my guardsmen won money on him. What has happened?"

"Have you not heard?"

She was suddenly impatient with the slyness in Sien's voice. "Obviously I have not heard."

"Then your informants need better training."

She made an impatient gesture. "What has happened?"

"You saw how unwell the prince looks."

"Yes."

"He was attacked by this slave. Beaten grievously before the attack was stopped by the other servants."

Her mouth opened. She tried to imagine such an event, and remembered again the brutal crushing of her throat by those strong fingers.

"Yes, Majesty," Sien said. "His highness has been much shaken. He trusted this slave, dispensed favors to him, granted him much more freedom than he should have. Only to be turned on viciously, like a mad dog."

Sien was almost smiling as he spoke. Satisfaction radiated from him. She could not understand how he could derive so much pleasure from a horror like this.

"Therefore," the priest continued, leaning toward her, "do not toy with the idea of acquiring the brute. His head will be adorning the spikes over the city gates soon enough. Look among your own loyal guardsmen for your protector, and do not delay. Kostimon has lived a long time thanks in part to the diligence of his Hovet. If you value survival, on the advice of your esteemed mother, you will heed my counsel in this matter."

She bowed her head. "Thank you, Lord Sien, for your trouble and for your wisdom. I shall pay great heed to your advice."

He left her soon afterward, and Elandra stood up to dance with her father. Her head was spinning. She did not know whether to believe Sien or not. Perhaps the Traulander slave was mad. Perhaps he had invented the story of his master's treason, planning this attack all along. Or perhaps none of it was true.

She felt too confused to sort it out.

Lord Albain was not a good dancer. He stumbled through the intricate steps, red-faced and swearing under his breath.

She would have laughed, but she knew he would misunderstand her amusement and be hurt by it.

"Father, please," she said at last, out of pity. "Let us step out of the line and watch."

"By Murdeth, I won't!" he replied stubbornly, hopping against the beat of the song. "If my daughter wants to dance, I'll be hanged if I don't see that she gets to."

He was endearing, but so miserable she shook her head. "But I am too tired to dance, Father. Truly. Let us stand aside and talk."

Grumbling and mopping perspiration from his face, he followed her from the dance floor. The music faltered and died, and everyone stopped.

Mortified, Elandra signaled hastily for a chancellor. "Please instruct the musicians to play on," she said. "I am too fatigued to dance and shall retire soon, but the festivities must continue as long as the guests wish. That is my command."

The man bowed deeply. "Yes, Majesty."

He hastened away to confer with the musicians. The tune struck up again, and slowly the couples resumed the reel.

Elandra took her father's arm and walked with him toward a shadowy alcove, where they might have a small amount of privacy.

"I have longed to talk to you all day," she said.

He gripped her hand in his large, calloused ones. Now he raised it to his lips and kissed her knuckles. "My little Elandra," he said gruffly. "Empress of the land. I am proud, very proud."

"Thank you. Father, about—"

"You must take care, Elandra. Guard yourself well, and do not form alliances within the court too hastily. Consider situations from all sides before you become involved."

"Yes, Father. But—"

"Intrigues are a nasty business. But they can't be avoided, not here. The place is rife with them."

"I have learned."

"Have you? Good. You were always a clever girl. You will show good judgment now."

"Yes, but, Father," she said, gripping his sleeve. "I need to ask your advice—"

He shook his head. "No, child."

"But—"

"No. I am not the man to advise you. I am just an old warmonger. Fighting is all I know about. The ways and wherefores I leave to others."

Exasperation rose in her. If he would just listen for a moment, but then he never had. "I need a *jinja*," she said hastily before he could cut her off again.

That got his attention. His single eye narrowed at her. "A *jinja*? Why?"

"There are strange portents," she said wearily. "You've seen the cloud on the horizon."

He sighed. "All have seen it. An era is ending, child. We all know that."

"Yes, and I feel the need for protection, for help."

Albain's craggy face grew fierce. "Albain blood flows in your veins. Have you forgotten that? Are you afraid?"

She wanted to scream at him to drop this pretense that there should be no fear, ever. She wanted to confess that she *was* afraid, horribly afraid. She wanted to be held in his arms and reassured. She wanted to find a place where she could feel safe.

But his scorn stiffened her spine. She flung up her head and looked him in the eye. "I have forgotten nothing," she said, making her voice haughty. "But if the emperor walks nowhere without a man at his back, whom am I to have at mine?"

"Ah. I see. But you need a flesh-and-blood protector, girl, not a *jinja*."

"I want both."

He considered it, pursing his lips. "You know *jinjas* are forbidden here. I have left mine at the city gates, squalling in a cage in the care of my baggage handlers. It is hard to walk about, feeling the magic that shifts through these halls, and have nothing to sound the alarm."

"Exactly."

"Would you defy the emperor?"

"Will you defy me?" she retorted.

He grew very still, his gaze arrested. Then slowly he smiled. "Your mother would have spoken to me in just that way, sharp as a spear, cutting to the heart of the matter. I will see what I can do."

She smiled at him in grateful relief. "Thank you."

He held up his forefinger. "There is one problem. You must return to Gialta to claim it."

"But I do not think I can."

"It is the only way. There must be the bonding, or a *jinja* will not serve well, not the way you require."

"Can there not be a bonding here?"

He shook his head. "It would not work."

Disappointment filled her. Frowning, she hissed a moment through her teeth. "Then the *jinja* must wait until I can come."

"All the more need to select a protector."

She nodded. "Lord Sien recommends I do so quickly. And he says I should not choose a Gialtan."

A slow smile spread across Albain's face. "But I think you do not always listen to this priest, do you?"

An identical smile appeared on her face as she looked up at him. "I listen. I may not heed."

Albain chuckled a moment, then sobered. "Be careful, girl. He makes a bad enemy."

"I know. He advises me to choose among my guardsmen, but they have not proven themselves yet. How can I test the one who will best serve me?"

"You are the daughter of a warrior, and the granddaughter of a warrior," Albain said gravely. "Your mother's house is very fierce. Listen to what sings in your blood, Elandra. Put your trust in your lineage, in the courage and good sense we have bequeathed you. Don't listen to the whispers of men. Listen inside."

She bit her lip and nodded, wishing he could tell her something more tangible. Instinct and guesswork were not always the most reassuring qualities to depend on.

Albain gave her cold hand a squeeze. "By Gault, you have confounded the world already. My girl an empress in her own right. My girl on the throne." He broke out in an unsuppressible chuckle, wheezing a little. "By Gault, I used to think myself poorly favored, with two girls and no sons, but now . . . Ha, ha! Show them what you're made of. Show them, Elandra! Let your mother's fire blaze forth. Do what you damned well please, and don't stand aside for any of them."

She wanted to. With all her heart she longed to seize

the world with both hands and make it her own. Yet she was so afraid of making a mistake.

It was like standing on the brink of a cliff. If she spread out her hands and believed in herself, she could soar like an eagle. If she clung to herself in doubt and worry, she would plummet like a stone.

"I will tell you this, and then I must go," he said, bending close to her ear. "The best course to confound the intriguers is to hew to your own truth. Do what they least expect and never back down. Remember you have the upper hand. And for the sake of Gault, do not offend the emperor. He has promised me extra lands on my western boundary."

She could have snapped in frustration. What good was his advice when he contradicted himself? Do as she pleased but don't offend the emperor? Still, what had she expected? His advice was better than anything else she'd been told.

"Will you send me your armies should I ever need them?" she asked in a very quiet voice.

Albain froze. His one good eye narrowed, and his jovial mood vanished. For an instant he was like a hawk sighting prey, still and dangerous.

"I swore an oath to you today. What more do you seek?"

"The oath was sworn to the throne," she replied, taut with nervousness at what she was daring to ask. "I ask you now for more than that."

"You mean when the cloud descends and you and the prince will fight for what's left of the empire?"

"Yes," she said.

Her senses seemed to heighten. She heard the music, glimpsed the dancing and laughter, but her being remained focused on him and his answer. Time came to a halt around her, and she almost ceased to breathe. She must have one piece of solid ground, one true assurance to count on for insurance against what might possibly come in the future. Even if it was only refuge.

Albain drew in a deep breath and glanced around slowly and openly to make sure they were out of earshot. He put his back to the company so that no one could read his lips.

"Elandra," he said in a quiet voice, "if ever you have need, I will unleash my armies and rend the empire from one end to the other. Merely send me word, and my sword arm is yours till death."

Chapter Fifteen

A DASH OF cold water in his face brought Caelan back to consciousness.

Suppressing a groan, he slitted open one eye and found that nothing had changed. He was still hanging by his shackled wrists from a hook, his feet swinging above the floor. His dripping hair hung in his eyes. He was naked to the waist and freezing cold. His amulet pouch still hung safely around his neck, untouched in this dungeon hell where only superstition received respect.

The blurred face of his torturer peered up at him, a pale orb of flesh with merciless eyes bobbing above a brown leather jerkin stained with dried blood and grime.

"Man ready speak some?" the torturer asked.

His voice was a ruined croak, as though his throat had been crushed long ago. His accent was strange, his words barely understandable. He seemed to speak an odd mixture of Lingua and pidgin. And although the man was no longer quite in focus, Caelan would never forget his first sight of him. The torturer's ears came to slight points that jutted up through his greasy hair. His fingers had delicate webs between them.

A shudder ran through Caelan. This was some kind of demon-spawn, a creature half human and half of shadow, as horrifying in its way as a moag or a lurker. To find it here in the heart of the city, clothed and employed, had shocked Caelan deeply.

Yet why should he be surprised at anything in Imperia? After all, the gladiators consorted with the monstrous Haggai—female creatures with siren voices and the bodies of huge, slug-like worms. The Vindicants exercised an official religion for the public, and a very different kind of blasphemous observance for private ceremonies. The empire was based on hypocrisy, and the emperor himself lived only through some kind of unholy bargain with the darkness itself.

But such things were hidden away for the most part, not talked about openly, concealed from all except those who actively sought them.

The torturer, however, was an official of the palace— no matter how lowly his status. Corruption was spreading; truly the end of the world must be nigh.

Even to look on the creature's pallid face filled Caelan with revulsion. As for the torturer, he knew Caelan was afraid and why.

Baring his teeth, the torturer laughed softly in Caelan's face, close enough for him to feel the creature's warm, fetid breath on his skin. Caelan averted his face, but the torturer gripped his jaw with viselike fingers and wrenched him back.

"Speak some!" he said angrily. "Man die slow. Man die hard way. Speak some, man die not. No speak, man die hard."

Caelan met the thing's eyes. They were human eyes, green and round, fringed with lashes as thick as a woman's. But the light in them was madness. Gathering himself, Caelan spat in the torturer's face.

"Gah!" Howling, the torturer struck him across the mouth.

Caelan's head rang, and the world melted into dizzying colors, shapes gone crazy against his half-closed eyelids. He swung back and forth by his shackle-chain, and his wrenched shoulder sockets screamed in agony.

A sharp command rang out, and the icy water dashed

over Caelan, bringing him back yet again. Coughing and shivering, he sputtered and squinted against the water dripping into his eyes from his matted hair.

Time had become lost to him. He did not know how long he had been here. As yet they had not put him on the rack or in the glove, a large wooden vise that could crack him like a nut.

The dungeons were a foul, gloomy maze of holes sunk in the floor and fitted with iron grates. The unfortunate inhabitants were dropped into the holes like rats down a well, and left in the dank coldness and filth until they were dragged out for questioning or until they died. Food was dropped in on top of them. They lived without light or warmth or hope, miserable wretches forgotten by all save their jailers. Their wailing went on all the time, an eerie, primal sound of raw anguish that never diminished.

Overlaying that were the screams of the tortured. A man currently lay stretched on the rack, babbling in delirium. A woman, recognizable as such only by her long, matted hair, sobbed in a cage that swung high from another rafter on the other side of the forge. The round stone pit glowed a dull red, hot with hissing coals, the smoke curling forth to blacken the ceiling. A short time past, some convicted thieves had been brought in, kicking and screaming for mercy, to be branded with the hot iron.

The torturer had picked up one of the irons, its tip white-hot fading to a dull red higher up the shaft, and he had held it close to Caelan's face, so close Caelan could smell the hot metal, could hear it singing and hissing, could feel its scorching warmth against his skin.

"Want this?" the torturer asked, moving the iron back and forth.

Caelan could not help watching it, his eyes shifting back and forth, mesmerized with horror.

"Man eyes, gone far!" The torturer grinned and let his tongue flick back and forth across the edges of his teeth. "Blackness, hot blind. All time blackness. Speak some!"

Sweat broke out along Caelan's temples, but he didn't flinch. After a few moments when the iron began to cool slightly, the torturer growled in disappointment and flung it back in the fire.

Now he returned, pacing and rubbing his webbed hands together. "Man think smart, but not smart. Think, master maybe change, maybe say torture not man. Maybe not!"

He laughed in Caelan's face, then drew back sharply as though afraid Caelan would spit at him again. "Speak some, or many hurts. Here!"

Drawing a flat, wide strap of leather from his belt, he swung it back and forth. One end was perforated with numerous holes. He brought it around with a rapid flick of his wrist. The leather struck Caelan's arm with a smack of fiery pain. He drew in his breath sharply, biting off a cry.

The torturer grinned. "Man speak some now. Man scream high!"

The beating commenced expertly, each blow landing on vulnerable flesh in an overlapping pattern of agony that only intensified. It was like a scourging, yet the wide strap inflicted a different kind of pain than a narrow whip did. After a few moments when Caelan felt himself begin to waver badly, he *severed* himself from the pain and endured it, detached in the cold void of elsewhere, and always waiting for a chance, however slim, to retaliate.

He had confessed hours ago, spilling all that he knew. But he had spoken too soon and too eagerly. The torturer had not believed him and was demanding another confession.

Caelan had nothing left to say. Gritting his teeth, he shut his eyes and tried to endure.

"Stop!"

The voice cried out the command loudly enough to silence the wails of the prisoners. The clatter and racket ceased as the jailers stopped their tasks and looked around. The torturer lowered his strap and turned sullenly, standing almost at attention.

Through the sudden silence, there came only the faint constant sound of dripping water and the soft moans of the man on the rack.

Swinging in place, Caelan struggled to turn his head so that he could see the visitor.

Through the smoke and gloom he glimpsed a figure in a soldier's breastplate, feet spread apart, head high with arrogance.

"Who is in charge here?"

The soldier's voice rang out strongly, sternly. It was a voice of command, and it sent jailers and turnkeys scurrying into a motley line as though for inspection.

A burly man, broad-shouldered, running to fat, shuffled forward. "I'm the head jailer," he said.

"Clear this room."

"What, of all—"

"Clear the room!" the soldier barked. "Immediately!"

Grumbling, the jailer turned around and gestured. His minions set to work unbuckling the unconscious man from the rack. The woman in the cage was lowered and dragged forth. She couldn't walk, and the men half dragged her, half carried her out of sight.

In the distance came the screeching of rusty metal as the grate of one of the holes was opened. Caelan heard the woman scream; then the sound was brutally silenced. The other prisoners resumed their wailing, crying out for mercy, pleading their innocence.

The torturer brought a stool and stood on it to reach the hook Caelan was swinging from. He fished out a key to unlock Caelan's shackles, and Caelan tensed himself in readiness. With even one hand free, he could attack.

"Not that one!" the soldier said, striding over. He paused before Caelan and looked him up and down. "Is this the Traulander? Prince Tirhin's property?"

"Is," the torturer admitted. He half turned away from the soldier and drew up a dirty hood over his head. "Not hurt."

"Leave him where he is." The soldier looked around, his face drawn with disgust. "Very well. All of you, clear out!"

The torturer glared at Caelan but went, along with the jailer and the others.

Caelan swung alone in front of the soldier, bruised and battered, his skin on fire, his shoulders bursting with agony. Even with the aid of *severance,* he found it hard to focus on anything more than a moment at a time. His wits were wandering. It would be so easy to sink away into unconsciousness, such a relief, but the soldier touched his chest lightly, setting him swinging again, and the resultant pain sent a choked cry slamming to the back of Caelan's throat. Gray and yellow misery washed through him, and the world was on fire. There was no passing out, no escaping it. Even *severance* did not contain it.

A voice spoke in the distance, and the soldier stepped away from Caelan. "He is ready, Majesty."

By the time Caelan managed to lift his head again and somehow throttle back his misery, the emperor had come down the steps and crossed the dingy, splattered room. He circled the forge, where the glow of the coals threw a ruddy glow across his face. At last he stopped in front of Caelan.

The emperor wore a tunic of cloth of gold and a crown on his head. He seemed to blaze in the gloom, and his jewels winked and sparkled at his slightest movement. His yellow eyes gleamed balefully at Caelan, and his face might have been carved from stone.

"You dared attack my son," he said in a low, furious voice. "You miserable wretch."

Caelan struggled to pull his wits together. By some miracle, he had his audience with the emperor. It was not what he had hoped for, but it would have to do. "Majesty," he said, his voice a hoarse croak, "I must denounce your son as a traitor and a—"

"Silence!" the soldier shouted, and struck him.

The man's fist slammed into Caelan's jaw like a battering ram. He spun around on the chain, the pressure sawing through his armpits, and felt his consciousness dribbling away.

"Get back, Captain," the emperor said as though from far away. "I do not require your assistance."

A murmured apology, and retreating footsteps.

Then a hand gripped Caelan's hair and jerked up his head. "Talk to me, you overgrown brute," the emperor muttered. "But take care. I have risked enough, giving you this chance to defend yourself when by rights your entrails should have already been fed to the gulls. Talk!"

Caelan tried, but his brain felt as though it had come loose in his skull. He gasped, struggling for the breath to answer, praying he could pull himself together one last time.

The emperor shook his head impatiently. It felt as though he might pull Caelan's hair out by the roots. "Talk, damn you! Is your confession the truth?"

"Yes," Caelan whispered thickly. "Traitor . . . it's true. I saw."

"What did you see?" the emperor demanded, his voice lower now, still tight with anger and impatience. "Tell me quickly!"

"Bargain . . . Madruns to come . . . take city." Caelan drew in a shaky breath, knowing he needed to be more articulate. He tried harder. "Sien and the prince . . . secret meeting on *Sidraigh-hal* . . . met with Madruns. Prince wants throne. Resents the—the lady empress." His mind stumbled and failed him for a moment. Then it came back. He frowned. "Prince plotted against you. Made alliance. Gave them . . . gave them . . ."

To his frustration his strength petered out, and he could not finish. Panting, he hung there and railed mentally against his own weakness.

"And you were there?" the emperor said grimly. "You participated in this plot?"

Caelan rested his cheek against his arm, his eyes half-closed. "No. Followed master. To protect . . . didn't know. Watched outside the hut. Heard. Saw him give them the paper."

The emperor's face turned pale. "The passwords?"

"And forged orders . . . strategy . . . way through the border. Everything. City in danger. Five days, then they will come."

The emperor's grip shifted to his throat. "When did this occur?"

"Day before coronation. I tried to warn you. Couldn't. Only to you could I speak. No way to reach you. Prince hurt."

"He will hurt even more," the emperor said furiously. His eyes were blazing, and he dropped his grip from Caelan's throat. "You're a slave. You could say anything. Why should I trust you?"

Caelan managed to meet his eyes. "You believed me. You came to see me for yourself."

The emperor's mouth quirked in a thin smile before he turned serious again. "I have seen you in the Dance of Death.

Only men of great courage attempt it. Courage and honor are sometimes found together." His eyes narrowed. "Then you attacked my son when you found he was a traitor."

Caelan shook his head. "No attack," he said wearily. "Lies."

"But the servants witnessed it."

"No attack."

Disbelief filled the emperor's face.

Caelan grew desperate. "Please," he whispered. "The accusation made by the healer against me is a lie. The servants saw nothing. There was nothing to see. Ask Orlo, my trainer. He will tell you the truth."

"Why should the servants tell this falsehood, lay accusations against you? My son has been injured. You struck him—"

"No!" Caelan said vehemently, daring to interrupt. "I swear to you on all my gods that I did not strike the prince. I brought him back from the mountain and sent for my cousin—for the healer Agel to tend him. The prince was attacked by the *shyrieas*. They hurt him, not I."

"None of this makes sense," the emperor complained. "It is all babble, as I feared it would be. You accuse a man, yet you carried him back and sought help for him? Bah!"

"Could I accuse him unconscious?" Caelan asked, his desperation rising. "Could I be heard unless he were in a condition to be judged? I have no reason to lie. My very life is endangered by what I have said. If you do not believe me, then I am a dead man. I would be safe had I kept silent."

"And why has the healer accused you?"

"I do not know."

"You say he is your cousin?"

Caelan found the emperor's eyes to be more penetrating than ever, as though the man wanted to peel open his skull and peer inside. "Yes," he said bleakly. Unwanted memories of Agel, of racing together through the spruce forests, of stealing apples, flitted through his mind momentarily and were gone, ghost voices laughing merrily before fading behind. "But I can call him kinsman no longer."

"He must have a reason for betraying you, *if* he has betrayed you."

Caelan frowned. "The reasons are old ones. When jealousy and grief entwine through a man's heart, who can say why he does one thing or another? Our feud does not affect this matter—"

"I think it does. I will know everything."

Caelan sighed. He did not understand why the old man had to probe into matters that were personal. "May I have a drink of water?"

"No," the emperor said in an implacable voice. "Talk."

"We were at school together, to be healers," Caelan said in a low, toneless voice, trying to shut off the pain. "I— my father wished me to be there, although I wanted to be a soldier in your army."

His gaze flicked to the emperor, who watched him impassively. Caelan shrugged. "A boyish dream. I was rebellious. The elders of the school eventually disrobed me—cast me out. Agel stayed, a model student, but he never forgave me. I had more talent than he did; he considered my actions a waste."

Spoken aloud, it did not seem like much of a motivation. Caelan hesitated a moment, then added, "There is more to it than a boyhood rivalry. Agel is ambitious. He thought this matter would bring him the gratitude of his highness. As a slave, I embarrass him."

The emperor turned away from him, hands clasped at his back. Back and forth he paced, deep in thought. Finally he stopped and faced Caelan again.

"If I had not seen you fight the Madrun, I would not have come down here. My son offered you a magical potion to strengthen you against your opponent, but you refused it. Why?"

Caelan blinked in surprise. Did the emperor know everything? "I—I do not believe in such things, Majesty," he said.

"Yes, you believe," the emperor said, turning the meaning of his remark. "You believe all right, and you're afraid. Why?"

Caelan's heart started pounding. Yet he could not escape. "I will not sip of the shadows, Majesty," he said, gasping a little.

"Hah!" The emperor drew back as though struck. His scowl was fearsome. "Self-righteous bastard, what do you know of the world? What do you know of shadows? Do you judge me, you piece of dung?"

Caelan dropped his gaze hastily. "No, Majesty," he whispered.

"No," the emperor said more calmly. "No, you do not. So you fought without magic. You fought with valor and courage and skill. You fought like a damned fool. And you used the Dance of Death, you, a mere slave, with no military service behind you. I know it is believed by some that my son taught you that move. But I happen to know that Tirhin is unacquainted with it, except in theory. It was never taught to him. How did you know it, slave?"

Caelan swallowed hard and had no answer.

"How did you know it?" the emperor demanded more harshly, forcing Caelan to look at him. His yellow eyes bored in. "A Traulander, bred to peace, the son of a master healer committed to pacifism."

Caelan's mouth dropped open. "You knew my father?"

"I did," the emperor said grimly. "The proud fool refused my offer of an appointment. How did you learn that sword move?"

Caelan's gaze shifted away, then came back to his. He said nothing.

The emperor leaned closer. "Was it the sword?" he asked in a scratchy whisper. "A blade of many combats. Did it sing to your blood? Did it share its secrets?"

Caelan's eyes widened.

The emperor laughed at him. "Do you think I don't recognize *sevaisin* when I see it? Do you think Sien would not know?"

Caelan's mouth was suddenly dry. "It is a great shame in my country."

"So is using *severance* to kill."

Caelan felt jolted. The denial rose to his lips, but he held it back.

"But, no, you fight fair," the emperor said. "Always you fight fair, although there are no rules in the arena. You have won the championship every time, and by rights my son should have freed you for that. You do not drink excessively. You do not sport with the Haggai. You do not spend the gold my son has given you. Except for being a slave, you conduct yourself with honor and honesty. Rare qualities rarely seen these days."

Caelan had no answer. He waited, hoping for the emperor's mercy.

"What did Tirhin do to destroy your loyalty?" the emperor mused. "Was it treachery alone?"

Hope filled Caelan. "Then your Majesty does believe me?"

"Hah!" Anger returned to the emperor's face. He spun on his heel and strode away, trotting up the steps and sweeping out past the soldier at the door, who stiffened to attention.

Caelan watched him go, chilled with dismay. It was

over. His chance had come and gone. He had failed to convince the man, and with him went Caelan's last hope.

His consciousness of his surroundings returned. The wailing sawed on his nerves, and he could once again smell the filth and despair. Like a beetle, the torturer came scuttling forth from the shadows and grimaced in his face.

"Speak plenty now!" he said petulantly, and struck Caelan.

The pain and gray misery swept through him again. He was choking, coughing, balanced halfway between oblivion and agony when he heard the rattle of his shackles. One of them opened, and his right arm dropped to his side.

Fire lanced through him, piercing straight through his shoulder with such intensity he could not find enough breath to scream. His left arm dropped too, borne down by the weight of the shackles and the chain that thumped him a glancing blow on the side of his face. He tumbled to the floor, unable to catch himself, lost in the fire of his wrenched shoulder sockets.

The torturer kicked him, grunted, and scuttled away. After a moment the intense pain abated slightly, only to flare again when a pair of turnkeys grabbed him by his elbows and lifted him.

Caelan bit off a cry, sweating and unable to walk. They propelled him forward, shoving him across the chamber and up the steps into the hands of some soldiers.

Barely conscious, Caelan glimpsed their cold eyes and taut mouths and knew they were taking him to execution. He'd been a fool all his life. He would die a fool. He should never have spoken the truth, not even to the emperor. What good had it done him but bring him to this misery and shame?

"Come on, get on your feet," one of the soldiers snarled at him. "If you can't get to barracks on your own strength, you don't deserve to be a member of the guard."

Caelan didn't understand at first. He stumbled, found himself jerked up, and broke out in a cold sweat. One of them slammed him against the wall, and he managed to brace himself there.

"What?" he asked in bewilderment, not certain he had heard right.

"Gault, but you stink," one of them said, wrinkling his nose.

"He'll be crawling with lice. Watch him," another warned.

"Arena scum—"

"No, no, Zoma," a man said. "He's a champion. I won money on you, Giant. But you'll have to change your ways now."

Caelan still couldn't believe it, although slowly comprehension was beginning to sink in. He looked at their faces, seeing neither friendliness nor condemnation. "I'm not going to be beheaded?"

They laughed in a roar that made his head ring.

"He's out of his wits," Zoma said. "Move on. The sergeant will cut you down to size soon enough."

Gathering him up, they shoved him onward, taking him out of the dungeons and out across the grounds toward the barracks. It was night, and very cold. Shivering and still wet, Caelan stumbled along as though in a dream. If he was to live, he found he could not let himself believe it yet. He was afraid it might vanish like ashes blowing through his fingers. It could be another cruel joke, a final measure of hope meted out to him before the axe fell. But with every step he began to believe despite his caution.

"Have I been pardoned?" he finally asked.

"From what?" Zoma asked, giving him another shove. "Is this man accused of any crimes?"

"No official charges."

"No, just that he stinks."

"You stink," Zoma said with a smirk. "Your punishment is a bath and severe scrubbing. If I catch any of your vermin, I'll peel your skull."

Caelan grinned. He straightened, his legs suddenly finding strength. He was to be a soldier, he realized. After all these years, after all this struggle, it was finally coming true. He could not be a soldier unless he was free. No slaves served in the army.

His heart filled up fast, ready to burst with intense happiness. Right then none of his aches mattered. He went staggering across the immense parade ground, managing to keep up with their long strides. He couldn't stop grinning, not even when they stripped him naked and threw him bodily into a trough of icy water.

"Get clean," he was told.

Shivering and sputtering, he scrubbed until his hide felt raw. Then, wrapping himself in a blanket, he dashed indoors only to find himself surrounded by a circle of brawny men.

Every face looked hostile. Not a smile of welcome flickered from one of them. A set of clothing came hurtling through the air and smacked him in the face.

He caught it clumsily, still unable to raise his hands higher than his elbows.

"Get dressed," he was told.

Someone else kicked a bucket his way. "The floor is dirty, slave. Scrub it."

Caelan stood there his hopes and dreams dying away while they laughed in open scorn and turned their backs on him.

When he didn't move, Zoma came over and gave him a hard shove that nearly overbalanced him. "Are you deaf? You heard the sergeant. Get to scrubbing."

"But I—I thought—"

"You thought what?" Zoma asked him scathingly.

There was no answer. Caelan's protest died in his throat. He looked down, his face hot, his hands clumsy with the clothing.

Zoma shoved him again, sending him stumbling against the empty bucket. It fell over with a clatter. "Get to work! Or you'll stay up all night, scrubbing in the dark."

Chapter Sixteen

WHEN THE MORNING bugles sounded, Caelan awakened with a start, forgetting at first where he was. Then the door to the barracks banged open, and an officer came striding in.

"Attention!" bawled the barracks sergeant, looking as startled as any of them.

The soldiers scrambled from their bunks and hastily assembled themselves in a line. Wearing only their nethers, their hairy chests pimpled with cold, their hair standing on end, and their jaws unshaved, they looked a bleary lot.

Caelan, who had slept on the floor in the uncaring slumber of exhaustion, climbed to his feet also but stood slightly apart from the others. The homespun tunic they'd given him was ridiculously small, and his wrists dangled from the sleeves like an overgrown boy's. In the clear early light his arms showed their bruises and shackle sores plainly. His shoulders still ached, but he could move his arms in a near-normal range of motion again. *Fast healer*, he thought derisively to himself. *Hurry up and recover so you can take the next round of abuse*.

The officer's gaze swept around the barrack like a cold northern wind and came to rest on Caelan. "Is this the man?"

The sergeant stepped forward smartly. "New recruit, yes, sir."

The officer looked Caelan up and down, his eyes missing nothing, not even the pail of dirty scrub water with the brush floating on top of the scum.

His mouth tightened. "In my day, sergeant, the recruits were set to polishing armor as part of their initiation. Floors don't seem quite in keeping with the dignity of the Imperial Guard, do they?"

The sergeant's face stayed as blank as the wall. "No, sir."

"Present the men for inspection by second bugle."

The sergeant's fist slammed against his left shoulder. "Yes, sir."

The officer pointed at Caelan. "You, come with me."

Caelan stepped forward warily and walked past the silent row of men. He no longer knew what to think. Their cruelty in letting him believe he was still a slave stoked his growing resentment. He remembered the brutality of the soldiers he had met as a boy and how they had robbed him on the road like common brigands. These men were no better, and as guardsmen, they were the elite of the emperor's fighting forces. He glanced at their stoic faces as he walked past and wondered how many more unpleasant surprises they had in store for him.

Outside, the air was frosty and still. Caelan's breath streamed about his face as he looked around. A small cluster of men in crimson cloaks and armor stood waiting.

"Get it done quickly, Sergeant Balter," the officer said to a short, burly individual who saluted.

The officer walked away without another glance at Caelan.

Frowning, Caelan stared at the others. "What am I—"

"Silence!" the burly sergeant snapped at him. "Fall in."

The other two guardsmen stepped behind Caelan, and he had no choice but to follow Balter down the long row of barracks to a sort of courtyard formed in the angle between the last barracks and the stables. Paved with flat stones, the area held a set of stocks, a whipping post, a fountain stilled beneath a skim of ice, and a smithy.

It was to the last that Caelan was taken.

He stepped into the open-sided hut, ducking his head beneath the low ceiling. The smith, muscular and sweating, already had his bellows going and a fire burning in his forge. The air in the hut smelled of charred hair, hot metal, and ash. Caelan suddenly suspected what was coming. He tensed, swallowing hard, and made his mind a blank.

Sergeant Balter exchanged a brief word with the smith, then snapped his fingers at Caelan. "He will remove your slave chain."

Caelan's throat was too full and tight to answer. He nodded silently, his eyes full of what he could not say.

"Come o'er," the smith said. Bearded and taciturn, he pointed at an anvil.

Caelan stepped over to it.

"Show us, then," the smith commanded.

Caelan fished out the golden chain around his throat. The smith's blackened hand fingered it.

"Pity to break that," he said, but pointed again at the anvil. "Lay yer head to it. Hold still, else the chisel'll go through yer throat 'stead of next it."

Swallowing, Caelan felt tremors go through him. His emotions were threatening to overwhelm him, and almost savagely he forced them down. He must not think. He must not feel. If he was to be freed, then let it be done. Until the chain was taken off his throat, he would believe in nothing.

Bending over, he pressed the side of his face to the cold, hard surface of the steel anvil. The smith moved Caelan's head so he could loop the slight amount of slack in the chain over the narrow, pointed end of the anvil. It was an uncomfortable position, but Caelan remembered the smith's warning and held himself absolutely still, hardly even breathing.

The smith took his time. He positioned the chisel on the links of the chain. It was an intricate piece of work, thick and very fine, fashioned of many strands braided together. Shifting the chisel a bit, the smith pressed the flat side of it against Caelan's jaw.

He suppressed a shiver and closed his eyes as the smith raised his hammer.

There came a swift, sure bang as hammer struck chisel with one blow. The chain broke and fell to the ground.

Caelan opened his eyes and slowly lifted himself. The smith bent and picked up the chain.

Its golden length caught the strengthening sunlight and gleamed richly against the man's dirty fingers. He cupped it in his palm, making a shimmering heap of it, and handed it to Caelan.

"Keep it," he said with a sudden grin through his beard. "To remind yourself of when times was harder."

Slowly Caelan's fingers closed around the chain. He had a lump in his throat. After all these years, he thought he would feel something when the day of release came. He expected to be different, transformed. Instead, everything seemed ordinary and unchanged. It was almost disappointing.

"Take off your tunic," Balter said. "Let's see if you've got any ownership brands."

Caelan wanted to hesitate, but he had too much pride before these men of war. He would exhibit no cowardice before them.

Swiftly he pulled off the small tunic and let it dangle from one hand. At the sight of his deep, muscular chest, broad shoulders, and sun-bronzed skin, the sergeant's eyes widened slightly.

The smith emitted a low whistle. "Aye, could play hammer to anvil all day and never tire, with those arms."

He reached out for the leather thong holding Caelan's amulet pouch. "What's this?"

Quicker than thought, Caelan gripped his wrist and held it with crushing strength. Anger blazed in him. "Don't touch that."

The smith's eyes grew round. "Sure," he said mildly.

Caelan released him, shoving him slightly backward. "It has nothing to do with this."

The smith held up both hands in a placating manner. "No offense to you."

"Here's a rower's brand," Balter said from behind Caelan.

Caelan knew exactly where it was; he would never forget the day the iron had been stamped into the flesh over his right shoulder blade, burning that small circle into his hide.

"Easy," the smith said. "Any others? Any fancy, foreign marks with them curlicues an' such?"

"No."

"Easy."

The sergeant stepped around to face Caelan. His face was pudgy and youthful despite the age in his eyes. With a frown, he said, "To serve in the army, all ownership marks have to be canceled. You understand?"

Caelan's tongue seemed stuck to the roof of his mouth. "Yes."

"Some slaves, when they're manumitted, they keep their tunics on the rest of their lives, so nothing will show, and they don't go through with crossing out the brand. A few runaway slaves pay smiths to cross out their brands, but such won't have the imperial mark at the edge to show it's official. Do you see?"

"Yes."

"In the army, you don't have any choice. I can see plenty of stripes on your back. You're hard to handle, are you?"

Caelan almost smiled; then suddenly it did not seem funny. "Sometimes."

"Sure. All fighters are, if they're worth anything. I've seen you in the arena. Spirited. Means you're spirited out of the ring too."

Caelan wasn't feeling very spirited just then. He was praying for courage.

"In the army, men are stripped. Men are inspected. Men are flogged. Men sometimes have to dig ditches to entrench a camp or lay siege. You strip down with an uncanceled brand on your back, and you could find yourself turned in as a runaway. You see?"

"I understand."

The sergeant went on staring at him hard, waiting.

Caelan managed to nod. "Go ahead."

"Good man." Stepping back, Balter signaled to the other two soldiers. "Come and hold him."

"No," Caelan said. "There's no need."

The smith, who had gone back to his bellows, glanced over his shoulder. "You can't stand still enough. You'll blur it when you jerk, and it'll make a bad sore."

"I'll stand still," Caelan said grimly. "I don't want to be held."

The soldiers' eyes held doubt, but when the sergeant shrugged, they backed off.

Caelan walked over to the anvil, drawing in deep breaths as he cleared his mind. It had to be done, he told himself. Freedom had to be absolute. He wanted no ownership marks left on him. He wanted no arguments in the future with overzealous bounty hunters coming after him by mistake.

Focusing, he pulled his mind into *severance*, entering the coldness of detachment. He gripped either side of the anvil and braced his feet apart, trying not to listen to the rattle of the irons or the hot sizzle of the fire.

His heart was racing, and his knees felt weak. He almost wished he had agreed to let the men hold him down. He could yell then and kick, knowing that their strength would be greater than his.

But he dared not have their grip on him. Because he was likely to flow into *sevaisin*, and if he joined with them or with the fiery metal at such a vulnerable moment, he might never return to himself.

He could not risk that; therefore, he had to be strong. He had to find courage, whether from desperation or pride.

"I'm coming," the smith said. "Make yerself ready."

Tensing his back, Caelan lowered his head between his shoulders and tightened his grip on the anvil. He could hear the hissing metal. He could smell the heat of it. He could feel it as it neared his back. He shut his eyes, detaching even farther, driving himself deep into the coldness.

"Now," the smith said and put the brand to him.

The stench of burning flesh choked his nostrils before he felt the fire burning away the coldness of *severance*. It came at him fast, pursuing him, melting down his strength, dissolving his control.

Just when it reached him and consumed him, a hand gripped his left shoulder and tried to pull him away from his death grip on the anvil.

"It's over," a voice said kindly. "Turn loose, lad. It's over."

He fell out of *severance* with a gasp and dropped to his knees. His back burned as though a fire had been kindled there. Coughing, he rested his cheek against the rough wooden base supporting the anvil.

"Here."

A cup was pressed to his lips. He tasted water, metallic and cold, and drank thirstily. Opening his eyes, he saw the face of the sergeant bending over him. Respect and a little awe lay in the man's eyes.

"You did well," Balter said. "The cross mark is clean and sharp, the best I've seen. Ice is good for it, but try to find ice in Imperia." He snorted. "Come, then. Back to barracks to kit up. We'll put a bandage on either side to hold your tunic off the burn. When it's healed, you can be fitted for armor."

"Standard issue won't fit," the smith said, plunging his irons into a pail of water that hissed. Steam curled from the surface. "He'll have to have his own armor made, same as an officer."

"Get to your feet, lad," the sergeant said kindly.

As Caelan pulled himself up shakily, Balter slung a glance at the smith.

"He'll be an officer soon enough. He was a champion in the arena. Them as is champions in one way of living usually can be champions in others."

The smith put his fist against his left shoulder in a mocking salute, then winked at Caelan to show his jest was well intentioned. "I'll measure fer that armor come end of week," he promised.

The three soldiers surrounded Caelan and walked out slowly with him, as though they were guarding him. He could feel their respect and admiration, although they did not say much. He felt warmed by them, and he found himself wishing he had been assigned to their barracks last night instead of where he'd been.

They took him to the quartermaster, who fitted him with good clothing and boots. They took him to the armory, where one-handed he tried out daggers and swords until he made his selection.

Balter exchanged an awed glance with his men. "You swing that broadsword about like a feather, lad."

Caelan grunted. It felt good to handle weapons again. He liked the armory, its neatness and order with racks of clean, well-oiled weapons hanging on the walls. Swinging the broadsword in a wider arc, he felt his stiff muscles beginning to loosen and grow limber.

"Not too much," the sergeant said in warning. "You'll waste your strength."

Caelan nodded reluctantly, missing Orlo's rough advice. He wondered if the trainer would stay in Tirhin's service, or leave it.

Sliding his new sword into its scabbard, he made one last circuit of the armory, communing silently with the weapons, admiring them. His fingers slid across a few last blades; then he settled his hand on the hilt of his own new possession. Pride straightened his shoulders. He walked out with the others, beginning to feel like a new man.

On the parade ground, guardsmen were lined up at stiff attention, armor and helmets shining, hands on sword hilts, chests out, eyes straight ahead.

A trio of officers, their crimson cloaks whipping in the breeze, walked along the line. Occasionally they pulled out a man, who walked over to join a small cluster of soldiers who were chatting and jesting with each other, flexing muscles and spitting between boasts. A fourth officer, wearing a cloak of gold wool, stood to one side with his arms crossed over his chest. He was scowling at the selections.

Balter tapped Caelan's arm to hurry him past. "This is for the seasoned men only. Nothing to do with you."

But the officers swung around and one of them said, "Sergeant Balter, halt."

Stopping in his tracks, the sergeant saluted smartly. "Sir!"

"Why aren't you at inspection?"

"Just delivering a new recruit to his quarters, sir," Balter said.

The officer asked another question, but Caelan stopped listening. In the distance he heard a bugle note, and idly he turned his head toward it.

He supposed it was just another signal for the military, but it had been far away, so faint as to be barely carried over the wind.

Another glance around showed no squadron tumbling forth. The parade ground remained deserted except for the Crimson Guard at attention here. Wind whistled desolately across its expanse, and at the far end, tattered garlands of yesterday's festivities swung from the temple doorways.

He heard the bugle note again, louder, as though borne by the wind itself. The hairs on the back of his neck prickled.

"Come on," the sergeant said, tapping Caelan's arm.

He shook his head, looking up at the sky.

"I said come."

"Wait," Caelan said, indifferent to Balter's swift look of annoyance or the surprise that flashed across the faces of the other soldiers. "I hear something."

"You'll have a lash across your back if you don't step out *now!*" the sergeant commanded.

That got Caelan's attention. He brought his gaze down to the sergeant's. Heat filled his face, and he barely stopped himself from bowing in a slave's manner of apology. Obediently he stepped forward.

The sound came again, closer and louder. It was a thunderous cry, echoing down from the heavens, a cry that had cut across his nightmares for years.

He whirled around with a shout of his own, reaching for his sword and drawing it before anyone else could react.

"Restrain him!" the sergeant shouted, but Caelan strong-armed his way past the men who reached for him.

He scanned the sky again, and saw it now, a small black dot borne on the air, coming steadily closer.

Fury swelled his throat, and he forgot everything except this chance for revenge.

"You fool! It's only a Thyzarene—"

Not listening, Caelan ran across the parade ground, angling to intercept the approaching dragon and its rider.

Swearing, soldiers ran after him, but Caelan was like the wind itself, too fleet to catch. He kept his gaze on his prey, marking where it was likely to land. He intended to be there when it did, waiting with a blade of vengeance.

The dragon screamed savagely overhead, its black, leathery wings broad against the sky as it skimmed over the walls and descended toward the broad front steps of the palace.

"Catch him!" the sergeant shouted. "Stop him!"

Swearing, the soldiers pounded after Caelan, but he was too far ahead to catch. He ducked reflexively as the dragon sailed over him, stinking of sulfur, its taloned limbs tucked up close against its belly. Its long, barbed tail stiffened, helping to guide it down.

It was going to land at the very top of the steps. Practically in the front door of the palace. Caelan took the steps three at a time, his long legs driving him forward.

The sentries at the door saw him coming. He saw their faces in a blur, saw the pikes being lowered from their shoulders.

The wiry Thyzarene rider glanced over his shoulder. The dragon's snakelike head whipped around, and it hissed, baring its fangs.

Shouts rang out in all directions. More guards were coming from within the palace. They ran at Caelan even as the dragon hopped sideways and lashed out with its barbed tail.

Without a shield to block that blow, Caelan had no choice but to duck. He did so, rolling across the marble pavement too quickly to be caught by that dangerous tail, and launched himself at the vulnerable side of the dragon.

The Thyzarene shouted something furious in his own heathen tongue and leaned over his mount to strike back at Caelan with his sword.

Caelan's weapon met it, one-handed, and the clash of steel rang out loudly enough to echo off the buildings.

Then the soldiers were upon Caelan, gripping him and pulling him back bodily. He struggled against them, but by sheer numbers they held him back.

Enraged, Caelan swore at them in his own language. "It is my right to kill him!" he shouted. "My right!"

By now Sergeant Balter came running up, breathless and red-faced. He backhanded Caelan across the face.

"Are you mad?" he yelled. "Come to order now! You, disarm him."

One of the guardsmen wrenched the sword from Caelan's grip. Furious, he glared past them at the Thyzarene, who jumped lightly down from the back of his dragon and slung a pouch over his shoulder. The Thyzarene glared back at Caelan and gestured an insult.

Caelan heaved himself forward, but the men held him back once again.

By now the officers had reached them. "What in Faure's name is the meaning of this?" one of them demanded.

The sergeant whirled smartly on his heel. "I do not know, sir. He saw the dragon and went berserk."

"Is he mad?"

"Must be, sir."

"No, I am not mad," Caelan said in exasperation.

With a smirk the Thyzarene strolled into the palace, and Caelan stopped struggling. Reason was returning to him by degrees. He realized this must be a messenger, coming in with dispatches. He didn't care. He had seen Thyzarenes turned loose on helpless women and children. He would never forget it. He would never forgive.

"Sergeant Balter, take this man to detention and sort this out."

The sergeant saluted. "Yes, sir."

"Wait," said the officer in the gold cloak. He shouldered his way forward. "Who is this man?"

"New recruit, sir," Balter replied woodenly.

"He looks familiar. Who is he?"

The sergeant glanced at Caelan, still rigid with anger and embarrassment. "Speak your name, but nothing else," he said to Caelan.

Caelan faced the officer in gold. "I am Caelan E'non."

Recognition leaped into the man's eyes. "Of course. The champion of the games. I knew I had seen that speed and that sword swing before. So you've left the games."

"He has. Recruited to the Crimson Guard," Sergeant Balter said possessively.

"Freed?"

Caelan raised his chin. "Yes, sir."

The officer nodded. "Put this man with the other selections."

"But, Captain Vysal!" protested one of the officers in crimson. "He must go to detention. He's oblivious to discipline. He would have killed that messenger if he hadn't been stopped."

"Yes, General Paz, and a few days ago I saw him kill a Madrun in the arena," Vysal said, undaunted. "I want him among the selections."

"But he can't possibly be—"

"Is there a man in this army with his size and his speed?" Vysal demanded. "He's a ferocious fighter. You've seen him."

"He's a savage," the general said with disdain. "Untrained. Undisciplined. He doesn't belong in the Imperial Guard at all, Crimson or Gold."

Around him Caelan heard mutters of assent from the men, until the sergeant quelled them with a glare.

"Perhaps not," Vysal said. "But I intend to include him in the selections just the same. Sergeant."

Balter pulled his shoulders back and saluted, then signaled for the men to release Caelan. Scowling ferociously, Balter marched Caelan down the steps.

The dragon watched them go by with glowing eyes. It hissed, letting little sparks of flames curl through its pointed teeth.

Caelan's heart boiled. He glared back at it with equal savagery, ready to attack if he got the chance.

"Come on," Balter muttered. "You've caused enough trouble."

They went on, moving fast, and with every step Balter muttered more.

"I should have known. Those stripes on your back. If the trainers in the arenas couldn't handle you, I should have known you'd be a discipline problem from the first. And in front of General Paz, no less. But there'll be no more of your nonsense here."

"You said you valued spirit," Caelan retorted.

"Silence! A soldier who can't follow orders is useless. Useless! You do what you're told, nothing else."

Caelan set his jaw. "I will fight my enemies."

"The Thyzarenes are allies."

"Not to me."

"Personal vendettas have no place here. You will follow orders and you will carry them out. Nothing more, nothing less. You do not think on your own. You do not act on your own."

A muscle worked in Caelan's jaw, but he made no reply. He had no intention of complying with such nonsense. Not when it stood between him and what was right.

"The captain is mad to select you," Balter muttered, shoving Caelan over to the others, who were still standing on the parade ground where they'd been left. "You'll never be chosen to serve the empress. Never."

Caelan flicked him a resentful glance. "They killed my family," he said harshly. "They burned and pillaged. I saw them slit my father's throat."

"I don't care," Balter said, equally angry. "You made a fool out of me. Now the officers will think I can't control my own men. It's the lash you need, and the lash you'll have if you don't calm down and do as you're told. Stand here. And cause no more trouble. You understand?"

Seething, Caelan stepped onto the precise spot the sergeant was pointing to. "Yes, sir."

Chapter Seventeen

BY THE END of the week, the coronation festivities were but a memory and even an unexplained flurry of war councils had tapered off. Elandra was putting on her cloak and gloves to go riding, when a chancellor came to her chambers with a low bow.

"Majesty, the emperor summons your presence at once."

She nodded and turned to one of her ladies. "Please send word to the stables to dismiss my groom."

The woman curtsied and went out.

Elandra reached for the strings of her cloak. "A moment, if you please, sir, while I remove my cloak and gloves."

"Nay, Majesty, the day is cold and you will need them. The emperor awaits you in the armory."

She glanced up in quick anticipation, her heart speeding up. A dozen speculations ran through her mind, but she knew what this meant. Smiling, she said, "I am ready."

With the man to escort her, she hurried out of the palace and down the broad steps to the immense parade ground. Her guardsmen followed close.

It was an overcast day, gloomy and bitterly cold. Little pellets of sleet hit her face as she walked. She drew up her hood, huddling inside her fur-lined cloak, and wondered if winter would ever end. She hated the cold.

But at least on a dreary day like this she couldn't see the black cloud that stretched across the horizon. As an omen, it was bleak indeed. She tried not to think about it, yet what good did ignoring it do?

As for the rumors of a Madrun invasion, they had dwindled and were now dismissed as gossip among the courtiers. Tirhin had not been cast in prison, so Elandra supposed the whole matter had been a falsehood from the first. She was glad now she had not involved herself deeply.

The emperor had been busy and preoccupied. She had scarcely seen him since the coronation. It was as though she were a detail that had taken much of his attention for a time, but now could be dispensed with. Her life had changed little from the way it had been before the festivities, except she could come and go largely as she pleased.

But where was there to go? What was there to do?

She was angry at being barred from the council meetings when the chancellors came daily to advise the emperor. Thus far, her complaints had not been heeded.

Reaching the armory, she paused while the sentries saluted and opened the doors for her. Walking inside, she found the air damp and chilly, not much more welcoming than the outdoors. The chancellor left her with a bow, and she and her guardsmen walked up the twisting stone stairs to the upper gallery that overlooked the fighting arena. The air smelled of men's sweat, horse droppings, and tangy sawdust.

This was where she rode her horse when the weather permitted no other option. She found riding around the rectangular arena boring exercise, but it was better than nothing. Sometimes, the Imperial Guard trained in here.

When she reached the gallery, she saw Kostimon standing at the railing, gazing down at the activity below. Hovet, looking as sour-faced as ever, paced restlessly about with his hand resting on his sword hilt. Tirhin, handsomely dressed as always, stood near the emperor.

Surprised, Elandra paused. She had heard that Tirhin was in disgrace with his father, but evidently that was not true.

Lord Sien, looking bored, was also present. She felt distinctly uneasy at seeing him, and more than a little displeased. Choosing a protector was her business, not his. She did not want him here.

But she could not dismiss the man, and that irked her also.

Masking her emotions as best she could, she approached the party. Tirhin was the first to notice her arrival.

His expression was sullen, and he appeared to have lost weight. He was still pale, and he did not stand quite as straight as usual. He bowed to her, and she curtsied very slightly.

Hovet and Sien turned around, both bowing to her. She nodded her head in response and walked up to Kostimon.

"So the time has finally come," she said softly, not wishing to startle him.

He didn't look around. "Yes," he said.

Both of his hands were clamped on the railing. He seemed intent on watching the light skirmishing going on below, but at last his yellow eyes swung around to meet hers.

"It is a special day, when a protector is chosen," he said.

Over his shoulder she could see Hovet lift his chin proudly.

"Yes," she agreed.

"It must be someone to whom you can entrust your life," Kostimon went on. "Someone you will never doubt." He pointed at the arena. "Five men. See them? The officers have worked hard to winnow out all but the very best, in terms of intelligence, ability, and fighting prowess."

Her gaze ran over the men shifting about constantly on the sand. The pattern of their grappling confused her, but she did not wish to show it.

"And I, Majesty," Sien said from behind her, "have brought truth-light by which to seal your choice."

She forced herself to give the man a glance of courtesy. "Thank you," she replied. "That is extra assurance, which I shall need."

Her gaze moved to Hovet, and she gestured for him to come closer. He frowned nervously and approached, eying the emperor as he did so.

"You can give me the most practical advice," she said, smiling at him in hopes of thawing his icy heart just a little. "What should I look for? What qualities should I expect?"

For a moment Hovet looked almost human. He softened visibly and his chest puffed out a bit. Nodding, he said, "Look at them, and I'll show your Majesty. See, now, they're all good men. Quick on their feet, well muscled. Look at those two, circling. See how when one moves, the other anticipates him? That's what you need, Majesty. A man with instincts and the good sense to act on them. Someone who talks himself out of his own intuition is no good at your back."

"I see." Fascinated, Elandra watched a moment.

Hovet pointed. "That big one, over there. The tallest one, see? Now he's got good reach on him. But maybe he won't move as fast as a more compact man. No, he's quick. Look at that!"

A flurry broke out, and one of the men was thrown to the ground. Elandra watched intently, wishing she understood what she was seeing.

"Well done!" the emperor called out.

The tall man glanced up, and Elandra blinked. Disbelieving, she leaned a little farther over the railing. He looked like the Traulander slave, the man who had begged her to get him an audience with the emperor. But it couldn't be.

"Yes, Majesty, it is," Lord Sien said softly over her shoulder.

Startled, she turned around and found the priest much too close. His deep-set eyes were gleaming as though at a joke.

He nodded. "Yes, that is the man."

Wondering anew if the priest could read minds, she frowned at him. "What do you mean?"

"We have been talking about that man," Sien said smoothly. "He looks very like Prince Tirhin's gladiator. We are curious to see the man more closely."

Now she did not have to pretend she was bewildered, for she truly was. "I do not understand. How could a gladiator be among our guardsmen?"

At her question, the emperor chuckled. Prince Tirhin turned red and swung away from the rest of them.

Elandra frowned. "Are they not drawn from the elite of our fighting forces? Or have I been misled?"

Her voice was sharper than she intended, but she didn't care. She was suspicious of all of them now.

"No, Majesty," said a new voice, one she did not immediately recognize.

Vysal, captain of her guard, walked into the gallery and bowed to them. Wearing his gold cloak, with her coat of arms half-hidden on his sleeve, he walked forward with a faint swagger common to military men.

"All of these candidates are members of the Guard," he said to her.

Kostimon turned around to stare at the man. "Are the men ready?"

"Yes, Majesty," Captain Vysal said respectfully.

Kostimon grunted. "The last time I chose a protector, I had the old one fight the candidates, one at a time. The one who defeated him took his place." He tossed a grin at Hovet, who was looking grim again. "That was Hovet, who has been at my side ever since."

"Is that what you wish?" the captain asked. "Some kind of trial by combat?"

"No," Elandra said quickly before the emperor could reply. "I prefer to talk to the men, one at a time."

The men exchanged glances, and Kostimon scowled.

"Talk!" he said impatiently. "Ela, for Gault's sake. That's no way to choose a protector."

"Why not?" she asked. "If they are all equally good at fighting, and equally intelligent, how am I to choose among them, save one I feel I can trust?"

"Don't forget, Majesty," Sien said smoothly, "that I have the truth-light to determine who you can trust."

"It must be my judgment. No one else's," she said with growing vehemence. "How am I to judge if I cannot see them for myself?"

The prince murmured something too soft for her to hear, but Kostimon heard it. His face darkened.

"Tirhin!" he snapped, and the prince widened his eyes in feigned innocence. "If you cannot be useful, you may leave us," the emperor said.

Tirhin bowed, but did not depart.

Kostimon glared at his son for a long, tense moment before he returned his gaze to Elandra. "Very well," he said grouchily. "If you must, do so. But I do not like it."

She smiled at him. "May Hovet accompany me?"

"I would rather Hovet fought them!" Kostimon snapped.

Something flashed through the protector's eyes, and Elandra felt a moment of pity for him. Hovet was old, a man clearly struggling to maintain his usefulness. How he must fear that any day Kostimon would decide to replace him with a younger, stronger man.

"Please," she said.

"Bah!" Kostimon said, but he gave Hovet a curt nod.

Hovet seemed reluctant to leave him, but he followed Elandra down the steps and into the arena. Her guards trailed behind them.

Picking up her skirts slightly to keep them out of the dirt, she approached the soldiers, who were swiftly lined up by the sergeants.

Not exactly sure how to go about her inspection, Elandra copied her father's manner of stopping before each man and staring at him openly, rudely, almost combatively.

The first man was brawny and built square, with massive shoulders like a bull's. He was also hairy and coarse, with a thick, brutish face she disliked instantly.

The second man looked competent and well bred, but his face was cold and impassive. She gestured at one of the sergeants.

"Walk him back and forth, please."

It was as though she were buying a horse, or a slave. There was an insult implied in her request, and the man did not completely succeed in masking his flash of resentment.

Tight-lipped, eyes straight ahead, he strode past her, then came back again and resumed his place in line. He moved well, but he was angry. She did not want a man who detested her standing always at her back.

The third man had curly hair and a square, open face. His eyes twinkled, although he kept his demeanor impassive according to regulations. He was built strong and straight. He might do very well.

The fourth man was still sweating, although the others were beginning to dry out after their exertions. His gaze shifted warily when she stopped to stare at him. He seemed nervous.

The fifth man towered over her, blond, deeply tanned, and blue-eyed. It was Caelan E'non, the slave who had tried to choke her, who had insulted her, who had pleaded with her. His fancy gold slavery chain no longer hung around his neck. Clean-shaven, his face free of soot and dried mud, his hair sleeked back from his face, he looked handsome today . . . too handsome.

She glanced away, biting her lip in consternation. She must not permit herself thoughts like that.

Steeling herself, she met his eyes. They were wary but unafraid. A predator's eyes, she reminded herself, and shivered.

She wanted to ask him how he had changed fortunes so quickly, but she could not without giving away the fact that she had previously met him. That she was not prepared to do. Her questions had to remain unspoken.

She struggled to think of something else. "Sergeant, please have this man walk for me."

Caelan moved obediently, his long limbs graceful and quick, like a panther's. If he felt shamed by her examination, he did not show it. He seemed indifferent, as though long ago he had reconciled himself to certain indignities. Or perhaps as a champion gladiator, he was used to being stared at and judged.

His face was lean and chiseled of feature. She found herself studying the straight line of his brows, the slant of his cheekbones, the firmness of his chin. How fair he was, yet how completely masculine.

Again she had to look away, annoyed with herself.

She turned abruptly and walked away from them, then remembered she had Hovet with her.

Flustered, she started over, picking out the three men who had caught her eye and dismissing the two she disliked. "Hovet?" she asked.

With a respectful nod, he moved past her and walked up to the cold, resentful man. Hovet looked old and a little stooped in comparison to these young soldiers, but he was still tough, still a warrior with more experience under his belt than they would ever know.

"Name?" Hovet asked.

The cold man answered, "Thal Brintel."

"Lord Brintel's son?"

The man's eyes flickered with another muted flash of resentment. "A younger son, sir."

Hovet pursed his lips and moved to the curly-headed man with the twinkling eyes. "Name?"

"Rander Malk," the man replied. His voice was sunny and assured. He almost smiled as he answered.

"Coastal-born, are you?"

Rander blinked, then did smile. "Aye, I am."

Hovet grunted and moved to the Traulander. He squinted up at the man. "Name?"

"Caelan E'non."

It was said evenly, but with a touch of pride. She saw the unconscious lift of his chin, the squaring of his shoulders, the quirk of defiance at the corner of his mouth. He was probably used to hearing cheers every time his name was mentioned.

Elandra sniffed to herself. She would not compete with her protector for attention.

"Traulander?" Hovet barked.

"Yes."

"What made you leave the games for the service?"

Caelan's attention focused hard on the man. Warily he replied, "A chance to fight for honor rather than entertainment."

The other men stirred slightly, and even Elandra was

impressed by the honesty of Caelan's answer. This was a complex man, not easy to handle, and far too good-looking.

She did not trust her own interest, or the way her pulse quickened when she merely stood within a short distance of him. He reminded her of the mysterious lover in her dreams, and she liked that least of all.

"Majesty?" Hovet asked. "Will you have them spar again?"

She hesitated, her gaze sweeping the three candidates. Then she shook her head. "No. Have them cleaned up and brought to the gallery in a few minutes."

Turning her back on them, she left the arena and found she was walking a little too fast, breathing a little too rapidly. Her hands were sweating inside her gloves.

She hurried up the spiral of steps, although there was no need to go so fast, and rejoined her husband with a sense of having returned to refuge.

"Well?" he asked her. "What do you think? You were quick in making the initial cut."

"I must consider."

Kostimon smiled at her indulgently and patted her clenched hand. "Take your time, my dear."

She looked away. She did not want to be patted and patronized. But this was no time to indulge in bad temper.

"Hovet?" the emperor asked. "What did you think of them?"

The protector shrugged. "I could take any of them in a fight."

"Of course," Kostimon agreed, suppressing a smile. "That's not the point, is it?"

Hovet shrugged. "She'll make a good decision."

He stalked away, and Kostimon smiled at Elandra. "Cold weather makes him grouchy. His bones ache, as do mine."

She was immediately concerned. "Are you chilled? Am I taking too long?"

"Hush, my child. Hush," he said, waving away her questions. "It is of no importance. I am in a tolerant mood. We have driven back our enemies, and all is well."

She looked at him, dying to shower him with questions, but he held up his finger.

"No, I will not discuss it. All is well. That is sufficient for you to know."

She settled back in her chair, trying not to be petulant. So the invasion had failed. She could not help glancing at Tirhin, but he was toying morosely with his dagger and did not look up.

Captain Vysal cleared his throat to gain her attention. "The men are here, Majesty."

Kostimon gestured, and Hovet immediately went on the alert, hovering discreetly a short distance away. Led by their stern-faced sergeant, the three candidates filed into the gallery and stood at attention in the same order as before. They now wore crimson tunics and plain breastplates. Their helmets were tucked under their right elbows, with their hands resting on their empty sword scabbards. They had not been permitted to come armed into the presence of the emperor. Their chins jutted at the correct angle, and their eyes were focused on the distance. They looked well trained and ready to serve.

"Your decision, my dear," Kostimon said.

Lord Sien walked forward to hover directly behind her. She felt a chill touch her spine and wished he would move where she could see him.

"Majesty, shall I use the truth-light now?" the priest asked.

Of the three, only Caelan E'non showed the slightest reaction.

She noticed and wondered why he should care.

Tirhin had risen to his feet. He glared at Caelan, who returned his gaze impassively, without shame, without appeasement.

Elandra remembered the Traulander's anguish only a few days ago, when he had been torn between duty and a personal sense of loyalty to the prince.

She needed loyalty. Above all things, she needed that.

Her father had told her to confound the others with her choice, to do the unexpected.

Lord Sien had urged her to pick from any province save that of Gialta.

Prince Tirhin was standing rigidly, his fists clenched at his sides while his father smiled benignly at the entire situation.

Elandra sensed dangerous crosscurrents around her. Angers and resentments smoldering beneath the surface.

She wanted the Traulander. He was the best fighter because he was arena trained. That alone made him more ruthless, more dangerous than the others. He was loyal, perhaps to extremes. He was fierce, as fierce as Hovet any day. He was strong, with incredible stamina, and he healed quickly. He had been a champion, which meant he was a survivor, yet he possessed integrity and honesty. He was intelligent and perhaps sensitive. There was nothing of the brute in him, although his manners needed work.

He was ideal for her purposes, but she dared not select him. For one thing, he had belonged to Tirhin only a few days ago. She did not understand whether the prince had sold him or freed him or why, but she suspected from the look on Tirhin's face that it had not been by choice. Tirhin already considered her his enemy and direct rival. She did not wish to fuel the flames of his resentment.

Besides, she was extremely disconcerted by her personal reaction to Caelan E'non today. Disconcerted and angry. Passion was not a quality she expected to find in herself. She would not permit it to exist if she could not feel it for her husband.

No, Caelan was too dangerous, in too many ways.

Without further hesitation, she looked at the curly-headed man. "I choose Rander Malk."

Rander's mouth dropped open in disbelief, only to spread wide in a grin.

Thal Brintel sneered, hooding his eyes but not before she saw contempt in their depths, mingled with a dose of self-pity. She was glad to be rid of him.

Caelan E'non was looking at Tirhin; then his gaze brushed against hers and again she felt oddly breathless. He nodded to her very slightly, and it was like a tiny salute of respect and acceptance.

That, more than anything else, reassured her that she had done the right thing.

Then all was confusion. The sergeant hustled the others away, leaving Rander Malk with only his captain for support. Rander looked overwhelmed and delighted. He could not stop grinning.

When she rose to her feet and walked over to speak to him, he bowed deeply to her.

"My lady—Majesty," he stammered. "I am honored. I will serve you till death. I swear it."

She returned his smile, gratified by his eagerness, but held up her hand. "The truth-light first. Lord Sien?"

The priest gathered a shimmering ball of unearthly light in his palm, then tossed it at the suddenly serious Rander. The light shimmered down over the soldier and spilled in a radiant glow at his feet.

"He is true, Majesty," Sien said.

She nodded and held out her hand to Rander, who knelt and kissed her fingers clumsily. But all the while, she was thinking of a tall, kingly man with blue eyes who was walking away from her at this moment, a man who would have served her beyond duty and ordinary courage, a man who might have given her his heart and his soul.

She wanted to change her mind and call him back, but she couldn't, not with Rander kneeling at her feet and humbly swearing his oath of allegiance. Not with her aged husband standing beside her with a benign smile of approval.

Chapter Eighteen

A STRANGE NOISE awakened Elandra from the depths of sleep. It was a soft susurration of sound, like the rubbing of cloth across a hard surface, almost inaudible, yet unusual enough to have pricked through the layers of her sleep. At the same time she also became conscious of a disturbing warmth against her chest.

She stirred, burrowing her face deeper against her pillow, and slitted one eye open.

A strange golden glow shone from beneath her, reflecting off the pale surfaces of her pillow and bedclothes.

Puzzled and only semiawake, she groped for the jewel pouch hanging around her neck. When her fingers closed on it, she was startled by its warmth. It was as though the jewel had taken on a life of its own. The light glowing from it spilled through the drawn top of the pouch and grew increasingly brighter.

Elandra raised her head and yawned, wondering what magic was working on the jewel.

Just then, she heard a slight scrape of the bed curtain rings upon the brass rod fitted to the canopy of her bed.

Elandra rolled over and saw a shadow looming over her.

It was like nothing she had ever seen before. In that split second of frozen time, she saw it clearly in the unearthly light cast by the topaz. It was the shadow of a man, yet only the shadow. There was no man standing there to cast it. Dark and opaque, it was thin enough to look almost invisible when viewed from the side.

Elandra opened her mouth, but with impossible quickness it surged closer, engulfing her.

Its ghostly fingers reached for the cord around her neck.

Elandra screamed and flailed against it, trying to drive it back. But her hands passed through it as though it was made of air.

She screamed again, rolling away from its unearthly touch, but it snagged the cord in its fingers and held fast.

She did not know how it could do so, but this was not a time to question what she was witnessing. The tug of the cord around her throat frightened her, and she suddenly feared this creature meant to strangle her.

She screamed a third time, but its dark fingers dug instead inside the pouch for the topaz.

"No!" Elandra shouted, but a burst of light shot forth from the jewel, filling the interior of her bed and almost blinding her.

She heard a scream inside her head, scree-thin and horrifying.

The shadow dropped the pouch. The topaz was blazing now, and Elandra cupped her hand protectively over it as she scrambled back.

She seized pillows and flung them at the shadow, only to see them pass harmlessly through it. Then she was tumbling off the opposite side of the bed, landing in an awkward tangle on the floor, as frightened as she was furious.

Where was her protector?

"Majesty!" Rander cried, crashing into the room. Holding a lamp aloft with one hand, he ripped open the bed curtains just as she picked herself up and came around to the foot of the bed.

"Rander, take care!" she tried to warn him.

The lamp fell from his hands, shattering on the floor and spilling burning oil across the carpets. Little flames danced up like imps, reaching for the floor-length bed curtains. One blazed with a sudden whoosh of fire up to the canopy.

Rander went stumbling back from the bed with the shadow on top of him. It had him by the throat, and he grunted in increasing desperation, hurling himself about in an effort to throw it off.

Chairs went crashing as he flailed and fought.

"Rander!" she called in horror.

The protector staggered and dropped to his knees, gasping and wheezing. Elandra ran for the door, wondering where her ladies were, wondering where the guards were; then she ran back toward him, her long hair flying.

Rander had drawn his dagger, but the weapon had no effect on the shadow that perched on his chest. His body convulsed violently, then went slack. The dagger fell from his fingers.

"No!" Elandra cried.

She dodged the flames that were now roaring in the middle of a fine carpet and knelt at his side. Taking the jewel pouch in both hands, she pulled open the top and touched the topaz to the shadow.

Again she heard that thin scream in her mind. It flew off Rander and went sliding across the floor, flowing up one wall with liquid rapidity.

Elandra bent over Rander, gripping his sleeve. But his protruding tongue and staring eyes told her she had not been quick enough to save him. Protector less than a day, dead already in her service.

"No!" she cried, shaking him although she knew it was futile. "Please, no!"

The shadow leaped onto her back, clinging cold and surprisingly heavy. She nearly fell across Rander from the impact of its landing and caught herself just in time.

The cord around her neck drew tight, and in a panic she twisted around to thrust the topaz at it.

The shadow sprang off her and flowed away.

An eerie sound from behind her made her spin around, crouching low even as she picked up Rander's dagger.

More shadows spread into the room through the open doorway, sliding across the floor, half-seen against the leaping flames and thickening smoke.

Coughing, Elandra crept backward until her back bumped against the wall. The shadows converged on her, driving her down one side of the room toward the doorway leading to the secret passageway. She thought about plunging into it, realized how easily these things could trap her in the narrow, unlit space, and shuddered in fear. Better to stay here in the smoke and the fire, where she could at least see these things.

One leaped at her, but she fended it off by holding the topaz aloft. The jewel's fierce glow spread around her like a golden nimbus, protecting her. Its heat nearly burned her hand, but she dared not drop it.

She worked her way back across the room, dodging the fire as best she could, until she reached her clothes chest. Throwing open the lid with one hand, she rummaged swiftly for a gown, shoes, and the golden cloak given her by the Mahirans.

As she pulled it forth, the shadows shrank back, fleeing to the corners of the room.

Elandra tossed the cloak swiftly about her shoulders, ducked her head against the stinging smoke, and fled.

They pursued her, silent and terrifying, moving quicker than thought. Yet the next time one leaped at her, it bounced off the cloak and shriveled to nothing.

Heart pounding in satisfaction, Elandra whirled around defiantly to face the remainder. "Get back from me, things of hell!" she cried, brandishing the glowing topaz. "I am not your prey."

The shadows fell back as though they understood her threat, and Elandra turned and ran again.

None of her ladies-in-waiting were to be found anywhere in her chambers. And when she burst out into the main passageway, she found her guards slumped on the floor. Dead or unconscious, she had no time to find out.

She stepped over them and looked both ways. In the distance she heard shouts. Her heart leaped with hope, but then she realized they were not sounds of imminent rescue but instead sounds of battle.

Smoke poured from the doorway behind her, reminding her she must not linger.

She brandished her topaz at the shadows following her, and they seemed reluctant to venture forth into the lit passageway. Seizing her opportunity to escape, Elandra ran full tilt past the throne room, where flames were licking around the edges of the doors as though a fire had been started inside it also.

The lamps were not lit in the passageway ahead of her, and she slowed down, renewed fear making her cautious.

Shouting men stormed along a cross-passageway, brandishing torches and drawn swords. They looked foreign, barbaric.

Elandra flinched back, pressing herself against the wall. To her relief, none of them noticed her. But it had been a close call, and her heart would not stop pounding. She dared not continue forward, but she feared to turn back.

Who were those men? Hadn't Kostimon boasted to her only hours ago that the invading Madruns had been turned back?

"Majesty," whispered a voice from behind her.

She whirled around with a muffled cry, only to sag with

relief at the sight of one of her guardsmen. He was missing his helmet, and his gold cloak was ripped and stained, but he was an ally.

She ran to him, grateful. "Take me to the emperor, at once."

"Not this way," he replied, his eyes darting back and forth on the alert. "Come, I must get you to the stables."

He hurried her back the way she'd come, then pulled her down a short flight of steps into the servants' corridor. They wound through a series of seemingly endless passageway, sometimes using the main ways, sometimes the servants'.

After several minutes, when Elandra was quite breathless from keeping up with his loping stride, the guardsman abruptly turned and pushed her into the scant protection of a doorway. She stood there beside him, trembling, her gown and shoes still clutched in her arms, and listened to the sounds of approaching men.

He touched her arm lightly. When she looked up, he put his finger to his lips.

He was very grim as he drew his sword, taking care to make no sound. "I'm sorry," he mouthed to her.

She realized he meant to confront the band approaching. He would fight them, outnumbered, to give her a chance to run. She wanted to weep for his courage, but she could not indulge in her emotions now. She must not waste the gift of his life. She must be ready to run faster than she had ever run before.

His hand gripped her arm above the elbow, tightening too hard. Both tense, they waited.

Then the men were upon them, striding hard and purposefully.

The guardsman shoved Elandra so hard she stumbled and nearly fell, and flung himself in the path of the men.

"Hold!" snapped a voice. "We're friends, you fool."

"My lady, wait!"

But Elandra was already spinning around, breathless with relief to see the red cloaks of the Imperial Guard looming out of the shadows. Their swords were bloody. Their eyes were blazing and brutal.

Her guardsman spoke to them rapidly, reporting to the sergeant in command. He pointed at Elandra, who returned to his side with as much dignity as she could muster.

"I must be at the side of the emperor," she said, making her voice sound far more steady and assured than she really was. "What has happened?"

"We've no time to waste on this. Reinforcements must be got through to the eastern side of the palace," the sergeant said, his gaze sliding past her impatiently to the guardsman. "Can you get us there?"

"Aye, but I'm responsible for her Majesty."

The sergeant scowled. "Where's the protector?"

His impatience angered Elandra. She glared at him. "My protector is dead, killed defending my life."

Their eyes flickered, and for a moment they were human beings again, chastened and respectful.

"Damned savages," the sergeant muttered. "We'll have to split up—"

Another group of guardsmen joined them, taut and wild-looking, bringing some of their wounded with them.

"Move on!" one shouted. "We're falling back. The central part of the palace is lost. They've started to loot now."

Horror spread across every face, and Elandra shared the shame and impotent fury all of them were feeling. To have barbarians in the palace that had stood untouched for nearly a thousand years was a desecration, a nightmare that could not be believed and yet was happening.

"Majesty!" said an accented voice that made her head snap around.

She looked and saw a man pushing his way through the soldiers, head and shoulders above the other men, his blue eyes vivid in the silhouette of his face.

"Caelan!" she said in relief, feeling safe for the first time tonight. "Give me your aid in reaching my husband."

"She cannot fall into their hands. She must be protected," the sergeant said, turning about to see who Caelan was. He grunted and jerked his head in an unspoken command.

Caelan stepped clear of the others, and they marched on.

The guardsman in gold lingered behind only to bow to her. "Please, Majesty, give me leave to fight."

"Go," she said.

He saluted her and swung around after the departing men, giving Caelan one quick, meaningful glance as though to pass his responsibility into Caelan's hands.

She faced the Traulander, who was alert, standing high, his nostrils quivering and his eyes keen and bright. He loved this, she realized. The danger, the excitement, the threat of combat . . . these all combined to bring him alive.

"Is the palace truly lost?" she asked, unable to believe it still.

"It will be soon," he replied. "We were betrayed. Someone let them in, and they gained a stranglehold before the alarm was sounded."

Elandra drew in a sharp breath, angry and shamed. "Tirhin?"

He nodded, looking grim. "I saw him leading the opposing forces. The emperor fell back twice, cursing him before gods and men, trying to hold."

"The emperor has not been taken?" she asked in sudden fear.

"No," Caelan said grimly. "He has been persuaded to save himself, in order that we can regroup the army elsewhere."

"But to leave the palace—"

"It has to be done, and you must hurry if you're not to be left behind as part of the spoils."

She glared at him, outraged that he would even think it, much less say it, but she didn't protest. There wasn't time for an argument.

He gripped her elbow through her cloak, only to release her in startlement. He frowned, started to touch the magic cloth again, then did not.

"It comes from Mahira," she said. "It has a protective spell on it. I am surprised you could feel it. No one else has."

"I can do many things most cannot," he said grimly. "Have you shoes?"

"Yes."

"Put them on. We'll be outside in a moment, if the gods favor us. Put your gown on too, over your nightclothes."

She knew he was right. Hurriedly she crammed her bare feet into her shoes. "Help me."

"Better that I should stand guard," he said, and retreated a short distance from her. "Hurry."

Mouthing a curse to herself, she slipped off her cloak and pulled the gown over her head. It was awkward, doing this alone, not because she was incapable of dressing herself but because the gown's design made it difficult to handle the lacings alone. It did not fit well over her sleeping robes, but she shook the folds of the skirt down impatiently and put on her cloak again.

"Ready," she said, trying to braid her hair so it wouldn't fly into her face.

He turned to look at her over his shoulder. Wreathed in shadow, his face concealed, he stood tall and formidable in his long cloak and breastplate, the sword shifting alertly in his strong grip. His long hair swung free about his shoulders, and she could feel danger radiating from him, directed not at her but at any potential foe, a savage readiness to attack and rend.

Was it fate that continued to cross her path with his? Or something else?

This was not the time to seek answers to those questions. She trusted him to protect her; that was all that mattered.

"Come," he said.

She joined his side, feeling reassured by his size. "There is something else you should know."

"Hurry," he said, striding forward.

She had to trot to keep up. "There are forces of the darkness at work here tonight."

That got his attention. He stopped in mid-step and stared at her. "Explain."

She described the shadows and how they had killed Rander and attacked her. "If you have any special means of protection from the gods you believe in, I beg you will call on it. We have more enemies than just the Madruns."

He was scowling, his eyes deep in thought. Almost absently he touched the throat of his breastplate in the manner of a man who wears an amulet. "Who calls forth the shadows?" he wondered aloud. "Who commands them?"

"I know not. Indeed, I will never see a man's shadow again and feel safe."

Caelan's brows knotted tighter, but he speculated no further. He seemed suddenly remote from her, as though he had stepped into a place where she could not follow.

He reached out and gripped her hand hard in his. It was a liberty that ordinarily she would not have permitted. Right now, however, it was a reassuring link from one human being to another. She gripped back just as tightly.

"No matter what, you must stay close to me," he said, his voice colder and harsher than usual. "You must follow orders, on the instant, with no hesitation, no argument."

She felt breathless with fear. Fighting the cowardly urge to retreat, she forced herself to nod. "I will," she promised.

"Then come." And he strode forward again.

Chapter Nineteen

WITH THE HAND of Empress Elandra clamped firmly in his, Caelan pushed himself deeper into *severance* to heighten his senses, but also to protect himself against the distraction she presented.

He hurried her along the passageway, questing constantly for trouble, more aware than she of how much danger they were in. She obviously believed the palace was still held by the guards, but Caelan knew differently. Most of the Imperial Guard on duty inside the palace itself were now dead, killed by poison or in savage hand-to-hand fighting.

Worst of all were the traitors, guardsmen who had joined Tirhin at the last minute, turning unexpectedly on their comrades to slay them before running to the ranks of the Madruns. At this stage, it was nearly impossible to tell friend from foe. Many of the traitors wore the empress's gold colors, and a few minutes before when Caelan had seen her standing trustingly next to a Gold guardsman, his heart had stopped. He expected to see her die of a quick knife thrust then and there, but the man had been loyal. He might well be the last loyal Gold alive.

So much betrayal . . . with every stride, Caelan's fury beat harder. Who had convinced the emperor the Madrun invaders had been turned back? Who had told him such lies? And why had the emperor believed them despite clear warnings?

The truth was, the Madruns had swept across the borders exactly as Tirhin had worked out. All the daily dispatches received by the emperor this week, including those brought by the Thyzarene, held false reports, which meant this plot had pervaded the government in every corner of the empire.

Kostimon's throne had seemed secure, but it wasn't. How many men had plotted with Tirhin, silently shifting over to his side while concealing their change of loyalties? Who had counseled the emperor to be merciful toward his son and not punish him for his betrayal?

That night in the dungeons, the emperor had believed what Caelan told him. Caelan had seen it in the man's eyes. Moreover, the emperor knew his son had conspired years before, in an earlier, abortive plot. Yet this week he did not even attempt to punish Tirhin, much less stop him. Gault above, how many warnings did a man require before he would listen?

It was like the last days of E'nonhold again, when Caelan had begged his father to arm the hold and stand prepared in case of attack. Ample warnings of Thyzarene raiding had come, but Beva E'non wouldn't listen. And in the end, everyone in the hold had been either slaughtered or carried off into slavery by the Thyzarenes.

Now it was the same thing happening again, only on a bigger scale.

Caelan felt his emotions surging up, threatening his control. He swore beneath his breath. He could not think about the past, and should not think about the present. What mattered right now was getting out of here alive.

He saw fire raging ahead, blocking the passageway. Caelan turned back to take another route. He did not know his way well, but he had a good sense of direction even in this maze of rooms and passages. He did not fear becoming lost.

Indeed, he must not fail his duties tonight, for entrusted to him by the fates was the largest responsibility he had known since he abandoned his little sister at the ice caves.

Caelan glanced down at the empress, hurrying breathlessly along at his side. She must be tiring, but she did not complain. There was fear in her face, but courage also. He noticed the dagger she clutched, and he admired her determination to survive.

Even now he still felt like the biggest fool alive for how he'd acted toward her the other day in Agel's quarters. Like an idiot, he had refused to believe she was the empress, when he knew nothing about it. And then to come face to face with her again the day she chose a protector . . . he had been mortified with no means of apologizing to her. She could have destroyed him that day with a word of complaint to the emperor, but she did not.

She had not chosen him as her protector either, but that had been a relief. He would have felt obliged to crawl on his belly for her forgiveness, and he did not want that. He'd swallowed enough humiliations for a lifetime. Nor did he have any wish to be a lapdog protector tagging at the heels of his mistress. All he wanted was to be a simple soldier, fighting the enemy, far from intrigues and hidden motives.

Still, despite everything, here she was in his keeping tonight. His fear was like a lump of ice in his gut. What if he failed to save her, the way he'd failed Lea?

He'd seen the relief and trust in her Majesty's eyes when he'd walked up tonight. In that moment he had felt a strange weakness flood his loins, and he would have lain down his life for hers.

It was strange, this desire to guard and protect her. He had felt nothing akin to this since he'd lost Lea, and yet this woman was completely unlike his sister.

It was not really for the sake of her beauty. He had seen beautiful faces before. Nor did it have much to do with how fierce her eyes could be one moment or how vulnerable they turned the next.

No, it was her courage he admired. Her steely determination. Her resolute ability to face facts, no matter how unpleasant. She did not wail and weep, wringing her hands and demanding rescue.

Somehow she had fought off the attack of the shadows, and she had searched until she found men to help her. She was far from helpless, and he valued that more than he could describe.

Besides, above all else, she was empress sovereign, ruler of this land after the emperor himself. She could not be lost, must not be lost. She represented order and stability. Along with the emperor, she *was* the empire. And as such, she constituted its most precious resource.

But why was he the only one who realized it?

Caelan's anger boiled hotter, and he quickened his pace until she was almost running to keep up.

"Please," she said, panting.

His gaze flicked to hers. "Your pardon," he murmured, and slowed down for a moment, only to unconsciously speed up again as his sense of urgency grew.

He had seen the panicky chancellors milling around; had seen the emperor protest one last time, then give in to their entreaties with an expression of bleak despair. Even now the man was probably mounting his horse at the stables, seizing his final opportunity to escape this carnage, with no thought at all for the wife he was leaving behind.

Not once had Elandra's name been mentioned in all the chaos. Not once had Caelan overheard the emperor ask about her. Was the man that shallow, that selfish, that he could forget her?

Caelan's fingers tightened on hers. It was insupportable, this cowardice, and he vowed that he would not let the emperor abandon her.

"Hurry," he urged her when she flagged.

She nodded, looking pale with fatigue, and quickened her pace obediently again.

They hastened down a flight of stairs and rounded a corner, only to come face to face with a small band of roving Madruns.

Caelan plunged to a halt so abruptly the empress bumped into him. He ignored her, ignored how she involuntarily clutched at his sleeve with a tiny gasp.

Dismay surged into his throat like sour bile. He hadn't heard these three, hadn't even sensed them. Were they shielded within some kind of spell, that they could pass like shadows?

They looked equally startled. The Madruns wore heavy leather breastplates and loin straps. Their bare legs were black with dried mire to the knees, and their weapons and arms were splattered with blood and gore. With their filed teeth and red eyes, clustered there in the gloom of the badly lit passageway, they were creatures from a nightmare.

Everyone stood momentarily frozen; then the Madruns' gazes fell on Elandra, and they grinned.

The primal lust in their savage faces enraged Caelan. He shoved the empress back from him, hard enough to almost overbalance her, and faced them with both his sword and dagger drawn.

Gathering up her skirts, Elandra scrambled back up the steps to give him maneuvering room. He had one last glimpse of her white, fearful face before he gave all his attention to the Madruns.

They shrilled out war cries and attacked together, three against one. Undaunted by the odds, Caelan threw his dagger, quick and hard. It hit its target in the foremost man's eye, quivering there as it penetrated his brain.

Screaming, the Madrun fell back, momentarily blocking the progress of the other two. Caelan charged them, swinging his sword up and across in a swipe that just missed decapitating the one on the left. Following through with his swing, he aimed it at the second man, who ducked and stumbled back with a howl.

Caelan stepped back in a half-pivot and parried the sword of the man on his left, now bleeding copiously from the wound at the base of his neck. Caelan hopped nimbly over the body of the fallen Madrun and forced his opponents down the stairs with a brutal, driving attack.

The passageway was too narrow for him to use his sword to its fullest extent. Hampered by the close quarters and lack of sufficient maneuvering room, he had to adjust his swing to avoid nicking his blade on the stone walls. However, neither could the Madruns circle behind him the way they so obviously wanted. He knew well their pattern of attack fighting: outnumber, surround, and maul.

The Madruns were equipped with shorter swords, designed for thrusting and fighting hand to hand. Under Caelan's attack, they fell back once more, then held their position shoulder to shoulder before him. Caelan fought them together, his blows driven by the sense of time running out. Every moment he delayed here kept him from his objective and put the empress in greater danger of being left behind.

His longer reach enabled him to finally slide over the guard of the bleeding man on the left. Caelan's sword ripped open the man's chest. The Madrun croaked out a final incomprehensible word of defiance, probably a curse, and fell.

The remaining one screamed defiance and charged, but Caelan had seen that move before. He ducked recklessly under the man's arm and spitted him full length on his sword.

The Madrun's eyes flew open wide. He stared at Caelan in disbelief; then blood filled his mouth, and he sank into death.

Caelan pulled free his sword and wiped it clean on the man's back.

Straightening, breathing hard, he slung sweat from his eyes and glanced over his shoulder.

His eyes met those of the girl's. Hers were clear, horrified, and steady.

"Come," he said.

She hurried to him, sidestepping the dead men without hesitation, and took his hand again. "Well done," she said, and only the breathlessness of her voice betrayed how fearful she'd been.

It was a warrior's compliment she gave, and her understated praise pleased him. He wondered where she had learned to do that. Perhaps from her warlord father. Perhaps she, alone of all the women he had met, understood what it meant to glory in the combat, yet to suffer for the aftermath of death and silence.

"We must hurry" was all he said as he swung away from the fallen men. He would not grieve for this enemy.

Together, he and the empress hastened onward.

A few minutes later, he pushed through a door and stumbled outside into the darkness. Barrels, stone amphoras, and casks filled the area. Dragging in a deep breath, Caelan looked around to get his bearings. They were somewhere along the rear of the palace, on the northwestern side, close to the delivery entrances for provisions. The mighty walls of the compound towered above him, seemingly invincible, their dark sides reaching up to the inky sky.

But no matter how thick or how high the walls, if the gates were opened, they counted not at all.

Caelan swung left, pulling her after him. "This way," he whispered.

They ran down an alley stacked with barrels and crates, half-seen obstacles in the darkness.

At the corner, however, torchlight flared orange in the distance, and behind them tongues of fire began to lick at upper-story windows.

Caelan plunged to a halt and peered around the corner. The parade ground stretched out ahead of him on his left, a vast distance filled with a melee of fighting men. The sight heartened him. If the Guard could hold the Madruns here, there was a chance of regaining the palace.

But right now, that was not his concern. He swung his gaze right, toward the stables, and saw bunches of Madruns trotting past. Fire could be seen blazing through the windows, and there came the neighs of panicked horses.

Elandra clutched at his cloak, her shoulder brushing against his armored back. "You said the stables," she told him. "How can we reach them?"

Caelan shook his head. "Too late. The emperor is gone."

"But—"

A wave of sudden exhaustion, borne by defeat, rolled over him. He pushed it off and measured the distance to the stables with his eye, only to swear in frustration. Impossible to get there with so many of the enemy around.

"I will leave you here," he said, thinking aloud. "If I can get a horse, there is still—"

"No," the empress said firmly. "They will kill you."

"But—"

"Look at the main gates," she said, pointing. "Can we ride through them even if you did get horses?"

He turned his head and saw the massive bronze gates shining in the light of the bonfires and burning barracks. A group of guardsmen fought valiantly there, but they were outnumbered. As Caelan watched, screaming Madruns cut down the guardsmen and swarmed at the gates, pushing them open.

Caelan's breath caught in his throat. He stared in horror as more Madrun troops poured in from outside.

It was over. The few pockets of resistance remaining in the compound would be hunted down soon enough. Already the enemy was running, swarming inside with their weapons held aloft in victory. They howled strange war cries that sent chills up the back of Caelan's neck.

He growled in his throat, gripping his sword tighter.

Beside him, Elandra was weeping. "Oh, Gault, no . . . *no*!" she cried softly.

Caelan knew an insane urge to run full tilt out into the open and attack as many as he could, to kill and slash and destroy. Then he withdrew from the corner and pressed his back against the wall, breathing hard as he fought the *sevaisin*. To surrender to his grief and outrage, to go mad and fight now, was to die.

And he did not intend to be defeated—or killed—yet.

"It is over," Elandra said in a disbelieving whisper. "We are finished."

"No, there is still a chance," he said. He pressed his fingers to her lips when she tried to protest. "Hush. Don't argue. We must hurry."

When he pulled on her hand, she hung back. "I will die if I run much farther."

Caelan had no patience with that. "You'll die for certain if you don't. Now come!"

"But where can we go?"

He pointed at the dark and silent temples at the far end of the compound. The looting had not reached them yet; perhaps the superstitious Madruns were avoiding them for now. Caelan knew there were underground chambers beneath the temples, at least the Temple of Gault. They could take refuge there. If nothing else, it would buy them some time until he figured out a plan.

The empress gave him a nod, her protests stilled.

Keeping to the shadows at the base of the walls, he trotted along as fast as he dared, freezing in place each time he spied another band of Madruns. More of them were scattering from the general conflict, intent on pillaging and destroying. Many carried torches, and they were laughing, talking loudly and arrogantly in their native tongue.

The riches waiting for them inside the palace clearly had them distracted, although as yet several were busy using their daggers to perform atrocities on the corpses of the fallen guardsmen. More than once Caelan tried to shield the empress from witnessing these horrors, but it was impossible. She made no sound, no outcry. When he glanced at her through the gloom, he saw only the pale blur of her face.

They crept on, hurrying as fast as they dared while keeping to the scant cover available. The darkness was their ally, and the farther they ran from the palace, the less torchlight and firelight there was to expose them.

Caelan found himself wishing for an army to command. If only he could wing his thoughts to the imperial troops camped and deployed elsewhere in the empire. If only he could bend the mysterious forces of time and distance to his will, and bring them here—instantly.

He would have given his soul right then to be able to turn the tables on these brutes and crush them. But the main army was far away, and only the Imperial Guard was stationed here. Now that esteemed fighting force lay massacred.

Stupid, Caelan thought, the word beating in his temples like his pulse. Stupid. Stupid.

But he was not the Lord Commander of the armies. He was not the one responsible for the deployment of troops.

He was not the one who had declined to bring extra protection back to the capital city.

In the distance the screaming of men and women told Caelan of more horrors. He resisted the urge to look back, but the empress stopped and stared over her shoulder.

"The servants," she whispered in anguish. "The courtiers. My ladies—"

"Don't," he told her, tugging at her hand. "Hurry."

It was a long way around the perimeter of the walls. The farther they went, the more exposed and vulnerable Caelan felt. The edges of his consciousness sensed dangers lurking in the darkness around him, dangers not of this world, dangers he could not fight with sword and strength. Dry-mouthed, Caelan tried to shut off his own imagination. But for the first time in years, he longed for warding keys. The darkness cloaked him and the empress, but it was no friend.

Praying under his breath, he kept moving, refusing to let fear stop him.

At last, the grouping of temples loomed ahead, silent and unlit, ignored by the combat at the other end of the compound. To reach the Temple of Gault, Caelan would have to run across the open. He hesitated, caught between the steady trickle of time and the intense need for caution.

Beside him, Elandra sank to her knees, sobbing for air. Yet her grip never slackened on his. "The Penestrican temple is closest," she whispered.

"Are there underground chambers, for the secret rites?" She nodded. "Yes."

He considered it, a trifle uneasy about invading the sanctum of the women priestesses. He knew nothing about the Penestricans, save that they were barely tolerated officially. The cults surrounding the earth mother were very primitive and old. He shivered a little, but hesitated no longer.

"We'll go there," he said.

Looking in all directions, his heart in his mouth, he led her out from cover and ran across the open distance. Overhead, the clouds parted to release a finger of moonlight along the steps. Caelan loped up them, two at a time, the empress's feet pattering swiftly beside his.

They reached the top, darting past the columns, and he lunged across the vestibule for the inky shadows behind the altar. Slinging the empress around it, he crouched beside her and pressed his sweating face against the gritty stone side of the altar. His breath came in loud, hoarse gusts. The empress had doubled over, pressing her face against her skirts, but still he could hear her muffled sobbing and panting.

He listened hard, every sense straining, but heard no sound of discovery or pursuit.

They had made it.

His taut shoulders sagged in relief, and he rolled his head back against the stone. Time to take stock. How long could they reasonably expect to hide?

There was a chance they might elude discovery altogether, especially if there were numerous hiding places below the temple, and depending on the degree of Madrun superstition and caution.

But what good was hiding? And how long could they last without food and water? Caelan knew he could hold out for several days. The empress was another matter. If they starved beneath the ground, what was accomplished except they did not die by Madrun hands?

Again, he drove such defeatist thoughts away. His goal was to keep this woman alive and well. Thus far, he had done that. If the gods were kind, he would find a way to get her out of here. Every moment of survival he carved out gave them a better chance.

Regaining his breath, he touched her arm gently. "Come."

She rose to her feet, although she swayed in his hold. Worried about her, he let her lead the way to the temple's entry.

A stout door of thick wood blocked the way. Though he put all his strength against it, it would not budge. Refusing to let a mere lock stop him, Caelan traced the metal with his fingertips, intending to pick it with the empress's dagger.

But intense heat seared into his fingertips.

Biting back a cry of pain, Caelan jerked his hand away.

"What happened?" Elandra asked. "What's wrong?"

Grimly he reached out again. Once more, his hand was repelled by a blast of heat.

He stepped back, wary and respectful now, and nursed his aching fingers.

"What's the matter?" Elandra asked insistently.

"It is spell-locked," he replied, flexing his hand. Although his fingers still hurt, there was no actual burn. "We cannot enter."

She drew in her breath audibly. "Even here, so close to the palace, the sisters fear desecration of the sacred places. By order of the emperor they are not permitted to keep this temple open, and so when they leave they lock it tight. It is a pity—"

"Pity for us," he said angrily. "We are denied refuge."

"Then we'll go to Gault," she retorted. "The Vindicants are always here. Surely it is open, unless the priests are cowards and have locked themselves inside."

He thought of the Vindicants, thought of Lord Sien, who was one of the traitors. "I do not think they will give us the help we want."

"Where, then, will we go?" she demanded. "To the treasuries? They will be looted. The priests are our last hope."

"Sien cannot be trusted."

"No one can be trusted," she said. Turning from him, she started down the steps alone.

The moonlight shone across her, and she hadn't even noticed. Swearing to himself, Caelan ran after her and shoved her to one side of the steps.

"Take care," he whispered furiously.

She stiffened under his hand, but did not waste her breath arguing.

Together they hurried to the imposing, larger temple, standing tall against the night sky. Its auxiliary buildings, containing living quarters and instructional rooms, stretched out behind it. Caelan considered circling around to the back and entering that way, but Elandra still hastened a step or two in front of him.

Picking up her skirts, she went up the wide marble steps with confidence. Caelan followed, watching for trouble, knowing they could be walking into a trap yet having no alternative to offer.

At the top, he moved ahead of her, keeping his arm outstretched to hold her back, and went first to the door.

Its lock was normal. No spell protected it. Caelan fitted the dagger's tip into the keyhole. A stiletto would have served his purpose better, but he had no such weapon.

Crouching there in the darkness, working by feel, the sweat of urgency running down his temples, Caelan felt the hand of the empress close upon his upper arm.

It was a silent warning. He reacted without looking, whipping his sword off his knees and coming up and around in one swift movement of defense.

The moonlight shone full upon the steps now, lighting

their pale marble surface in silvery radiance. Skimming upward over the steps came the shadows of men, only no men walked the ground to cast them.

Caelan's blood congealed in his veins. Staring in astonishment and rising dread, he straightened fully upright, and for a moment his grip slackened on his sword. Although the empress had described these shadows to him previously, nothing she had said truly prepared him for the horror of seeing them coming so fast and silently.

He took one cautious step back, retreating deeper into the dark, and brought up his sword.

The empress did not retreat, however. Fumbling at the bodice of her gown, she drew out something secured on a cord about her neck. "Hurry and break the lock," she said softly. "I'll try to hold them off."

He stared at her, wondering what kind of talisman she held. "Do you have a warding key?"

"What is that?" she asked, then gestured at him. "Hurry! You cannot fight them with swords. I told you. Get the door open as soon as you can."

But Caelan knew that doors would not protect them from the unbound shadows of men. Even if they got inside, these creatures would follow. He shivered involuntarily and braced himself for the fight to come.

A faint golden glow appeared on Elandra's palm. He looked and saw that she was holding a large, square-cut jewel, and it was emitting the light. Astonishment spread through Caelan. He had not realized she possessed powers of her own.

Above the light spreading out from her hands, Elandra's face looked set and purposeful. She raised her hands to cast the light from the jewel a little farther, and the racing shadows stopped and curled back from the light as though burned.

Inside his amulet pouch, Caelan's fused emeralds grew warm against his chest. They had warned and protected him before. Now he marveled to see that the empress carried something similar. Even better, she knew how to utilize the powers within hers. Although he was long familiar with the magical ability of his emeralds to conceal their true shape and worth from the eyes of other men, Caelan had never dreamed his emeralds contained a force such as this. He had kept them all these years as a token of hope, as a reminder of his little sister. But perhaps they had other uses.

The shadows raced around behind him, and Elandra turned quickly in a small circle, casting the golden glow over both Caelan and herself. She was using her jewel exactly like a warding key. Its light kept the shadows back, although Caelan could feel danger pulsing at him. The shadows were vicious, angry, and intent on their prey. He could almost sense thought in them, a simple, hammering thrust of purpose—kill, kill, kill.

The heat cast by his emeralds intensified to an almost unbearable degree beneath his breastplate. Tempted to draw them forth and join their power to that of Elandra's jewel, Caelan tugged at the cord around his throat; then the corner of his eye caught movement to one side.

He plunged deep into *severance*, and pivoted sideways quicker than thought.

The thrown dagger came hurtling through the air, plunging through the spot where he'd been standing only a split second before. It thunked into the wooden panels of the door and quivered there.

"What—" Elandra cried.

In her startlement, she let her hands drop. The circle of light dipped low, and in that instant one of the shadows leaped at her.

She fell back, screaming.

Caelan's arm went around her, and he dragged her close even as she kicked and screamed against the onslaught of the shadow. The thing seemed wrapped around her throat. Caelan could hear her choking.

He shifted to *sevaisin* and found nothing to join with. The shadow had no substance, no existence of its own. Caelan caught only a faint effusion of someone else . . . a man familiar, yet no one he could recognize. It was like looking at a reflection in a pool of water, hazy and indistinct. In frustration, Caelan sought to join with the source of the shadow.

And found himself suddenly sucked into a tide pool of surging emotions, hatreds, vile passions, and perversions. Overwhelmed by the fury of them, Caelan temporarily lost himself. He was being sucked in . . . he was becoming . . . he was one with . . .

"*No!*" he shouted, and *severed*.

The shadow screamed in his mind, a mortal cry that went through him like a knife plunge. Freed of that which had controlled it and had tried to control him, Caelan came to himself with an abrupt jolt.

He found himself on his knees at the top of the temple steps. The moonlight bathed him in silvery radiance and coated his sword where he had dropped it. The empress lay on the stones, unconscious or dead, he did not know.

Chapter Twenty

FRANTICALLY CAELAN PRESSED his fingers against Elandra's throat and found a pulse. He sagged with relief and gathered her still body in his arms, drawing her back into the concealment of the darkness.

Across the parade ground, a group of Madruns were coming now, having been alerted by the screams and the flash of light. Bearing torches, they ran with their uncanny speed, and more joined them. It would be scant minutes before they arrived to finish what the shadows had begun.

Laying Elandra down next to the door, Caelan retrieved his sword, then remembered the half-seen assailant who had thrown the dagger at him.

Breathing out short and hard, Caelan closed his fist around the hilt of the dagger and plucked it from the wood. Using *sevaisin* he joined with the weapon, learning who owned it and who had thrown it.

Agel.

The answer made him ill, but he snapped from the joining and gazed around swiftly without sparing time for his emotions. His nostrils flared, drawing in scents, sifting them. He spared one more glance at the approaching Madruns, then hurried off to the right, in the direction from which the dagger had been thrown.

At the front corner of the temple vestibule, he found a narrow flight of steps heading down the side of the temple. At the foot of them crouched a man in pale robes, struggling with a broken shoe lacing.

Agel.

Caelan's heart felt like stone in his chest. Gripping his sword, he went hurtling down the steps.

Agel sprang up to run, but he was hampered by his shoe. He went no more than a few paces before Caelan caught him and drove him full force to the ground.

Crying out, Agel lay unmoving beneath him. Caelan scrambled up, seizing his cousin by his robes and hauling him upright. He shook Agel the way a dog would shake a rat.

"Give us the way in!" he said through his teeth.

Agel moaned something, reeling bonelessly in Caelan's grip.

"Damn you to hell if you do not get us inside! Agel!"

At that moment he was ready to strangle his cousin from sheer rage if nothing else. He had nothing to lose now, nothing to care about.

As though sensing that, in silence Agel pulled a large metal key from his pocket.

Caelan seized it and turned, dragging his cousin with him as he ran back up the steps.

The Madruns were less than fifty paces from the main ceremonial steps. They roared at the sight of him and quickened their pace.

Stepping over Elandra's unconscious form, Caelan slammed the key into the lock and turned it. The heavy door opened with a creak of its hinges.

He shoved Agel inside and picked up the girl. Her head lolled over his arm, her long hair spilling down like a curtain. Caelan carried her inside, then propped her against him while he pulled the door shut and locked it again. A heavy bar leaned against the wall. He threw that into the brackets as additional security.

A heavy thump against the panels made him flinch back. More thuds and kicks resounded off the door, and he could hear the cries of the enemy outside.

On a pedestal near the door, a single lamp cast a feeble glow. Caelan turned around and saw a narrow foyer with an open doorway at the opposite end. The air smelled musty and unclean. He heard unfamiliar sounds in the distance, and his skin crawled.

Agel stood erect once more, no longer stunned. His eyes met Caelan's stonily even as a fresh barrage of kicks and thumps came from the door.

"That won't hold against them long," Agel said.

"Even with a spell-lock?"

"I know nothing of such things."

Caelan didn't trouble to argue. "Lead us below, to the hiding place of the priests."

Agel frowned in defiance. "You'll find no refuge here, disbeliever."

Caelan's final shreds of respect for this man faded. So Agel had joined the ranks of the blasphemers. His healer's robes were a sham, his piety fake.

"Liar," Caelan said harshly. "You have sipped the blood of the damned."

Agel's eyes flinched slightly, as though Caelan's knowledge surprised him.

"You belong to Sien," Caelan accused him. "Admit it!"

Agel inclined his head.

Grief knotted itself in Caelan's heart, but he stayed remote from it. There was no time to deal with Agel now. Nor did he intend to discuss Agel's attempt to kill him. Instead, he met his cousin's wary eyes. "In the name of the empress, give her the assistance you would deny me."

"The empress has no authority here," Agel said sharply.

"What is this?" Another, deeper voice broke in.

Caelan turned quickly to face the doorway at the far end of the foyer.

Sien emerged, his deep set eyes luminous and alert in

the gloom. His saffron robes had been discarded. He wore instead a tunic and leggings beneath a heavy traveling cloak.

At the sight of Caelan he checked, stared, then frowned. "You have brought the enemy to us," he said. "You fool! Could you not lead them away long enough for—"

Caelan hefted the girl higher in his arms. "I ask help for the empress."

Sien's frown deepened. "The empress," he said as though he did not recognize Elandra.

"Great Gault, man!" Caelan cried. "The empress! Your sovereign ruler."

"Yes, of course," Sien said, blinking. "Her arrival is unexpected. It will alter things—" Breaking off his sentence, he seemed to recover his court manners. With a slight bow, he gestured toward the doorway behind him. "This way."

Caelan strode forward without hesitation. Beyond the doorway, a flight of steps descended steeply. He could see a feeble glow of light below, and he went down the steps as fast as he could with his burden. Behind him, he heard a low murmur of voices as though Sien was giving Agel a set of instructions.

I am mad to come here, Caelan thought, but he shoved his doubts away. There was no choice. He could not reason with the Madruns, or ask for civilized treatment if they were to take Elandra prisoner. They would defile and kill her, and the very thought of such a fate made him tighten his hold involuntarily.

He would not fail this woman, he vowed silently, still going down steps. He would not.

At the bottom of the steps, he stopped and gazed around apprehensively. The place was featureless, swept clean. Aside from the small lamp on its pedestal, he saw no furnishings. Three doors surrounded him, all firmly shut. The smell down here was worse, hinting of decay and death.

He could tell himself that it was only the stench associated with blood sacrifices, that entrails for the auguries had to be cleaned and disposed of somewhere, that carcasses of dead animals had to be butchered for daily distribution to the poor.

But his instincts knew there was more to the smell than innocent surface explanations. There was something darker at work down here. Something he did not want to meet, or know.

He swallowed hard, half-ready to retreat, but Sien joined him and walked across to a door carved with the faces of unnamed spirits. He pulled it open.

"Through here. Is she injured?"

"I don't know," Caelan replied, carrying her through.

He found himself in a narrow passageway, unlit except for the lamplight cast from behind him. When Sien shut the door, they were plunged into cold darkness.

"Wait," Sien said, and a second later a dim radiance appeared. It spread, pushing back the encompassing darkness.

The light glowed from Sien's left hand, faint but steady, just enough to show their way.

Caelan found his heartbeat thudding too fast. He swallowed again, but it did not ease the dryness in his throat.

"You were nearly too late," the priest remarked. "They will be leaving soon. Or so they intended before you led the Madruns here. Now there may not be an opportunity. We are not as well hidden down here as we should be."

"What do you mean?" Caelan asked quickly with a sharp look at the priest. "Is the emperor here?"

"Of course."

Caelan blinked, too astonished at his luck to speak.

It was Sien's turn to frown at him. "Is that not why you brought her to the temple?"

Confused, Caelan swung his gaze away. "Yes. But I— I thought we were too late."

"You nearly were. If she is hurt, I had better examine her. Or let Agel attend her. It will not do for the emperor to see her in this state."

Unwillingly Caelan halted. He knelt and gently propped the girl against his knee, supporting her while Sien bent over her.

She looked so young and vulnerable. Even smudged with dirt and soot, she was breathtaking. He could have gazed at her for hours, marveling at the delicacy of her bone structure, at the wide, clear expanse of her brow, at the thick crescent of her dark lashes against her cheekbones. Tall and slender, she lay against him with no more weight than a feather. Even in her bedraggled clothes and tangled hair, her high lineage showed plainly in her narrow wrists and ankles, in the tapering perfection of her hands that all evening had gripped his with such strength and determination.

Caelan prayed for her now, worried that the shadow had damaged her irreparably.

"It was choking her," he said softly. "I don't—"

"What was?" Sien asked.

Only then did Caelan realize he had spoken aloud. He looked up and met the priest's yellow gaze. An unnameable fear took hold of Caelan's entrails and squeezed, but he forced himself not to look away.

"A shadow," he replied. "A shadow of a man, but unattached to anyone alive or present."

Sien did not seem surprised. He went on gazing into Caelan's eyes as though to probe to his very soul. "Was it?" he asked.

His voice held only interest, nothing more.

Suspicion came alive in Caelan. He frowned. "You—"

"It did not act by my command," Sien said, lifting his hand. "Cast no accusations at me."

His remarks confirmed Caelan's suspicions. "So you *can* command these creatures?" he asked. "You can bring them away from the person who casts them and make them do your bidding?"

Sien frowned at the empress, letting his hands hover just above her. "What is this material, this cloak?" he asked. "I cannot touch her."

"Her cloak is Mahiran-made," Caelan said. He found it interesting that the cloak's spell could repel the priest. That alone told Caelan to not trust Sien. Not that he intended to anyway. He wished she had been wearing her hood. Perhaps then the shadow could not have reached her throat.

"For someone so young, she is remarkably resource-ful," Sien said.

"Yes, she is. And I asked you if you can separate men from their shadows."

Looking cool and unruffled by Caelan's questions, Sien went on gazing at the empress. "You are an unbeliever," he replied. "I have no answers to give you."

"But did you set this thing loose on her?" Caelan persisted with growing horror.

"No."

"Do you know who—or what—did?"

Again Sien paused to glance at him. "An interesting phrasing of that question. What is your name, guardsman?"

Caelan was surprised that Sien had forgotten him. "Caelan E'non."

"Ah, yes. You were rejected by this lady as a possible protector. Yet here you are. How interesting." There was an idle note of amusement woven in Sien's tone.

Caelan caught it, and his lips tightened. "You toy with me, Lord Sien," he said grimly. "You know me from before that. You have seen me often at the heels of my former master."

"Yes, I have. And now you serve the empress instead. Although you were not her chosen protector, and you do not wear her colors."

"Rander Malk is dead," Caelan said evasively. "Killed by shadows. Will she recover?"

Sien stared intently at him. "What will you pay for her recovery?"

Confused, Caelan reached for his belt. If it was a matter of a healing fee—

"No," Sien said as though he had read the thought in Caelan's mind. "Put away your coinage, fool. It is answers I want. Where do you come from? What spawned you? Why do you serve those who are doomed? Why do you resist us? Resist even your own kinsman Agel? What powers enable you to fight like no other man alive?"

Caelan's chin lifted, and his eyes grew steely. "I have no answers for you."

Sien backed away from the empress and stood up. "Then I have no help for her Majesty."

Furiously Caelan moved on him fast, pinning him with enough force to make the priest's shaved head thump against the wall. Eyes narrowed, Caelan glared at Sien. "No matter what unholy shadows you serve, your duty still lies here. Attend her Majesty now, or—"

Sien's long fingers curled around Caelan's, and Caelan felt *sevaisin* leap into him from the other man.

For the first time in his life, he experienced the joining from the other direction. It was strong but clumsily done. It was an invasion, a violation. And he could feel himself shifting also to *sevaisin*, as though to make the link doubly strong.

Horrified, Caelan held himself back, refusing to cooperate with what called to him.

He could have snapped the link with *severance*, but caution warned him not to reveal the other side of his gift.

That left him with no choice but to endure Sien's exploration of his feelings and his thoughts, even parts of his memories.

Then the priest withdrew with sinuous slowness, his questing coldness fading away. Shuddering, Caelan broke free of the man, shoving himself back. His legs felt wobbly and weak. His stomach was roiling. He felt both chilled and hot, as though a fever had seized him. Most of all, he felt defiled, as though he had been bathed in slime.

A slow smile of satisfaction spread across Sien's face. "Thank you," he whispered. "That was very informative."

Caelan jerked out his dagger and held it on the man, ready to plunge it deep to end that smirk forever.

"I have a piece of you now," Sien said fearlessly. "If you want it back, you must come to me of your own free will and ask for it."

"No," Caelan said hoarsely.

"You will come," Sien said with soft assurance. "And you will give me the rest of your secrets in exchange."

"Never."

Laughter ghosted from Sien's throat. His deep-set eyes glowed at Caelan with a madman's fervor. "The shadow god wants you. He knows of you now. You are marked, and you cannot escape what awaits you."

"You're lying," Caelan said defiantly. He closed his ears to what Sien was saying, refusing to believe it. "I know what you serve. You are darkness and blasphemy. You have betrayed the emperor and brought destruction down on the city. You'll pay for it."

Sien spread out his arms, the smile still lingering on his

lips. "Why not now? Take vengeance for all those who have died tonight, and strike me down. It will teach you much."

Caelan's hand tightened on the hilt. Thoughts of the guardsmen, courtiers, women, and servants who had died needlessly tonight boiled through his mind, igniting his rage anew. He knew Sien was mocking him now, egging him on as though to test the limits of his temper. With all his heart he craved the satisfaction of killing the priest, but he stayed his hand. He would not do it, if only because the priest asked for it.

"Oh, come," Sien said in false disappointment. "Do not hesitate. You are a champion in the arena. You have killed more men than you can count. Death walks at your shoulder. You call him friend. Are you not his best reaper?"

"No," Caelan whispered, but his mouth quivered as he spoke.

"You take life so efficiently," Sien said. "It is your talent. Tell me, in your culture what is a taker called?"

Caelan stared at him, skewered with guilt exactly as Sien intended. Loathing against both Sien and himself burned in his throat.

"Take my life," Sien taunted him, "and learn. So much awaits you. Besides, do you not crave vengeance against your enemies? And I have conspired with them, have I not?"

"Why aren't you with Tirhin right now?" Caelan asked around the lump choking his throat. "Why aren't you out there, enjoying your triumph? The empire is destroyed—"

"Oh, not by half," Sien said impatiently. "The head has been severed from the body, but neither are dead yet. They could easily be rejoined. Especially since the emperor is preparing to take the secret ways to safety at this moment. And the empress lies here at our feet, very close to joining her sovereign lord." Anger flashed in Sien's yellow eyes. "My work is far from finished."

Caelan felt his entrails drawing into a cold knot. Drawing on his courage, he forced himself to go on facing the priest with defiance and contempt. "If you are so busy," he said, "why don't you run to Tirhin and help him?"

Sien laughed. "Can you really be so naive, so stupid as to think I want the prince to assume the throne?"

Caelan frowned at this monster in human guise. This was the man who had persuaded Tirhin to trust the Madruns and to ally his cause with theirs. This was the man who had abandoned his prince to the attack of the *shyrieas* that night on the mountainside. This was the man who had counseled Emperor Kostimon for years, yet tonight had turned on him in betrayal.

"You want the complete destruction of everything," Caelan said slowly. "You want everything pulled down. You are working against everyone in the imperial family."

A smile spread across Sien's face. "Perhaps I have given you a small piece of myself in our joining," he said in approval. "Your perception has improved."

"It isn't hard to fit the pieces together," Caelan said angrily.

"No, it isn't. Especially when I make it easy for you."

A soft moan from the empress kept Caelan from retorting. He turned and knelt beside her as she stirred.

Moaning again, she lifted one hand to her brow and opened her eyes. She seemed lost and confused for a moment; then comprehension flooded her gaze and her eyes filled with tears.

She sat up, choking, and Caelan wished he could gather her tightly in his arms and hold her.

But she was the empress, and he was no one with the right to offer her such comfort.

"You are safe, Majesty," Caelan said quickly, putting reassurance in his voice. As he spoke, he glanced up at Sien standing apart from them in the gloom, and hoped he told the truth. "We are beneath the temple."

She glanced at Caelan fearfully and brushed back a strand of hair from her face. "The shadow—"

"It is gone," Caelan reassured her.

She groped for the embroidered pouch that hung around her neck, gripping it so hard her knuckles turned white. "Did you destroy the creature?"

He had a sudden fear that she might reveal to Sien the magical jewel she carried. "The shadow is gone," Caelan said firmly.

Her eyes met his, and she seemed to see the warning in his gaze. Frowning, she looked away and swallowed. Her shoulders were trembling, and she drew up her knees, trying weakly to stand up. "It will return."

"Not down here, Majesty," Sien said with an unctuous bow.

At the sound of his voice, she gasped and stiffened. Caelan put a large hand on her shoulder and squeezed gently.

Sien stepped closer to them. "Nor can the Madruns break through our safeguards for a short time yet. Your guardsman has spoken the truth when he said you are safe. Are you ready to join the emperor?"

Elandra ignored the priest and looked at Caelan. "Assist me to my feet," she said.

Although her voice was sharp and imperious, he could see how frightened she really was. In silence, he obeyed her and steadied her when she swayed. Then she squared her shoulders and lifted her chin regally, looking every inch an empress. Only her pallor and her tight grip on Caelan's fingers betrayed her.

"Lord Sien," she said unsteadily, "are you saying my husband is nearby?"

"Yes, Majesty."

"Is he—is he alive or dead?"

Sien's eyes widened. "Why, alive. Your Majesty need not fear."

A reverberating crash from overhead made all of them look up.

Caelan's throat tightened, and he reached for the hilt of his dagger. "The Madruns have broken through. Go on, Majesty. I will try to hold them as long as possible—"

"You fool!" Sien said sharply before Elandra could respond. "There are sufficient safeguards in their path that will hold the barbarians better than even you can. Let us go forward, however. The emperor cannot wait much longer."

As he spoke, he gestured at the shadowy corridor stretching ahead of them. Caelan moved to take the lead, all his senses alert, his dagger in his hand. He had the edgy, uneasy feeling that they were walking into a trap. Sien could not be trusted, whether he helped them or not. The priest was far more dangerous than he appeared, and his dark powers made him formidable. As Caelan strode along with Elandra and the priest following, he glanced often at the dagger in his hand. Could mere steel, even if thrown swift and true, destroy this minion of the shadow god? Caelan had the feeling that at any moment he might have to find out. Sweating, he tried to stay calm and ready for anything.

"Stop," Sien said.

Caelan obeyed so quickly Elandra nearly bumped into him from behind. He stepped aside with a murmured apology to her. Inclining her head, she flashed her eyes to his, then looked away.

Caelan faced the priest. "What now?" he asked suspiciously.

Sien smiled, his yellow eyes glittering. He gestured. "Open the door."

Caelan had seen no door, but now as he spun around in surprise, a carved wooden barrier blocked the corridor where none had been before. Astonished and more wary than ever, Caelan stared at it. He could not tell if it was real or imagined. He dared not touch it to find out.

"Open it," Sien said softly. "The emperor is just on the other side in the cavern."

Elandra's face lit up. "He's been waiting for me?"

"Yes," Sien said. "Twice his officers have had to dissuade him from going back to search for your Majesty. His distress has been great. But naturally he could not be allowed to jeopardize himself. If the enemy manages to break through my special defenses within the temple and get this far, it is possible they will be able to follow him even through the secret ways."

"I must join Kostimon," Elandra said. New strength filled her voice. She stood tall and queenly, her grace and confidence returned.

Caelan gazed at her, glad she so readily believed the priest's smooth lies. He met Sien's gaze, and the truth flickered between them for just an instant. In the initial confusion of tonight's attack, Caelan had seen the emperor refuse to send guardsmen to rescue Elandra, claiming he could not afford to split his meager forces unnecessarily. Caelan knew the emperor had not waited for her, had thought only of his own safety, had abandoned her with his concubines and his staff. It was better she did not know. Caelan himself would not give her such hurt for the world.

Gathering up her skirts, Elandra stepped right up to the door and stopped there. She glanced at Caelan over her shoulder. "Open it."

He hesitated just long enough to bring a frown to her eyes; then he stepped forward to obey. It was hinged to swing toward them.

Cautiously, not trusting what might perhaps really await them on the other side, Caelan gestured for the empress to stand back.

She did so, and he reached for the latch.

Before his fingers actually touched it, however, it opened itself. The door swung inward on its own.

Caelan flinched back from it, then crouched with his dagger ready.

Past the doorway stood a spacious cavern filled with men and milling horses. The area hummed with frenzied activity. On the opposite side of the cavern, the emperor's banner hung limply from a staff, and the guardsmen themselves were men Caelan recognized as loyal. Relief swelled in his throat.

He stood aside to let Elandra precede him.

On the threshold, however, she seemed to bump into something unseen.

Gasping, she recoiled and backed away quickly.

Cursing himself, Caelan reached her side immediately. "Is your Majesty hurt?" he demanded.

She shook her head. Her eyes were still wide with fear. "What in Gault's name is it?" she whispered, clutching her jewel bag.

Caelan returned to the doorway. When he reached out, his hand struck an invisible barrier that was as firm as a stone wall. It was neither cold nor hot to his touch. It was simply impassable.

Gazing through it in mounting frustration, he could see the guardsmen saddling horses and loading provisions, but he could not step through to join them.

No one in the cavern glanced his way. Caelan decided they could not see him. The thought stirred fresh worry inside him. Were the guardsmen really out there, or was this all an illusion?

He turned around to face Sien. Inside him, rage and resignation were building. He'd known all along the priest was going to pull some trickery. Now it had to be dealt with.

"Careful, warrior," Sien said softly. "Do not make a mistake you will regret."

Caelan bared his teeth as he brandished his dagger. "Did you not ask me to strike you down just a few minutes ago? Your memory is short, priest."

"On the contrary," Sien replied, "my memory is excellent. I recall asking you what price you would pay for the lady's recovery."

Elandra's head whipped around sharply. "What?"

Caelan felt a slow rage heating inside him, molten in his loins, burning hotter and hotter in his chest, rising through his neck, his cheeks, his eyes. He glared at the priest, in no mood for games.

"You didn't cure her," he said hoarsely.

Sien smiled with pity, and Caelan suddenly understood that the priest meant Elandra's return to the side of the emperor. It was a cold drenching of comprehension that left him standing there stricken and silent.

"No," Elandra said softly, horror in her voice. She looked from one man to the other. "No."

Caelan ignored her. His gaze was only for the priest, whose eyes were now rapacious and gleaming. Sien licked his lips, and something in the air smelled burned.

"Dark magic!" Elandra cried in warning. She stumbled against Caelan, perhaps to push him to safety or perhaps to grip him for reassurance.

He swept her aside with his free arm and moved toward Sien slowly on the balls of his feet. In his temple his pulse throbbed with the desire to kill this bald old viper, but he kept his emotions in check. He must use his wits here, not his brawn. Physical attack was not the answer; if Sien used magic to defend himself, Caelan knew he would not stand much chance against the priest.

"I ask again," Sien said. "What price will you pay?"

"What price do you ask?" Caelan countered.

"No!" Elandra said. "Caelan, I forbid this. Do not bargain with this traitor."

Caelan frowned, wishing she would be quiet. She was distracting him. He narrowed his gaze on the priest, wondering how he could make the man drop the spell on the doorway. "You wanted answers from me, and you took those. What is your price now?"

Sien laughed, a horrible gloating sound. "If I could give you a way to go back and save the life of your father, would you take it?"

Caelan froze in revulsion. His fingers clenched knuckle-white on his dagger. *Don't listen*, a voice in the back of his head warned him.

"If I could give you a way to go back and change your decisions?" Sien continued, his voice insinuating and soft. "What is the child's name? Lea? Do you want to know exactly how she died in the forest?"

Caelan shut his eyes. "Be quiet."

"But if I let you go back to save her, would you go?"

The never-healed wound broke open afresh, welling raw hurt. Caelan clenched his eyes shut harder, and tears stung against his eyelids. If only he had stayed with her. If only he had remembered his responsibility was to protect her. If only he hadn't thought he could make a difference at the hold.

"I was just a boy," he whispered aloud. "I did my best."

"You made a mistake," Sien said. "Undo it. Go back and save your sister. Forget this woman who stands here. Think of Lea. She loved you so much, Caelan. She trusted you. And you promised to return for her. Why not keep that promise now? I can send you back to her."

Caelan shivered. Inside, he felt as though he were breaking in half. It hurt, and it would always hurt. To be able to undo his mistakes. To be able to change the course of his life . . . but such longing was only a belief in falsehood. Change was not possible.

"It *is* possible," Sien whispered. "Trust me."

Caelan forced open his eyes. Tears spilled hot down his cheeks, and he turned his back on the priest. Inside, he struggled away from temptation and tried to harden himself against the priest's lies. He understood what Sien wanted now. Sien wanted him to abandon Elandra in these corridors, to leave her able to see her husband and his soldiers yet barred from reaching them until the Madruns eventually found her.

He could save Elandra, or he could believe this lying priest possessed the ability to manipulate the past enough for Lea to be saved.

Caelan clenched his free hand at his side until his powerful body trembled. Either way, the price was too high. How could he make such a choice?

"Caelan." Elandra whispered his name.

He turned his head toward her. The way she stood before him would be forever etched in his memory. Her ivory skin, the flawless beauty of her face, the burnished glints of candlelight in her auburn hair. Caelan felt emotions stir and awaken in him, a force fiery and hard to control. It was as though he were suddenly dipped in heat, his ears on fire and roaring, his eyes burning in their sockets, his breath seared in his lungs. He stood suspended in the spell of her luminous eyes, helpless in his new knowledge of himself and her.

Her eyes glistened as she gazed back at him with understanding and compassion. A tear brimmed over and fell down her cheek. Still meeting his gaze, she shook her head. "Don't—"

"Caelan."

A different voice uttered his name this time. The sound of it gave him a profound shock. His gaze snapped away from Elandra, and he saw Lea kneeling on the ground less than two strides away.

The child crouched there, hugging herself beneath her scarlet cloak and shivering violently. Her golden curls straggled from the edge of her hood, as bright and pretty as ever, but her face was pinched and gray; her lips were bloodless with cold. Dark smudges lay under her eyes, which were dull with suffering. She was starving to death, freezing to death. He could feel the icy blast of wind off the glacier. Its force was brutal, merciless.

Lea whimpered. Shivering so hard her teeth chattered, she knelt there for what seemed like an eternity, while he watched helplessly, his grief like a stone in his chest. Finally she struggled to her feet and walked on, bent nearly double against the howling wind.

Caelan opened his mouth, but no sound came out. He could smell the crisp scent of the pines. He could smell the sickly sweet scent of the child's skin, and knew it signified starvation. How long had she been walking in the snowy woods? Her boots were ragged and worn through. She staggered in a zigzag pattern, floundering in the deep snow, and fell.

"Caelan!" she cried, lifting her face to the heavens. "Help me!"

Her plea tore his heart. With a wordless moan, Caelan ran to her and reached out.

The vision of Lea vanished as though she had never been there. Anguished, he dropped to his knees and wept for her.

"I'm sorry," he whispered. "I'm sorry."

"What good are apologies?" Sien asked from behind him. "You and I can walk around time and go back to that fateful day in the snowy forests of Trau, when you abandoned the only person you loved. Save her, Caelan. You seem to have a strong urge to save people, like an overgrown dog. You could save the empress by turning on me and striking me down. My spell on the doorway would end, and she could go through. But why not save the one person who really mattered to you? Why not save the one person who needed you? Who depended on you? Lea. A pretty name. A pretty, precious child. Lea."

Caelan gulped, his throat working. "Don't say her name."

"Lea."

He jumped to his feet and whirled on the priest with insane fury, striking the man with his fist and sending Sien reeling against the wall. "Don't say her name!"

The invisible barrier across the doorway suddenly shimmered into a tangible rainbow of color, like a bubbled pane of mouth-blown glass. The guardsmen on the other side blurred and nearly faded from sight.

Dabbing at the trickle of blood running from the corner of his mouth, Sien nodded. "Anger is a good step. Take another. Embrace the rage, Caelan."

Caelan glared at him through a murderous haze, the dagger pulsing as though alive in his fist. He felt the tug at his emotions, felt the seduction calling to him from Sien. The need for completion, for *sevaisin*, stirred within him. It would be so easy to surrender to it, so easy . . .

He *severed*, going deep into the coldness as though he plunged himself into a glacial lake. This time he did not care if he *severed* so far he could never return. All he wanted was an end to the hurting, an end to the memories, an end to the guilty attempts to serve others in atonement. He would put himself where Sien could never reach him.

A wall of ice appeared before him. He saw how it separated him from the priest. Through its transparent sides he could see the priest gesturing, could see Sien's lips moving. But he heard no more insidious urgings, no more vile persuasions. He felt no more temptations. He could not see Elandra at all. There was only the void and the compelling coldness that made him brittle, calm, and unapproachable.

In the very great distance, far, far beyond the wall of ice, he saw a column of icy mist that eventually transformed itself into the vague figure of a man.

The figure beckoned to him.

Caelan recognized Beva, and his heart grew even colder. He did not want his father's approval. He had not come into this place to earn that.

Turning his back on both his father and the priest, Caelan set his face into a bitter wind and trudged away. He would go deep into the void, never to return. He would vanish. He would cease to exist. He would escape all responsibility forever.

But before him stretched the threads of life, a shining network of iridescent strands stretching into the sky and vanishing out of sight in the gray clouds. Frowning, Caelan stopped and looked back.

He saw Sien's silhouette against the icy mist, a dark shadow standing near the entrance to a cavern. One of Sien's hands was outstretched. From each of his fingers stretched multiple threads, and the black strands were woven across the mouth of the cavern.

Caelan hesitated only a moment, knowing that *severance* was his last true secret kept from the priest. If he used it, Sien would seek him out again to wrest the gift from him or turn it into something evil.

But there was no other way. He could not vanish into the void. Escape was not possible, for even here in *severance* he carried himself with him. All his guilt and feelings journeyed with him, as though in a basket he could not drop on the wayside.

Gathering his strength, Caelan advanced on Sien. He *severed* the threads of the spell. Fire exploded in the mouth of the cavern, sending him reeling back; then reality snapped around him, and he found himself stumbling into the corridor wall. Gasping, he pressed his hands to the wall and struggled to regain his equilibrium.

To his right, Elandra stood staring at him with her hands pressed to her mouth. Her eyes were huge with fear and something he could not identify.

Sien was huddled down, swearing to himself and clutching his hand. The skin was charred black, as though he had stuck it into a fire.

Regaining his wits, Caelan strode to the doorway and stepped through it. He paused there and glanced back at Elandra.

He reached out to her. "Come. Quickly."

She hesitated, still staring at him as though he was a monster, but she came. Slowly at first, then running the last few steps. She clutched his hand, and he pulled her through the doorway.

The cavern rang with noise as men hurried about their tasks. There were fewer soldiers than Caelan had hoped to see. Too few, in fact, but at that moment he didn't care.

Relieved, he smiled down at Elandra. The fear vanished from her eyes, and she smiled back. Then her smile faded, and she looked troubled again. She squeezed his hand. "Your sister—Lea—what Lord Sien said about her—"

"He was lying," Caelan said, forcing his voice to be light. "Think no more about it."

She searched his eyes. "Are you sure? I—"

"The empress!" someone shouted. "Look! It's her Majesty. She's alive!"

Elandra broke off what she'd been about to say and dropped Caelan's hand. She frowned, looking flustered.

He bowed to her. "Go to your husband, Majesty. Let him know you are safely delivered."

Several expressions flitted across her face. Finally she smiled again. "Thank you," she said with heartfelt sincerity. "I shall never forget all you have done for me."

Then she was gone, hurrying into the confusion only to be met by Sergeant Balter, who saluted her with a beaming smile and led her toward the emperor's banner.

Caelan watched her for a moment, filled with the bittersweet satisfaction of knowing this time he had done the right thing. He had not failed his true responsibilities.

"Caelan E'non."

Startled, he turned and warily faced Sien. The priest stood on the other side of the doorway, gazing out at him.

Still nursing his burned hand, Sien looked wide-eyed and astonished. "You vanished," he said. He reached out his hand, then drew it back without touching Caelan. "For an instant, as I was talking to you, you simply ceased to exist. Where did you go? How did you break the power of Beloth to stop the spell?"

Caelan stared hard at him without any emotion at all. "You have already taken all the answers you will ever get from me."

Anger replaced the astonishment in Sien's leathery face. "Impertinent fool! You are trampling on that which you do not understand. You—"

"She is out of your hands," Caelan broke in. "Whatever meddling you wrought with Kostimon's mind to make him forget her has ceased to work. She is back where she belongs, despite your plots, shadows, invaders, and spells."

Fury twisted Sien's face. He lifted his burned hand as though to hurl magic at Caelan. "Yo—"

Caelan sprang at him and gripped his injured hand, squeezing it with all his strength.

A strangled scream of agony burst from Sien. He crumpled at Caelan's feet without resistance.

Caelan released him and stood glaring down at the man without any mercy. "Save your spells for the Madruns," he said harshly. "Conceal this entrance once again, so that when they come at last to this cavern, they will never find it. Nor will they find the secret ways. Nor will they follow where Kostimon goes."

Breathing hard, his eyes still slitted with pain, Sien glared up at him. "You dare order me?"

"I dare," Caelan said coldly. "I could have taken your life as easily as I took away the spell. Remember that you called me a taker. Remember that you taunted me for enjoying what I do. Now consider our new bargain. You will conceal this cavern so that when the savages come, they will look but never see what lies here. Do it, or I swear I will destroy you."

Hatred filled Sien's face. "You cannot!" he boasted hoarsely. "Not while I serve the darkness."

"Can you find the darkness now?" Caelan mocked him. "Can you feel it strong and powerful within you as it was a few moments before? While its connection to you is withered and damaged, you are merely a man. Nothing more."

Sien's scowl deepened. Finally, resentfully, he nodded. "Very well, I shall do as you say. I have enough strength left to cast the spell that you request. But this is not the last of us, Traulander. When I am once again fully rejoined with my master, I shall hunt you down. No matter how far you journey, I will find you. Remember that I have a piece of you. It will lead me to you, anywhere on this earth, or beyond it."

Caelan listened to his threat without fear. He thought of that future encounter and knew he would welcome it. Right now, as much as he would like to finish Sien once and for all, he knew it was not the time. They needed Sien and his despicable dark magic to fool the Madruns searching for them.

Meeting Sien's gaze, Caelan held it a long while, until the priest's gaze dropped first. Color suffused Sien's cheeks, and he started to say something else, but Caelan was finished with the man. It was time to seek out the emperor, time to rejoin his fellow guardsmen, time to resume his duty.

There was, after all, an empire to rebuild.

Turning his back on the defeated priest, Caelan walked away.